Praise for the Novels of Barry Eisler

Requiem for an Assassin

"It's a nifty plot . . . punctuated with interesting and sophisticated touches. . . . *Requiem for an Assassin* is a skillful spy novel." —*The Washington Post*

"Nifty black ops scenes . . . and emotional explosiveness." —*Entertainment Weekly*

"The action is slick and fast, and the plot tightly choreographed." —*The Economist*

"Fast, fun fighting . . . a brilliant and extremely conflicted protagonist." —*Kirkus Reviews*

"Tense and well crafted." —*Library Journal*

"This one is as good as its five forerunners, and here's hoping the author has a few more stories to tell." — *Booklist*

The Last Assassin

"Body Count: a whopping 20. Worst Death: a double beheading via katana blade. Lowdown: [*The Last Assassin*] . . . certainly gives good gunplay. And don't let that extreme body count fool you: Eisler is just as keen on inner angst as on executions." —*Entertainment Weekly*

"[A] grippingly turbulent plot." —*San Francisco Chronicle*

"Full of modern spy craft . . . exotic locales, hot sex, and violence." —*San Jose Mercury News*

"I have been an addict ever since the first one, *Rain Fall.* . . . Reminiscent of James Bond's greatest hits." —*The New York Sun*

continued . . .

Killing Rain

"Eisler unspools a plot full of warring secret government connections, cool spy paraphernalia, and vivid martial-arts sequences . . . exhilarating."
—*Entertainment Weekly*

"Steeped in exotic locales, charged with spasms of violence . . . unique and entertaining."
—*Rocky Mountain News*

"High-octane action."   —*South Florida Sun-Sentinel*

"Pulse-pounding. . . . Rain should have a bright, bloody, nerve-racking future."   —*Lansing State Journal*

"Freelance assassin Rain, now an established presence on the thriller scene, confronts both menace and morality . . . plenty of good action . . . a thriller as straight as an arrow . . . Thankfully, expect more Rain."
—*Kirkus Reviews*

Rain Storm

"If Quentin Tarantino ever got to take a crack at the James Bond franchise, chances are the resulting film would resemble one of Eisler's novels about John Rain."   —*Entertainment Weekly*

"[A] superb thriller . . . an ultra-cool assassin."
—*New York Daily News*

"A propulsive thriller plot . . . plausible, au courant, and creepy."   —*Kirkus Reviews*

"What truly sets Eisler's series apart is its near total absence of formula and stereotype. Rain is a wholly original, cliché-free character operating in a world created only for him, serving as both his folly and his foil."
—*Publishers Weekly*

Books by Barry Eisler

Rain Fall
Hard Rain
Rain Storm
Killing Rain
The Last Assassin

REQUIEM FOR AN ASSASSIN

BARRY EISLER

AN ONYX BOOK

ONYX
Published by New American Library, a division of
Penguin Group (USA) Inc., 375 Hudson Street,
New York, New York 10014, USA
Penguin Group (Canada), 90 Eglinton Avenue East, Suite 700, Toronto,
Ontario M4P 2Y3, Canada (a division of Pearson Penguin Canada Inc.)
Penguin Books Ltd., 80 Strand, London WC2R 0RL, England
Penguin Ireland, 25 St. Stephen's Green, Dublin 2,
Ireland (a division of Penguin Books Ltd.)
Penguin Group (Australia), 250 Camberwell Road, Camberwell, Victoria 3124,
Australia (a division of Pearson Australia Group Pty. Ltd.)
Penguin Books India Pvt. Ltd., 11 Community Centre, Panchsheel Park,
New Delhi - 110 017, India
Penguin Group (NZ), 67 Apollo Drive, Rosedale, North Shore 0632,
New Zealand (a division of Pearson New Zealand Ltd.)
Penguin Books (South Africa) (Pty.) Ltd., 24 Sturdee Avenue,
Rosebank, Johannesburg 2196, South Africa

Penguin Books Ltd., Registered Offices:
80 Strand, London WC2R 0RL, England

Published by Onyx, an imprint of New American Library, a division of Penguin
Group (USA) Inc. Previously published in a G. P. Putnam's Sons edition.

First Onyx Printing, May 2008
10 9 8 7 6 5 4 3 2 1

Copyright © Barry Eisler, 2007
All rights reserved

 REGISTERED TRADEMARK—MARCA REGISTRADA

Printed in the United States of America

For Owen, Rachel, and Sandy, with love

1

JIM HILGER and his team sat hunched over a group of surveillance photos in a budget hotel room in Kuta, on Bali's famed west coast. The late-afternoon monsoon rains had given way to a clear night sky, and the adjacent beach was still noisy with revelers—Australians, drinking away the last night of a holiday before returning to the grind back home; American frat kids, a bit more adventurous than their peers in Fort Lauderdale, lured to Kuta by true stories of cheap accommodations and oceanside discos and like-minded young people searching for sin; dark-skinned Balinese beauties in bikini tops and sarongs, looking for rich white boyfriends, or, failing that, a night or even an hour in exchange for a proper tip in convertible currency. In fact, the hotel was a popular stop for tourists who had found a local "date" nearby and were in a hurry to consummate the transaction, and the high turnover, cash basis, and reluctance of patrons to meet each other's eyes made places like this one good expedient safehouses, not just here in Indonesia, but in many other countries where Hilger operated. Sex could be a good cover for secrecy; salaciousness, for murder.

For security, the five of them had arrived one by one earlier that evening at staggered times, and, so as not to stand out, each had come accompanied by an appropriately nubile Balinese companion. Indeed, Hilger knew that two of the men had arrived early enough to fully indulge the cover their temporary girlfriends provided, but Hilger was untroubled by their behavior. He had commanded men in war and understood their needs, and besides, he would rather they get a taste of the local fauna early so they would be less inclined to chase after it late at night. The man they were hunting was dangerous, and Hilger wanted everyone sharp.

Hilger knew the man as Dox, said to be short for "unorthodox," a nom de guerre the man had acquired during his unsung service in Reagan-era Afghanistan. Once upon a time, Dox had been a Marine sniper, one of the best, but these days worked freelance. Hilger had used him three times. On the first two occasions, Dox had performed superbly. The third had been a disaster, and was what the present operation was all about.

"Look at this," the man sitting across from Hilger said, pointing at a photo taken through a 500mm lens. "We've seen him coming and going from his villa. It's isolated. I think we could take him there."

Hilger nodded. The man's suggestion was sensible. His name was Demeere—a big, blond Belgian bastard and veteran of his country's Détachement d'Agents de Sécurité. The DAS guys provided security at Belgian embassies. They were trained by Belgian special forces, comfortable in urban environments, and typically multilingual. Demeere had been one of their standouts. As adept in a particularly rigorous form of tai chi as he was with a knife, he had, over the years, assisted Hilger with four successful "renditions" of terror suspects, and Hilger knew his counsel was worth considering.

"I like the villa," the man behind Demeere said. "Go with what you know, that's what I say."

It took some effort on Hilger's part not to grimace. Demeere, whose back was to the speaker, evinced slightly less facial control.

Hilger looked up and observed the man for a moment. He was standing apart from the rest of them, leaning against the wall by the window while the others sat across from each other on the room's twin beds. No one responded to his comment. Even pointing out its vapidity would have been more engagement than any of them seemed willing to grant him.

The man liked to refer to himself as Drano, and Hilger hadn't liked that from the start. Nicknames bestowed by comrades were an honor. If you tried to invent one for yourself, it was a joke, a sign of narcissism and an underlying lack of confidence. Hilger had known better at the time, but he'd lost so many men in the last two years that he'd ignored the warning from his gut as he went about restaffing. Stupid. Never time to do it right, always time to do it over.

The guy had come highly recommended, true. Former Navy SEAL, combat duty in Afghanistan. But that kind of background was merely necessary, and not always sufficient, for what Hilger demanded of his men. Anyway, even among SEALs there was an occasional loser. Apparently, it had been Hilger's bad luck to come across one of them.

The man to Demeere's left rotated his bald head, breaking the silence by cracking the joints in his neck. "Better to wait," he said, looking first at Demeere, then at Hilger, and ignoring Drano completely. "His villa would be convenient, sure, but it's no coincidence he built the place in the middle of all those rice paddies. You know how long it'll take us to slog all the way through to his house? If he's got sensors deployed and sees us coming, he'll turn us into fertilizer one at a time. And I don't want to go in on that zigzagging little access road, either. He knows that's the only approach, he's got to have it rigged. And trying to set up there while he's gone would be worse. I guarantee you he's got layered systems that would warn him. Better to take him on unfamiliar ground. The downside is more potential witnesses and the other risks you get rendering someone in public, but overall our odds are better."

The man's name was Frank Garza, but he was known in Hilger's organization as Pancho, the name given him by his Mexican mother. While Demeere had a deceptively placid exterior, Pancho tended to radiate a not-to-be-fucked-with aura that he had a hard time concealing. A former All-Marine boxing champion, he also had a fourth degree black belt in Kenpo. One night he and Demeere had gotten into a sparring match that had started out playful and then become serious. To Hilger, it had been like watching an irresistible force and an immovable object. If Hilger hadn't stopped it, the two of them might have crippled each other and destroyed a hotel room in the process.

"The question is, how much time do we have," the fifth man said, leafing through the photographs. "That town he lives in, Ubud, isn't exactly huge, so sooner or later he'll wind up where we want him. But if we need to move fast, we have to go where we know he'll be. Right now that means the villa."

The man's name was Guthrie. His boyish good looks

had made for excellent cover during his service as a
Federal Air Marshal, and the training he'd received
then, along with ferocious natural ability, made him
their best combat shooter. Unlike Demeere and Pancho, he was no martial artist, but nor did he believe in
fighting, preferring to settle disputes amicably with the
Wilson Combat .45 he carried in a belly band under an
untucked shirt.

Hilger nodded, considering. There was a lot he hadn't
told them yet. They all hailed from careers in need-to-
know environments, and understood his reticence. But
maybe he had given them too little. At this point, keeping them in the dark made them unable to properly
weigh the costs and benefits, to plan effectively. Yes, he
decided. They needed to understand . . . if not the full
picture, then at least a larger part of it.

"You're all being too cautious," Drano said, still leaning against the wall and looking down on them as
though bored, or in judgment.

Hilger looked up, liking neither the man's tone nor
his choice of "you're" instead of "we're." The other men
glanced at one another. Their expressions were too subtle to be called disgusted, but Hilger knew disgust was
what they felt. This was hardly the first time Drano had
insisted on offering his unsolicited and useless "exper-
tise," and they were sick of his weak bullshit. The man
had been a mistake. And if Hilger didn't deal with it
soon, his men would rightly judge him for it.

"Really," Hilger said, mildly.

"Really," Drano said, nodding his head aggressively.
"One man, night-vision goggles, just before dawn, a
kerosene bomb on that thatched roof of his. We take
him when he runs outside."

"You going to take the neighbors, too?" Hilger asked,

his tone even milder now, bordering on gentle. "They'll come out when they see fire. And do you know which way Dox'll run? Tell us, so we can be in position. Oh, and police and firefighters, we can expect a few of them to show up, so we'll need a plan for that, too. And the attention we'll get during and after from a nocturnal blazing Ubud villa, we'd all appreciate any pointers you could offer us there. This is all assuming you don't trip a sensor and get your head blown off on the approach to the house, of course. But you could probably bat the bullet out of the air with your own dick if it came to that, right?"

The man shrugged, too stupid, or proud, to admit his mistake. "Sometimes you have to take a chance if you want to get something done," he said.

The other men weren't even looking at Drano now. In fact, they'd been making their distrust apparent through body language for a while now, and Drano had picked up on it. It was why he was standing apart—he knew he wasn't welcome. And the stupid criticism was really just a misguided bid for attention, to be accepted among company to which he aspired to belong.

Hilger suddenly recognized the reason he'd been withholding information from the men, information they needed to plan the operation. It was because he knew this bozo was untrustworthy. And rather than fix the problem, he'd been living with it, hoping it would magically take care of itself. Now that he realized it, he was quietly furious at his own weakness. But all right, better late than never. The man had to go.

He turned to Demeere. "How are we staffed for this?"

"Three is the bare minimum," Demeere said without hesitating, and Hilger knew from the readiness of the answer that the big Belgian already understood. "Four is comfortable. Five is a hundred percent."

Hilger nodded. "All right. Then we're in good shape." He glanced behind Drano. "Close those drapes, will you?" he said. "They're open at the edges, it's sloppy."

Drano turned and adjusted the drapes. Even without all the other faults that had combined to disqualify him, the cluelessness he displayed right then would have been enough.

In the two seconds during which Drano's back was turned, Hilger reached with his right hand for the SIG P232 he kept as backup in an ankle holster; grabbed a pillow with his left; and pulled the pillow around the muzzle of the gun, holding the ends tight at his right wrist so that the gun was completely enclosed within it. He raised both arms, aiming at Drano's head.

Drano turned back. He saw the pillow and the way Hilger was holding it. Without giving him time to process the information or react in any way, Hilger pressed the trigger. There was the crack of a muffled gunshot, and a small, dark hole appeared in Drano's forehead. His body jerked as though something had shocked him, then he buckled and collapsed to the floor.

The sound of the shot was loud, but not terribly so. The P232 was chambered in .380, a smaller round than the .357 Hilger carried in his primary, a full-size P226. He had chosen the backup just now precisely for its reduced noise profile. And of course the pillow muffled some of the report. Maybe some guy in the next room would look up and wonder what he'd just heard, but when there was no follow-up, he'd happily go back to fucking and sucking and whatever else he was doing that brought him here in the first place.

Drano was lying on his back now, his legs folded under him, his eyes open. A small trickle of blood began to run down his face from the hole in his forehead. Not much, though. The other reason Hilger had selected the P232 was to lessen the chance of the round blowing out the back of Drano's head, which would have made a mess.

Demeere pulled several tissues out of a box on the nightstand, knelt, and, with his thumb, wadded the paper into the forehead hole, stanching the trickle of blood. Hilger nodded slightly in admiration. There was nothing flashy about Demeere. There didn't need to be; he was rock solid. How many men could prevent a mess as calmly as he just did?

Hilger collected and pocketed the spent casing, then decocked the pistol and returned it to his ankle. The room was quiet for a moment while they listened for sounds of disturbance, for any sign that someone might want to investigate. There were none.

Pancho said, "Looks like Drano's gone down the drain."

Pancho and Demeere laughed. Only Guthrie looked at all discomfited. But he hadn't been with Hilger as long as the other men.

"Well," Pancho said, "I'm glad that's done. Been wanting to do it myself."

Hilger nodded. "I should have taken care of it sooner."

"Don't worry about it," Pancho said with a shrug. "It's not the kind of thing I'd want you doing lightly."

They laughed again. After a moment, Hilger said, "We'll pull up the van when we're done. Load him in, take him to the boat, punch holes in him and dump him at sea. We'll be better with just the four of us than we would have been with a weak link like that one."

Everyone nodded. Demeere tossed a blanket over the corpse and sat back on the bed.

"All right," Hilger said, after a moment. "Dox . . . isn't the ultimate objective. If he were, we could take our time. But our interest in him is secondary."

Pancho hunched forward, his head dropping as though he were zeroing in for a knockout. "Access agent, then?"

Hilger nodded. "An unwilling one."

"Who's the primary?" Pancho asked.

Hilger looked at Demeere, who he suspected had already guessed.

Demeere said, "John Rain."

Pancho looked at Hilger. "The freelancer? The one who took out Winters?"

Hilger nodded. "And Calver and Gibbons, too. Those losses were why I had to dig so deep and bring in a mistake like Drano. It's hard to find good people."

Pancho returned his gaze to Demeere. "How'd you know?"

Demeere shook his head to indicate he wasn't privy to any knowledge Pancho lacked. "I didn't. I guessed."

Pancho cracked his knuckles and stared at Demeere as though considering how much credence to give the man's response.

Guthrie said, "Rain . . . this is the Japanese assassin, right?"

Demeere nodded. "Half Japanese. His mother was American. But he looks Japanese. At least, that's what I've heard. I've never seen him. Not many people have."

Hilger said, "I have."

The third time Hilger had used Dox, the man was supposed to eliminate Rain. Dox knew Rain from Afghanistan, a connection Hilger thought would enable the former sniper to get close enough to do the job. He'd gotten close enough, all right, so close that Rain and Dox had joined forces and then in the space of a single year had torn apart two of Hilger's operations. True, it hadn't been personal—neither man had understood what those operations were really about—but Hilger's losses had been considerable. Among other things, he had been forced to abandon the Hong Kong cover he had been living and relocate to Shanghai.

Also, at the disastrous conclusion of that second blown op, Dox had leveled Hilger from behind with a chair launched from the top of a riser of stairs. It could have been worse—if Dox had been properly armed, Hilger would be dead now. As it was, the massive bruise from the impact had lasted for a month; the memory, considerably longer. Hilger couldn't deny that he took some pleasure in imagining how he would soon squeeze Dox for the information he wanted.

Pancho was still staring at Demeere. The half-Mexican was a reliable operator, but prone to feel slighted easily and to react with anger.

Hilger decided to cut short a possible argument. "Demeere was in charge of the op to try to render Rain out of Bangkok. He was running Winters and a local team there. That's how he knew just now. How he guessed."

Pancho eased back an inch on the bed. "How'd it go down?"

"We don't know all the details," Demeere said. "It seems Rain spotted the ambush Winters had set, and attacked. Two of the locals got away. Two others Rain killed with a knife. Winters was found in an alley with defensive wounds on his arms and a slashed subclavian artery. Bled out internally."

"Rain beat Winters in a fucking *knife* fight?" Pancho

asked. "I knew Winters. He had a kali background. Trained in the Philippines. He was good with a blade."

"Rain's had a lot of training, too," Hilger said. "Judo. Boxing. Edged weapons when he was with Special Forces. And a hell of a lot of practical experience."

Pancho nodded as though considering. Demeere looked at him and asked, "Does that make you nervous?"

Pancho returned the look. "No."

Demeere offered a slight, chilly smile. "It should."

Pancho smiled back. "Maybe Rain just got lucky. Or maybe Winters wasn't being run properly."

Guthrie said, "Anyway, the point is, Winters was good."

Demeere, his eyes still on Pancho, said in lightly accented but otherwise perfect English, "Fuck-all good."

"What about Calver and Gibbons?" Guthrie asked.

"Shot to death," Hilger said. "In a Manila restroom, while they were trying to protect an agent in another op."

Pancho looked at Hilger. "So you're looking for payback. To take Rain out."

Hilger shook his head. "I want him to do a job."

Pancho squinted and pursed his lips as though thinking. Hilger didn't know whether he was confused or disappointed or both.

"If he's freelance," Guthrie asked, "why not just hire him, through channels?"

"Two problems," Hilger said. "First, I don't know how to contact him. I tried to locate him, and couldn't even find out where he is. At one point he was known to be in Tokyo, then supposedly in São Paulo or Rio. The reports are all several years out of date, though, and I doubt he's still living in either country. And even if he were, it wouldn't be enough to go on. Brazil has the world's largest Japanese expatriate community. Rain would be invisible there. More so in Japan. He always kept a low profile, but these days he might as well be a ghost."

Guthrie said, "What's the second problem?"

Hilger shrugged. "For now, let's just say that I doubt what I want him for is something he'd do voluntarily. Dox is his friend, one of only a few. That means Dox knows how to contact him, and it means Dox is the leverage to make Rain cooperate."

"They're that close?" Guthrie said.

Hilger nodded. "I saw Dox carry Rain over his shoulder out of a firefight at Kwai Chung harbor in Hong Kong. Five million dollars in play, and Dox walked away from it to save his partner when he got hit. So I'd say they're close, yeah."

Pancho said, "What you've got in mind, the thing you want Rain for, you can't handle in-house?"

Again, Hilger detected disappointment. He shook his head. "Rain is the right resource for this. We just have to get to him."

They were all quiet for a moment. Guthrie said, "How much time do we have, then? To snatch Dox."

Hilger shuffled through a few more of the photos, looking for a pattern. He felt something beginning to cohere.

"We can give it a few more days," Hilger said. "If we haven't had an opening at that point, we can work the villa angle. But I agree with Pancho, it's high risk and I'd prefer something else. The main thing is that we take him totally unaware. Because without the element of surprise, taking him alive and functioning is going to be bloody. Close quarters he's not Rain, but believe me, he's plenty dangerous."

Pancho squinted. "Rain is that good?"

Hilger nodded, remembering how Rain had tracked

him to Hong Kong. No one had ever turned the tables on Hilger like that before, and Hilger knew he was lucky to have survived it. The experience had spooked him, he had to admit, and for this, along with his more concrete rationales, he wasn't going to let Rain continue to roam the earth when the current operation was done.

"He must be getting old," Guthrie said. "He's a Vietnam vet, isn't he?"

Hilger nodded. "He went in late, though, when he was seventeen, so he's young for that conflict. But even if his best years are past him, tell me, do you know of anyone else who's survived in this business, on his own, with no organization to protect him, for as long as Rain?"

The room was silent.

"There's a reason he's survived all this time," Hilger went on. "And it's not luck. No one stays lucky that long. It's because he's good. He's better than all the people he's killed, and he's killed plenty—more than we have all together. So you don't want to think of him as old, or slow, or used up, or burnt out, or anything else he wants you to think so you'll underestimate him. You do, and you'll wind up another one of his statistics."

"Like Winters," Demeere said.

"Like Winters," Hilger said, looking at each of them. "We don't want any more losses like that. So we're going to be patient for a few more days. With three of us on motorcycles and one in the van, we can cover the likely spots and converge quickly on wherever Dox is spotted. Like Guthrie said, Ubud's not that big a town."

Everyone nodded, accepting the matter as settled, at least temporarily. Pancho tilted his head toward the body on the floor. "You want me to bring around the van?"

Hilger nodded and started to collect the surveillance photos. They all stood.

Guthrie asked, "Where do you think we'll spot him?"

Hilger considered one of the photos. "Look at this guy. If he weren't such a good sniper, he'd probably be playing professional football. How much does a guy like this eat every day?"

Demeere smiled and said, "Plenty."

Hilger nodded. "Exactly. I don't know what kind of food supplies he's got laid in, but sooner or later, he's going to have to go out for more. That's what we're waiting for."

2

DOX WOKE WITH a long, pleasant groan. He stretched out across the king bed, curling his toes, liking the feel of the cotton sheets against his body. From the sun on the gauze curtains, it must have been past seven. He'd slept late. But why not? He wasn't on a job. He deserved to take it easy. Taking it easy was what Bali was all about. Hell, it was why he'd come here. It was why he'd built this villa.

He got up and walked naked across the sisal rug to the bathroom to take a leak. It was funny, when he'd first imagined this place, he thought it would be the ultimate bachelor pad. But now that it was done, he found he was reluctant to share it. Bedding down with someone inside a place he'd built himself would feel more intimate than he was ready for. Or rather, he hadn't met anyone yet whom he was ready to be that intimate with. He wanted to meet someone good, someone right, but of the many women he'd known and enjoyed, he just couldn't get that close with any of them. There was

Rain's lady, of course, Delilah, and a man would have to be gay or in a coma not to have some kind of thing for her, but even acknowledging to yourself that you had a hankering for your bro's woman was a dangerous thing. And doing anything to act on it would be an unpardonable sin, not to mention a declaration of war against the kind of man you'd have to be insane to want for an enemy.

Anyway, it wasn't like he pined for Delilah or anything like that. It was more like, she was just the kind of woman he wished he could meet. Smart, confident, and of course drop-dead gorgeous. Semi-mysterious, with a tasty little edge to keep you on your toes. Like what Angelina Jolie might be if she were blond and had taken up spy work for the Mossad instead of acting.

Well, he'd keep looking. And it wasn't like he was suffering in the meantime. He had a couple of honeys tucked away in Kuta, only an hour away, and several in Bangkok and Jakarta who went into paroxysms whenever he called to say he was coming to town.

He finished urinating, then looked at himself in the mirror. He liked what he saw: just shy of six feet and a solid two hundred twenty-five pounds, with a six-pack and no fat other than a pair of moderate love handles the ladies seemed to find endearing. Exercise was the key. He liked to do something different every day: weights, the jump rope, a Cross Fit routine, some kettlebell stuff he'd learned from the Russians and bodyweight exercises Rain had shown him. He figured his body looked about ten years younger than the forty he actually was, which was good. He wanted to be able to keep chasing twenty-five-year-olds for as long as possible without feeling like a dirty old man.

He knew he wouldn't be able to maintain himself forever, but that didn't really bother him. He didn't care if he lost his hair, either, although at this point it didn't look like he was going to. There were only two things he would miss, when the time came: being able to take out a dime-size target at five hundred yards in low light, and getting it up as quick as a fourteen-year-old with a can of Crisco and a Carmen Electra video. Young enough to get wood right away, but old enough to last pretty much as long as he wanted, that was the best thing about being forty. Waiting to come until you'd given some pretty lady as much pleasure as she could stand, until she was practically dying from it and begging you for mercy, well, if there was a better high than that on this earth, he'd like to know what it could be.

Of course, when that day came, when his hands got shaky and his pecker turned weak, he'd have to remind himself he was lucky. Not everyone lived long enough to have to deal with such eventualities. He was planning to, but you never really knew. The main thing was to enjoy yourself while you could, because in the end, everybody's moment was brief. Especially in the line of work he was in.

He walked over to the window and opened the curtain, letting the sun warm his body. God, what a vista. Nothing but blue skies, white clouds, and green rice fields dotted with coconut trees. He loved standing here and surveying his realm, not just because the view was so good, but because this was one of the few places in the world where he felt comfortable silhouetting himself this way. He'd taken out enough people through the glass of their own windows to have developed a permanent shyness about any room with a view. Sure, he could have spent a lifetime in therapy doing successive aversion training or some other bullshit to get over his nervousness, or he could just have all his windows custom-built out of aluminum oxynitride by a company called Surmet. They called their product ALON and it could stop multiple .50 caliber armor-piercing rounds, meaning an ordinary sniper bullet had about the same chance of getting through as a mosquito. How did those MasterCard ads go? "Aluminum oxynitride bullet-resistant glass—ten dollars a square inch. Peace of mind that no one's about to blow your brains out with a scoped rifle—priceless."

He pulled on shorts and a tee-shirt and spent an hour hitting the weights in his first-floor exercise room, then showered and made himself a giant protein smoothie for breakfast. A cup of milk, a couple bananas, papayas, mangos, and four raw eggs. The eggs were his last, he noted—he'd have to pick up some more. And he was getting low on fruit, too.

He drank it all down while using the laptop he kept on the kitchen table to catch up on the latest horseshit in the Middle East and elsewhere. A long time ago he'd been troubled over the way he'd left the Marines, but these days you couldn't pay him enough to be part of the government. The hypocrisy of it all was enough to make you sick. He wondered how people could stand for it. If he were a philosopher king or a benevolent dictator, the only jobs he thought he might enjoy more than his current occupation, he'd have a rule that you could only authorize a war if you were actually going to go off and fight it. That'd get the politicians singing "Kumbaya" right quick.

When he was done with breakfast and the news, he checked the URL that ran a live feed from the four CCTV cameras he had positioned around the house. Everything was normal. Not that he was expecting any visitors, of course, but a little extra assurance never hurt anyone. He wished he could get a dog—for security, a low-tech little yapper was hard to beat—but he traveled too much for it to be feasible. Maybe if he settled down a little more, found a brown-skinned woman with almond-shaped eyes. Get her pregnant, raise a family, teach the kids to hunt and fish and shoot like he could. Yeah, maybe one day.

Getting dressed to go out in Bali didn't usually mean much—this morning, just shorts, a tee-shirt, and sandals. He would have preferred to accessorize with a baby Glock or one of the other pistols he kept handy, but you always had to weigh accessibility, concealability, the likelihood of need, and the likelihood of getting busted for violating Indonesia's draconian gun laws. This morning, he felt the balance was against the Glock. But that didn't mean he would be unarmed: he put a Spyderco Clipit Civilian in his front right pocket and hung a Fred Perrin La Griffe with a two-inch spear-point blade around his neck inside the shirt. He grabbed the big backpack he used for groceries, opened the garage, and took out his motorcycle, a 250cc wine-colored Honda Rebel, beat-up, dirty, and reliable as hell.

It was still morning but it was already getting hot, and the air was plenty sticky. He stood there for a moment, just appreciating the feeling of another day in paradise. He liked everything about it, the smell of the mud, even of the duck excrement that fertilized the paddies. It didn't smell like shit to him at all, it smelled like life, real life far away from all the places covered in concrete and asphalt and choking on diesel. It smelled like the earth itself.

He pulled on his helmet, hating the thing as always because of the heat. The locals didn't always adhere to

Indonesia's helmet ordinances, but as an obvious foreigner he found it best to do what he could to avoid standing out, especially when standing out meant disrespecting the host country's laws.

There was no driveway as such; just a quarter-mile-long dirt road. He fired up the bike and motored slowly forward, looking around automatically as he moved, noting the hot spots, checking to see if anything seemed out of order, if anything rubbed him the wrong way. There was no good way to get to him at the villa, which was half the point of its location and design, but the least worst place for an ambush would be somewhere along this road, and so he was always extra alert coming and going here. But nothing was at all amiss this morning, just the usual dogs barking agreeably in the background, the usual farmers sweating at their labors amid the thigh-high rice.

He turned right at the end of the road and picked up speed. A 250cc bike was small for a guy his size, but it's what everyone around here used and the roads were too narrow and winding to go very fast anyway.

He pulled into the parking lot of the Bintang supermarket on Jalan Raya Ubud and killed the engine. The Bintang was in a two-story stone building with a wood-and-red-tile roof, surrounded by ferns and bamboo trees. It was by far the biggest market in town, and the one Dox liked when he needed more than just a few supplies. Out front were the usual complement of motorbikes, bicycles, and cars. A small dog, one of the scores that roamed Ubud unsupervised, lay in the shade under the front awning, conserving its energy in the gathering tropical heat.

Inside the store, a couple of mothers with diapered toddlers in tow prowled the cramped aisles, shopping for tonight's dinner, a few household supplies, maybe a bit of candy to keep the baby smiling. Dox had nowhere special to go, and spent a leisurely half-hour moving methodically through the store and loading up a small cart. When he was done, he rolled up to the register, where a pretty girl he knew as Wan was working.

"How are you today, Mr. Dox?" the girl asked him with a beautiful Bali smile.

Dox smiled back, but kept a little distance in his expression. Wan was a tasty-looking little treat, no question, but a sensible man knew not to shit where he ate. Or in this case, shopped. Besides, he could get all he wanted and more an hour away, in Kuta and Sanur.

"Fine, Wan, and how about you? Putting up okay with the heat?"

The girl laughed, her eyes sparkling. "Oh, Mr. Dox, this isn't hot today, you know that."

He made a show of mopping his brow. "Darlin', you're tougher than I am."

The groceries cost him a whopping four hundred thousand rupiah—about forty bucks. He wondered if anyone had ever done a study on the prospects of countries where buying groceries cost half a million of the local unit of currency. He doubted there was much correlation between economic health and all those zeros.

He loaded the groceries into his backpack, shouldered it, said goodbye to Wan, and headed outside.

A foreigner, a big blond dude, was pacing in front of the building near where Dox had parked the Honda, a mobile phone to his ear. He was wearing shades and speaking a language Dox didn't recognize—not German, not French, Dutch, maybe? When he looked up and saw Dox, he closed the phone and smiled.

"Hello, maybe you can help me," he said, with a slight, indeterminate accent. "Do you speak English?"

"Depends on who you ask," Dox said. The guy seemed like your typical lost European tourist—not exactly an unknown species in the area—but still, Dox immediately glanced left and right. The perimeter check was a learned reflex, triggered whenever a stranger tried to engage him. The danger is that the person asking for directions, or the time, or a light, or whatever, is there to distract you from his cohorts, who are flanking you from your blind side, and Dox wasn't about to get caught that way.

To Dox's left, a guy in a full-face motorcycle helmet was leaning against the wall under the awning, doing nothing in particular. On the right—another guy in a full-face helmet, moving leisurely in Dox's direction.

Later, his conscious mind would articulate all the factors that his unconscious had just instantly, wordlessly spotted and assessed. He would be able to describe what was wrong with this picture: the positions of the guys in the helmets relative to the blond dude; the way they were waiting in places in which they had no ostensible reason to wait; that they were wearing helmets in the heat even though they were off their bikes; how smoothly and deliberately the one on the right was closing the distance.

But for now, his understanding took the form only of a sudden heat in his gut. He knew the feeling. He especially knew not to doubt it. A single word—*fuck!*—blaring in his mind like a klaxon, he braced and reached for the Civilian.

The blond guy moved—much faster than Dox thought he'd be able to, given his size. He took a long step forward and pivoted, and then his right foot crashed into Dox's midsection like a freight train.

Dox had just enough time to react by tightening his stomach, and that saved him from having the wind knocked out of him entirely. But the kick still blasted him backward and cost him his grip on the knife. The Civilian clattered to the ground, and Dox struggled to regain his balance. A part of him understood that he was already far behind, that whatever this was, it was going very badly.

One of the guys in helmets latched onto his right wrist. Dox found his footing, pivoted, and smashed his free elbow into the guy's head. If he had connected with the guy's skull the blow might have killed him, or at least knocked him off, but the helmet kept the guy in the game, and now he was dragging on Dox's arm, trying to pull him off balance. Dox spun clockwise, getting behind the guy, sucking him in close with his giant forearm, and reached under the tee-shirt with his left hand. He pulled free the La Griffe, its ring handle encircling his first two fingers and its razor-sharp blade protruding from his fist like a claw. But before he could get it under helmet boy's chin and rip out his throat, the blond guy had wrapped himself around Dox's left arm, both hands securing the wrist. Something stung Dox in the neck from behind and he knew with a sickening lurch what it was. He struggled against the men on his arms. They felt heavier, and his vision blurred. He staggered and thought, *John, fuck, I'm sorry.* And then he was gone.

3

I SHOULD HAVE known they'd get to me through Dox. He was no soft target, true, but he was easier than I am, and a little easier is sometimes all it takes.

I was living with Delilah in Paris at the time. Or living with her separately, you could say. Her job was such that security required different apartments, and various other minor inconveniences. Although I suppose that when half the romance is a retired contract killer and the other half a committed Mossad agent, separate dwellings can be the least of your troubles.

I liked Paris, liked almost everything about it. Along with Barcelona, where I'd spent a month with Delilah a year earlier, it was as beautiful a city as I've ever seen, the architecture and the open spaces and the endlessly walkable streets. I loved the coffee culture, and relished a place where I could indulge my enthusiasm for the bean in an endless profusion of sidewalk cafés. I wondered at little mysteries, like the abandoned bicycles chained to the park gates at the place des Vosges, slumped insensate against their shackles, their wheels bent and broken, like crippled pets whose owners cared too much to kill them and who compromised instead by leaving them to die. I thought of the generations that had visited the city before me, dreamers and cynics, romantics and radicals, the ones who had come here to find something, and the ones who wanted only to forget what they had lost or left behind.

I'd never been to Paris before, and when I first arrived, my impressions were all secondhand. I expected an ambience born of architecture, romance, history, gustation. I pictured the Louvre and its glass pyramid; the Seine and Notre Dame; intellectuals arguing over philosophy and smoking ceaselessly in clusters of Left Bank cafés.

What I saw on the train ride from the airport, therefore, was unsettling. Paris, it seemed, was besieged, ringed with tenement towns not unlike Rio's favelas. Many of these were walled off, at least from the highways and the train tracks, and the gray concrete barriers, some topped with razor wire, were covered, every inch of them, with ugly, angry graffiti, like sea walls braced against a seething tide. By the time I arrived at Gare du Nord in Paris proper, the graffitied walls had abated, but their import lingered: this was a civilization encircled by its enemies, living uneasily under some implicit, eroding truce, slowly losing a war the signs of which were everywhere but that its citizens preferred to ignore.

I took a small apartment on rue Beautrellis in the Fourth Arrondissement, the same block where Jim Morrison had once lived, on the edge of the Marais. The rent was high, but I'd walked away from an operation in Japan a year earlier with two million tax-free dollars, and I could afford it. I liked the feel of the neighborhood, the glow of its streetlamps, the sounds of laughter and conversation from its bars and bistros. In a strange way, the area reminded me in its intimacy of Sengoku, the Tokyo neighborhood I'd been forced to leave a thousand years earlier.

Delilah's work kept her busy, and we had to be careful about seeing each other regardless, so I had ample time alone. That was good: partly because being alone suits me; partly because in Paris it gave me time to adjust to the new sensation of having someone in my life. It wasn't just the unfamiliarity of plans several times a week—dinner at Le Petit Célestin on the quai des Célestins; a walk on the narrow streets of the Ile Saint-Louis; a night at my apartment; sometimes a night at hers. It was the whole notion, the feeling, of being someplace primarily because of another person's presence there. There was a lot I liked about that feeling, but it was taking me a while to get used to it, and I was glad circumstances permitted me to go slowly. I used the time alone to explore the city, and read, and practice French with tapes. It was my fourth language, after Japanese, English, and Portuguese, and I remembered some of it from high school. It was coming back quickly.

I'd been telling myself for a long time that I wanted out of the life, but it was only recently, with Delilah, that the longing had become real. For a while, she had been heading in the same direction. Her organization blamed her for losing a colleague, an assassin called Gil, in an otherwise successful terrorist takedown in Hong Kong, and was set to cut her loose. But she'd faced them down and forced her way back in, and now she was more determined than ever to stay.

I was ambivalent about her work. On the one hand, it gave me space, which I liked. On the other hand, her continued presence in the life inhibited my own efforts to leave it. Part of it was the behavioral cues—the need for a ready cover story when I was with her in case she ran into someone she knew, and her routine perimeter checks and other tactics—which continued to remind me of who I'd always been. Part of it was ongoing operational necessity, because as long as she was in the life, she was at risk, and if you're with someone at risk, you'd better believe you're at risk, too. And part of it was notional: if I was this involved with someone still in the life, how far could I have left the life behind?

I pushed her sometimes, but not too hard. I'd learned Delilah was a fighter, and if she felt she was being doubted, or second-guessed, or in any way talked down to, she had a tendency to come out swinging.

"Why not retire?" I asked her once, over café-crèmes and croissants at Le Loir dans la Théière, a restaurant on the rue des Rosiers named after the dormouse in the teacup in *Alice in Wonderland*. Delilah had introduced me to the place, and I loved the mismatched chairs and small wooden tables, the eclectic wall art, the wonderful smell of years of fresh ground coffee. "We could buy an apartment on the beach in Barcelona. Make love to the sounds of the waves at night, walk on the beach in the morning. Nothing but the feel of the sun and the smell of coffee and cava and no bad memories."

She smiled and pushed back a strand of blond hair. Her blue eyes were lit by sunlight coming through the restaurant's large front windows. "You make it sound enticing. Especially the making love part."

"That was my favorite, too."

She laughed. "I don't know, John. I don't know."

I took a sip of coffee and watched her. I liked it when she called me John. My Rolodex is slim, and the few people in it tend not to use my first name. Midori had called me Jun, short for Junichi, my Japanese given name, and at the time I had liked that very much, too. But that was before she had betrayed me to protect our infant son, and thereby denied me a part in his life. Among the bad memories I had just mentioned, Midori held a prominent position.

"What would you do if you were doing something else?" I asked. "If you'd never gotten into the life. Do you ever think about that?"

"Sometimes," she allowed.

"What would it be?"

"I don't know," she said again. "Maybe fashion photography. That's the cover I've been living in Paris, and I like it. I suppose I could have done it for real."

"Then do it now."

She took my hand. "You know I can't. Iran is poised to go nuclear, we have Hamas in the territories and Hezbollah in Lebanon. Things are going to get worse before they get better, if they ever get better at all. I can't just walk away to photograph anorexic girls on catwalks."

"Is that all you'd be walking away for?"

"You know what I mean."

I tried again one evening as we stood pressed together on Pont Sully, taking in the glowing lights of the Ile Saint-Louis and the illuminated buttresses of Notre Dame. "Your organization is using you," I told her. "You've said so yourself. Why don't you just walk away?"

I felt her stiffen, and she took a half-step back. "I've told you before," she said, looking at me. "The 'organization' isn't the point. This is about my country. My people."

I shook my head. "I don't buy it. I think this is about

you standing up to the men who blamed you for Gil getting killed in Hong Kong. Showing them you're tougher than they are, that they can't drive you out."

"Why does everything have to be so one-dimensional with you? Yes, I have personal reasons for staying. My dignity is involved, fine, I admit it. But why can't you at least acknowledge there are other reasons, too?"

"Because . . ."

"I'll tell you why. It's because you've never been tied to anything larger than yourself. You don't believe in anything. So you can't imagine someone who does. She must be either deluded or lying or naive."

I felt myself flush. "I understand your selfless reasons better than you know. I also understand the more devotion you give to the organization or the corps or the country, the more it'll hollow you out when you realize your love was always unrequited. The more you'll feel betrayed."

We were quiet for a moment. She said, "It doesn't have to be that way for everyone."

"You know anyone whose experience has been different?"

We stared at each other. Her eyes were narrowed and her nostrils flared slightly with her breathing. That's the way it was with us. We could go from bliss and harmony to anger and recriminations as fast and with as little warning as a tropical storm. What made it bearable, what made it good, was that the foul weather would pass with equal suddenness, usually leaving something glorious in its wake.

"Anyway," I said, "I am tied to something larger than myself. I'm tied to you."

Her eyes softened. Then she stepped in close and kissed me. I turned my head away, still irritated, but she reached up and turned me back. I resisted for another moment, mostly for form's sake, and then gave in.

We stood like that for a minute or so, and the kiss grew into something more. I could feel her breasts, the heat of her skin, and suddenly I wanted badly to be alone with her someplace.

She broke the kiss and hooked her fingers through my belt. "Let's go to your apartment," she said. "We can fight better there."

We did. And things were good again, until next time, when the pattern would repeat itself.

But between the periodic swings from bitter argument to sweet resolution, things were mostly good. I haven't been deeply involved with many women, but among them, only Delilah really knew about, and accepted, what I was beginning to try to think of as my past. The surprising depth of our mutual chemistry, and the improbability of the romance it led to, was a quiet miracle for me. Delilah shared with me intimacies that I sensed came from the deepest places within her, aspects of her mind and her body that by long habit she had learned to protect ferociously and that she conceded now only slowly, cautiously, with fear-tinged hope.

I found myself opening up with her, as well. I'd meant it when I told her I was getting attached. I'd been alone so long, I'd learned to conceive of myself that way, but slowly and strangely, my conception of myself was beginning to include someone else. Sometimes the attachment scared me, and felt like a burden. Other times it seemed like a life raft, or at least like ballast. Either way, it was real, and deepening.

But one thing I didn't share with Delilah was the onset of periodic ... anxiety attacks, for want of a better description. Occasionally, I would get so lost in a book in a café that I would neglect to look up when I heard someone come in, or so lost in thought on a morning stroll that I'd suddenly realize an entire minute had elapsed and I hadn't checked my back. At those moments, I'd be gripped by a kind of horror, the feeling you get if you accidentally run a red light at full speed and miraculously manage to breeze through the intersection unscathed. You can tell yourself no harm, no foul, but still you know you fucked up, that in another universe you were annihilated by a truck coming from your left, or you mowed down a young mother stepping off the curb, or were overtaken by some similar catastrophe. A primal part of your mind screams, *How could you be so careless? Do you want to die?*

I was used to living with fear, and there was always a reason for it, typically that someone was trying to kill me. Now that the causes of fear were growing distant, the fear itself diminishing, anxiety was filling the vacuum. Had I been afraid so long that I needed something to be afraid of, something the fear could focus on?

I tried taking long walks at night, the more deserted the streets, the better. There was an area in the Eighteenth Arrondissement, known as La Goutte d'Or, near Barbès, that I particularly favored. Decorated with the incinerated husks of cars the locals had torched, and inhabited by dealers, beggars, and illegals from the Maghreb, the area had a dangerous, desperate edge that kept me on my toes. Its street denizens would observe me as I moved through, not knowing what to make of me. I was in France, but my face was Japanese; my attire was civilian, but my vibe was anything but. Aside from occasional offers of drugs, they mostly left me alone.

Once, a tall Moroccan with a shaved head and ears

weighed down by multiple metal studs started pacing me from behind while I walked. I calmly glanced back at him, and at the two friends trailing in his wake, to let them know I was aware of their presence, and to signal thereby that I wasn't afraid, stupid, or likely to be easy. He mistook my cautionary glance as an opening, though, and called out to me in Moroccan-accented French, "What you doing here, man? You want to buy something? I help you find it. What you want?"

I checked the area to ensure I wasn't being flanked, then stopped and turned to him. "I'm not what you're looking for," I said in French.

But he kept coming. He might have been too stupid to have understood my signals. Or maybe he had decided to resolve his cognitive dissonance over my appearance and vibe by more closely examining me, rather than just shrugging and moving on.

"No, man," he said. "Wait up. I just want to help."

His friends were fanning out now, moving toward my flanks. I felt adrenaline churn through my system, and damn if its hot rush wasn't almost sweet. I checked my rear again. All clear.

It was going to be a fast interview, I could tell. One, maybe two more questions to distract me and confirm my vulnerability; a sucker punch to drop me and signal his friends to move in; a joyous multiple stomping; then off with my wallet, watch, and anything else I would no longer be needing.

"It's cool," he said, coming into range. "I know you come for something here in La Goutte. I want . . ."

Most people find it hard to do two things at once, like complete a sentence and avoid a palm heel to the nose. Which was why I nailed him that way in mid-thought. It wasn't the world's hardest shot, but as a simple setup, it didn't need to be. It just needed to disrupt his focus and rock him back onto his heels. Which it did.

I stepped past him, my right hand catching his throat in an eagle claw grip and my right leg sweeping both his legs from under him. But for the throat grab and substitution of concrete for a mat, it was pretty much the classic *osoto-gari*, or big outer leg reap, I had performed hundreds of thousands of times in my years at the Kodokan. Basic, but still one of my favorite throws.

For a split second, Mr. Helper was suspended horizontally. Then he was accelerating downward, assisted substantially by the downward force I was exerting on his neck. The back of his skull blasted into the sidewalk with a resounding *crack*, like the sound a thick book makes when someone slams it closed.

Palming the folding knife I had clipped to my front pocket, I checked my perimeter. Still clear. I took a step toward his two friends, who were rooted in place. "Do you still want to help me?" I asked, my voice calm.

"No, man," one of them answered, his hands raised palms out in supplication. They started backing away. "It's cool, man."

I checked the papers the next day, and there was nothing about a killing in La Goutte. So Mr. Helper must have had a hard head. The only downside of the whole thing, from my perspective, was that prudence required I steer clear of the area for a while.

There were other places, though, and I continued to visit them at night. Still, the nocturnal prowling helped only so much. Situational awareness for countering potential street crime is one thing. The fever pitch alertness required to survive professionals who are patiently, dispassionately, specifically, maneuvering to take your life is something else. If you're addicted to the latter, and maybe I was, the former is no more than an occasional dose of methadone in the face of a long-term heroin habit.

As my relationship with Delilah deepened, and as I gradually eased myself away from the mindset you need to survive in the life, it was as though the part of myself that was so adept in dangerous environments, the part that had kept me alive in the jungle in Vietnam and then in countless urban jungles afterward, didn't like what was going on. That killer inside me, that iceman who could always do what needed to be done, felt he was being marginalized, disenfranchised. But what could I do? I didn't know how to propitiate him, or even if I could. All I knew was that he was deadly, as deadly as anyone I've ever known, and capable of almost anything if he felt his survival required it. I could feel him looking for a reason, a rationale, an excuse to come surging back and shove me out of the way.

Someone who needed him, say. Someone in danger. Someone like Dox.

4

DOX CAME TO SUDDENLY. One moment he was out, gone, and then it was as though someone had pressed his reboot button. He blinked and swallowed, and for a moment he thought maybe it had been a nightmare. He had that kind of dream from time to time, where the bullets would just plop out of his rifle, or his knives would all get stuck in their sheaths, and when it happened he knew he needed to train, because hard training was the only way to sleep well again. But this time, as he came around, the images in his mind only grew sharper, and he knew it had really happened. He'd gotten grabbed.

Christ, he was sore all over. Must have gotten bounced around some while he was out. He tried to move and couldn't, then realized why. His wrists and ankles were secured, and his hands were stretched back above his head. Actually, below his head was more like it, because as he recovered his senses he saw that he was strapped to a declined board, with his feet about a foot higher than his head. Well, that wasn't a good sign.

Where the hell was he? A small room, maybe ten by

ten. Wood walls. Fluorescent lights. Nothing else to go on. He felt like he was rising and falling and thought it was because he was woozy, but then he recognized the rhythm for what it was. He was on a boat, and the movement he felt was of swells underneath him.

Who had taken him? Whoever they were, they were good. They hadn't wasted a second once the blond guy engaged him. The flankers were ready and knew exactly when to move in. Coordination like that showed not just skill, but the kind of unit confidence and cohesion you get only after a lot of training together. These weren't freelancers. They'd worked together as a team before.

He wondered if that asshole Jim Hilger had something to do with it. He'd sensed as much in the instant before he blacked out, and he'd learned to trust his instincts on these things. First answer, best answer, that was usually his experience. And now that he was awake and thinking, he saw there was some logic behind that initial, unconscious conclusion. The coordination and skill, for one thing, that felt like Hilger. After all, the man had been Special Forces and then CIA before going off the reservation. And there was a motive that could explain things, too. He and Rain had killed two very bad men in Hilger's network, one an arms dealer, the other a terrorist trying to buy nuclear matériel, forcing Hilger to go to ground in the process, and it was possible the man was the type to hold a grudge. Yeah, this was probably about Rain, too, otherwise why didn't they just kill him outright in front of the Bintang? Why run all the extra risks of a snatch? Well, whatever, he'd find out who did it and what they wanted soon enough.

He was furious at himself for being stupid enough to get nailed like this. He'd waited too long, that was his first mistake. He hadn't checked his perimeter until the blond guy asked for his help, when he should have checked it from within the store, or, failing that, then as soon as he'd stepped outside. Dumb, just fucking dumb. If he'd seen those guys standing around in their helmets, he would have gone to code red with an extra two seconds to spare, before they'd even gotten a chance to move on him, and that would have made all the difference.

And he shouldn't have gone for the knife immediately when he saw something was off—that was reflex, to reach for a weapon, but there it was the wrong reflex. He should have moved first, moved off the X, the killing spot, made them react, chase after him, whatever. He would have had plenty of time to get to the knife, and hold on to it, after that. Wasn't that one of the things John was always telling him? *Move. Never give them a stationary target.* Sometimes he felt like Rain was lecturing him and bristled at it, but he had to admit the man knew what he was talking about.

He wondered how they had traced him. Well, there were a lot of ways they might have learned he was in Ubud, if they had enough resources. From there, they probably deployed a watcher at every grocery store in town, knowing he would have to show eventually. When he did, someone used a radio or a mobile phone to alert the others, and they converged on the Bintang while he was inside. When was the last time he'd been there? Four days earlier . . . no, five. So they'd probably been in town close to a week. Had he seen anyone who set off his radar? No, but there were always tourists passing through Ubud, and besides, if these guys were in helmets and on motorcycles, they would have been damn near impossible to spot.

At least one of them must have been driving a van. They'd injected him with fentanyl or Rohypnol, something like that, that was the sting in his neck. Shove him into the van after knocking him out, and they're off before anyone could intervene or even be sure what was happening. Change vehicles somewhere close by, then head for the coast where they'd moored the boat. Which pretty much brought things up to date.

He took a deep breath. All right, he'd fucked up. Hard to argue about it at this point. But there was no use beating up on himself—he had a feeling someone else would be taking care of that, and more, soon enough. Being demoralized would only make it harder for him to keep his shit wired tight.

And he could keep it tight, he knew that. It wasn't how far you fell, it was how high you bounced—his dad had once told him that and he'd never forgotten it. If he could survive sniper school, he could survive anything. He could certainly survive this, whatever it was. He just had to remember who he was and what he was made of. He had to hold that close and not let them separate him from it.

He waited a long time, silently telling himself jokes he liked. That one he'd told Rain about the bear was great. The guy didn't like to laugh much, which made it all the more satisfying to get to him. When Dox got out of this, he'd be sure to tell Rain the one about *kabunga*. That would be apt, under the circumstances.

He reminded himself from time to time that the waiting was part of it, part of how they hoped to wear him down, with uncertainty about everything, who had taken him, what this was about, where he was, what might happen next, when it might happen. He'd been trained to resist interrogation, and knowing what to expect was half the battle. He was pleasantly surprised, even bolstered, to realize the training was really helping.

After what he estimated was three hours, the door to the room opened. The blond dude, whom he recognized from the parking lot, came in first, followed by a scary-looking bald guy, and then a smaller specimen who looked way too young to be mixed up in any of this. The bald guy and the young one he assumed had been wearing the helmets in front of the Bintang. He heard another set of footsteps, and sure enough, there he was—Hilger, just as Dox had suspected. Okay, check off the *who* box. *Why* and *where* were still open.

The four of them stood around him, observing him silently. About fifteen seconds passed.

Dox yawned. "If this is nothing pressing," he said, "I'd like to ask you boys to give me another twenty minutes or so to continue my nap. I'm sure you didn't mean to, but you've interrupted me."

He chuckled, enjoying fucking with them while he could. He might not be able to keep it up, but half of what they planned to do to him involved the infliction of dread, and damned if he would accommodate them by actually feeling it.

Not unless he absolutely had to.

5

HILGER SLID a wooden chair over and sat facing Dox. He observed the big man for a moment, as silently and dispassionately as a scientist studying a microbe. He wanted Dox to understand that he viewed him not as a man, but merely as a subject, the focus of a series of impending if/then sequences that meant nothing to Hilger other than his desire for a certain result.

"I'm going to make this as easy for you as I can," Hilger said, his voice low, his tone reasonable. "There's no need for you to suffer, or even to be uncomfortable. The information I want isn't going to compromise anyone. It's not going to put anyone in danger. It's just going to enable me to contact someone. That's all."

Dox smiled. "The ladies in my little black book wouldn't be interested in you, amigo, I'm sorry to be the one to tell you. They seem to prefer their men handsome and virile."

Hilger sighed. He'd seen men in Dox's position before, many of them. What they all had in common was fear. What differed, what was interesting, was the way they tried to cope with it.

Some men, faced with torture, would bluster. Some men begged. Both types were really two sides of the same coin: their focus was the interrogator, and because of this they tended to crack easily. As soon as they saw that their bluster and begging were useless, that they couldn't make a human connection that would stop the pain and torment, their psyches folded and information began to spill out.

There was another type that would go silent even before the interrogation began, who wouldn't utter a word even later, even while screaming. These men were more self-contained, and therefore more difficult to crack. They didn't expect anything from their interrogator. They conceived of him not so much as a human agent, but as more of a natural force, like foul weather or a disease. Not as something that could be reasoned with or negotiated with or otherwise influenced, but rather as something that could only be ridden out.

There was a third type, also very tough, and, in Hilger's experience, the rarest variety. These were the men who under duress defaulted to some core personality setting from which they derived strength and comfort. Dox, it seemed, was part of this last group. They didn't disengage from the interrogator the way the stoics did, but their behavior wasn't calculated to affect the interrogator like that of the beggars and blusterers, either. Its function instead was self-referential. What Dox was doing, although Hilger wasn't sure if he was even conscious of it, was proving that if he could still crack jokes, he was still himself. If he was still himself, he was still in control, and things couldn't be that bad.

Which was what made breaking men like Dox so hard. It wasn't just a question of pain. Pain was a surface thing. To break a man like Dox, you had to break him down deep. Even with a jihadist, it was an unpleasant thing to have to do. With an American, a former service-man like Dox, it could be grim.

"I know from your file you've been through SERE," Hilger said. "Did they waterboard you?"

SERE was the military's Survival, Evasion, Resis-tance, Escape program. The purpose of the question was twofold: first, to bring forth memories that would trig-ger anxiety; second, to suggest that Hilger knew a great deal about Dox, that he was in complete control.

"You tell me," Dox said, and Hilger thought, *Touché.*

"They did," Hilger continued. "You held out for al-most five minutes. Your instructors were impressed."

Dox smiled. "They gave me a gold star."

"It's different when it's not in the classroom. Worse."

Dox glanced up at his bound feet. "You know, just be-cause the latest chickenshit legislation says it's okay to do this sort of thing doesn't mean you should be doing it. Shame on y'all."

Pancho laughed. "Why not? The legislation even promises to indemnify us, if we get in trouble."

Dox looked at him. "Especially shame on you, son. You're a disgrace to the Marines."

Pancho startled for a moment, then glanced at the Semper Fi tattoo on his forearm, realizing where Dox had gotten his information.

Hilger could almost have smiled. Dox was playing the same "I know more than I'm letting on" game Hilger was.

"And where's that accent from?" Dox said. "You from Mexico?"

Pancho's eyes narrowed. "You have a problem with that?"

Dox turned his head and spat. "Well, it explains a few things."

Pancho started to move forward. Demeere stepped in front of him and said, "Easy, easy."

"Go ahead," Dox said. "You might be able to take me, tied up as I am." Then he added something in Spanish that made the blood drain from Pancho's face and scalp. Pancho tried to move around Demeere, but the big man kept him back.

Hilger was impressed. Dox was using what he could to control what he could, and steadying himself in the process. Before he could manipulate the environment any further, Hilger said, "You're right, it's strange there was such a fuss over these . . . what did the president call them? 'Alternative interrogation techniques,' that's right. Because mostly they're ineffective, it's true. You haul in a fishing trawl's worth of field-level jihadists? You don't know who they are, much less what they know? Hook up the alligator clips and crank the generator and they spew so much bullshit that even if there's some real intel mixed in with it, you'll never know, much less be able to make use of it."

He paused as though in thought. "But when you know who you've captured? And you know he's got the information you're after? And you can immediately verify the quality of that information as soon as you extract it? Well, when you've got all that, alligator clips and a generator are pretty much a man's best friend."

"Listen to what you just said," Dox said. "Really, listen. Alligator clips and a generator are a man's best friend? You've been out in the field too long, amigo. All of you have. You've got to get yourself some help. You need it."

Hilger was getting irritated despite himself. "What I need," he said, "is information. Tell me how I contact Rain."

Dox chuckled. "Yeah, I thought you might be pissed about Hong Kong. How's the back, by the way? That was a heavy chair."

Hilger cautioned himself not to take the bait. He had to be smarter than that. If he reacted like Pancho, they'd all just wind up beating the shit out of the subject and get nothing of any value.

"The back is fine," Hilger said. "Thanks for asking."

"What do you want with Rain? You mad at him for killing that guy Al-Jib? Boy wanted to make an atomic bomb for Al-Qaeda. And you were going to give him the matériel. I'll tell you the truth, it's hard for me not to be sick just talking to you from this close."

"What you don't know about Al-Jib," Hilger said, "would fill a book. And when AQ does get a bomb or a radiological device, you and your friend can thank yourselves for it. You fucked up an operation that would have stopped it."

"That what you tell yourself when the Ambien's not working and you're lying awake at night?"

It was strange. Initially, seeing Dox helpless had eclipsed Hilger's anger at the man's previous interference, at the long recovery Hilger had endured after getting hit with that chair. But now that brief and improbable moment of sympathy was receding so quickly, it almost seemed not to have happened at all.

Hilger was beginning to accept that this wasn't going to be an easy one. True, the information he wanted from Dox would entail only a minor betrayal, but the man's honor and self-image required him to part with nothing without a fight. And, although his repeated requests now were likely to prove as futile as Dox's resistance later, Hilger had his own reasons for trying one more time. It would make the memories of what happened next easier to deal with.

"I'd prefer a phone number," he said, his tone still reasonable. "Or an e-mail address. Or the URL for a secure electronic bulletin board. Why don't you give me one of those instead?"

"I don't know how to contact him," Dox said. "He contacts me."

"How?"

"He calls me. Always from a different number. But I haven't heard from him in months."

"Not true, Dox. You saw him three months ago. In Barcelona."

Dox blinked, then instantly recovered. "I was in Barcelona to take in the Gaudí architecture and meet some nice Spanish ladies. You're fishing and you know it."

Hilger had been fishing—he knew from customs records Dox had spent four days in Barcelona, and had no idea whether he'd seen Rain there. But the gambit had paid off with that single, involuntary blink.

A long moment went by. Hilger said, "Last chance. Do you have something you want to say?"

Dox glanced at his feet again, then turned his head to Hilger and smiled. "It looks bleak for our hero, I'll say that."

Pancho smiled and picked up a bath towel. He started to move in.

"No," Hilger said. "You're running too hot, and you know it." He nodded to Demeere. "Do it."

Demeere took the towel from Pancho. Pancho looked at Dox and said, "You're lucky, *pendejo*. This time."

Dox smiled and said something in Spanish again.

Pancho's nostrils twitched and he strained forward like a Doberman on a leash.

"Outside," Hilger said.

Pancho shook his head. "No, I'm okay. If you're not going to let me do it, at least let me watch. I want to hear him blubbering with his voice as high as a little girl's."

"Out," Hilger said again.

Pancho shot one more glance at Dox, then nodded and started to head for the door. Dox said, "I'm going to miss you, Uncle Fester. Y'all come back and visit, you hear?"

Then Demeere was lifting Dox's head, wrapping the towel around it with clinical ease. Dox tried to twist away, but the reflex was useless. Guthrie stood astride him on the table and turned on the hose. He looked at Hilger. Hilger nodded.

Guthrie aimed the hose onto Dox's chest. The cold water hit the towel and immediately soaked through it. Dox twisted his head left and right, but Guthrie kept the water flowing onto the towel. A minute passed, during which Hilger knew Dox was holding his breath. Then suddenly the big man was choking and coughing, his body bucking against the table and the restraints around his wrists and ankles. Guthrie kept the water flowing for a few more seconds, then diverted it to the side.

The advantage of the towel was that it modulated the amount of water the subject could actually swallow, while still causing suffocation and thus the sensation of drowning. The sensation was what you wanted because that was enough to produce the panic response. Actual drowning was counterproductive because when you're unconscious, you're no longer panicking, and being revived from drowning can sometimes produce euphoria—

not exactly the goal of a hostile interrogation. Actual drowning was also risky: if the subject died, you sure as hell couldn't interrogate him. Besides, performing mouth-to-mouth resuscitation to save Abdul the terrorist suspect you were torturing a minute earlier wasn't considered good form in the community.

"Anything you want to tell me?" Hilger said, no more loudly than was necessary to get Dox's attention. "Or do you want to do it again?"

The coughing subsided, but Dox didn't answer. Hilger nodded to Guthrie, who turned the hose onto Dox's face again.

They repeated the process twice more, then again. On the fifth time, when Guthrie diverted the hose, they saw vomit flowing from under the towel. Hilger judged this the right moment. If they went on much longer, panic would be replaced by exhaustion, and Hilger would have to change to more brutal tactics, which he preferred not to do—more, he recognized, for his own sake than for Dox's.

Hilger nodded to Demeere, who stepped in and peeled the towel away. Guthrie hosed the mess off Dox's face. Dox jerked back and forth, blindly trying to avoid the spray. Guthrie turned aside the hose. Dox wheezed and gagged, then threw up again with a choking, strangled scream.

"Nothing funny to say?" Hilger asked, and was immediately ashamed of himself.

But Dox was past humor now. His chest heaved in the cadences of barely controlled panic. His teeth were chattering and his hands shook in their manacles. His breath whistled in and out in whimpers, and Hilger realized the man was crying.

Hilger pushed aside his shame and disgust. He leaned

forward and said, "I don't want to know where he is, just how to contact him."

Dox shook his head.

Hilger said, "You've already held out longer than Khaled Sheikh fucking Mohammed, you know that? And he held out as long as anyone I've ever seen. But no one can hold out against this forever. No one. Why don't you tell me what I need to know. Otherwise we're going to do it again. And again."

Hilger waited a long moment, then nodded to Demeere. The Belgian stepped forward with the towel. He lifted Dox's head, but Dox shook free.

"All right!" Dox shouted, his voice hoarse. "All right." He let out a stream of foul words that Hilger had never heard strung together quite so inventively, not even during his time with the linguistically creative men of Third Special Forces in the first Gulf War.

They waited. When the invective had subsided, Dox said, "It's a secure bulletin board." He told them the URL, and Demeere wrote it down.

"How often does he check it?" Hilger asked.

"I don't know. We're not in touch that often. I'd guess once a day, if that."

"Good. That means we've got twenty-four hours."

"For what?"

"For Rain to get back to us. If I haven't heard from him by then, I'll assume what you've given me is inaccurate. In which case, I'll have to ask you again. And probably not as nicely as I did just now."

Dox turned his head and spat. "Yeah? What are you going to do, behead me and sell the videotape to Al Jazeera?"

Hilger looked at him. "I think you're confusing me with someone else."

"Really? Why don't you tell me the difference? Because I can't see it."

Hilger waited a long moment. When he spoke, his voice was cold.

"The ends," he said. He was still looking at Dox, but it was Rain he was thinking of. "It's all about the ends."

6

ALTHOUGH THE martial arts world is vastly bigger today than it was when I got started in judo in the seventies, I still had to be careful. My face was known not only at the Kodokan in Tokyo, but also at Carlinhos Gracie's jiu-jitsu academy, where I'd trained obsessively for the year I'd lived in Rio. No one at either club knew my name, but if someone from either happened to be training in Paris, I didn't want to deal with questions about what I was doing here or where I was living.

There's a cost/benefit equation in all decisions, though, and my need to train was strong enough to outweigh the risks involved. It wasn't just a question of keeping my skills sharp, although that was part of it. Like my nocturnal excursions, training soothed an anxious part of me. So I worked out five afternoons a week at a place called the RD Sporting Club, on the boulevard Saint-Denis near the Saint-Martin canal. The club had a variety of equipment—mats, gloves, bags—and plenty of tough partners to train with. And I was glad for the opportunity to use my French, too.

Every day, usually after a workout, I would stop by an

Internet café, always a different one, to check the bulletin board I used with Dox. We weren't in touch that often, but I liked the routine. I'd done something similar for a long time with Midori before our rupture, at which point I'd shut that board down. I realized afterward that I missed the possibility of a message, that I had grown used to living with the pleasure of a small quotidian hope.

I almost hated to admit it, because Dox's boisterousness, wisecracking, and willingness to wing it on tradecraft drove me crazy, but he was now as close a friend as I'd ever had. I hadn't much cared for him when we'd first met, in Afghanistan. He was damn capable in the field, but his constant antics and outsized personality grated on me. Then, a few years ago, some elements in the CIA had tried to draw on the Afghan connection in sending Dox after me in Rio. Instead, the two of us wound up working together. The partnership was of necessity at first, and I distrusted him. But at Kwai Chung harbor in Hong Kong, he'd walked away from a bag with five million dollars in it to save my life. With that one remarkable act, he'd blasted through my defenses and altered my whole worldview. I still struggled with the aftermath. Would I have done the same for him? Today I wouldn't hesitate, but at the time . . . no, I had to admit, at the time I wouldn't have. I didn't trust anyone back then, didn't think anyone was worthy of trust. I believed in preemptive betrayal. There was a line I heard in a movie once: "Hell, I'll kill a man in a fair fight . . . or if I think he's gonna start a fair fight." That was me. There was nothing wrong with betrayal, just with letting the other guy beat you to it. But Dox had changed my view. The only person I could think of who had affected me as profoundly was Delilah.

One day, on one of these forays to an Internet café, I saw there was a message waiting from the big sniper. I smiled and opened it, expecting nothing more than a report on the weather in Bali and maybe a hint of some fresh sexual conquest. The usual, from Dox.

I couldn't have been more wrong. The message said, *We got to your friend near his villa on Bali. He's with us, and for now he's okay. But if we haven't heard from you within twenty-four hours from posting this message, we can't guarantee his continued comfort.*

I felt the blood draining from my face, an adrenaline dump in my gut. There was no way it was a joke. Dox liked to give me a hard time, but this would be crossing a line. I looked up from the terminal and glanced around, instinctively, uselessly, then looked back at the message. There was a phone number—Dox's mobile. That was all.

The message had been left at 2:00 A.M. Greenwich Mean Time. That was 3:00 A.M. in Paris. So . . . shit, over twelve hours ago. Less than twelve to go.

I purged and closed the browser, then walked outside. Cars shot along the boulevard de Magenta, dead leaves skittering in their backwash. Pedestrians dodged me, intent on their destinations, heads down against the chill winter breeze, shoulders hunched. A multitude of urgent questions and frightened thoughts were crowding me, trying to get inside, and for a few minutes I concentrated only on my breathing, letting the cold air work to clear my mind.

What do you know, I thought. *Not what you suspect; what you know. Start with that.*

What it boiled down to wasn't very much. Someone had gotten to Dox. Whoever it was, they were good. They'd forced him to give up the bulletin board, which meant they were ruthless. Now they wanted something from me.

What else? The board was compromised. If they were good enough to take out Dox, they'd be good enough to hack the site and determine the location of the terminal from which I'd just accessed it. In fact, I had to assume they'd just gotten a ping confirming for them that I was currently in Paris.

Shit, I thought. *Shit.*

If I called from Paris, it would give them a second means of determining my current position. But if they'd already hacked the bulletin board, what they'd get from a phone call would be redundant.

I thought about using the remaining time to go somewhere else, another city in France, maybe, or a quick train trip to Brussels, or Frankfurt. But I immediately rejected the notion. If they logged the time and location of the bulletin board access and then the call came hours later from elsewhere, it would look like I was trying to obscure my current location, which would mean Paris was in some way significant to me. Better to act as though my presence here was as fleeting as it was irrelevant. Which meant making the call right now, right here.

I turned on the prepaid GSM phone I was carrying. I had bought it in New York months earlier, and hadn't yet used it in Paris, or even in Barcelona. If they tracked its provenance it would create another distracting datapoint about where I might be found.

I slipped a Bluetooth earpiece in place, input Dox's number, and waited. It rang once, twice, three times. This was theater, I knew. The people who had set this up would have the phone close at hand. The wait was intended to suggest nonchalance, power, control.

On the fourth ring, someone picked up. A voice I didn't recognize said simply, "Yes."

"I got your message," I said.

"Wait a moment," the voice said. There was a slight, indeterminate European accent.

I looked at my watch, tracking the second hand's gradual sweep. Five seconds, ten. The wait was supposed to put me on edge. Having the underling answer was intended to let me know I was dealing with a group, an organization, and to make me feel alone and powerless by comparison.

That's all right, I thought. *I've gone up against groups before. Maybe I'll get to show you how it's done.*

But intelligence first. Action after.

A full minute went by. Then a voice I did recognize said, "Hello, John."

I waited a moment, then said, "Hello, Hilger."

If he was surprised I knew it was him, he didn't reveal it. Not that he had too much cause for astonishment, after the way we'd locked horns in the past. The first time, Dox and I had killed a half-French, half-Algerian arms dealer named Belghazi whom Hilger was working with; then, just a few months later, Delilah, Dox, and I had taken out another bad guy Hilger had recruited, a terrorist named Al-Jib, along with a bad-apple Israeli access agent called Manny. That was the op in which Delilah's colleague, Gil, had died. Hilger had shot him.

I realized that with someone as dangerous and connected as Hilger, I never should have treated any of it as concluded. My understanding was that he'd left the government and opened up his own shop, a kind of privatized intelligence operation, more shadowy, better connected, and substantially less accountable than private security firms like Blackwater and Triple Canopy. I thought Hong Kong had blown his operation out of the water, but apparently Hilger had been wearing a life vest.

A long moment went by. The silence was intended to get me to blurt something out, to betray eagerness. *More tactics*, I thought. *He's still shaping the battlefield.*

I looked at my watch again. It was a stainless steel Jaeger-LeCoultre Reverso Grande Taille with a brown leather band. I might have worn a Traser, but I tend to avoid anything that could be recognized as tactical. People who know, know. Besides, I just have a weakness for a fine watch like the Grande Taille. I thought about all the care that went into its design and its manufacture, imagined the craftsmen working on it, wearing spectacles, using magnifying glasses and precision tools to get the complications just right . . .

"I have a job I want you to do," Hilger said, finally. "Three of them, in fact. Do the jobs, and Dox lives. Don't do them, and he dies."

"Put him on the phone," I said, keeping my voice casual.

I wondered if he would refuse. I would have judged that stupid—I wasn't going to do a damn thing without what's known in the kidnap trade as "proof of life"— but on the other hand, in a negotiation, you don't give anything away for free. Hilger might want to position a few words with Dox as a concession. He'd been staging this thing carefully so far; maybe he'd want to stage it a bit more.

But he didn't. He just said, "Wait."

Thirty seconds later, I heard Dox's baritone twang. "Howdy, partner."

I was about to admonish him not to call me that because I didn't want Hilger to think we were close. But he went on: "Just so you know, these four boys have got us on the speakerphone."

Speakerphone. I should have anticipated that, and it was smart of Dox to tell me. It was also smart to slip in the mention of their numbers. Hilger might not have minded that; he probably hoped to intimidate me with the odds.

There was a down note in Dox's tone that was entirely unlike the rampantly cocksure persona I had come to tolerate, and eventually to like. A flood of emotions wanted to engulf me again: relief that he was alive, worry about what might happen next, anger that he'd allowed himself to be taken. I struggled to push it all aside, then felt that deep, icy part of me breaking through to the surface and taking the controls. And the feeling that came with it was nothing but relief. Finally, a reason for my fear. A reason not to struggle against the creature inside me.

"You all right?" I asked.

"I'm alive. I reckon that's what this conversation is intended to establish."

"You know where you are?"

"On a boat. Wish I could tell you more."

Then he was gone, and Hilger was back on the line. "We'll use the bulletin board," he said.

From the suddenness with which he'd grabbed the phone, I gathered he was concerned Dox might tell me something more, something useful. But what?

"No," I told him. "What you've got to tell me, you can tell me to my face."

"No. We do it my way, or . . ."

"Or you can fuck off." And with that, I pressed the "End call" button.

Or rather, the iceman did. The iceman knew that if I

didn't establish some measure of control early on, I'd always be reacting, always trying to recover, every step of the way, until finally, no matter how desperate my efforts, or feverish my hope, Dox would be dead, and probably I along with him.

I looked at the Grande Taille again, watching the second hand's smooth sweep. I could feel my heart beating steadily, my pulse rate just a little above normal. I was inside myself, suspended somewhere only I could recognize, disconnected, severed from events.

I watched the second hand's slow sweep. One circuit. Two. Another. The street was gone. My focus was no larger than the movement on the watch face.

The second hand was beginning its fifth rotation when the phone buzzed. I saw Dox's number on the screen and pressed "Answer."

Hilger said, "You're lucky your number got stored in this phone's caller ID just now. Otherwise your friend would already be dead. Now listen, there's something I want you to hear."

In the background, Dox started screaming. I held the phone far from my ear and looked at the watch again.

Whatever they were doing, they did it for ten seconds. Then the screaming stopped. Hilger said, "I hope you won't do that to him again."

"Where do you want to meet?" I said, my voice as flat as a hockey rink and twice as cold.

"We're not going to meet. I told you, the bulletin board. It's nonnegotiable."

"Then we have nothing to negotiate."

There was a pause. He said, "You want to hear him scream again?"

"You can make him scream all you want. You want me to work for you, you'll give me the assignment in person. I want to look in your eyes when you tell me. I'll know from that how much I can trust you to let him go when this is done."

There was another pause, longer this time. I could feel him considering, weighing the odds. He was thinking, *I'd ask for the same thing. And I'd be looking for a way to take a run at me, sure. But that's a dead end . . . hit me while my men have Dox, and Dox dies, too. Besides, if I choose the time and place, I can control the situation.*

Of course, there was another possibility: Hilger's reticence was feigned. He didn't want me to kill anyone; he had grabbed Dox simply to flush me into the open so he could kill me. In which case, by insisting on a meeting, I was giving him exactly what he wanted.

But I would have to take the chance. Dox had saved my life twice. Playing it safe now would be no way to return the favor. Because if I didn't keep Hilger moving, if I couldn't get him to depart from his game plan, I would always be one step behind on this thing, all the way to its bitter end.

"Hong Kong," he said.

Hong Kong was his territory. He could control it too well. But I wanted an Asian background. It would make it easier for me to blend, and harder for him. I said, "Tokyo."

"No good," he said, knowing he would be at as least as much of a disadvantage in Tokyo as I would be in Hong Kong. "Bangkok."

We were getting closer. But not long ago he'd fielded a team in Bangkok on short notice, a team that had very nearly gotten to Dox and me after we'd spoiled one of his ops. I knew he had reach there. It wouldn't do.

I needed a place that was familiar to me, but where he was unlikely to have much local capability. Something inside me spoke up, and before I could think more about it, I said, "Saigon."

There was a pause. He said, "When?"

"The night after tomorrow."

"I can't make it that fast. For Vietnam, I'll need a visa."

I know, I thought. *And that'll give me one more data-point I can use to track you.* "One of the services can get you one in a day," I said.

"What about you?"

I'd be traveling under a Japanese passport, which doesn't require a visa. But Hilger didn't need to know that. Better to let him think I was going to arrive the day of our meeting. That way, not only would I have time to reconnoiter, but he wouldn't know I'd had time.

"I can get one in a day," I said. "Keep Dox's phone with you, and I'll keep this one. The bulletin board will be backup. We'll meet somewhere public, somewhere we can trust each other not to misbehave."

"I trust you. Because if there's a problem, the screaming you just heard is going to sound like music by comparison."

I clenched my jaw and exhaled. "Careful how you use that leverage, Hilger. Right now, it's the only thing keeping you alive."

"Maybe. But you're what's keeping Dox alive. If you step out of line, you'll kill him."

"Put him on again."

"After the first job. Assuming there aren't any problems." I started to protest, but he had already clicked off.

I walked in the direction of the place de la République, where I knew there was a travel agency. My survival paranoia felt like a brewing riot, and I didn't want to be on the Internet searching for and purchasing flights to Saigon so soon after being tagged in Paris. Better to have the transaction done on a closed system.

From what I knew of Hilger and the number of government officials he had in his pocket, I guessed he might have access to customs information. If he knew what flight I was coming in on, it would be too easy for him to have a team waiting at the airport in Saigon. In fact, the safer alternative would be to fly to Hanoi and arrive in Saigon by some land connection. But there was no time for that. So the best I could do was to avoid leaving directly from Paris. That would at least obscure my arrival time.

There was a flight from Frankfurt at 7:20 that evening, with a change in Bangkok that would put me into Saigon at 3:25 the following afternoon, and of course my pick of flights on other airlines from Paris to Frankfurt. The woman who helped me was a little confused about why I wouldn't want to just fly nonstop from Paris on Air France. Miles, I told her. I wanted to be able to upgrade to first. But damn, I didn't have my frequent flyer number with me. . . . I would take care of it later, directly with the airline. I booked the flight for Taro Yamada, the name on the passport I would be using and the Japanese equivalent of John Smith. Yamada was currently my most solid alter ego, fully nurtured into a mature identity, including driver's license, credit cards, bank accounts, and the other indicia of unremarkable citizenship.

I hadn't been to Saigon in over three decades, and I knew there would be a lot to learn, and not much time to learn it. Well, I could pick up a guidebook at the airport and read it on the plane. With that, plus the time I'd already spent there, plus the extra day I'd have on Hilger, I'd have an advantage.

I was actually in my apartment packing a bag—a few

changes of clothes, a little less than ten thousand dollars in cash—when I realized I was supposed to meet Delilah for a drink in Montparnasse. *Shit.* I thought for a moment. Call her on her mobile? And tell her what?

I checked my watch. With just a carry-on, I could meet her and still make my plane. I went out to boulevard Henri IV and caught a cab.

Now that the logistics were taken care of, I was gripped by a creeping unease, entirely separate from the fear I felt for Dox. Maybe Vietnam was a bad idea. Saigon offered security advantages, yes, but for me it would also be a land of unburied memories, of a world that could never be forgotten, only, perhaps, left behind. I wondered why the iceman would want to go back there, what he was trying to accomplish in doing so.

I would have to let it go for now, and trust him as I always had before. What mattered is that he was here, invoked by crisis. The trick would be to get him to leave when the crisis was done.

7

DELILAH SAT AT a corner table in the brasserie of La
Closerie des Lilas in Montparnasse. She liked that
John wasn't there yet. For a long time she had always
been able to count on him to come early. She would ask
him about it, and he would tell her he had some extra
time, that he just wanted to read the paper or people-
watch. She knew better, and knew he knew, too, but
what was the point of saying anything? He arrived early
because it was an old habit, a means of avoiding an ambush. She engaged in similar tradecraft herself, of
course, but Rain was extreme.

Even when he was on time, she would sense that
he'd been nearby, watching their meeting place before-
hand, wanting to see her arrive first. Once she'd actually gotten in position two hours early and sure
enough, she had barely arrived in time to watch him
move through the area, checking the hot spots. The last
one he checked was hers, and rightly so, because she
had chosen a less obvious place, farther down the
street, not a particularly good view. She'd given up
after that, knowing that if he knew she was going to

show up two hours early, he would just come an hour earlier still.

The nice thing was, he'd been getting better, to the point where every now and then he seemed comfortable arriving on time. He wasn't going to sit with his back to a door, not soon, maybe not ever. And she knew never to come up behind him, or approach him from his blind side, not that approaching his blind side was easy because he tended not to keep his head trained in one direction for very long. She'd also learned not to stand close if she had to wake him. She'd made that mistake once, and Rain had sprung on her like a panther. He hadn't hurt her—he'd managed to pull back in time—and although he hadn't said anything beyond an embarrassed apology, she could tell he was horrified at what he'd very nearly done. She was careful after that, as much for his sake as for hers.

Still, he was changing. She noticed it in little things. He always had a great way of listening, with his eyes, even his whole body, a quality that made him rare among males. It was still there, but now he was more inclined to talk, too, and when he did, he gestured more with his hands. She hadn't seen that before Paris, and knew it was part of the chameleon in him, or what a colleague of hers had once referred to as the shape-shifter, because chameleons change only color, while Rain's ability to blend with his environment ran much deeper than that. She liked the taste he was developing in French music—Jean-Louis Murat, Patricia Kaas—and the way it was symptomatic of a more general openness to an unfamiliar culture. She wondered to what extent his ability to embrace the new, to make it part of himself and himself part of it, was attributable to his Japaneseness, and to what extent it was attributable simply to his own nature. She wanted to ask, but was afraid to, lest he become self-conscious, which might impede the very changes that pleased her so much.

It wasn't easy for him, she could tell. While he was effecting changes, the changes were affecting him. What did Nietzsche say? "When you look into an abyss, the abyss also looks into you." But the phenomenon expressed itself in more positive ways, too.

She wondered sometimes what had happened with Midori and Rain's son, who as far as she knew were still living in New York. Rain had never told her exactly how the situation had been resolved, only that they were no longer in danger and that he could never see them again. Delilah was secretly pleased on both counts and recognized, from the time he told her, that the subject would be taboo. What had happened, though? Whatever it was, he seemed reconciled to it. Perhaps he was satisfied, consciously or unconsciously, that he had done the right thing in going to see them and in protecting them afterward, and simultaneously relieved that, for reasons beyond his control, he didn't have to have them in his life. She could respect him for the first while being glad at the second.

She looked up and there he was, and the instant she saw him she knew something was seriously wrong. He was dressed nicely as always, in this case a blue cashmere blazer and a striped shirt she had bought for him at Charvet. And his features were the same, of course, Asian with a hint of something else, a nice head of dark hair with just a little gray over the ears. The difference she had immediately spotted was in his eyes. They were businesslike, almost blank, which in Rain's case made him look dangerous for anyone attuned to such things.

And his body, she realized. He kept in shape and was always light on his feet, but now he looked almost too ready, with his shoulders rolling slightly and his head swiveling, eyes logging details as he moved. It was all back, as if the months in Paris had been suddenly emptied out of him, leaving the killer ascendant.

He sat down and glanced at her, then scanned the café.

"What is it?" she asked.

"Hilger's got Dox."

"What do you mean, 'got'?" she asked, feeling the blood drain from her face, already suspecting the worst.

"Rendered him. Kidnapped him. They're holding him on a boat somewhere. I got a message from them on the bulletin board I use with Dox. I don't know what they did to make him give it up and I'm trying not to imagine. I . . ."

He stopped for a moment as though confused. "I have to go. But I thought I should tell you."

"Of course you should tell me. What were you going to do, just disappear without saying a word?" Even as she said it, she knew that was precisely what he had almost done. In fact, he had done it before. It was his realization that he had to account for himself, that he couldn't just drop everything, that had produced his confused expression.

He didn't say anything, and she realized he was struggling just to stay there. "Where are you going?" she asked.

"To meet Hilger."

"Are you crazy? He might have . . ."

"Yes, I've already thought about all that. I'm taking steps to mitigate."

"He's got you reacting. You need to slow it down."

"I know what I'm doing."

"John, don't . . ."

"Don't tell me what to do. You run risks all the time, and you've never listened to me when I've asked you to get out."

"It's different. My country . . ."

"I don't want to hear about your country. This is my friend."

He stood up. Suddenly she was afraid, and she didn't even know of what. She said, "At least tell me where you're going."

He shook his head. "I can't."

She stood, too. "Let me help."

He shook his head again. "You've helped me too many times on too many things. This isn't your problem."

"I'm not offering you charity, damn it. I care about Dox, too. And my organization has a score to settle with Hilger, don't you realize? For killing Gil. I could call Boaz. He would help."

Boaz was a colleague, and an ally, too, a competent, dangerous field operative and bomb specialist with a deceptively easy laugh. Along with Gil, Boaz had brought Rain into the Manila op that initially had gone so wrong her organization tried to kill Rain for it.

"I don't trust Boaz," he said.

"I trust him."

"I don't want him involved, or anyone else on his end. They wouldn't care about saving Dox. Only killing Hilger."

"You're wrong," she said, but without conviction.

She wanted to argue with him, but knew if she did he would just play tit-for-tat again. He was being stupid, and childish, and she didn't know how to get through to him.

She tried to think of something to say, some way of reasoning with him. But before she could, he turned and walked away. She watched, stunned. It was as though he'd already forgotten her.

8

I HAD HOPED to sleep on the thirteen-hour flight from Frankfurt, but for a long time I couldn't. My mind was too preoccupied with Dox, with where I was going, with what I was walking into. And with Delilah. Maybe I'd been too . . . abrupt with her. She'd only been trying to help. I should have been grateful, should have found a way to show her I was grateful. But her intentions, good as they were, wouldn't overrule her organization's imperatives. When Gil had gotten killed in Hong Kong, he'd been hunting me. The same kind of thing could easily happen here. And although the Mossad's reasons for wanting me dead—a job that had gone sideways in Manila before I finished it in Hong Kong—no longer applied, I wasn't enthusiastic about reappearing on the organization's radar screen, either.

Yeah, but Delilah herself could help. Discreetly. She's helped before. Dox is her friend, too, like she said.

Bullshit. She's compromised. Look how devoted she is to her organization. How many times have you tried to convince her to leave?

But I trust her. If I thought she would say anything

about the two of us, to be safe I'd have to leave Paris. Leave her.

That's different. She has no obligation to them about you. Hilger killed one of their own. Anything you tell her about Hilger, she'll feed to them.

I put my fists to my temples and squeezed my eyes shut. Christ, it was like two different people, struggling inside my head. Trust and suspicion. Hope and fear. The rationalist and the iceman.

Eventually I slept. When I woke, we were landing in Saigon, Ho Chi Minh City only in name. I don't think it was until I got off the plane that I really understood where I was, what I had returned to. I walked across the tarmac to a waiting bus, and the thing that brought it all home was the wet heat, the heat and that fecund earth smell, mud and competing tropical growth and rot. Then the doors closed and for a moment it was gone. But of course it was all still there. It always had been.

Outside the airport was tumult. Crowds and honking taxis and the wet heat again. The weirdly familiar cadences of the language itself, tonal like Chinese but softer, lower-pitched. I smelled diesel and spices and that jungle smell again, the mud that had caught in my mind the way it had once stuck in my boots.

I doubted Hilger could have put anyone in position quickly enough to intercept me here. Even if he'd wanted to, the way I'd traveled, he couldn't have known quite when I was arriving. And even if he'd guessed right, the airport, with all its cameras and other security, would be a poor place for a hit. Still, I haven't survived this long by taking anything for granted, and the first thing I wanted to do was make sure I was clean.

I shouldered my overnight bag and asked a taxi driver who seemed to speak decent English to take me downtown. I stayed with a Japanese persona and used a Japanese accent. With Hilger I'd be American. At all other times I wanted to be Japanese. The two personas have always been subtly distinct for me, and slipping from one to another would make me harder to describe, and therefore to track.

I watched behind us as we left the airport. Several cabs followed us into the thick traffic. I waited three minutes, then said, "Wait, go back, go back! Forgot sunglasses!"

The driver looked at me, unsure. "Sunglasses!" I said again, gesturing to my eyes. "Airport, please."

He nodded, then turned into the oncoming traffic with a U-turn that for an older passenger might have meant a coronary. I watched behind us as we returned to the airport. No one, not even one of the motorcyclists in their hundreds, replicated the U-turn.

I paid the driver five dollars—still the street's preferred currency, and about what the trip downtown would have cost had we completed it—went back into the terminal, and waited inside, watching. No one tried to follow me in, and I saw no one setting up outside. I found another cab and had it take me to the Rex Hotel.

In the thick traffic, the five-mile trip took almost an hour. I sat in the backseat, jostled by the occasional pothole, surrounded by the buzzing and honking of armadas of motorcycles, with nothing to do but watch and think.

I hadn't ever intended to come back here. It's not that I hated these people, although there are plenty of soldiers who still do—hell, there are American World War II vets who still hate the Japanese. I hated them at the time, yes. I wanted to hate them, to prove that despite my Asian face I was different, I was American, more

American even than the soldiers who suffered and fought alongside me.

And there were plenty of opportunities to hate, plenty of reasons. The Vietnamese were masters of psychological torture. They could turn anything, any harmless, neutral thing in your environment, into something deadly, until the world itself started to seem like your enemy. They booby-trapped pens, C-ration cans, the bodies of dead soldiers. They hid trip wires behind branches and mines under the dirt. They would lay spikes alongside a road and then ambush you so when you dove for cover you'd be impaled.

Imagine losing a buddy that way, one of the men whose smile could always cheer you up, who'd saved your life, who had your back no matter what. Imagine how you would hate. But then imagine this. Before you've even had a chance to process what's happened, while your uniform is still soaked with your friend's hot blood, two guys you've never seen before and never will again have zipped him into a bag and tossed him rudely onto a medevac chopper, and an instant later he's gone, so gone you wonder where all that blood could have come from. There's no funeral, no burial, just a grief so confusing and bitter you start to choke on it, and the only thing that saves you from being paralyzed by that grief, being killed by it, is a rage so white-hot the sane can barely begin to imagine it.

The rage has a purpose, you see: it offers an outlet. But it carries a heavy price. You do things you couldn't have imagined doing, couldn't have imagined anyone doing, things you can't talk about afterward, not even with the men who acted with you. In that state, the things that make you human, your empathy, even your fear, they're gone. You feel like you've died already, and you're right in a way, part of you has died and will never come back. At that point, being killed is almost a mercy. Because if you survive it, if you survive your own death, the path back to life is almost impossible. After the war, there were men, hollowed-out men whose means of negotiating the world had been reduced to alternating silence and rage, who would try with earnest futility to explain themselves that way. "I died there," they would say.

I thought that, too, for a long time after. But now, watching from the back of a cab images of that stark country that had swallowed up my innocence, I thought, *No, I didn't die here. Vietnam is where I was born.*

And I'd never left. Not really. I'd been back to the States, then all around the world, then finally settled, at least for a time, in Japan. But the person who was born here had never grown up, never fundamentally changed. His body had wandered, but his mind had remained in the place that had formed it.

Once, when I told Midori I wanted out of the business, she had asked me how hard I was trying. I felt my jaw clench at the memory. What horror had she ever endured? How could she, how could anyone who wasn't there, imagine the way war changes you?

Losing people, and not being able to properly grieve them, shrinks your world. You try to avoid attachments, anything that could hurt if you lose it. You start to say *don't mean nothing* about everything, the important things especially. You learn that only a few people can be trusted, fewer and fewer, in fact. You feel used by your own government. The equipment sucks, the orders suck, you know the politicians don't give a shit if you live or die as long as they're reelected. And then, if you're special, the way I apparently was, you get sent on a certain mission, where you can kill your own out-of-control best friend: my blood brother Crazy Jake, still the most dangerous man I've ever known. That brings it all together: the horror, the stifled grief, the silence, the distrust, the raging, all-consuming hatred.

I got out of the cab in front of the Rex and declined a bellboy's offer to help me with my bag. I wasn't going to stay here, but I remembered the hotel from leave in Saigon and thought it would be a good starting point from which to refamiliarize myself with the city. I was glad it was still here, the silly crown over the marquee and all. Not just because it was inherently comforting to know that my memories weren't only of relics, but also because familiar terrain would save me time and help keep me safe.

I looked across Le Loi Street and smiled. The oddly named Saigon Tax shopping center was still there, looking much as it did in my memory, the main difference being the replacement of a Sony neon sign by one advertising Motorola instead. The French-designed City Hall to the Rex's right also remained, its cream-colored balustraded façade illuminated grandly in the day's fading light.

I went into the hotel. The lobby had gotten a face-lift, but in its déclassé essentials it remained unchanged. I smiled in quiet amazement that a place could survive war, and communism, and the passing of decades so unperturbed. I moved in from the entryway, feeling like I was stepping back in time. The young man I was had come here with a prostitute, more than once. I was astonished at the clarity with which I could remember faces, and moments, even the names they had called themselves ten thousand nights ago.

I took an interior staircase to the fifth floor, and

then, ignoring the signs warning that only registered guests were permitted beyond, I explored the mazelike interior of the hotel. Beyond the public areas, it was all as it had been: hallways with open balconies at their ends; faded wood paneling and stalwart tiled floors; empty couches facing upholstered chairs in hidden antechambers, coffee tables and ashtrays absurdly at the ready, set out in melancholy hopes of a party that had moved on decades before. Even the fat geckos, feasting on insects attracted to the corridors' stark fluorescent lighting. It was as though it had all been waiting for me.

I followed one of the staircases down to the third floor, then made my way to a balcony at the end of the corridor. I had a perfect view of City Hall and the plaza in front of it. Excellent.

There was only one problem: a single inset incandescent light in the ceiling directly above me. I took out a handkerchief and unscrewed it a few turns until it went out. I doubted anyone would notice and fix it before tomorrow. If they did, I would just unscrew it again.

I took the stairs back down and walked over to the statue of Ho Chi Minh on the plaza in front of City Hall. I looked up at the hotel. The balcony I had darkened was noticeable, but not egregiously so. There were plenty of other lightless patches in the hotel's façade, and I doubted Hilger would zero in on this one. Even if he did, he'd have no way of knowing I was standing there, shrouded in darkness.

Saigon Tax was a little less familiar, primarily because it had gone upscale since I had last seen it. In addition to jewelry, watches, plasma televisions, and home theater systems, there was a section selling Panasonic massage chairs. Slowly but surely, Saigon was getting rich. But the layout was as I remembered: four floors, with an

open atrium from the ground floor all the way up; three
sets of staircases, two escalators, one elevator; entrances
and exits on three sides. Perfect.

Long into the night, I wandered District 1, the city
center, refamiliarizing myself, absorbing details. It
wasn't just the Rex: I was astonished at how little the
city itself had changed. I'd been to Bangkok less than a
year earlier and the place was barely recognizable as
the city I had first visited during the war, but communism had retarded things here, and it was only recently
that Saigon had begun to take off. Some of the street
names had changed, yes. And there were a few new
high-rises—a Citibank building, one for HSBC—but
the low skyline was largely the same. I recognized some
of the Rex's contemporaries: the Caravelle, with a tall
new wing; the Majestic, still perched above the Saigon
River. The presidential palace, whose wrought-iron
gates had come crashing down under the North's tank
treads when the South fell in 1975, had been preserved
and renamed the Reunification Palace, and was now a
tourist attraction. I was amazed at the almost palpable
presence of the young man who had walked these
streets and seen these sights. I no longer was that man,
but his memories were now mine, his dark gift to me;
they united us as surely as the progeny of a dissolved
and loveless marriage.

I walked. The ubiquity of commerce, I noted, that too
was unchanged: motorcyclists offering impromptu taxi
rides; stores selling a few spare feet in a corner for
someone to park a scooter; street vendors hawking secondhand watches and rebuilt engines and coconut milk
in plastic cups. The raw capitalism, the economic dy-
namism, of the place was stunning. I wondered why anyone had ever feared that communism could take root in

this culture. The North had swallowed Saigon like a diner ingesting a virus, and within twenty years the virus had so infected the host that Hanoi was calling for *doi moi,* politely described as "reforms," more accurately understood simply as "capitalism." Save these people from communism? Christ, it was Hanoi that needed saving now. We could have just sat back and enjoyed the show.

But that would have required patience, I supposed, and perspective, too, neither of which was ever likely to feature prominently in anyone's list of the top ten American virtues. Well, at least I wouldn't have to participate in the current sequel: America Uses Military to Remake the Middle East and End Tyranny in Our Time.

Sequel, my ass, I thought. *It's a fucking remake. And the end is going to be just the same.*

I was pleased to find the Opera House I remembered, now known as the Municipal Theater. Likewise, the Notre Dame cathedral, a remnant, along with City Hall, of French rule. I liked that the locals hadn't tried to eradicate the country's colonial heritage. Their acceptance, even embrace of the past suggested a cultural maturity I found I admired.

I smiled. Maybe I was giving them too much credit. Maybe they were just too busy making money to care.

I found a store that sold knives, where for ten dollars I bought a nameless folder with a four-inch blade. I would have preferred something higher-quality, but I had to settle for what was available. I slapped the spine of the blade against my palm a few times, and was satisfied the lock was adequate. Certainly the edge was sharp enough, at least for the time being. Dox, who could be almost fetishistic about what he carried, probably would have sneered at it. But I tend to be a meat-

and-potatoes guy about blades: insert pointy end in target. Repeat as necessary. It's always worked for me
before.

The thought of the burly sniper bore down on me. I
didn't want to think of him just now—there was nothing
I could do for him, so the thinking was a distraction, a
waste. But for a moment, the sound of that last scream
echoed in my mind, and my worry broke through. I
paused and concentrated on where I was, what I was
planning, until the emotion had passed.

As the night grew late, fatigue crept closer. Darkness
softened the contours of the city around me, and my
emboldened memories emerged like insistent stars in a
fading sky. Kids, ten thousand miles from home and
fresh from the jungle, delirious with sudden freedom
and the absence of fear, loosed upon the city and looking for booze, girls, any kind of trouble. Crazy Jake, in a
bar on Dong Khoi, berserking on a navy guy who'd said
something stupid to him, then denying everything to the
MPs after the guy had been ambulanced off, persuading
them, his shark's smile and the insanity in his eyes letting them know *you fuck with me you better be ready to
die.* Everyone laughing nervously after the MPs had ac-
knowledged their mistake and shoved off, everyone but
Crazy Jake himself, who'd been ready to die right then,
who'd actually expected it, and maybe was disappointed
that yet again it hadn't happened, that the gods of war
had plans for him far from the artifice of the city with its
lights and laughter and otherworldly rules.

I hadn't thought of Crazy Jake in years. He had
thrived on the madness of war, going deeper and deeper
into that heart of darkness until he was possessed by it,
until it infused his sinews and coursed in his veins. I was
the only remaining person he trusted, and that's why

they sent me for him. He knew. I couldn't have done it if he hadn't let me. He couldn't kill what he'd become. Someone else had to do it for him.

All at once I wanted badly to have four plain walls around me and to sleep, especially to sleep. I caught a ride on a motorcycle cab to the New World hotel, which my guidebook had informed me was large, anonymous, and popular with Japanese tour groups. I took a hot bath, fell into the adequate but unspectacular bed, and was gone as instantly as if I'd been humping a sixty-pound ruck through the jungle, rather than wandering streets haunted by the restless ghosts of that earlier time.

9

THE NEXT DAY, I continued to familiarize myself with the terrain: the patterns of traffic (there weren't any); presence of security (in front of banks, jewelry stores, and higher-end hotels); the best vantage points (the Rex, Saigon Tax, some of the hotel restaurants). I looked for anything out of place, any signs of a set-up. I experimented with different personas. As an American, and carrying a map, I was assailed with offers of rides on motorcycles and in cyclos; as a Japanese, less so; when I'd bought some local clothes and started imitating the walk, the posture, the expressions of the natives, I was left alone entirely.

I had a lunch of *pho* noodle soup and watermelon juice, then bought a camera tripod to augment the Nikon D70 digital SLR I had brought with me. I finished mapping things out and was satisfied. After that, I had nothing to do but wait.

AT SIX O'CLOCK that evening, the sun had set, but the air was still hot and wet. The back and chest of my shirt were dark with sweat, the shifting crowds and insectile drone of motorcycles close upon me. I stopped in an ice cream shop around the corner from the Rex to rest and wait. I bought a cone and enjoyed it, along with the scant, periodic relief offered by a lone oscillating ceiling fan. Thirty people were crammed into the seats around me, but they paid me no heed. I'd picked up the local vibe and faded right into it.

My phone buzzed. I glanced at the readout—Dox's mobile—and picked up. "Yeah."

"I'm here," Hilger said. "In the city. Where are you?"

I put a fifty-thousand dong note on the table and started moving. "District One. You?"

"The same. Where are we going to do this?"

I kept moving, watching the sidewalk and street. "You know the HSBC building?"

"No, but I'm sure I can find it."

"Ask anyone. You can see it from most of District One—there aren't many high-rises. There's a coffee shop on the ground floor. Meet me there in ten minutes."

I clicked off and headed into the Rex. Two minutes later, I was in my third-floor balcony perch. No one had fixed the lightbulb. I set up the camera and tripod, then looked down at the statue of Ho through the 400mm telephoto lens. I could see every detail. If anyone asked, I was just a Japanese photography hobbyist, trying to capture the essence of the plaza below me. But I didn't expect to be challenged. The Rex was never that kind of place.

Ten minutes later, my phone rang again. It was Hilger. "You're not here," he said.

"I got nervous. I wanted something more public."

There was a pause. "Don't fuck with me, Rain. If I abort this meeting, your friend is going to die."

That was a bluff. Whatever he wanted from me, he

wanted it badly enough to have come this far. I could safely take him along a little farther.

"I'm not fucking with you," I said. "Just walk to the City Hall, the huge French building a block south of you. There's a plaza in front of the building with a statue of Ho Chi Minh. Lots of people around. Meet me in front of the statue."

Two minutes later, he showed. Through the camera lens, I could see everything in the brightly lit plaza, even the beads of perspiration on Hilger's face. His right side was to me. I didn't see an earpiece. So far, so good.

This time I called him. "Are you there yet?" I asked.

He looked around. "Yeah, I'm here. Why aren't you?"

"I'm being careful."

"You're being too careful. You're going to blow this whole thing."

"How do I know you're not setting me up?"

"You're the one who asked for this meeting, remember?"

There was a pause. I said, "There's a shopping center right in front of you, if your back is to City Hall. Saigon Tax, the one with the big Motorola sign on the façade, across the street from the Sheraton. With a Citibank building visible behind it. I'm inside, in the Góc Saigon café. Rooftop of the shopping center. Come on up and you can find me."

I watched him glance behind, then to the sides, then up at the buildings around him. I waited, and was rewarded with a close view of his left ear—empty, like his right. His eyes swept right over the dark spot where I stood. *That's right,* I thought. *I might be here. Or in Saigon Tax. Or in a room at the Sheraton. Or maybe I set up video in one of the vans in front of the Rex and I'm*

*watching you remotely. Or I'm not watching you at all.
The point is, you don't fucking know.*

He clicked off without a word and headed up the
plaza, toward Saigon Tax. I tracked him through the
camera for a moment, then watched the plaza unaided.

A few seconds later, I spotted a burly blond guy moving casually behind Hilger and in the same direction. I
looked through the camera and saw that his eyes were
everywhere, taking in all the details, his head tracking
slowly left and right as he walked. The visual alertness
was out of sync with the casual gait, and I made him as
Hilger's backup. I made him so fast, in fact, that I wondered for a moment whether he was supposed to serve
not just as backup, but also as a distraction. The idea is,
the opposition knows you're looking for backup, or for
surveillance, or whatever, so it serves up exactly what
you expect. And because you've now spotted the danger
you knew was going to be there, your mind unconsciously closes to other, less obvious possibilities. *I knew
there was going to be something . . . oh, there it is!* is the
mindset of amateurs and others without much hope of
longevity in this business. *I knew there was going to be
something . . . there's one, now where are the others?* is
the mindset of survivors.

The guy kept gliding forward like a panther, confident, balanced. He was wearing rectangular, wireless
glasses, and felt vaguely European to me. I wondered if
he was the one who had picked up the phone when I
first called from Paris. There was a readiness about him,
not just in his alertness but in his balance, his stride. If I
had to take him out, I would definitely use a tool, along
with as much surprise as I could muster.

I snapped a dozen photos, then examined the plaza
for any other possibles in Hilger's wake. This was the

hotel district, and there were foreigners around, but none of them tickled my radar. They were either too old, or too flabby, or with women and children. Most relevantly, none of them had that quality, no matter how subtle, of exceptional awareness that's almost impossible to conceal when you're moving and operational. I folded up the tripod, put it in my backpack, and headed up to the Rex's rooftop bar. Concealed behind a garden that hadn't existed back in the day, I had a perfect view of the sidewalk in front of Saigon Tax. Mr. Blond was waiting on the sidewalk outside.

If Hilger was willing to let Mr. Blond drift that far behind him, he really must have been confident I wouldn't try to take him out while he held Dox. Or else Mr. Blond really was a distraction, in which case someone more subtle would shortly follow Hilger into the building. I waited, but saw no one I identified as a problem.

I headed down an internal staircase, cut southwest on Le Loi, then crossed the street with fifty other pedestrians, motorcycles buzzing around us. On the other side of the street was a parking garage with its own entrance into Saigon Tax. I slipped inside, checking hot spots as I moved. Nothing rubbed me the wrong way. I turned a corner and waited. No one came in behind me. I waited for another minute, making sure Hilger had time to get to the restaurant ahead of me.

I entered Saigon Tax and used one of the internal staircases, pausing at the balcony of each successive floor to look above and below. Still nothing out of place. I continued to the fourth floor, where I cut across to the northeast side of the building, scanning as I moved. Still clear.

I came to the stairs that led to the Góc Saigon. I took one last look around. All clear. Okay.

I turned off my phone and turned on the other miniature bit of electronics I was carrying, a bug detector my martyred friend Harry, a hacker adept at kluging together all kinds of improvised devices, had made for me in Tokyo. If Hilger was wired, the detector would vibrate in my pocket and let me know. I headed up the steps to the restaurant.

The place sprawled out in an L shape, partly under a roof, mostly under the dark Saigon sky. Wood floors, slatted wooden tables and chairs, twinkling lights strung out across plantings like Christmas ornaments. Diners, but only a handful because it was still early, and none who appeared to have just arrived.

A hostess approached. I glanced at her, saw she wasn't a threat, and went back to scanning the restaurant. The woman offered to seat me. I shook my head but otherwise ignored her and kept moving.

I hadn't seen Hilger yet, so if he was here, he must be around the corner, in the short end of the L. I kept close to the inner wall, came to the edge, and snuck a quick peek around. There he was, sitting in the corner, his back to the concrete wall, his feet planted under him, ready to move, his head up and his eyes alive. The surrounding tables were all empty, this end of the L momentarily deserted.

He stood when he saw me coming and took a step back from the table, but slowly, showing me his hands. They were empty, the fingers splayed slightly. I approached him in the same nonthreatening way.

I moved toward him until I was in front of his table, then turned and faced him so my side was to the corner of the L. I wanted to be able to see anyone who came in after me and still have time to react.

He angled slightly away from me so that I was facing

more of his left side than his front. He rubbed his chin
with his left hand, the forearm vertical across his body,
the other hand touching his elbow. I noted from the
stance that he was right-handed, confirming my recol-
lection of what I'd learned while witnessing his pistol
craft at the China Club and at Kwai Chung the last two
times we'd crossed paths. Although it was intended to
look thoughtful and nonthreatening, the stance covered
up most of his vital points. He was concerned I might attack. He was right to be.

Not for the first time, it occurred to me that he must
be highly motivated to incur the risks he was running. I
wondered what he was after, and who he could be working for.

"Let's go," I said.

He looked doubtful. "Where?"

"Someplace else. You might have called someone and
told him where we are."

"I'm alone."

I wasn't going to tip my hand by asking about Mr.
Blond. "That's good to hear," I said. "Indulge me anyway."

I'm not getting any younger, but I still have two advantages. First, I've always been unusually quick—
partly the result of genetics, partly of obsessive training.
Second, I can go from stonelike stillness to explosive violence without any of the usual precursors. The signs
people know to look for—obvious ones, like shouting,
gesticulating, and other posturing, and less obvious
ones, like the face going white and the pupils dilating—
I don't exhibit, or have learned to mask. I can hurt you,
or worse, and the only sign you'll have of what's coming
is that I was close enough to do it.

Hilger didn't know that. I was close, sure, but the sum

total of his experience would be telling him that there'd be some warning, some noticeable transition, and that therefore he would have the necessary moment to react. So it really wasn't his fault that he wasn't ready for what happened next.

"You need to . . ." he started to say.

I closed the distance with one long step, my lead hand feinting for his face. His eyes popped open in surprise and his arms flinched upward—away from my trailing knee, which arced up and slightly around on the way to its abrupt run-in with his balls. He made a sound you might describe as *vomitus interruptus* and doubled over into me. I shoved him into the wall and had the folder open against his neck in an instant. The edge might not have offered longevity, but it was plenty sharp at the moment, and I pressed it against his carotid, the pressure just short of breaking the skin, my fist in his Adam's apple, my left hand securing his right wrist and keeping it away from anything he might have in his pocket.

"Hands up, shitbag," I breathed. "Against the wall, alongside your head. Move for a weapon and I'll open you down to your spine."

Beyond my substantive need to check him for weapons, it was important that I give him an option other than resistance or death. If he were convinced I was going to kill him, I couldn't expect cooperation. As it was, he decided to comply. He grimaced and slowly got his arms up against the wall. His head was pressed back, his chin tucked in against my fist, his nostrils flaring with his breathing. His eyes were narrowed to slits, coldly observing me.

I stared back at him, and realized with a start how close I was to doing it. Grab his hair, shove his head to

the left, rip right, sidestep to avoid the spray. Walk outside, fillet Mr. Blond before he had a chance to react.
Go Keyser Söze on them, let the remnants of Hilger's
team understand who they were fucking with and what
was coming for them next.

"I don't check in, my men do Dox," he said, as though
reading my thoughts. "It's automatic."

Maybe, I thought. *Or maybe your men let Dox go at
that point, to mollify me. What good is he to them, anyway, if you're dead? Yeah, let him go. A quitclaim, a
peace offering.*

Jesus. I wanted to kill him so badly I was actually
panting a little. And rationalizing everything else, even
Dox's life, to give myself permission.

*Do it. Just fucking do it. End it now and you can
walk away.*

I imagined Dox, helpless somewhere, cut off, in pain,
and somehow the thought stayed my hand. My whole
body trembling with ambivalence, I turned Hilger
around and patted him down. He was carrying two
knives, a folder and a belt unit. I pocketed both. Next,
Dox's mobile phone. I turned it off and pocketed it, too.
Other than a roll of dong and greenbacks, he was carrying nothing else, not even a wallet.

I backed away from him, closing the knife as I moved.
I put it back in my pants, noting that Harry's bug detec-
tor had stopped vibrating the moment I had turned off
Dox's phone. Hilger was clean.

I watched him, dumbfounded, on some level, that he
was still alive, that I'd managed to hold back. He swallowed and his right hand drifted to his throat, rubbing it,
caressing the undamaged skin. He was breathing hard.

The hostess turned the corner and pulled up short.
She hadn't seen what had happened a second earlier,

but she could feel the aftermath. I glanced at her and said, "Give us a minute." She nodded and backed away.

I looked at Hilger. "Let's go."

He shook his head. "Out of the question," he rasped.

"You're not thinking clearly," I said, a part of me shouting *It's not too late—just step back in and fucking finish him!* "If I wanted to kill you, you'd be bleeding out right now. You said it yourself: I can't touch you while you're holding Dox. I'm the one who has to worry about surprises, not you. There's no reason we can't walk out of here together. Unless you want to keep me here because you've got backup you told about this meeting place. In which case, I'm going to assume this was a setup."

What I'd said was logical. Which is why I wanted him to refuse. If he did, I would have no choice. I could butcher him and whatever happened to Dox after wouldn't be my fault.

He didn't say anything. He might have been considering my point. He might have been thinking about the hostess, and wondering whether she was freaked out enough to call the police. He might have seen in my eyes how much I was hoping he would refuse. Regardless, after a moment he nodded.

We left Saigon Tax through the garage entrance, heading southwest on Le Loi and then turning left on Pasteur. I flagged down a cab and had it take us to the Ben Thanh Market, a labyrinthine produce emporium stretching out over an entire city block. I watched behind us as we moved, but couldn't be sure amid all the motorcycles that no one was following us. Inside the market, there were hundreds of Vietnamese, shuffling along. Hilger and I moved fast and directly, and I didn't see anyone trying to match our pace, but still, I wasn't as

sure as I usually am, or as I like to be. I reminded myself Hilger had been in the city only for a day. Hiring
and deploying local talent that fast would have been a
hell of a stretch.

Hilger kept up and didn't give me any more trouble.
We got another cab on the Le Thanh Ton side of the
market, which I had take us to the Park Hyatt. The
route gave me another opportunity to check behind us,
when we turned right on Hai Ba Trung. I didn't think I
saw anyone follow us from the market, but . . . damn it,
there were just so many motorcycles, and so many dark
stretches of street, and so many of the riders were wearing face masks against the pollution. Did I see that guy
earlier, the skinny one in the white tee-shirt, with the
black bandanna around his face? Or had that been
someone else?

We rode in silence. I noted again that, whatever was
motivating Hilger to do all this, it had to be powerful.
But what?

I hadn't counted on so much motorcycle traffic. When
I was here during the war, it had been mostly cars, along
with jeeps and lumbering deuce-and-a-halfs, of course.
The countersurveillance environment was tougher now.
I would have to use extraordinary caution later, when I
left the meeting. But at least I'd be safe inside. The reason I had chosen the hotel, Saigon's newest and most
deluxe, was that it offered the kind of camera surveillance, guards, and other security that would inhibit an
on-the-premises hit.

The cab deposited us at the midpoint of a semicircu-
lar driveway. Twin bellmen opened the hotel's wide
double doors and welcomed us. We made our way to the
lobby lounge along polished wood floors and muted
Persian rugs. There was some jockeying for position as

we chose where to sit. In the end, we wound up adjacent to each other at a table along the exterior wall, both of us facing the expansive, two-storied room. The lounge was lit softly by several hammered-metal chandeliers high overhead, and we were surrounded by the sounds of conversation and laughter from the mostly expat crowd around us. It was a safe scene, and therefore surreal.

We sat silently for a few moments, each trying to wait the other out. A pretty waitress broke the standoff by coming to our table and handing us menus. "My name is Ngan," she said. "May I bring you something to drink?"

Hilger surprised me by asking, "Are you hungry?"

In fact, I was. I'd been keyed up all afternoon and evening, and hadn't realized that my *pho* lunch was long gone. And now that the immediate danger was under control, my stomach was demanding attention.

I nodded warily.

"Why don't you order for us," he said. "You know the cuisine better than I do."

I took a quick glance at the menu and selected a variety of spring rolls and dumplings. Hilger surprised me again by ordering a beer. I stayed with orange juice.

Neither of us spoke until Ngan had returned with the drinks and food. When she was gone, Hilger took a sip of his beer and said, "It must feel strange for you to be back here."

I figured the comment was an elicitation ploy, an attempt to draw something out of me. But I wasn't sure what. "Why do you say that?" I asked.

He shrugged. "Memories. My place was the desert. I was in Iraq for the first go-round, and now, you put me someplace with a lot of sand and superheated dry wind, and bam, I go all the way back, body and soul. Like I never left. People who haven't had that kind of experience ... they don't understand. It's like they live in two dimensions and you live in three."

I knew what he was talking about. The part of you that's formed in battle will always respond to being back on the battlefield. And when you return, I was learning, it feels as though some fitfully sleeping part of you stirs to wakefulness, while the person you thought you were surrenders as quietly as a dream. Maybe that was the paranoia I was feeling. That older self, the self that had kept me alive in the jungle, in places and circumstances where so many other men had died.

We started in on the spring rolls. A table full of Americans to our right erupted in loud laughter at something one of their party had said. Hilger glanced over and shook his head.

"Look at those people," he said. "Think they own this place, don't they, think they own the world. Makes me sick sometimes."

I watched them for a moment, and found I couldn't disagree. What I saw was a collection of overfed, overprivileged sheep who were born to whatever they had and whose only understanding of real fear and privation was what they received from images broadcast on CNN between commercial breaks for smile-whitening toothpaste and mountain-fresh fabric softeners. They condescended to the locals because the locals needed their money and had to serve them to get it. They didn't understand that the service was like what the staff provides to the inhabitants of a nursing home. They confused stoicism with passivity, service with servility, the current world order with some ordained plan. They didn't realize the people they looked down on now were going to own them a little later this century. Or, at the rate the West was going, maybe just bury them, instead.

He popped a dumpling into his mouth, chewed, and swallowed it. He shook his head. "Makes me wonder why I bother."

I looked at him, intrigued that he was able to laugh and break bread with someone who not an hour earlier had very nearly executed him. I didn't read this as weakness. On the contrary, Hilger's easy recovery from our earlier encounter suggested a long and comfortable acquaintance with violence. And more than that, a man so ruthlessly adept at compartmentalizing the personal and the professional that he would be capable of almost anything. If he deemed something necessary, I expected he would act with little compunction and even less warning.

"Why do you bother?" I asked.

He looked away, and for a moment his gaze was distant. I wondered what he was seeing.

"Because things are broken," he said. "People used to think broken meant a system that could only respond to a crisis. But that's not broken. Broken is a system that can't *even* respond to a crisis."

"What crisis are you talking about?"

He took a swallow of beer. He glanced at me, then shook his head as though disappointed. "If you have to ask, you wouldn't understand."

"Why don't you try me?"

"I'm talking about America. The wheels are coming off, haven't you noticed? And what are you supposed to do if you care? Join a protest march? A letter to your gerrymandered congressman? What?"

It's been my experience that people who can express their political views only in metaphors and passionate generalizations are fanatics. Hilger might have been one of them. Or maybe he was trying to obscure his true affiliations, or his lack of any at all. Or this whole conversation was his attempt to draw me out, to gather intelligence about me. Or all of the above.

"I don't know," I said. "What are you supposed to do?"

Therapists call it reflection: repeating the patient's words, rephrased as a question. I had dealt with enough Army shrinks back in the day to find the technique stupid and annoying, and it's so basic that even machines have been programmed to do it. But it can create a sense of empathy, or in this case its illusion, and draw a subject out.

It didn't work with Hilger. He said only, "What you can."

Which in his case, I gathered, was a lot.

I waited, hoping he would add something I could use. After a moment, he said, "It's too bad it has to be this way with us. I respect you. We ought to be able to work together. I work with a lot of guys like you."

"Like me how?"

He shrugged. "Smart. Independent. With the insight to understand the way things really work."

I felt the manipulation, but didn't know where he was trying to steer me. "I don't know what you mean."

"Sure you do. You know democracy's just a pretty picture. And that to ensure its survival and preserve its appearance, certain men have always done things that no one else can know."

"Assassinations."

"Exactly."

"Coups."

"Sure."

"Kidnapping?"

He shrugged. "We call them 'extraordinary renditions.'"

"Abu Ghraib."

He shook his head. "I'm not talking about Abu Ghraib. AG was exactly the way not to go about it. People say what happened there is immoral. Shit, it's worse than immoral. It's incompetent. The whole thing was nothing but a fishing expedition. Widespread and sanctioned. And once it got out, predictably, we had to bend over backward in the other direction because of all the media scrutiny."

"I thought the VP said waterboarding was a 'no-brainer.' And that was after AG."

"Believe me, the right people had a lot more freedom before AG. Anyway, the VP doesn't know what he's talking about. None of them do. That's the point. With guys like that in the limelight, more than ever you need the right things done in the dark."

Okay, so this was "you and I are the pros and everyone else is incompetent." If he thought that would save him when this was done, he was wrong.

I looked at him. "Yeah? How do you know when it's right?"

He returned the look. "When it's necessary."

"And when is that?"

"When you need something, and there's no other way to get it."

"How did you know there was no other way here? You never asked me."

"Some things you just know."

"Why don't you ask me now."

He shook his head. "Now I'm not asking. I'm telling you. That's why I had to go through Dox. Because it has to get done."

A long silent moment passed. I tried not to think of
Dox. It helped me keep the latent lust to kill Hilger momentarily on a leash.

"All right," I said. "Tell me what you want."

He glanced around, then leaned forward. "Three jobs,
like I told you. When you're done with the first, I'll give
you the second. When you're done with the second, I'll
give you the third. When you're done with the third, I'll
release Dox."

I looked at him. When I spoke, it was half directed at
Hilger, half to appease the iceman.

"If you do anything permanent to him," I said, "you
know I'll find you. And you know what I'll do to you."

He offered a faint, humorless smile. "You're being
generous. You're going to try to find me the moment I
let him go, if not before."

"There's something you need to understand. I've
been trying to get out of the life. If I have to revert to
protect a friend, I will. But I don't want to go any further than I have to. Yeah, right now I'm upset. I don't
like the way you got me to the negotiating table. But if
you play it straight from here, we might all be able to
walk away from this."

There was a lot of truth in there. Which made it the
best kind of lie.

Hilger nodded, but that was all. I didn't know
whether he'd bought it.

"Let me talk to him again," I said.

He shook his head. "You've talked to him once. You
can talk to him again after. After each one."

Something told me I wasn't going to win on this point
and I let it go. I rotated my head, cracking the neck
joints. "All right," I said, "the first one. Who, where,
when, how."

"Who is Jan Jannick, Dutch national, male, forty-five years old. Where is the San Francisco Bay Area, where he's temporarily resident. When is within five days from today. And how is something that absolutely looks natural."

The appearance of natural causes is my specialty, and the reason I've always been able to charge a premium. Except, of course, when I'm working under duress, when my fees tend to be ... waived. I assumed it was the "naturalness" imperative that made Hilger need me, but there might have been more.

"Why natural?"

"You know why. I don't want anyone asking questions."

"I'm asking why you don't want the questions."

"That's not something you need to know."

I thought for a moment. "Five days to get to San Francisco, track this guy, find him, identify a pattern, select an opportunity, plan for an escape ... there's no way. You know that."

"We already have a lot of the information you'll need. Home and work addresses, things like that. It'll save you time. I'll upload it to the bulletin board."

"Even so ..."

"Jannick is a civilian. He has no surveillance consciousness at all, no security, no clue. He's as soft a target as you've ever gone after. The only trick is making it look natural. That's why I want you."

"If he's that easy, anyone could have done it the way you want."

"He's only one of three, remember. And you're wrong about just anyone being able to do it. Making it look natural is harder than hell, except in the movies, and you know it. You've got a talent. It's why we're here."

There was a lot he wasn't telling me, of course. So all

I could do was continue to engage him, continue to try
to gather the information that would get Dox out of
this. After all, I understood profoundly that Hilger would
kill Dox the moment I was done with whatever he
wanted doing. Even if I were inclined to give Hilger a
pass for his transgression, he couldn't count on one
from Dox. And if Dox and I came after him together, his
prospects would be bleak indeed.

Hilger, of course, could do this math as well as I
could. And the ruthlessness I sensed in his poise would
turn the situation into a simple equation for him, an
equation for which the solution set would be obvious,
and therefore imperative.

He knew I knew all this. Which meant the third target
might be fictitious. I would kill the first two to buy time,
thinking I had one more to go before Hilger killed Dox,
but in fact I'd have unwittingly finished the whole job at
the second target, at which point Dox would die. The
third job, then, would be a setup. They'd feed me coordinates on some easy-to-track civilian on terrain they
knew well, and when I showed up to take out the red
herring, I'd walk into an ambush. Meaning, in effect,
that the third target would be me.

Or maybe I'd be the second. Maybe Jannick was
Hilger's only objective, and when he was done, so was
Dox. So was I. There were a lot of possibilities, none of
them good.

"Are you satisfied?" Hilger asked, as though reading
my thoughts.

"With what?"

"With having looked in my eyes. Trusting me to let
Dox go when this is done."

"No. I don't trust you to do that. But I learned something else from your eyes."

"Yeah? What's that?"

From his tone, I knew he was concerned that I might have picked up some piece of information he didn't want me to have. Why else would I have insisted on a meeting? Trusting someone because of what you see in his eyes is a load of shit, although the latest bozo in the White House claimed to have managed a view of Vladimir Putin's soul that way. And it was clear after what happened in Góc Saigon that I wasn't going to kill him. What else could I have been after, if not information?

I thought of Mr. Blond. Maybe I'd lost him. Maybe not. Maybe there had been others I hadn't spotted. I realized now that I'd been wrong in thinking Mr. Blond, and any others, were only backup for Hilger, or part of a setup. More likely, they were a plan B. If I refused to follow instructions, they would have tried to kill me here. Then they would do Dox immediately after.

I took a deep breath, then let it go. "I learned I don't have a choice."

He nodded. "You got that right."

I stood up and took out his knives. I wiped them off with a napkin—I don't like leaving my fingerprints on weapons—and placed them on the table. He made no immediate move for them, which was smart. I put Dox's phone on the table, too. There was no way Hilger would have been stupid enough to have used it for any sensitive calls, so there was nothing to gain by taking it. And I wanted a way to reach him quickly if necessary.

"When will the information be on the bulletin board?" I asked.

"It's there now."

I looked at him. For the moment, the urge to kill him

had faded into the background, like what happens when you get so hungry your appetite temporarily dissipates.

"I'll be in touch when it's done," I said.

He nodded. "I know."

I turned and walked away. He could damn well pay for the spring rolls himself.

10

DOX SAT ON the cot in the cramped, windowless boat cabin, the lights off, his eyes closed, a small smile on his face. He'd long since told himself every joke he'd ever known, three times over, four or five for his favorites. He'd recollected the layout of his childhood house, and imagined himself building it, starting with the foundation, then brick by brick, all the way to the roof and the detail work. Now he was trying to remember the name of every girl he'd ever slept with, but it just wasn't possible because, well, there had been quite a few. The first ten were easy to come up with, even though it had been a long time ago, but once he got up into the double digits, things got tricky. He tried a different tack, focusing only on the ones who'd been lucky enough to surrender him their virginity, but the truth was, that was a reasonably lengthy list, too. He knew he'd never remember them all, and that was sad, but still it was fun to try, and it wasn't like he had anything else to occupy his mind here.

He was shackled like a federal prisoner: leg irons, wrist manacles, and a chain connecting the two. They weren't being overly generous about the length of chain involved, either. He couldn't so much walk as shuffle along, bent over like an old man. If he got an itch on his nose, the only way to scratch it was to push his face against the wall and rub. The room had its own head, and he supposed he ought to be grateful for that, but wiping his ass chained as he was wasn't exactly the high point of his day. He was half-tempted to beat the bishop, more than half-tempted, if the truth be told, especially with all these thoughts of girls he'd deflowered, and with his hands stuck right in front of his crotch, he could have, too. But the possibility of his captors sniggering at the sounds of his chains clanking in the dark would be an unbearable indignity. Besides, how the hell would he clean up the mess.

The one thing he wanted to do more than anything when he got out of this, well, besides standing up straight and stretching, that was the main thing, but besides that, the thing he wanted most was just to brush his teeth. The last time he'd had a chance had been the morning they'd grabbed him, and at this point it felt like he had a moss forest growing in his mouth.

He'd considered every variety of possible escape, but he couldn't see a way out. The door was always locked. He'd tested it with his shoulder and knew it was heavy and solid. Unshackled, he might have been able to bust it open, although it opened inward so maybe not, but in these chains he could develop all the momentum of a pregnant penguin, and he certainly couldn't kick. The door had a small window, too, and they were careful always to look in on him before entering. But hell, they could come in blindfolded and what could he do, shuffle over and head-butt them in the shoulders like the friggin' Black Knight in *Monty Python and the Holy Grail*? Call them dirty names?

He might have tried bellowing like a madman when he sensed they were in port, but he doubted anyone would hear. He didn't know how big the boat was—they'd kept him blindfolded while they were moving him about—but they'd taken him down some steps and then across a short corridor to put him in this room, so he knew he was on a lower level and almost certainly in an interior room. No, the chances of any good coming from shouting were awfully remote, while the chances of someone coming in and smacking him in the guts with a truncheon and duct-taping his mouth shut and hooding him after for good measure were fairly high. It just wasn't a percentage move.

He hadn't been much mistreated, he had to admit, if he was willing to discount that initial waterboarding and some electric shock they'd applied to his feet after to get him to scream over the phone for Rain's benefit. Jesus Christ almighty, the waterboarding was flat-out awful. The hell of it was how short-lived the effects were. One second you're pissing-your-pants-panicked, and then a minute later you're rational again, swearing you won't break this time. Except you do. It was unnerving to be swept away by blind fear that way—it was like losing control of your bowels or something, but a hundred times worse. Hilger was right, going through it at SERE was one thing, having the bad guys do it to you with real intent was something else entirely. That vice president who'd called it "a dunking" ought to have his head pulled out of his ass.

They'd left him in his cold, wet, soiled clothes for about a day and hadn't fed him at first, either. That meant they were still checking on the information he'd given them, wanting to keep him uncomfortable and mindful of his recent ordeal so they could break him again more easily if it turned out he'd been bullshitting them. When they hosed him off, changed him into a clean, dry track suit, and left him food and water, he knew something had been worked out. And whatever it was, his life was part of the bargain.

They'd pretty much left him alone after that, except when they'd put him on the phone with Rain. That conversation had been hard. Rain was his buddy, and he knew the man wouldn't quit until he'd gotten him free or died himself in the process. He was ashamed his carelessness had put his partner in this position, and it was awful knowing Rain was out there doing God knows what, while he was here, chained up and helpless to change the odds even a little.

They were even feeding him well enough, he supposed, with two hot meals a day in styrofoam containers that he ate hunched over with a plastic spoon. Sometimes the food was Chinese, sometimes Malay, sometimes Indian. Which didn't mean much, because you could get all three at pretty much any food stall in Southeast Asia, and it all froze and microwaved just fine. They could be anywhere. There was no porthole in his room, and his only sense of place was the rise and fall of the swells beneath them and the sound of the engine when they were moving. He didn't even know what time of day it was, or night, for that matter.

His worst immediate problem, aside from shame, boredom, and the feeling that his tongue was cultivating lichens, was the Mexican, whom Dox thought of as Uncle Fester for both his bald head and his crazy eyes. The man had a touch of the sadist in him—more than a touch, in fact. Every now and then he liked to pop into the cabin and get in a cheap shot. The first time it had been in the gut, but Dox had seen it coming and even though the fuckwit knew how to punch, the damage hadn't been too bad. But there were other places to hit. He'd kneed Dox in the coccyx once and the spot still hurt like hell and made sitting in his chains even less pleasant than it otherwise would have been. The man was picking his targets, Dox realized early on, so as not to leave marks. He figured Hilger, who while clearly being a four-alarm psycho in his own special way also seemed to be guided by some sort of professional ethos, would have taken a dim view of gratuitous mistreatment of a prisoner, and the bald guy was being careful because of it.

The last two days had been particularly bad. The only people he saw were the bald guy and the boyish-looking one, who Dox knew goddamn well at this point was anything but boyish, and he figured Hilger and the blond dude had gone somewhere. With fewer people around, Uncle Fester seemed to be emboldened.

The punishment hadn't stopped him from provoking the dude with insults, though. On the contrary, more than ever his dignity required that he prove he was unbowed. There wasn't much he could be proud of at the moment, but standing up to that piece of shit, insulting him grievously enough to make him an enemy, that was something. His body was paying for it, but it was helping keep his spirit alive.

He shifted on the cot and winced at the pain in his lower back. Yeah, he liked putting that fucker down, and he didn't mind suffering for it, either. 'Cause when this was over, he was going to make Uncle Fester pay for all of it, and with more interest than the man could ever hope to come up with.

He just had to live through it first.

11

I WENT OUT the back of the hotel and made a variety of aggressive moves until satisfied I was clean. Then I found an Internet café where, after the usual examination for spyware, I checked the bulletin board I used with my contact in the CIA, a young Japanese-American in Tokyo Station named Tomohisa "Tom" Kanezaki. Kanezaki and I had first run into each other a few years earlier, when he'd been a green, idealistic Agency recruit newly posted to Tokyo. He'd quickly figured out the way his superiors were using him, though, and was a sufficiently quick study to turn the tables on them and survive. Since then, I'd helped him with a few off-the-books matters, and could typically count on him for information, and sometimes equipment, albeit always at a price. I wondered what the price would be this time. Whatever it was, I'd have to pay it. I knew I couldn't get Dox out of the jam he was in without Kanezaki's help.

The bulletin board was empty. I didn't know when Kanezaki might check it, so I sent him a text message from an e-mail account he would recognize as mine:

You in Tokyo? Need to meet. Although over the years
Kanezaki had managed to achieve a relatively mild rat-
ing on my threat assessment matrix, I would have preferred not to warn him I was coming. But I also wanted
to make sure he was in town when I arrived, not on temporary duty someplace else.

I thought. Hilger must have had family somewhere.
Find them, take them . . . offer them up as a hostage exchange? Maybe. Kanezaki could probably point me in
the right direction, assuming he didn't balk at the nature
of my interest. But if there were family, how close were
they to Hilger? How much would he care? And even if
he did care, how likely was it that I could kidnap someone, hold him, and negotiate Dox's release, all on my
own? While faced with a five-day deadline?

Maybe I could use family as a threat: Kill Dox, and I'll
slaughter your aging parents, or your adorable nieces, or
whatever. Hilger might know about my rules regarding
women and children, but what he saw in my eyes in the
Góc Saigon would have shaken his confidence.

But no, that kind of threat could take things in unpredictable directions. I'd given Hilger a slim reed of hope
with my talk about getting out of the life. Better to leave
it at that, play along for time, and work my way back to
him, and wherever he was holding Dox.

After five minutes, I checked the e-mail account
again. Kanezaki's reply was already waiting, a simple,
I'm here.

I purged the e-mail account and purged and shut
down the browser, then left for another Internet café.
My paranoia was running hot, and I didn't want to do
anything else on the same computer, with the same
identifiable IP address, I had just used to contact
Kanezaki. I doubted Hilger would be able to trace me

through a Saigon Internet café IP address, and even if he could, at most he'd only be able to tell where I'd gone on the Net, not what I'd done or said there. But I've lived as long as I have by not taking risks without good reasons.

From the second café, I checked on flights out of Saigon. There was a 9:10 P.M. ANA flight to Bangkok that night. Perfect. From Bangkok I would have my pick of flights to Tokyo. I booked the flight, purged again, and went to a third café.

This time, I Googled Jannick. The first hit identified him as the founder and CEO of a Silicon Valley startup called Deus Ex Technologies. "From God" Technologies . . . whatever they were selling, they weren't modest about it.

I followed the link and perused the site. Once I finished sorting through the jargon about migration automation and cross-platform schema and backpropagation and Bayesian theory, I understood that DET's focus was databases, specifically database search. They were trying to use neural networks—computers modeled on the cortex of the human brain—to spot previously hidden patterns in massive databases.

Jannick had earned a Ph.D. in computer science at Stanford University in 1982. Since then he'd worked for Microsoft, Oracle, and several small companies I hadn't heard of. DET was his first startup. I checked the funding page, and was surprised to see that Jannick was funded by In-Q-Tel—the CIA's venture capital fund. I didn't know what it meant, but it had to mean something.

I thought about what Kanezaki had once told me about Hilger's privatized intelligence outfit. Unencumbered by congressional oversight, he could go places and do things the CIA couldn't. It wasn't clear how he had gotten started—on his own, or with his own version of governmental venture capital backing. Whatever the answer, the funds would be untraceable now, deniable. If Hilger's activities got out, his customers, or his paymasters, would simply express shock and dismay at the uncovering of this "rogue" operation; reaffirm the importance of proper oversight; and, if necessary, convene a blue ribbon commission to whitewash the government's complicity and decide on an appropriate fall guy. Thank you for playing, Mr. Hilger. Next contestant.

It was natural enough, I supposed. Democracy is about checks and balances. But if the policymakers find they're being checked and balanced a little too much, they look for what the software types call workarounds. Can you blame them? You might as well blame water for trying to go around a rock. It's not a question of blame and fault; it's a question of nature and proclivities. If there were no demand for Hilger's services, or for mine, for that matter, there wouldn't be a supply.

I wondered why Hilger would want to eliminate the CEO of a CIA-funded outfit offering neural net database technology. Was Jannick competition of some sort? Did his work interfere with something Hilger was trying to do, or threaten a market Hilger wanted to get into? No way to know, not yet.

I considered how Hilger might try to trace me, making sure I hadn't missed anything. He would expect me to Google Jannick right away. If he had access to the data, he could start with searches for Jan Jannick that occurred, say, one hour after our meeting at the Park Hyatt. Cross-reference the hits with servers in Vietnam, and you'd have the IP address of the computer I used. A long shot, maybe, but not impossible. But now, even if he had the access, he could confirm no more than that I'd checked out Jannick, as he would have suspected. My other Internet activity would remain sterile.

I caught a cab back to my hotel, collected my gear, and headed directly to the airport. Hilger might have anticipated the move and put people at one of the choke points inside—check-in, maybe, or outside customs—but I doubted it. Too many cameras, too much security. Also, my gut told me he really wanted Jannick dead. If so, I'd be safe until it happened.

Afterward was a different story.

12

HILGER DID a surveillance detection route, and, when he was satisfied neither Rain nor anyone else was following him, headed to the Sheraton, his rendezvous point with Demeere. He walked slowly, sweating in the tropical evening heat, only dimly aware of the humidity and the smell of diesel and spices he couldn't name, ignoring the incessant horns, the shouted invitations from motorcycle cabs, the dizzying whine of two-stroke engines.

That had been a close thing with Rain, a hell of a close thing. If the man had been bluffing at the Góc Saigon, it was the best bluff Hilger had ever seen. When Rain held that knife to his neck, and he saw what was in Rain's eyes, he really thought he was done. He had thought, *I miscalculated, he doesn't care about Dox, the crazy bastard's going to kill me right here.*

Hilger had been an inch from death twice before. The first time was in Baghdad, when a sudden sneeze from the omnipresent sand and dust had jerked his head a fraction, just far enough for a sniper round to crease his scalp instead of his skull. He'd called in artillery, and a minute later the sniper was vaporized. The second time, his rifle had jammed and he had to engage one of Saddam's Fedayeen hand-to-hand. The man had tried to gut Hilger with a Bedouin knife that broke off on Hilger's flak jacket, and Hilger knocked the man down with his rifle stock, then beat him to death with the butt, pulverizing his skull. Both times, the initial elation had given way to a feeling of wonderment at the miracle of still being alive, and then to a long period of reflection on the fragility of everything. He'd dodged two bullets, one of them literally, but those were only the two he knew about. How many went right by us, every day, without our even knowing?

Well, he'd just survived his third, and now that he was out of Rain's presence, now that the operational exigencies were behind him and he could acknowledge what had happened, that post-combat giddiness was kicking in. His legs felt rubbery and his hands were trembling. He'd known Rain by reputation, and by their one brief encounter in Hong Kong, but this was the first time he'd really seen him up close and personal. He recognized the type, although he'd known only a very few: Rain was a killer, a natural predator. The hesitation, the hand-wringing, even the paralysis that afflicts ordinary men, it was all absent from what he'd seen in Rain's eyes.

Hilger had done his share of killing, most recently that idiot Drano in Bali, but he didn't consider himself to be in Rain's class. He knew his own ability to kill, while formidable, was also something cerebral, something he had learned. Rain was a different breed. Killing was in him, down deep, and whatever that quality was, whatever name could be ascribed to it, Hilger suspected Rain had been born with it. He wasn't sure if that would be a blessing or a curse. What he did know

was that he wouldn't want it for himself. He valued
control too highly, and Rain's control of that killing
part of himself was clearly questionable. He'd been
struggling with it in the restaurant, and it could easily
have gone the wrong way.

He crossed the street and saw Demeere, waiting in
front of the hotel as though for an acquaintance or a
cab. Vigilant as always. Hilger gave him the slightest nod
as he passed to let him know everything was fine, then
took the elevator to the bar on the twenty-third floor.
Demeere arrived a few minutes later. They sat on the
terrace, a sticky breeze rustling the tablecloths, the
sounds of traffic diminished now, pleasant, the lights of
the city twinkling all around them.

"You want something to drink?" Hilger asked. "I
could use something."

"Sure," Demeere said. They ordered a pair of Bom-
bay Sapphires, doubles, and when the waiter had de-
parted, Demeere said, "I couldn't stay with you. He
would have made me, I could feel it."

Hilger nodded. "You played it right and we knew
you'd probably have to let me go. It worked out."

"He's going to do it, then?"

"It looks like it."

"Can he really manage it in five days?"

Hilger thought again of what he'd seen in Rain's eyes.
"Yeah. I think he can."

"And then?"

"Then things start to open up for us. And we give him
the second target."

"And then the third?"

Hilger looked at him, and understood that, as usual,
Demeere's intuition was sound.

"The third target is Rain," Demeere said.

Hilger nodded. "He's too dangerous to leave alone. Especially after what he's doing for us now."

The drinks came and they sipped them in silence. The gin was just what Hilger needed. He could feel it relaxing him, anesthetizing his still slightly jangled nerves. He'd been planning this for a long time and a lot of things still had to play out just right before it was over. But they were off to a good start. It was strange to think how much good it was going to do the country, and yet everyone would believe it was the work of the country's enemies. Well, strong medicine could be like that. It wasn't the bitter taste that mattered. It was the beneficial effect.

13

I CHANGED PLANES in Bangkok and slept most of the six hours to Tokyo. I arrived at Narita at seven-thirty the next morning. An hour and a half later, I was at Tokyo Station. I emerged from four stories underground into a cold, sunlit morning. I stood for a few minutes outside the massive red brick façade of the building, my carry-on bag slung over my shoulder, watching and listening. Truck engines and car horns. Construction equipment, jackhammers. Commuters flowing by me in their nameless thousands, squinting against the harsh morning light, hunched into the wind, briefcases gripped like life preservers. The moment I felt it, I realized how I missed the overwhelming energy of the place, missed it like the perfume of a woman I secretly loved, who slowly crushed me with her indifference.

I sighed. Tokyo was a sad place for me now, the people connecting me to it disappearing one by one, like lights going out at night in the windows of an almost empty building. First, Midori. Then Harry, set up and thrown off the roof of a building. Then Naomi, the sweet

Brazilian Japanese dancer I'd gotten involved with while hunting a *yakuza* assassin named Murakami, and whom I'd left in Rio after discovering she'd told the CIA where to find me. And then, only a year ago, Tatsu, my onetime nemesis and then loyal friend with the Keisatsuche, the Japanese FBI, to cancer. After that, Tokyo had become for me just another way station, a meeting venue. And soon, even that would be gone, when Kanezaki was recalled to headquarters or transferred to some other post or left for a career in industry. If I came back then, all I would find would be a graveyard of memories.

I called Kanezaki from a pay phone. "It's me," I told him.

"Didn't take you long."

"Can you meet?"

"Of course."

The "of course" was a perfect imitation of Tatsu, right down to the mildly exasperated tone, which was intended to only ill-conceal the vast reservoirs of patience needed in the face of so many stupid questions. Hearing Tatsu's quirks live on in Kanezaki, whom I knew Tatsu had mentored, and whom he had perhaps in his mind even adopted as a surrogate after losing his own son, caused me a pang of sadness, and a small smile.

"How about breakfast?" I asked.

"An early lunch would be better. I've got a few things to do."

I instantly disliked the counteroffer. It would give him time to arrange things, if . . .

If what? In the last few years, Kanezaki had a half-dozen opportunities to try to set me up. He never did, nor, as far as I could tell, did he have any reason to. I'd dropped in suddenly. He had things to do, like he said.

Still, I didn't like it. If I hadn't needed him so much right then, I might have bailed. Instead, I said, "All right. How about the place we met last time. When it opens."

That would be Ben's café in Takadanobaba, at eleven-thirty. A nice, out-of-the-way, neighborhood kind of place that served fresh bagels, quiche, and excellent coffee. I knew the area well. I'd get there early for countersur-veillance. Just in case.

"I'll see you there," he said, and clicked off.

I took the Yamanote line to Takadanobaba and got to Ben's a little less than two hours early. I set up just past the edge of the window in a convenience store across and slightly down from the café, my eyes on the street. Japanese convenience stores don't mind their maga-zines being used as a lending library, and I took full ad-vantage.

Nothing set off my radar, and Kanezaki showed right on time. He glanced back through the store window as he went by, doubtless seeing me in the corner but giving no sign of it.

Shit, I thought. I don't like getting nailed, even by a probable friendly. I watched to make sure he was alone, then drifted out of the store and caught him as he went into Ben's.

"Hey," I said, coming up behind him.

He turned without any sign of surprise. "Hey."

"You saw me in the convenience store."

He shrugged. "Yeah, it was where I would have set up, too. But I didn't figure you were one for the girlie magazines."

"What else do people read when they're loitering like that?" I said, still feeling a little defensive. "I was just being another middle-aged pervert. Blending."

"I think you were enjoying your work."

I realized that, not for the first time, I was underestimating this kid, this young man, rather, who was more seasoned every time I saw him. He was getting smarter, and I needed to get smarter about it. He knew my tactics now, knew that I wouldn't be waiting where I said I'd be. And he was becoming sufficiently tactical himself to know where I'd probably be, instead. I had to stop playing him as though he was still a beginner. He wasn't, and hadn't been for a long time.

I smiled. "Maybe a little. I was there for two hours. It wouldn't have gone by as fast with *Car and Driver*."

We shook hands, and I looked him over. I nodded in approval of what I saw: a slim, thirtysomething Japanese American with the kind of serious eyes you get from realizing the world isn't the innocent place you once imagined it to be, and from suspecting that what you do makes you complicit.

Over sandwiches and coffee, using English and keeping my voice low so as not to be overheard by the other patrons, I briefed him on everything that had happened with Hilger and Dox. I explained that there were three hits, but told him I didn't yet have any specifics. Given Jannick's CIA backing, I judged any mention of him too risky. The CIA connection might have been relevant to Kanezaki, for reasons I couldn't yet understand. He might have felt obligated to warn Jannick, or to otherwise prevent me from carrying out the hit. If protecting Jannick was important enough to Kanezaki, telling him might even have been dangerous. If someone wants to get to you, and he knows who your target is, he doesn't have to find you. He just has to find your target, and wait for you to show up.

When I was done, he said, "I'm sorry to hear about all this."

I looked at him. "Sorry isn't really what matters here. What matters is what you're going to do about it."

"What do you expect me to do?"

I felt a flush of irritation. "I expect you to help Dox."

"I don't really know how much I can."

"How many jobs has he done for you? Three? Four?"

"We've worked together. But that doesn't mean . . ."

"Cut the bullshit," I said, gripping the sides of the table and leaning forward. "He's in trouble now, bad trouble, what are you going to do, abandon him?"

I realized I was half out of my seat. The words themselves were fueling my rage. It was the iceman, wanting a reason to hurt someone, anyone, for Dox.

Easy, I thought. *Easy.* I exhaled sharply and slowly sat back down. I let go of the table and flexed my hands.

Kanezaki was as quiet as a man who turns a corner to find himself face-to-face with a growling attack dog. If he hadn't been sitting, he would have been backing up.

After a moment, he said, "Dox is a good man. I'm grateful to him professionally and I like him personally. But he's a contractor. That's his choice."

I looked at him, still trying to get a grip on myself. I thought about telling him it was fine, he could do anything he wanted. As long as he understood that if Dox died, so would he.

I shook my head. What was I thinking? Threats were the way I had played things when I was young and stupid. I was lucky to have lived long enough to find more effective means of persuasion. And the kind of help I needed here wasn't something I could extort.

Back off, I thought, as though actually talking to someone inside me. *Back off.*

"Look," he said, his hands up, palms forward, "I'm not saying I won't help. Just that you're still on the hook for the toys I got you guys last year."

He was referring to a tranquilizer gun and some considerably more lethal hardware he had procured for Dox and me in Tokyo. We had used it all to interrupt a drug deal in Wajima and touch off a small war between the Japanese *yakuza* and the Chinese triads. The war had forced a *yakuza* enemy of mine, Yamaoto, into the open, finally giving me the opportunity to kill him.

But his comment calmed me down. I realized, as I should have earlier, that his protestations weren't heartfelt. They were haggling. Irritating, yes, but not a bad sign, either.

"'On the hook'?" I asked. "Why do you think I just told you about Hilger? You mean knowing what he's up to isn't valuable to you? All right, next time I won't bother you with the information."

He sighed. "It's not valuable, really, not without more. Maybe if I knew who the targets were, that would be something. But without knowing who he's after . . . ?" He finished the sentence by turning his palms up to the ceiling, then dropping his hands back to the table.

Yeah, haggling, like I thought. But at least we were making progress.

"Like I said, I'm waiting on that information," I told him. "As soon as I have it, I'll let you know."

"I have your word on that?"

Well, his former naiveté hadn't been totally eradicated. I'd spent most of my life killing people for a living. Did he think I was going to lose sleep over a lie?

"You have my word," I told him. "And then we'll be square?"

"We'll be up to date. But if you want something else from me, you'll have to do something in return."

Ah, the moment of truth, I thought. *At last.*

"Yeah?" I said. "Who?"

"Don't you mean what?"

"I already know what."

He nodded, conceding the point. "Even if you get Dox out of this, you're going to take out Hilger, aren't you?"

"I don't know."

"You know. The only thing that worries me is how patient you are. Look how long you waited to do Yamaoto."

"I don't know why you think that was me. From what I read, he got shot, then died in the hospital of a cardiac arrest."

"Now who's bullshitting? I know Dox shot him. It was a 7.62 round, same as the rifle I procured for you. And you gave him the heart attack. Look, Tatsu and I were working together more closely than you know. He told me a lot."

He might have been bluffing. But the relationship with Tatsu was true, I knew.

"Tatsu told me you were doing something together," I said.

He nodded. "Call it unofficial counterpart relations."

"Is that what killing Hilger is about?"

"It's part of it."

"Why do you want him dead?"

"When did why start mattering to you?"

I shrugged. "It doesn't."

"Good. You want my help with Dox? Help me with Hilger. Don't wait when you find him. As soon as you have the shot, take it."

"All right," I said. "It sounds like we're on the same page. You want me to take out Hilger, and I want to find him. Hard to do one without the other."

"Good," he said again, nodding. "Now tell me what you need."

14

FROM TOKYO, I flew to Los Angeles, arriving on a cool, clear winter morning. San Francisco would have been more convenient, but Hilger knew I was coming and I didn't want to do anything that would help him anticipate me. It was bad enough he knew I'd be tracking Jannick; I wasn't going to offer up an additional datapoint unless I had no choice.

Before leaving, I'd gone to an Internet café and uploaded the photos of Mr. Blond to Kanezaki. It wouldn't be much to go on, but Mr. Blond and Hilger must have both applied for Vietnamese visas in the last seventy-two hours. That might be enough for Kanezaki to cross-reference. If it wasn't, I'd just have to get him more information. I included Dox's mobile number in the upload—the one Hilger was using now. Probably Hilger was keeping the phone off out of fear that I might have some means to triangulate on the signal, but it was still worth trying.

I might have given Kanezaki the URL of the compromised bulletin board, too. Maybe he could tell me where it was being accessed. But I decided to hold off on that.

Even if Kanezaki had the technical means, and I wasn't sure he did, I doubted Hilger would be sloppy enough to access the site from anywhere that would reveal his actual position. And if Kanezaki managed to hack the site itself, he'd be able to read my communications with Hilger, including the ones about Jannick. I didn't want to take that chance for so little probable gain. At least, not yet.

I had also checked the bulletin board I used with Dox, now compromised, of course, by Hilger. Hilger had uploaded a thorough dossier on Jannick: photos, home and work addresses, make and model of car, everything. I looked at the photos for a while. They had all been taken from public sources: his Stanford yearbook photo, company bios, some newspaper clippings. He was blond, with a round face, rectangular rimless glasses, and an uncertain smile balanced by a determination in his eyes. No surveillance photos. Apparently, Hilger had never gotten that close.

The home address was Christopher Lane; work, East Bayshore Road, both in Palo Alto. I'd never been to the town, but of course knew of it: birthplace of Hewlett-Packard and other technology giants; home of Stanford University; once a sleepy community of apricot groves, now the world's foremost technology center, the heart of Silicon Valley itself.

At LAX, I rented a Mercedes E500 with a navigation system. With the extra miles I was going to be driving, the car would run me about two thousand dollars, but it was worth it. I didn't know how much skulking around would be required before I figured out how to get close to Jannick, but there was a lot of money in Palo Alto and I expected the Mercedes and BMW quotient to be high. The locals, and local law enforcement, would take a lot less interest in a sixty-thousand-dollar car parked at the curb than they would in a Buick.

I stopped at a sporting goods store, where I equipped myself with a three-inch Benchmade folding knife. Tossing such quality knives every time I got on a plane was definitely an expensive habit, but it beat not having something sharp at hand when you needed it. Next, a Cingular shop, where I picked up an Apple iPhone. The mobile I had been using with Dox was now compromised, of course, and I needed something new and therefore sterile. The iPhone had a huge screen that made it useful for Internet access—not as versatile as a laptop, true, but it was a lot more portable and was always connected, too.

I drove north on Interstate 5 with the cruise control set for seventy-two—close enough to the seventy-mile-an-hour speed limit to ensure I wasn't risking a ticket; just enough over the limit to look normal. Plenty of cars passed me at eighty or better, and I silently thanked them for drawing off any prowling Highway Patrol cars and making me uninteresting by comparison.

I reminded myself of who I was, what I was doing here—the story I would use if anything went awry and I wound up facing questions from someone, a neighbor, a hotel clerk, a cop. Cover for action, the American spy agencies call it. It's the ostensible reason you have prepared in case you're caught doing something you're not supposed to. A fairly intuitive concept, actually, as anyone who's ever had an affair can tell you. When one of your colleagues shows up unexpectedly during your lunchtime assignation at your favorite out-of-the-way restaurant and says, "Jim! What a surprise to see you here. And who's your lovely companion?" you'd better have a prefabricated explanation, or your only response is likely be the time-honored slow suicide of "Uh, uh, uh . . ." or perhaps a variation of a "This isn't what it looks like" or an "I can explain this," both of which are universally understood to be confessions of full guilt.

The concept is easy, but effective execution is difficult. It requires imagination, a talent for acting, and experience. At this point, for me, the operation is second nature. I imagined myself as who I was: Taro Yamada, recently divorced, easing the pain of separation with a rambling holiday on America's West Coast. The camera I had with me would support the story, and I made sure to snap pictures of a few vistas along the way. It was a persona I'd used before, and I knew the details well, even the names of my ex-wife and our grown daughter, the location of my apartment building in Tokyo, the office where I worked as an executive in one of the big electronics concerns. None of it was well backstopped, but it didn't need to be. The popular American perception of Japan today is of a peaceful people, craving luxury brands, snapping pictures ceaselessly, polite, prosperous, deferential, supportive of America's war on terror. Nothing about my face or behavior would arouse any concerns. These days, it was the dark, bearded, Abdullah-looking types who got all the attention, never mind the protests of the antiprofiling crowd. And even if anyone wanted to check up on some of the details of my story, both the country and the language are opaque enough to throw off and eventually frustrate all but the most ardent and expert hunters.

If there had been time, I would have taken the Pacific Coast Highway, something I'd always wanted to do. But there wasn't, so I endured a fairly monotonous drive, instead. I passed flat expanses of farmland; scrub grass blackened by wildfires; a mile-long patch of earth trod to mud by the hooves of thousands of cows.

One place struck me: the San Luis reservoir, just west of I-5 along a winding stretch of Route 152. Amid the undifferentiated, rolling hills and gnarled, brooding trees, the sudden expanse of sparkling cobalt startled me. I drove along it for miles, watching it unfold on my left, fascinated by this improbable inland sea. As I came to its end and 152 began to curve away, I pulled over and got out.

The air smelled good, moist from the reservoir, cool and rich. I walked the hundred or so yards down to the water, my feet crunching in the gravel. A few cars whooshed by behind and then above me, but otherwise the area was utterly quiet.

The water sat within a basin of undulating stone walls stretching away for miles. Despite the afternoon sun it was cold down at the edge, and a sharp wind whistled in the crags of rock. The walls were scarred with horizontal grooves, nature's own graffiti, carved across the millennia by the ceaseless pressure of water and wind. I stood and watched, hidden now from the road, from everything behind me.

"I don't know who he is," I said aloud after a few minutes. "But it's him or my friend. I don't have a choice. You don't like it? Well, what would you do? Let Dox die, instead?"

I waited. But of course there was nothing. Just the coruscating sunlight and the caustic wind.

"Why do I even ask?" I said, shaking my head. "You're not there. You never were."

I turned and went back to the road.

I arrived in Palo Alto at a little before four. The first thing I did was go to a military-surplus store in nearby

Mountain View, where I bought a down parka with a hood and a pair of leather gloves. It was fifty-five degrees outside, according to the Mercedes' digital readout, so the parka would be a little excessive. But its bulk would conceal my body type, and its hood would obscure my face. The gloves I would need later.

Next, I drove to Jannick's house. Christopher Lane was a long, narrow hill ending in a cul-de-sac ringed by massive new mansions with equally massive yards and impressive views of the Palo Alto hills. I didn't see anyone about, but I was glad I was driving the Mercedes. It fit right into the neighborhood.

The house was close to the bottom of the hill. It was an older, two-story building, white painted clapboard with solar panels on the roof. No cars in the driveway. Maybe no one was home; maybe they parked in the garage. No way to know at the moment. It was a weekday and I expected Jannick to be at the office regardless.

I went past slowly, looking for a place I could set up. There was a gravel turnout on the right side of the road, about fifty yards down from his house. I could wait there and pick him up coming and going, but the spot would enable me only to see him, not to act. Worse, if I parked there, Jannick would go right past the driver's side of my car. Even if he were as oblivious to personal security as Hilger claimed, he might see my face, and he would certainly make the Mercedes.

I drove down to the end of the street. Christopher ended on Old Page Mill Road, a narrow, sleepy affair paralleled by a blacktopped, four-lane artery called Page Mill Road. I gathered the "old" version was what the locals relied on until the town grew and the small road was overtaken by the need for something wider

and faster. I made a left on what I decided to think of as
OPM and drove slowly north. A hundred yards up the
street, just south of another small road called Gerth
Lane, there was a dirt turnout. I did a U-turn into it and
stopped, facing Christopher. I looked around and decided I liked the spot. I wasn't in front of a house, so no
one was likely to pay me much attention. And I had a
good view of Christopher where it let out onto OPM.
Jannick couldn't come and go without my seeing him,
and I was far enough away so that he was unlikely to see
me, or to care particularly if he did.

A pack of bicyclists shot past me on Page Mill. They
were all helmeted, sleek in gaudy racing suits, and I had
a feeling their machines cost thousands of dollars apiece.
They reminded me of hiking clubs in Japan, whose members wouldn't consider a stroll even on a gentle grassy
hillside without hiking boots, walking sticks, and enough
North Face paraphernalia to make a seasoned alpinist
blush. Well, I could see why biking would be popular
around here. I understood the weather was wonderful
most of the year, although just now it was overcast, and
the hills were beautiful enough.

I was tired, but there was only about an hour of daylight left and I wanted to reconnoiter more before it got
dark. I plugged Jannick's office address into the nav system and drove there so I could get a feel for his likely
route. It was pretty direct: mostly a straight shot north
on Page Mill Road, five miles in all. There were no deserted stretches anywhere along the way. On the contrary, the route was heavily trafficked. Page Mill had
four lanes for cars, several miles of bike lanes, sidewalks,
and a mix of office buildings that gave way to residences
farther north. I could follow him easily enough in the
traffic, but unless he surprised me by veering off and

stopping somewhere deserted, I saw no locations that would serve for action.

East Bayshore turned out to be an access road paralleling Route 101, one of the main arteries between the Bay Area and southern California. I parked on a perpendicular street called Embarcadero, across from a Chinese restaurant named Ming's. Call me paranoid—I'd just take it as a compliment, anyway—but I didn't want to run even the smallest risk that the car I was driving, or its license plate, might be seen near Jannick's office, whether by an employee or a camera or both.

I slipped on the parka, pulled up the hood, and got out. I used the short walk to get into character. Thinking in Japanese, I reminded myself that I was Yamada again, altering certain details of the legend to fit the current circumstances. This time, I was being transferred to Silicon Valley by my employer, Matsushita Electric Industrial in Osaka, and was in town now to find a house and take care of school arrangements and otherwise prepare for the family move. I had a business card I could provide in case anyone asked for it, complete with a number that would be answered by a suitably incomprehensible Japanese message on the voice-mail system I continued to maintain back in Japan. My wife would need office space after our move for her work as a freelance translator. *This look like a good place, and so close to highway, too . . . what kind companies work here?* It wasn't very cold, so the parka was a little odd, sure, but Americans are tolerant of foreigners and their idiosyncrasies. Look at how much they put up with in that movie *Borat*.

Jannick's building was three down on East Bayshore, on the right side of the road. I strolled past the driveway, noting that it was shared by several office buildings, each an unremarkable, two-story glass-and-concrete box. From the size of the structures, I gathered Jannick was renting or subletting space. That, or DET was a much bigger company than its website suggested. I didn't like all the windows. If Hilger wanted me dead, he could have a sniper waiting in one of the buildings, knowing I would show up here while tracking Jannick. Or someone shooting photos instead of bullets, compiling evidence of my guilt, evidence they'd use for blackmail later. But I didn't have a choice. I kept going, my scalp prickling from the feeling of exposure to all those ominous windows.

I walked through the parking lot looking for Jannick's car, according to Hilger's dossier, a black Volvo S80. I didn't see it. I wondered if he was out at a meeting. Or if he'd left early for the day and I'd missed him on his way home. Or if he was traveling somewhere. In my experience, every predictable pattern you've analyzed goes to hell the moment you go operational. Imagination, backup plans, and an ability to improvise are the only countermeasures.

I thought about calling him from a pay phone, but didn't like the idea. I might come away with a better understanding of where he was, or even if he was in town right now, but I'd have to engage him or someone else with a story, too, leaving another potential piece of evidence for later. I decided to wait until a call would likely be more valuable.

I headed toward Jannick's building. As I got closer to the entrance, I saw that the windows next to the entrance doors were coated with some reflective material. There was a sign stuck to the window. It was too far for me to read from this distance, but I had a feeling it warned of CCTV monitoring. A security camera there, rather than in the parking lot, made sense. It was the building and what was inside it they'd want to secure. They didn't care about employees' cars.

I turned and walked away, considering. With a camera, I couldn't get to him in or directly in front of the building. That still left the parking lot. The problem was, to make a death look natural, you need some temporary control over the environment. If all that was required was walking up to Jannick and shooting him, I could have done it almost anywhere, the only real concern being escape. But I was going to need a few minutes alone with him. The parking lot wasn't great for that.

I kept walking. The light was fading from the sky, and it wasn't yet five o'clock. At this time of year, almost no one left work before nightfall. In the dark, I might be able to drag him behind his car, depending on where he was parked. But unless it were especially late and deserted, there was a worrisome chance that the person whose car was parked next to us might choose just that moment to head home, too. Plus, even the relatively clueless tend to be somewhat vigilant in parking lots at night. I could overcome that with Jannick, but if there were other people in the area, they'd likely be more watchful than I wanted.

Morning offered the opposite range of risks and benefits. On the one hand, people arriving at work are distracted by thoughts of the morning meeting, the day's tasks, what messages might be waiting for them. And parking lots aren't threatening in the morning, so no one pays any attention to their surroundings in them, anyway. But unless Jannick showed up for work very early indeed, it was hard to see how I could count on the privacy I needed. And then there were all the windows of all the buildings ... even aside from the possibility of one of Hilger's men lurking behind one of them, if just one person happened to be looking out at the parking lot at the wrong moment, there would be an eyewitness to the decidedly unnatural manner of Jannick's demise. Hilger and I hadn't discussed what would happen if Jannick's death was a success but its manner a failure. It didn't matter. I wasn't going to take the chance.

I walked another mile or so down East Bayshore, getting a feel for the area, its rhythms and rituals, what fit in and what might seem subtly out of place. My sense was that the neighborhood was transitional—office buildings on the south end, a new IKEA and shopping mall at the other, a trailer park and long-term storage facilities in between. Blending wasn't the problem here. The problem was access, and control.

I thought about using light disguise to enter Jannick's building. There might be opportunities inside—a restroom, a fitness facility, a closet. Somewhere Jannick's guard would be down and I could hold him long enough to do things the way they needed to be done. But I hated to create a connection between myself and the place where he worked, especially if that's where he was going to die.

I walked back to the Mercedes, cutting once again through the parking lot on the way. Jannick's car still wasn't there. It was dark now, but there was a lot of light from streetlamps. I was going to have to find a better place.

I drove back to Jannick's house. Still no car. Then back and forth again. I used slightly different routes each time, and after five such trips, I started to feel I had a reasonably good feel for the layout of the streets, the patterns of traffic. Within that layout and those patterns, there would be possibilities. There always were. Sometimes I recognized them immediately; sometimes I had to sleep on it first, and let my subconscious work the problem.

Sleep. I needed to get up early tomorrow to make sure I could catch Jannick before he left for work. And the time zone shifts were getting to me. It was time to call it a day.

I stopped at a phone booth in a gas station and checked the Yellow Pages, where I found a hotel called the Stanford Park. Menlo Park, the next town over. I called and was glad to hear they had a vacancy, a king room with a fireplace. No smoking, the clerk said apologetically, perhaps in response to the Japanese accent I was using. No problem, I assured him. No smoking was fine. It was only available for two nights? That would be fine, too. I didn't plan to be in town any longer than that.

I purged the car nav system before checking into the hotel, then had an excellent dinner at a place called Café Borrone, about a mile down the road: salad, lasagna, and a wonderful Napa Valley Cabernet called Emilio's Terrace, which, as globalization would have it, I had discovered a year earlier in Bangkok. The restaurant itself was a lively place, a bigger, smoke-free, California version of some of the Left Bank cafés I liked. There was a huge independent bookstore next to it, Kepler's, and after dinner I strolled among its offerings for a while, watching the people, absorbing details. Everyone looked so prosperous and satisfied and well intentioned. I felt like some secret foreign matter among them, a virus in the system, a germ in an operating room.

I asked one of the employees, a pretty woman named Cynthia, about Internet access. She directed me to the public library, less than a quarter mile away. I strolled over and checked the bulletin boards. Nothing.

The last thing I did before falling into an exhausted sleep was fire up my old cell phone and check its voice-mail account. There was a message from Delilah. "Don't push me away like this," she said. "Call me, please."

I didn't. I couldn't. I had to stay focused. I had to be who I always was.

15

I GOT UP at five o'clock the next morning, showered, shaved, fueled up on eggs and coffee in the hotel's restaurant, and went out. Unlikely that Jannick, or anyone else, would get to work this early, but still I drove past his parking lot to start with. It was deserted. Next, I stopped at a Starbucks in the shopping center at the other end of East Bayshore. I ordered a Venti Latte, wondering why they couldn't just call the damn thing a large, and dumped the contents in a drain a little ways from the store. It was the cup I needed: first, because I'd noticed that just about everyone in Palo Alto walked around attached to a Starbucks coffee, and carrying one of my own would make me look natural. Second, and more important, I didn't know how long I might have to wait for Jannick, and although no one was likely to pay attention to a quietly parked Mercedes, they might be discomfited by the sight of a man repeatedly stepping out of it to urinate on the curb.

I drove by Jannick's house. There was still no car in front, but my guess was that it was in the garage. The sun was just coming up, and the house was dark. I drove down to OPM and parked in my spot. I couldn't see his house from here, but I'd catch him when he pulled onto Page Mill.

While I waited, listening to a woman named Alisa Clancy on a radio show called *Morning Cup of Jazz,* I wondered who Jannick really was. A guy with an aptitude for technology? And where did his ambition come from? Did he miss his home in the Netherlands, or was this place, with its yoga-supple people and clean and prosperous streets, his home now?

One thing I didn't ask, though nor could I deny it, was whether he had a family. Of course he did. The house was too big, and too suburban, for anyone to live in it alone. And his car, a Volvo S80, had kids written all over it. But the less I knew about all that, the better. It's one thing to recognize something intellectually. It's quite another to see it—no, watch it—with your own eyes. The last time I'd gotten too close to the family of a target, in Manila, I'd frozen and damn near died. In unguarded moments, I still thought of the little boy whose father I'd taken. I wasn't going to go through that again.

I waited. No one disturbed me. I had to leave the engine off because if the car were running it might have attracted attention. The interior got cold, but the parka helped. The Venti cup proved handy.

At just past seven-thirty, someone on a bicycle came down Christopher and made a left onto OPM. He was wearing a white helmet and a fluorescent-yellow windbreaker, something designed both for warmth and to be visible to cars. I eased down in the seat a bit and watched through the windshield, thinking it was someone out for his morning exercise. But as he got closer, I realized *Christ, that might be him.* I'd been so fixated on the Volvo I was waiting for that it took me a moment to adjust. He passed me, not even giving the Mercedes a second look. I was going only on a bunch of out-of-date photos, but the shape of the face, the glasses . . . I was pretty sure it was Jannick.

Shit, the bike changed everything. Was this just exercise, or was it his commute? If the latter, I didn't know what route he might take, and I couldn't tail him effectively in a car even if I did.

I thought for a moment. Follow him down OPM? I didn't like the idea. The road was really nothing but an old jug handle to Page Mill. It wasn't closed to cars, but there was no reason a car would use it. Following him directly would be too conspicuous.

I fired up the Mercedes and cut left on Page Mill, paralleling OPM. I pushed it up to fifty, wanting to go faster but holding back because of the risk of a cop. Up ahead was a turnoff on Deer Creek Road; the light was red and I had to wait for it. *Come on, come on,* I thought. I wanted to get ahead of him before he came out on Page Mill so I could get another look.

The light changed and I shot forward. I got to the other end of the jug handle just in time to see the bicyclist pull out onto a bike lane on the other side of Page Mill. A hundred yards ahead was another intersection and another traffic light. *Good,* I thought. *We'll both have to stop and I'll get another look.*

I was half right. While I was stopped at the light, the bicyclist made a left onto the bike path on Junípero Serra. *Shit.*

It was a painfully long light. When the left turn signal finally changed to green, I cut into the turning lane and made a left onto Junípero Serra. A minute later, I'd caught up to him. I glanced over as I passed, but again I couldn't be totally sure.

I pulled ahead of him, wondering whether he was going to the Stanford campus. But instead, he made a right. *Damn.* I did a U-turn and backtracked to where he'd turned off, a road called Stanford Avenue. I made a left and drove forward but didn't see him. There were a number of smaller, residential streets snaking off on both sides. Unless I got lucky, for the moment I had probably lost him.

I thought for a moment. Maybe he was on his way to work. He avoided Page Mill because it was a busy road and farther north it had no bike lane. He was taking a more roundabout route, both for safety and for the exercise.

It felt right. I got back onto Junípero Serra, then Page Mill, and went straight to his office. There were a few cars in the parking lot now—enough to find concealment, not so many that I had to worry about too many people seeing and possibly remembering the Mercedes. I pulled in next to a Lexus SUV, putting it between me and the parking lot entrance, cut the engine, and waited.

Ten minutes later, the bicyclist pulled into the parking lot and rode straight to Jannick's building. Bingo.

I watched him carry the bike inside, then I drove down to the shopping center at the other end of East Bayshore. Now was the time for a call. From a pay phone, I dialed his office. One ring, two, then a voice: "Jan Jannick."

"Ah, sorry . . . wrong number," I mumbled, and hung up. I wiped down the pay phone and went back to the car.

I drove slowly back in the direction of his house, thinking. The office was no good. The house would be difficult at best. But he was on a bike. . . . That would create opportunities I hadn't considered before.

I thought about what I knew. Two locations, home and work, neither of them suitable. An unknown route in between. I considered buying a bicycle so I could follow him more closely and see what opportunities developed, but it felt too improvised, too uncertain. What I needed was a choke point. A place I could anticipate him, a place I could prepare and control.

I thought about OPM again. In a car you wouldn't bother; it would just be a slower alternative to the four lanes of Page Mill right next to it. But on a bike it would represent a shortcut. And not just theoretically: Jannick had used it this morning. There was at least a decent chance he would use it again on the way home.

I went back to OPM. I'd been on it earlier, of course, but I wanted to look again, this time through the prism of newly acquired information about how Jannick commuted to work.

I liked what I saw. The road consisted of two narrow lanes, and was obviously in disuse. Grass on either side had grown onto the shoulder, and scattered leaves that would ordinarily be swept aside by passing automobile traffic covered much of the surface. The trees crowding both sides had been pruned back to prevent dead branches from falling into the road, and the branches were now piled up here and there in large deadfalls. On the east side were trees and scrub that grew denser as the road curved away from Page Mill, until after about a half-mile the big artery was impossible to see and even the sounds of its automobile traffic had faded almost entirely. On the west side, there was a chain-link fence with signs warning, STANFORD UNIVERSITY ACADEMIC RESERVE, NO TRESPASSING. Beyond the chain-link fence, a series of empty, rolling hills, apparently the property upon which Stanford didn't want passersby to intrude.

Where the road connected with Page Mill, cars could
go right, but were prohibited from turning left at rush
hour—yet another reason a driver would be unlikely to
bother coming this way. But the west side of the road
tapered smoothly off into a bike trail that ran along
Page Mill and then curved left onto Junípero Serra.
Jannick's route. I looked up, and as if to prove my
point, two women on bicycles came down the Page Mill
bike path and rode past me. I nodded to myself. The
place felt right. Now I just had to find a way to make
it work.

I walked back in the direction I'd come from, dead
leaves crunching beneath my feet. There was a construction site between OPM and Page Mill, accessible by a
short bridge. I walked over and saw that the bridge ran
over a creek that curved away under OPM and into the
Stanford lands beyond. I walked down the embankment
and looked back, and damned if I wasn't invisible from
the road. Very nice indeed.

Under the bridge, there was a concrete wall marred
with graffiti. The paint looked old, though, and in some
places was only a few inches above the water line. I
gathered this place was used by kids in the summer,
when the nights would be warmer, the water lower or
nonexistent, the area more inviting for a shared joint
and adolescent fumblings or a bit of juvenile vandalism.

I walked back up to the bridge and then to the construction site. It was surrounded by a chain-link fence
and full of equipment, but there were no workers and
the site felt as disused as the road itself. A series of signs
on the fence warned, CAUTION: GAS PIPELINE STATION 3,
CITY OF PALO ALTO. In the shadows of the trees and the
utter quiet, the sign and the station felt like relics, future
artifacts to be encountered and puzzled over by what-

ever generations might discover this place long after today's drama was done.

I spent another hour walking the road, logging details, identifying backup routes, refining the plan. Then I went back to the car. It was time to go shopping.

At a place called the International Spy Shop in San Francisco, I bought a pair of Yukon Viking Pro 2x24 night-vision binoculars. At an REI sporting goods store in Mountain View, I picked up head-to-toe black Under Armour running gear—jacket, leggings, gloves; a black fleece cap; a large black fanny pack; and a roll of black photographer's tape. At a gun range called Reed's in Santa Clara, I acquired a SureFire M6 Guardian flashlight—less than eight inches long, 2.5 inches in diameter, and five hundred lumens. Finally, at a Nordstrom in a Palo Alto shopping center, I purchased a pair of Nike running shoes.

I finished at a little past three in the afternoon and, after a quick soup and sandwich at a restaurant in the shopping center, went back to the Stanford Park. I closed the drapes, turned off the lights, and checked the equipment. The night-vision binoculars illuminated everything. And the SureFire was absolutely blinding. Its light was so white and bright that even when the beam was pointed away from me, I had to squint to look at it.

I put black photographer's tape over the reflective surfaces of the Under Armour gear and the running shoes, checking it all by laying it on the bed in the dark and hitting it with the flashlight from various angles. No reflections. Then I suited up, putting the binoculars and the flashlight into the fanny pack and slipping the parka over the whole ensemble.

I drove back to Jannick's office and parked in the

Ming's parking lot so I was facing Embarcadero and East Bayshore. Unless Jannick made a right on East Bayshore, which would take him in the opposite direction of his house and which was a different route than the one he'd arrived by this morning, he would pass me on his way home. But if I missed him tonight, I could always get a little more aggressive tomorrow. In fact, it was possible I'd missed him already, that he had already headed home. But I doubted it. It was only four o'clock, earlier than regular people could get off work. As for people like Jannick, with the drive and passion to start their own companies, they tend not to quit until much later. I was less concerned that he'd gone home early than I was that he might keep me waiting past midnight. But either way, again, if things didn't work today, there was always tomorrow.

Just before dark, it started to rain. That might have been good news or it might have been bad. Good, because it would make the road slippery. Bad, because maybe Jannick's wife would pick him up, or he'd get a ride home from a colleague, or otherwise leave his bike at the office. But my guess was, the weather worked to my favor. There was the windbreaker he was wearing against the cold this morning, for one thing; it would do the trick in the rain, too. And there was the determination in the personality type of an entrepreneur, for another. Yeah, something told me Jannick wasn't someone to be dissuaded by a little precipitation. The rain felt like a good omen.

It was. At just past seven-thirty, the end of a twelve-hour day, I saw the fluorescent-yellow windbreaker and white helmet coming toward me. I checked through the night-vision binoculars to confirm. No question, it was him.

He made a right on Embarcadero. By the time I got
out of the parking lot and through the light, he was too
far ahead of me to see. But it was a safe bet he had
stayed on Embarcadero, the same route he had used
this morning. I peeled off onto the exit ramp to 101 and
Page Mill. Between the car and the shorter route, I estimated I'd get to OPM ten minutes ahead of him.

I parked in an office park just north of the corner of
Page Mill and Junípero Serra. I pulled on the hat and
the gloves, strapped on the fanny pack, and got out. I
walked for a minute, but as soon as I was clear of the
car, and anyone who might have seen me leave it, I
started jogging. The rain on my face was cold, and my
breath fogged in the chill air, but I felt warm and insu-
lated in the Under Armour. My heart was beating hard,
not from exertion.

I got to the construction site and was pleased to find
the area exceptionally dark. I could hear the patter of
the rain on the road and in the creek, the white noise of
it quieting the area, masking noises and reducing the distance sound could travel. I used the night-vision binoculars to scope out the road, the site, and the underside of
the bridge. I was alone. I still had to be careful about an
evening dog walker, or a determined jogger, or another
commuting bicyclist, but overall the chances that I would
have this little stretch of road to myself for the necessary
moments, and that I would remain unobserved even if
someone happened along, were as good as I could hope.

I set up next to the bridge by the construction site,
keeping low and scanning the area through the binoculars. Everything was illuminated beautifully. The fanny
pack was open, and the flashlight, like the binoculars,
was getting wet, but the equipment was top quality and
waterproof. I wasn't concerned.

Five minutes of waiting and scanning. And then I saw him, coming toward me on the bike path along Page Mill. I could make out his face perfectly through the night-vision magnification, all the way down to the droplets of water on his glasses. A headlight on the front of the bike showed up in the viewfinder like a glowing yellow flare.

I felt a hot rush of adrenaline through my gut, and my heart started kicking harder. I breathed in and out deeply several times and did one last scan of the area. All clear.

I dropped the binoculars into the fanny pack, pulled out the SureFire, and walked into the middle of the road. Without the night vision, I couldn't see Jannick himself, but his headlight shone like a beacon a hundred fifty yards out. One hundred. Fifty.

He slowed slightly as the bike path fed onto OPM, but he was still moving at what I guessed was close to fifteen miles an hour. More than fast enough.

Thirty yards now. I raised the SureFire to my shoulder. I closed one eye to protect it from the glare and preserve my night vision, and squinted with the other. Twenty. Ten.

Just before the forward edge of his headlight illumination reached my position, I pressed down on the flashlight's tailcap switch. Five hundred lumens hit him in the face, as momentarily bright and white as a bolt of lightning. I heard a cry of pain and surprise.

He must have instinctively hit the brakes, as I had hoped. I heard the tires skidding on the wet leaves and leaped out of the way. The headlight weaved crazily as Jannick fought to control the bike. But he was too startled, and too blinded. And the road was too wet. For an instant, the headlight gyrations grew wilder. Then the bike went over and Jannick hit the pavement.

I dropped the SureFire into the fanny pack next to the binoculars and zipped the pouch shut. I looked around, confirming once more that we were alone.

"Are you all right?" I asked, walking over. He was on his hands and knees, spitting out blood, trying to get up.

He moaned, sounding as though the wind had been knocked out of him.

I walked closer, my heart hammering. "Don't try to move," I said. "You might be hurt."

He started to say something back. I didn't hear what. I stepped over him and sat down hard on his back. He grunted and collapsed to the ground. I planted my feet solidly along either side of his head, reached with both gloved hands under his chin, and arched savagely back. His neck snapped with the sound of a thick piece of dry firewood and his body spasmed under me.

I stood and immediately moved back to the bridge, where I had some concealment. I took out the binoculars again and scanned the area. No one. Then I examined the tableau before me. Jannick's bike was on its side, the headlight shining uselessly upward into the falling rain, the front wheel slowly rotating. Jannick himself remained facedown, steam rising slowly off his body, the rain continuing its indifferent patter on and around him. It looked like a freak accident: a bicyclist, going a little too fast in the dark and the wet, loses control and falls the wrong way. There was no reason to think it was anything else, and no way to prove it, either.

16

I ZIPPED UP the binoculars and moved out to Page Mill. I waited a few minutes until there were no headlights coming from either direction, then jogged across the road and returned to the car.

I drove back to San Francisco, to the Tenderloin district, which I knew had a large homeless population. I left everything I'd worn that night next to garbage cans on a variety of street corners off Market, knowing the garments would be efficiently scavenged, distributed, and assimilated into the shifting ranks of the homeless within hours, perhaps minutes, of my passage. The binoculars and the SureFire went over the side of the San Mateo Bridge, into the dark, trackless waters of San Francisco Bay.

I found an Internet café called the NCK Cyber Lounge in San Mateo, where I checked the Kanezaki bulletin board. It was empty. I posted him a message: *Jan Jannick, Dutch national, CEO of Deus Ex Technologies in Palo Alto, California, In-Q-Tel backing.*

I'd wait until tomorrow to contact Hilger. There were two commodities I needed if I was going to find Dox: information and time. Immediately apprising Hilger of Jannick's demise would have cost me both. I couldn't wait too long to contact him, though, because sooner or later he was going to learn when Jannick had died and I didn't want it to look like I was playing for time. But I could slow things down. A message in the morning to set up a phone call for even later would buy me an additional twenty-four hours, maybe even more. Within which, with luck, Kanezaki might have some new information.

Kanezaki. He wasn't going to be happy to learn of the identity of the first target after the fact. I'd just have to finesse his suspicions as best I could. I went out and called him from a pay phone.

"You got anything?" I asked, when he picked up.

"No. Didn't you . . ."

"The phone number you're tracking?"

"He's keeping it turned off. Not a surprise. Look, didn't you check the bulletin board?"

"Yeah, I just left you a message there. Name and particulars of the first person on the list."

"Our friend gave you the list?"

"Just the first entry. And it's already taken care of."

"It's already . . . you were just here forty-eight hours ago. How could you have . . . you must be bullshitting me, you must have known who it was when you were out here. Otherwise you couldn't have done it so fast."

"I'm not bullshitting you. All I knew was I was supposed to go to California. The information was waiting for me when I arrived yesterday. I caught a lucky break and an opportunity presented itself. I didn't have a chance to tell you sooner and I'm telling you now."

There was a long silence. He knew I'd known earlier. But what could he do?

"I'm waiting on the second name now," I said. "As soon as I have it, I'll tell you. In the meantime, take what's on the bulletin board and see how it cross-references with what I've already given you. I'll drag things out as long as I can on my end."

"I hope you're not going to fuck me on this."

"Why would I? We both want the same thing. It's just a question of timing. I'll check in again tomorrow, okay?"

He waited a moment, then said, "Okay."

Back at the hotel, I took a long, hot shower. Then I got a fire going and sat with a towel around my waist, watching the flames. I hadn't eaten in more than eight hours, and I thought I should get something into my stomach. But I wasn't hungry.

I wanted to feel something. Relief that I'd bought Dox time. Horror that I'd just killed a man, probably a husband and father, not a mile from his house, on the very road he was taking home to his family. Fear that I'd missed some variable, that even now the local police, or worse, Hilger and his men, were mapping my coordinates, triangulating on my position, moving in for the kill.

But there was nothing. It was as though some emotional spinal cord had been severed, leaving my mind useless and numb.

The numbness disturbed me. It was how I always used to feel, or rather, not feel, after taking a life. Clinical, analytical, detached. The trouble in Manila, when I'd frozen rather than traumatize a child by killing his father in front of him, had actually been a kind of breakthrough for me, although I'd only realized it in retrospect. It had been the first sign that the killer might be less than all of me, the first crack in the ice of what I was. But now, the iceman was back. And not just for the work, it seemed. For the aftermath. For everything.

All of which was bad enough. But what was worse was how . . . comfortable it felt. Like a favorite chair, or the food you grew up on, or an old, perfectly sprung pair of boots that felt just right when you slipped them on after a long absence.

I told myself there was no reason to be concerned. Being myself again felt natural enough, and it was certainly easy. I thought maybe I should just give in and go with it. What was the point of fighting, anyway? In the long run, you can't win against yourself. I'd been up on points for a while, but the iceman was patient. He'd bided his time, and when he saw his moment, he'd found his way back.

No, not back. Maybe he'd just always been there. Like I supposed he always would be.

17

EARLY THE NEXT MORNING, I left the Stanford Park and headed south on 101. In an Internet café in San Jose, I checked the Kanezaki bulletin board. It was empty. I found another café and checked on Hilger. Again, nothing. I left him a message that read, "Tell me when I can reach you by phone." I didn't say Jannick was done. I didn't mention Dox. For the moment, I wanted to keep my options open.

It looked as though I had a little time on my hands. I decided to return to Los Angeles by the coastal route. Strange circumstances to fulfill my ambition to drive along the sea, but smoke 'em if you got 'em. And it would give me a chance to think.

The drive was beautiful. My appetite came back on the way, and I stopped in Carmel for lunch. I stumbled across an Italian place called Casanova in a cozy Mission-style building, and ate on their patio, warmed by the radiant sun. The food was superb: bruschetta with local heirloom tomatoes; linguini with fresh mussels and shallots; chocolate nougatine pie. All accompanied by a

'96 Hudson Vineyard Marcassin Chardonnay that alone
was worth the drive.

It was the kind of place Delilah liked, and the kind of
place I liked to take her. I realized I should probably call
her. But I didn't know what I would say. The work she
did, and the world she inhabited, necessitated compro-
mises, of course, but in her way Delilah was as ethical a
person as I've ever known. I didn't want to have to tell
her what I'd just done. And I didn't want to hear the suspicion in her voice if I refused to answer her questions. I
certainly didn't want her judging me. I'd dealt with
enough of that shit with Midori and wasn't going to put
up with it from Delilah, too. How could she understand,
anyway? How could anyone, who hadn't been there?

*Yeah, but Delilah knows you, better than anyone. She
would understand.*

*Bullshit. No one ever understands. They say they do,
but they don't.*

I kept heading south, the windows down, the sunroof
open, the wind in my hair. The road narrowed in Big
Sur, the traffic thinning, the stores and houses and other
signs of people slowly evaporating as I drove. Soon the
land was mostly quiet meadows and conifered hills, scal-
loped cliffs that wended along the Pacific, in and out,
back and forth, each curve in the road revealing some
new, spectacular vista. I watched the ocean sparkling a
thousand feet below and felt I was driving along the
edge of the earth, through some intensely private and
stoical place, beyond civilization's purview, beyond any
notion of redemption or regret, a place that existed only
for itself, that neither welcomed nor opposed nor held
in any regard at all the fragile creatures who intermit-
tently passed through in awe of it.

San Simeon. Pismo Beach. Santa Barbara. The sun set over the water as I drove, yellow, then pink, then finally a long red band at the horizon, fading to indigo. I wondered if Delilah had ever driven this route, and imagined what it would be like to have her here with me, watching as daylight yielded to a giant vault of stars. I tried to push away the thought, but the feeling persisted.

I drove on in the dark. Absent the distraction of the sunlit scenery, my mind began to wander, not to good places. I thought of Jannick, and all I had taken from him. I reminded myself that I had no choice, that it was either him or Dox. I thought of Hilger, and regret and ambivalence were eclipsed by hatred and cold rage.

First Dox, I reminded myself. *Then Hilger. Just be patient. That's what's going to make this work for you.*

I stopped in Santa Monica and checked the bulletin boards. Nothing from Kanezaki. A short message from Hilger: *Call me at 08:00 GMT.*

Eight o'clock Greenwich Mean Time . . . that would be midnight in California. Damn, it was almost eight out here already. A few more hours, and I would have missed the time for the call. I thought about skipping it entirely, telling him I hadn't gotten the message until too late, giving Kanezaki more time to work the data. But I decided not to. If Kanezaki hadn't found anything by now, he wasn't going to, at least not without more information. A call to Hilger might shake something loose. And besides, I wanted to check in on Dox, to see if he was okay.

I thought for a moment. Hilger's message was left at five o'clock that evening California time. I had posted at nine o'clock that morning, which would have been midnight or later throughout most of Asia. I imagined

Hilger going to sleep sometime before I posted the message, receiving it and responding in the evening my time . . . morning his. A reasonably safe bet, then, that he was still in Asia somewhere, on a boat as Dox had said. It wasn't much, but the more pieces I had, the better I'd be able to recognize and exploit each one of them, until hopefully, finally, they'd all add up to a breakthrough.

I called Kanezaki from a pay phone. "Heads up," I told him. "There's going to be a call at oh-eight-hundred GMT. Less than four hours from now. If you have a way to track the signal, that's your moment. I'll keep him on for as long as I can."

"I don't know," he said. "If our man is careful enough to keep the phone off the rest of the time, I doubt he'd be stupid enough to call from an insecure location."

Kanezaki had grown a lot since I'd first met him, but he still had an annoying tendency to try to show his smarts by stating the obvious. "Of course he wouldn't," I told him. "But it'll be one more piece of data to work with. I'd rather know where he places the call than not know, wouldn't you?"

There was a slight pause while he absorbed the rebuke. Then he said, "You're right."

"What about the guy I posted about? Any leads on that?"

"No."

"The government venture-capital backing? You don't think that's a coincidence, do you?"

"I don't think it's a coincidence, but I haven't turned it into anything workable yet, either."

"All right, then. Oh-eight-hundred GMT. I'll call you when it's done."

I had a burrito and a fruit smoothie at a place on the

pier, then killed time by strolling, loosening up after the long drive. I went to a pay phone at exactly midnight and made the call.

One ring, then Hilger's voice: "Yeah."

I noted that he picked up directly. Maybe he'd made his point about the strength of his numbers last time, and didn't feel the need to repeat it.

"It's done," I said.

"I know. Nice work. You complained about five days, but in the end you only needed two."

Maybe he already knew about Jannick. Maybe he was bluffing to impress me with his omniscience. It didn't really matter.

"Let me talk to Dox," I said.

There was a short pause, and then I heard the big sniper's baritone, tinny through the speakerphone. "Dox here."

"How are you doing?"

"Bored. This is one of the dullest groups of nitwits I've ever been forced to spend time with. It's a dark day to be a Marine."

He was telling me they weren't leaving him alone, that there was someone with him at all times. With a little luck, they'd notice only the insult, and not the substance it concealed. But why the mention of the Marines?

I heard static, then Hilger's voice again. "All right, you heard him, he's fine."

That was the second time he'd grabbed the phone in a hurry. The Marines . . . was that what Dox was going to say when Hilger had grabbed the phone from him last time? And what did he mean by it now? Hilger was former Army. But what about the people with him? Did Dox know one of them from his Marine days? Or did he

have some other way of knowing one of them was a jar-
head?

Why did Hilger keep cutting me off so fast? I had a
sudden, uncomfortable thought. Far-fetched, maybe,
but . . .

"Put him on again," I said.

"No."

"Put him on. You can listen, I just want to make sure
it's him and not one of your people imitating his voice."

There was a pause, then I heard Dox's voice. "Yeah."

"What's your favorite hotel in Bangkok?"

"What?"

"Your favorite hotel in Bangkok."

"What is this? You don't think it's me?"

"They're only letting me talk to you for a second at a
time and your accent is too easy to imitate."

"What accent?"

"Tell me."

"If they hear my answer, I won't be able to go there
after this. And that would be a tragedy."

It had to be Dox. No one else could be so obstreper-
ous. But still.

"The name, goddamnit."

"Look, I like the place because of the mirrors in the
bathrooms. I tried to tell you about a threesome I had in
one, all right? With two lovely Thai ladies. And you cut
me off 'cause you didn't want to hear."

I let out a long breath. It was him all right. The hotel
was the Sukothai, and yeah, I had cut him off the time
he tried to tell me the story.

I heard the phone being moved, then Hilger's voice.
"Satisfied?" he asked.

"All right," I said. "I've held up my end. Now let
him go."

"You're not done. There are two more."

Well, it was worth a try.

"Give me the particulars, then," I said.

"Not yet. You're a little ahead of schedule."

"We're doing this on a schedule?"

"The person's not in position yet. As soon as he is, I'll upload the information you need."

On the one hand, I liked the extra time. On the other hand, once again, I hated the idea that Hilger would be able to follow me by my efforts to track his target. I hoped Kanezaki would find something to help me short-circuit the whole thing.

"How long are we talking about?" I asked.

"Forty-eight hours. Check the bulletin board then."

He clicked off.

I called Kanezaki from a pay phone. "You get it?" I asked.

"I got it. He's in Jakarta. Or at least he was during the time you had him on the phone."

I was gripping the phone hard. "Where in Jakarta?"

"Pluit, it looks like. The marina."

"Can you be more precise than that?"

"What do you want, an address? All I know is he was near a cell tower in Pluit. Without a formal request to the NSA, which will create a lot of questions and take a month to process anyway, I can't triangulate. I can only give you a radius around a single tower. From what I can see, either he was in Pluit, or he was a little way out in the Java Sea."

I was quiet for a moment. He was right, I wasn't being reasonable. But damn, to feel like I was that close to having him in my sights . . .

"He's got our friend on a boat," I said. "They proba-bly docked in Jakarta to make the call, maybe use an Internet café, whatever. But with the boat, they could move anywhere, and keep moving. There are ten million people in Jakarta alone. Leave Jakarta, and you've got seventeen thousand islands, only six thousand of them inhabited, and probably twenty thousand miles of coast. And that's all assuming he stays somewhere in Indonesia and doesn't move on. Shit, this isn't much better than knowing he's in Asia."

"It's another piece," Kanezaki said, after a moment. "Like you said."

I sighed. He was right again. "Is this anything you can use with what you've already got?" I said. "The visas, the previous known location, the government backing?"

"I doubt it. I don't have a way to search travel records by location, only by names. It doesn't look like our friend was traveling as himself. So it's slow going."

"All right," I said, trying not to be frustrated. We had so many pieces . . . but they still added up to nothing. I fought the urge to just go to Jakarta, see what I could find there. Without more information it would be useless.

"What about you?" he asked. "You learn anything on the call? Anything new we can work with?"

"No. Well . . . maybe one of the people who's holding Dox is or was a Marine. I think Dox was trying to indicate that, but I'm not sure."

"All right, I'll see if that gets us anywhere."

Even as he said it, I knew it was unlikely. It was almost nothing.

"Anyway, that's all," I said. "Hilger told me he'd upload details about the next assignment two days from now."

"Two days from now? You're doing it again, aren't you? Giving yourself time to . . ."

"I'm not doing anything. He told me the person isn't in position yet and wouldn't be for forty-eight hours. I've got nothing to do but wait. If you could come up with something in that time, it sure would be handy."

"Otherwise . . ."

"Yeah, that's right. Otherwise we get to number two on the list."

"Jesus," I heard him breathe.

"Don't 'Jesus' me," I growled. "I'm not going to let something happen to my friend."

"Yeah, but . . ."

"Bullshit. I don't want to hear it. Not unless you've ever once gotten your own hands bloody. Have you? Ever? Or do you only send out other people for the nasty stuff so you can sleep like a fucking baby at night?"

A long moment went by. Then he said, "I wasn't judging you. I was just . . . a little awed. That's all. I'm trying to help, okay?"

I watched people strolling past me. A group of teenagers, laughing through orthodontic-perfect smiles, sauntering in distressed jeans that probably cost two hundred dollars a pair. Men whose faces bore the marks of nothing worse than overstretched mortgage worries beat back by too much Botox. Women with bare lipo-suctioned midriffs and Herculean plastic breasts. A river of well-fed selfishness, a contagion of insecure conceit. I hated them. I hated all of them.

"You there?" I heard Kanezaki ask.

"Yeah."

"If you don't mind my saying, and you probably will, you seem like you're on a short fuse lately."

"You're right, I mind."

"I'm only bringing it up because . . ."

"Because what?"

"Never mind."

"What? Just say it."

He sighed. "Don't push away the people who are trying to help you. You can't afford it. And neither can our friend who's in trouble."

"Oh, now you're trying to help me. Not use me. Help me."

"Look, there's something I want out of this, yes. I've been upfront with you about it. But that doesn't mean ..."

"That's exactly what it means," I shouted. "Exactly. When are you going to grow up and realize you can't fucking have it both ways?"

I slammed down the phone and clenched my hands into fists, fighting the urge to smash something. A sound rumbled up out of my throat. It might have been a snarl.

I looked up and saw three husky college kids watching from five yards away. White, dressed like gangsta wannabes. I realized they had stopped because of my outburst.

"Chill, dude," one of them said.

I stood perfectly still. Inside, a war raged: the need to avoid trouble so I could focus on Dox; the overwhelming urge to slaughter the three creatures looking at me like I was an animal in the zoo. I imagined myself tearing into them like a lawn mower up on its back wheels, slashing, ripping, gutting. I could almost hear their high-pitched wails of terror and surprise, could practically smell the hot blood pouring out of them. I gritted my teeth into an insane smile and stood staring at them, panting with the effort of holding back, praying for one of them to say something, do something, to tip the balance and make me lose control.

One of them smacked Mr. Chill on the back of the head and gave him a shove. "Let's go, man," he said. And Mr. Chill, perhaps guided by some reptile-brain recognition of the image of a predator just before it pounces, nodded and silently complied. The three of them walked away, and somehow I managed to let them.

I glanced around. A few other people in the area were studiously looking elsewhere. Goddamnit, I'd drawn attention to myself. Stupid. I pulled out a handkerchief and wiped down the phone receiver, obscuring the act with my torso, then walked away, keeping my head down.

I found another pay phone and called the toll-free number for Hilton hotels. Their property in Beverly Hills had a room available tonight, did I want that? I told them I did, and would be there shortly. One night was fine. I was just passing through.

I had the car for a week anyway, so I decided to hold on to it. It beat figuring out the bus system, or trying to get around by cabs. I had nowhere to go for two days. I might as well stay here.

The nav system took me onto the Santa Monica Boulevard and east toward Beverly Hills. I drove through alternating patches of feeble yellow light and serene urban darkness, the interior of the Mercedes strobing weakly with each passing lamppost. Fragments without were illuminated, revealed, then gone again: a shuffling homeless man, glancing up at me as indifferently as a sea creature outside a passing bathysphere. Shuttered storefronts, graffitied walls, construction sites suffocating under profusions of slapped-on posters. A homeless woman, sunk to her side in the shadows, her head in her hands, another soul swallowed up by the city.

A few miles from the hotel, as concrete gave way to palm trees and graffiti to the shiny windows of boutiques, I turned on my old cell phone to check the voicemail account. Part of me hoped for a message from Delilah. Part of me dreaded it.

What I got, though, wasn't a message. Just a second after I fired up the phone, it buzzed. I checked the readout, surprised, and saw that Delilah was calling me right then.

I hesitated for two full rings. Then I picked up and said, "Hey."

"You're hard to reach," she said. "And you don't return calls."

I thought of several things to say. What came out was just, "Sorry."

"You know how many times I've called you, hoping I'd catch you with your phone on?"

"A lot, I'm getting the feeling."

"Any news?"

"Some. He's okay for now."

"Did you meet with . . ."

"I met him."

"And?"

"I learned a few things. But not enough."

"Where are you now?"

"I . . ." I started to say. Then, "I don't know where I am."

"I want to see you. Just tell me where."

"I'm in California. But . . ."

"I have some time off. Tell me where on the bulletin board. I'll fly out."

I wanted her, and yet I didn't. "You shouldn't come," I said. "You don't want to be mixed up in this."

"You told me you feel tied to me. Did you mean it?"

I sighed. "Christ, you're stubborn."

"Did you mean it?"

I didn't say anything for a moment. Then: "You know I did."

"Then I'm coming to see you. Just tell me where."

"I've only got two days . . ."

"Post it now and I can be there tomorrow afternoon."

A dozen more protestations came to mind. But I said only, "I need to get to a computer."

"Okay. And give me the name you're using. I'll make a reservation somewhere and tell them to let you in. If you show them ID, you won't have to wait for me."

We were quiet for a moment. I said, "What are you wearing?"

She gave me a small laugh. "I'll see you tomorrow."

My gut roiled with conflicting emotions. I waited, wanting to say something more, for her to say something more, but she had already clicked off.

I found an Internet café in West Hollywood and told Delilah I was in L.A. Then I went to the hotel. I used their business center to check the Air France website—a safe bet Delilah would be flying the national carrier if she wanted her choice of nonstops. There were two flights she could use. One got in at 3:50 in the afternoon, the next, a few hours later at 6:55.

I lay in bed for a long time, thinking, trying to unwind. I wanted to see her, but at the same time I was afraid to. Afraid of what she'd make of me. Which was stupid, of course. Why should I even care what she thought, or anyone else? And if anyone could understand . . .

No one can understand. No one.

Lying in another anonymous bed in another random hotel room, back in the life as though I'd never left it, I thought I should just let Delilah go. Already my relationship with her felt improbable, inapplicable, absurd. What could I have with her, anyway? Separate apartments in a foreign city, thoughts and lives that we couldn't discuss?

It didn't matter. Whatever we had, it was gone, another moment alchemized to memory. I should just accept that. I should just move on, alone. It was all I was ever good for. It was all I could really trust.

18

DELILAH ARRIVED at LAX at a little before four in the afternoon California time. It was almost one in the morning now in Paris, but she'd napped on the flight and didn't feel tired at all. Flying west was easy. It was the trip back that could be a little rough.

She was carrying only a shoulder bag, a dark brown Bottega Veneta in classic woven leather, and was in a cab less than twenty minutes after touching down. She told the driver, a twentysomething with a nice smile who she guessed was from West Africa, to take her to the Beverly Wilshire, although the reservation she'd made was in fact at the Bel-Air. Unlikely anyone was waiting at the airport to try to follow her, but she wanted a chance to confirm anyway before going on to her true destination.

"And let's stay on Sepulveda to Jefferson Boulevard," she added.

"Are you sure, miss? The four-oh-five would be faster."

She knew that, which was exactly why she wanted to go through the city. In L.A. freeway traffic, it would be impossible to know whether anyone was following them; there could be fifty cars between the cab and a tail. The city route, by contrast, would have fewer cars and more local traffic. Every time the cab turned, Delilah would be able to check behind to see if anyone had stayed with them. A few instances of a car going the same way could be a coincidence. All the way from the airport to Beverly Hills would be a different matter.

"I'd just like to see the city," Delilah said.

The driver furrowed his brow and smiled. "Of course, of course. You . . . live in L.A.?"

Delilah understood what he was thinking. She obviously knew the city well, but if she lived here, why would she want to take the scenic route? And with her looks, he was wondering if she was a celebrity he couldn't quite place. Her clothes fit the celebrity theory, too: a classic Burberry trench coat, open now in the relative warmth of the southern California afternoon; a cream-colored, scoop-necked cashmere sweater, set off by a long, gold Faraone Mennella chain-link necklace; chocolate brown, platform-heeled boots worn over slim-cut jeans. She got that quizzical "Is she a celebrity?" look a lot. It neither gratified nor displeased her, but was occasionally something she could use.

"I've spent time here," she said, glancing behind as they turned onto Sepulveda, marking the cars that followed them.

"Oh, of course," the driver said, and she knew he would take the glance behind them as alertness for paparazzi, or, if not that, then wariness about being followed to an assignation with her lover. The second interpretation, she realized, wasn't so much inaccurate as it was incomplete.

She thought of John on the way, and Dox. She was

worried about both of them: Dox, for obvious reasons;
Rain, because she knew that precisely because he was
hell-bent on helping his friend, his judgment was likely
to be impaired. Look at the way he had blundered into
surveillance last year when he'd gone to see Midori
and their child. Delilah had tried to warn him then,
too, and he had ignored her. She wondered what it was
about men that wed them more to a way of doing
things than to achieving their ostensible goals. She
loved them, loved nothing more, but she had to admit
the world would be a better place if it were run by
women.

By the time they got to the Beverly Wilshire, she
knew she was clean. Still, she wanted to do a foot route
to be absolutely sure. She freshened up in a restroom,
then strolled through Beverly Hills as the sun set, using
a variety of countersurveillance moves to make certain
she was alone. After an hour, she was satisfied, and
found another cab.

When she had checked the bulletin board before
leaving Paris and learned that Rain was in L.A., she immediately thought of the Bel-Air, her favorite hotel in
southern California. She'd stayed there twice, and loved
it: a luxurious but low-key oasis of pink stucco Mission-
style buildings, improbably secluded in the heart of the
city among acres of flower and herb gardens, quietly
trickling fountains, and the canopies of ancient trees.
The hotel had been popular with stars since opening in
1946 because it was so serene, secure, and, of course, dis-
creet. She had posted John the name and location, and
the name she would be using. *Just say you're with Laure
Kupfer,* she had written, *and they'll check you in.* Then
she had called the hotel, paid in advance for the Garden
Suite, and explained that they should give a key to a Mr.

Ken, who might arrive before she did and ask to be let into her room.

The cab let her out on the quiet, residential street that fronted the property. She crossed a covered stone bridge to the main building within and was instantly enveloped by the beauty of the place. Water trickled somewhere in the dark beneath the bridge; to one side, the twisting branches of ancient sycamores were illuminated by spotlights from below. She caught the scent of orange blossoms and basil and suddenly realized she was ravenous.

The check-in area was furnished like a comfortable, tasteful living room, all upholstered furniture, landscape paintings in gilded frames, unostentatious objets d'art. The light was just right, not too bright, not too dim, and the room had a welcoming hush to it, along with a faint scent of wood and cut flowers. A fire crackled in an open fireplace.

Delilah walked over to the front desk and told them she was Laurè Kupfer. Of course, Ms. Kupfer, welcome, they told her. Mr. Ken had already arrived; would she like to be escorted to the Garden Suite? She thanked them and told them no, she would rather just stroll over alone.

She walked along a porticoed terrace, her footfalls echoing quietly. She heard the sounds of conversation and quiet laughter from a few people dining under the heat lamps on the patio outside the restaurant, but other than that, Delilah enjoyed the delicious sense that she had the place to herself.

She came to the Garden Suite, unlocked the door, and stepped into the living room. The lights were on, but she didn't see Rain. "John?" she called out.

There was no answer. A fire was burning in the stone fireplace, and she caught a faint, pleasant trace of smoke in the air. A thick contemporary Oriental rug with a floral design was spread across the expansive Saltillo-tiled floor. The upholstered chairs and couch arranged around a wooden coffee table at the center of the rug were all empty: not a newspaper, not a tossed-aside jacket, not an empty glass. Other than the lights and the fire, in fact, there was no sign that anyone had been using the room.

Suddenly, she was concerned. Rain had sophisticated enemies, and look what had happened to Dox. What if someone had . . .

Then she told herself she was being ridiculous. The hotel's security was designed to protect Hollywood glitterati. They were safe here. And even if his judgment were off, Rain was still the most thorough, cautious, paranoid tactician she'd ever known. He was just out—taking a swim, or using the gym, or maybe strolling in one of the gardens.

She walked into the bedroom, scanning reflexively. Still no sign of him—no clothes lying around, not even an impression in the bedspread where he might have been sitting. Ah, there, on one of the dressers—a bottle of 1971 Glenmorangie. A good single malt, that was John. She glanced inside the walk-in closet, and saw a navy cashmere blazer on a hanger, and a pair of Camper loafers she recognized as his tucked neatly into a corner. She smiled. She knew there were women who would kill to have a man so neat, but it could be a little spooky at times. It was in Rain's nature to move, and to live, without leaving sign.

She walked into the enormous bathroom with its soft white tile and mirrors and sensible light, and found a few toiletries in a drawer. And then, next to one of the sinks, a note. Okay. She picked it up.

On the grounds, the note read. *Back by 7:00.*

She looked at her watch. It was 6:15 now. She was mildly annoyed that he wasn't waiting for her, and wondered what he was doing. She recognized the note itself was a concession: he didn't like revealing anything that might enable someone to anticipate him, whether it was a restaurant reservation or a simple note describing his whereabouts. The vague reference was a compromise, but because she knew him, she could probably fill in the blanks, as he knew.

She guessed a workout. The gym was right around the corner. If he wasn't there, she would just wait for him here. She peeked out at the private patio—half security habit, half curiosity—and liked what she saw: a hot tub sunken among the flagstones, rising steam illuminated by an underwater light; a pair of chaise longues, surrounded by ferns and hibiscus flowers; a high brick wall surrounding it all. She imagined the hot tub with John later and it gave her a little shiver. She took a quick shower and went out to find him.

The gym was a large former cottage that had been gutted, carpeted, and outfitted with the latest equipment. It had a high ceiling and large windows. Delilah glanced inside, and immediately saw Rain. He was in a corner, barefoot, in shorts and a tee-shirt, doing squats. She watched, fascinated. She knew he worked out and he'd told her a bit about his solo routines, but she'd never seen him. He was going fast now, squat, stand, squat, stand, occasionally brushing a wet strand of hair back from his eyes. She didn't know how many he'd done before she started watching, but she counted two hundred and fifty, and then fifty more where at the end of every rep he leaped into the air.

He paused for a moment, and she sensed he was

going to scan the windows. She stepped to the side and waited for a moment so he wouldn't see her. She wanted to keep watching.

After a few seconds, she looked back inside. Rain was doing handstand push-ups, freestanding, not against the wall. Slowly this time: up, down onto his forehead, hold, then up again. She counted ten, and then he dropped over into a back bridge and did fifty more push-ups, inverted. A dark line of sweat ran down the front of his tee-shirt.

He flipped over and stood, and Delilah moved out of the way again. When she looked back inside, he was hanging from the horizontal bar of one of the machines, his hands spaced widely. She looked more closely . . . was he using just his fingertips? Yes, he was. He did twenty pull-ups, then dropped down and shadowboxed in front of the mirror. No, it wasn't just shadow boxing, she realized; he was incorporating other elements, ripping and grappling movements she recognized, like some kind of customized karate kata. As he circled around, she caught a glimpse of his face. His eyes were closed, and she was surprised, even disconcerted, at the intensity of his expression. This was no dance for him, she knew; the movements were techniques he could use, had used, to kill. She wondered what, or whom, he was picturing right then that would produce such mimed ferocity, and imagined it must be Hilger.

She knew there was a dark skein of intensity deep in Rain's nature, something that only rarely revealed itself at the surface. It was a quality that intrigued her, and, she had to admit, was part of what attracted her to him, but he never let her see it, and her only previous glimpses had been brief and inadvertent. She wondered why he was letting himself cut loose like this now, in a room with so many windows. It must have been the sense of privacy the hotel grounds fostered. Then she realized she had probably posed the wrong question: maybe he wasn't letting himself. Maybe right now he couldn't help it. Regardless, this was the longest she'd ever watched him unbeknownst, and it fascinated and excited her in equal measure.

After five minutes of the drills, Rain started stretching, and Delilah knew he was warming down. She eased away from the window and returned to the room.

A short while later, sitting in front of the fireplace, the lights turned low, she heard the key in the lock. She stood and watched the door open a crack, then swing wider when Rain saw it was her.

"Hey," he said, looking her over. He was pumped from the workout and she liked the way the tee-shirt clung to him.

"Hey," she said, smiling. She had planned on giving him a hard time about not being there when she arrived, but now she was just glad to see him.

He bolted the door, then walked over and kissed her lightly. She reached around for the back of his head, holding him there, prolonging the greeting, letting it turn into something more.

He raised his glistening arms like a doctor prepping for surgery. "I'm all wet," he said.

She let out a little laugh. "Me, too. But I'm starving . . . why don't you shower and we'll get something to eat?"

They decided on the low-key lounge rather than the more formal dining room, and sat adjacent to each other at a corner table amid dark paneling, low light, and a wood fire. He looked good to her after a week away, casual in faded jeans, a checked oxford cloth shirt, and the cashmere blazer, his dark hair still wet from the shower. Delilah ordered filet of beef with Stilton; Rain, roast chicken with polenta, and they shared terrine of foie gras and a lobster corn custard. Rain chose a bottle of '89 Lynch-Bages Bordeaux, and while they ate and drank, she asked him questions, and worked to sift through the responses.

"What does Hilger want?" she asked, quietly. "Why is he doing this?"

For almost a minute, Rain was silent, rolling the stem of his wineglass through his fingers, his eyes on the liquid inside. Just as Delilah thought he wasn't going to answer, he said, "He wants me to do three jobs."

There was no need to ask what the jobs would consist of. And she knew he wouldn't tell her the details. In fact, she wasn't sure she wanted to know.

"What are you going to do?" she asked.

Again he was silent for a long time. Then he said, "If I don't do the jobs, Hilger will kill Dox. If I do the jobs, he'll kill Dox as soon as I'm done."

"Not just that. He might . . ."

"Yes, he'll probably be using one of the jobs as a set-up to take me out, too. I know. That's why I have to find out where Dox is being held, and free him. There's no other way he's coming out of this alive."

She couldn't disagree with his assessment. She said, "You're playing for time, then."

Rain nodded. "Time, and information. Part of the reason I wanted to see Hilger in person was to make him move. Tracking someone who's frozen is hard. Moving, he'll leave a trail."

"Has he?"

"So far, only fragments. I know he's got Dox on a boat, and on one of our calls they were in Jakarta. He's probably moving among various Indonesian islands, and maybe ports in nearby countries. I'm trying to narrow it down."

She knew not to ask him whether he had already done one of the jobs. Her gut told her he had. And still it hadn't been enough. He was going to have to do it again. God.

She took a sip of wine, thinking. "And you're sure Dox is . . ."

He nodded. "I've spoken to him twice. The first time, Hilger did something to him to make him scream. He screamed for a long time."

From the flatness of his tone and the stillness of his expression, he might have been describing something he'd read about in the news, not the overheard torture of a friend. What was it costing him, to recall and relate a memory like that one with such dispassion?

She took his hand and looked at him. "I'm sorry, John."

He shook his head slightly, his eyes still on his wineglass.

"Hey," she said. With her other hand, she reached for his chin, and gently steered his face toward hers. He met her eyes, and the flatness she saw in his actually made her flinch. She'd seen eyes like that before, on Gil, her colleague, the frighteningly efficient killer who had died in Hong Kong. But Gil's eyes were like that all the time; it was all there was to him. It was worse to see the look on John, whom she knew so much better, whom she cared about so intimately.

He blinked, then suddenly was back, his eyes alive again. He swallowed and looked away. "You, uh, you want dessert?" he asked, glancing around for the waiter.

They finished with a Grand Marnier soufflé accompanied by glasses of an '85 Graham's Port, followed by

French-press coffee. That look she'd seen didn't return, but nor could she say he was being himself. It was almost as though someone was doing a good imitation of him, but the persona wasn't quite natural, with some acting, some effort showing through it. But why? What was he hiding?

Back at the suite, Rain poured them each a healthy measure of the Glenmorangie. The fire had burned low, and she sat on the couch, the lights off, watching him kneel in the glow of the embers, moving coals, adding logs, getting it going again. After a little while, there was a good blaze, and she thought he would join her. But he didn't. He stayed where he was, kneeling almost formally, one hand under the whiskey glass, the other on its side, watching the flames, his back to her.

"You going to come sit with me?" she asked.

After a moment, he came wordlessly to the couch and sat down a few inches away.

"What is it?" she asked, after a moment.

"I've just got a lot to think about."

"You want to talk about it?"

He took a swallow of whiskey. "I don't know how to."

She looked at him. "Maybe that's the problem."

He returned the look, his eyes narrowing. "No. The problem is the problem. Not my disinclination to discuss it."

"So you know how to, but don't want to."

For an instant, his face contorted in anger. He swallowed and seemed to get it under control. "What difference does it make?" he said.

"It makes a lot of difference. How is about you. Not wanting to is about me."

He flushed and looked away, and she realized she was pushing too hard, no matter the truth of her words. She could be enormously patient and subtle when she was eliciting information from a target, but she had a habit of reverting to a more primitive, more deep-seated self with Rain. She cared too much about him; that was the problem. Her feelings made her forget herself. They brought forth all her default settings, the bad along with the good.

A little more tactical, girl, she thought. *Not just for you. For him, too.*

"I'm sorry," she said. "It just . . . scares me when you keep everything bottled up. It makes me feel insecure. I'm not used to feeling that way."

He finished his Glenmorangie. Ordinarily, he savored a good single malt. Gulping it down like this, especially after a bottle of wine and a glass of port, wasn't like him. "What do you mean?" he asked.

She shook her head. "Just . . . there are parts of you that you don't let me see. And sometimes I feel like they're the most important parts." She was being tactical now, yes, but she wasn't lying, either.

He refilled his glass and topped off hers. They sat quietly for a while, Delilah sipping her whiskey, Rain drinking his down, the light from the fire playing on the walls.

"I don't know why you want to be with me," he said, staring into the flames.

"Why do you say that?"

He kept looking away from her. "Because of what I am."

"What are you?"

"You know."

"I don't. I only know how I feel about you."

He shook his head as though saying *No, you're missing the point,* then looked at her, his lips pursed, struggling with what he was trying to say. This time, what she saw in his eyes was utterly different from what she'd seen in the bar. She had never seen it before in him and wasn't entirely sure what it was. But if she had to attach a word to it, the word would be . . . pleading.

"I'm . . . a . . . killer!" he whispered emphatically, as though simultaneously ashamed at the admission and bewildered that she couldn't understand the point.

He looked away again. "Look at me," he said, his voice rising. "I can't stop. The most I can do is take breaks from the life, like an addict falling on and off the wagon. But it always finds me again. And you know why? Because it *is* me. It's what I am."

He drained the rest of his whiskey and slammed the empty glass down on the coffee table, then stood and started pacing, his head swiveling, his hands clenching. He was so wound up it looked like his body was fighting itself, the muscles bunched and writhing under the clothes.

She got up and intercepted him. He stopped in front of her and stood there, breathing hard, his hands balled into fists. No wonder he was working out the way he was. If he didn't burn some of this off, it was going to consume him.

"Hey," she said, trying to get him to meet her eyes. "Hey. I know you. As well as I've ever known anyone, maybe better. Don't tell me you're only that one thing."

He laughed harshly. "What else matters?"

She took his face in her hands and steered it so that he was looking into her eyes. "You," she said. "What you decide. That's what matters."

"I'm talking about what I am."

She shook her head. "What you choose is what matters. Not the things you've done, or your abilities, or the training you've had, or even your inclinations. You can atone for all the rest, but your choices are what make you who you are."

"You don't understand. . . ."

"I do. You're not Gil. Don't reduce yourself to that one thing. Find a way to be more than that. You have been, I've watched it happening in Paris."

"I was fooling myself in Paris. And I guess you, too."

"No, you're fooling yourself now, or trying to. You're in a bad situation and you're terribly worried about your friend. Don't let that . . ."

"I can't!" he shouted. "I can't be both. I have to be a certain way, or . . . or . . ."

"To save Dox, yes, you have to be that way, I understand," she said, staying with him. "And you will. But that's situational. It doesn't define what you are. Don't let it."

He squeezed his eyes shut and drew his lips back from his teeth as though the agony he felt were physical. "I don't know how," he whispered.

"By the choices you make."

He shook his head violently. "I don't have a choice."

"I know, and for the moment, you're doing what you have to do. But the moment is going to pass. It's a situation, it isn't you."

He looked up at the ceiling, his breath coming in short, sharp bursts, the muscles in his neck tight cords. He was fighting something, tears, terror, she didn't know what.

"I . . ." he said, and then the word was choked off. He shook his head and took hold of her wrists as though preparing to cast her aside, and she sensed that whatever battle was raging inside him, he was losing it.

"Stay with me, John," she said, trying to get him to look at her again. "Stay with me, please. . . ."

And then he had her face in his hands and he was kissing her, ferociously, desperately, ravening her as though she was the only connection keeping him from being sucked away into some nameless horror. She kissed him back, hard, her mouth open, her hands in his hair, letting him feel her, take whatever he needed from her, making him know with her mouth and her hands and her body that she was there and she wasn't going to let him go.

He backed her into the bedroom, his hands still on her face, his mouth not leaving hers for an instant. The feel of her jeans rubbing against her as she moved was suddenly maddening, electric, and she realized with a start that she was close to coming from nothing more than the way he was kissing her and the friction of a tight pair of jeans. For a moment, she forgot where they were, she wanted him to just keep kissing her like that, keep moving her like that, yes, just that way . . .

The back of her thighs bumped against the side of the bed. She was barely thinking now, she just wanted him naked, his skin against her, his weight on her, all of him inside her. He broke the kiss to lift her sweater over her head and was back before he had even tossed it aside, his tongue, his teeth, the taste of whiskey and his own taste, too. She managed to get his belt open, then his pants. She reached inside, and when she felt how hard he was, it excited her even more. She squeezed and felt his breath catch.

She pushed the jacket off his shoulders and tugged it down over his arms, then got his shirt off and threw it aside, never once letting him stop kissing her. He pushed her back on the bed and stepped out of his pants. She realized her bra was gone, she hadn't even been aware of his doing it. Her groin ached and she was panting. Without thinking, she put her hand on herself, over her jeans, and rubbed. "Hurry," she said.

Then he was naked, leaning over her, unbuttoning her jeans. He hooked his fingers inside the waistband and peeled the jeans and her panties down over her legs and flung them away. She scrambled back on the bed, spreading her legs and raising her knees, and Rain moved on top of her. She took hold to guide him and she was so wet that he didn't stop or even slow but buried himself inside her with one violent stroke. She gasped with the mixed pleasure and pain of it and he moved back and thrust again and this time she cried out because she was coming, her back arching, her body shuddering, her hands moving involuntarily to his ass to pull him deeper, deeper. She felt his arms go under hers and he took her face hard in both hands and spread her legs wider with his thighs, his weight on her now, holding her, pinning her to the bed, kissing her hard again, fucking her like some primitive natural force she'd conjured but could now no longer control. He was moaning in her mouth, she could hear it and feel it both, and his movements grew faster, more brutal, and she felt another orgasm welling up from the depths of her. He groaned and squeezed his eyes shut and hammered at her harder than ever, as though enraged, or enraptured, or punishing an enemy he didn't know how else to kill. Then the groan grew wilder and his body tensed and she felt him coming and she came, too, a shock wave of pleasure reverberating from her groin to her toes, her breasts, her fingertips, her mouth where he was kissing her still.

Slowly, gingerly, she settled back onto the bed, gasping as though she had just surfaced from the deep. Rain dropped his head next to hers and took some weight onto his elbows. She heard him mumble something, she didn't know what, and she smiled through near delirium.

He remained like that for a few moments, the only movement the gradually slowing rise and fall of his breathing. Then he rolled off her onto his back, but close this time, so their bodies were touching, not the way it had been on the couch. They lay there, and she imagined a pair of shipwreck survivors who had just washed up exhausted onto a beach.

He came to his side to face her and put a hand on her belly. A line of sweat was trickling down his forehead, and she wiped it away with a finger.

"You okay?" he asked.

She smiled. "Okay?"

"I didn't mean to be so . . . rough."

She laughed. "I think you did."

He dropped his eyes and a little color crept into his cheeks. "Well . . ."

He looked so appealing to her right then. The tousled hair . . . the sweat . . . the sudden shyness after a bout of demonic lovemaking. "Sometimes you're a little rough, John," she said, tracing the contours of his face with her fingertips. "It's part of you. It's part of what I . . . like about you."

Good God, in the raw, dazed honesty of the moment, she had almost said, "What I love about you." She had been close before to giving voice to those feelings, but had always pulled back out of fear of his reaction.

"Come sit with me in the hot tub," she said.

He looked at her, sidelong. "I don't know if I can move."

She smiled and punched him on the shoulder. "If I can, you can."

They switched off the patio lights and entered the water slowly, wincing from the heat at first, then enduring, and finally surrendering to it. They sat immersed in the near dark, steam rising into the cool air around them.

"It's good here, isn't it?" Delilah said. In the dim light, she could see his eyes, but not make out his expression.

He didn't answer for a while. He was looking past her, and just as she thought she would take a chance and ask him what he was thinking, he said, "How will I know?"

"Know what?"

"How to make the right choice. Because I never have before."

She reached through the water and took his hand. "I think you made a good one a few minutes ago. That's a start."

19

DOX HAD BECOME adept at reading sounds and other signals on the boat. Whose footsteps belonged to whom; whose muffled voices. The vibration of the engine when they were at sea; its silence when they were in port. The slight dip and rise of the craft when someone stepped on or off it. He knew they were in a port right now, somewhere. Hilger and the blond dude were off the boat; only Uncle Fester and the young-looking guy were still aboard.

He heard footsteps on the stairs and knew from the sound it was Fester. He glanced up a moment later and there he was, looking in through the door window. Dox smiled at him to let him know he wasn't afraid, and turned up both his hands to offer a double middle finger salute. He heard the lock turning, and Fester poked his head in.

"How you doing, Uncle Fester?" Dox asked, smiling as though the psycho were his best friend.

"I'm good, *pendejo*. I wanted you to know, I'm going to bring you a surprise."

"Oh, Fester, you don't have to put yourself out for

me. I know you've got important things to do, you know, lawns to mow, fruit to pick, things like that."

Fester reddened and Dox felt a rush of satisfaction. He had nothing against Mexicans or anyone else for that matter. It was just a good way to push Fester's buttons.

Fester recovered and broke out in a hundred-watt psycho smile. "Ordinarily, I'd fuck you up for that. But . . . I think now I'll wait until next time I see you. I'll bring the surprise then. I just want you to have it to think about."

Dox shook his head. "Fester, I'm disappointed in you. It's sad that a first-class sadist such as yourself should have to resort to such crude and obvious strategies as trying to instill dread in the prisoner. You've been reading too many books on interrogation, I think that's the problem."

Fester reddened again, and Dox thought he might be onto something. Before he could follow up, Fester said, "Oh, one more thing. You know, we're setting up your friend. He's doing some jobs for us, and then we're going to kill him. Should be just another day, maybe two. When he's dead, we won't need you anymore. I'm telling you because I want you to wonder every time I knock on your door. 'Is he here to give me my surprise? Or is he going to gut me and let me bleed over the side to attract sharks before throwing me in?'"

"That's more like it, Fester! See how you put some of your own special personality into it? That time, it didn't feel like it came from a book. Keep practicing, and soon you'll be able to terrorize any helpless, manacled prisoner you like. You'll be an inspiration to sadists everywhere."

Fester smiled. "Okay, *pendejo*. See you soon." He

closed the door and Dox listened to his footsteps as he went up the stairs.

He let out a long breath. Just because Fester had read it in a book, and it was crude and obvious, didn't make it ineffective. Knowing Fester's tactics, and provoking the man on top of it, was helping. But when that door closed, and the sound of footsteps receded, it was hard not to be scared.

Especially after that "See you soon." Something had kept Fester from losing his temper just now, something he was looking forward to. Dox hated to think of what it might be.

20

DELILAH LEFT the next afternoon. She had things going on in Paris, I knew, but still it wasn't easy to get her to go. She was worried about me, and about Dox. She wanted to help.

I appreciated the sentiment, but I was determined to keep her out of this. I'd accepted, even solicited, her help before, but that had always been operational. These killings for Hilger . . . no matter the reasons, no matter the coercion, there was a line I didn't want her to cross. She had no idea what would be waiting for her on the other side of it, or how difficult, maybe impossible, it is to find your way back.

I didn't want to face it, but the odds of my coming out of this thing intact weren't exactly encouraging. I'd established some room for maneuver, true, but overall Hilger was still calling the shots. He had no intention of letting me live when I was done with his work, and there were a hundred ways he could use Dox to get to me when he was ready. Even if I managed to survive, most likely Dox wouldn't, and losing him would fuck me up in ways I sensed but didn't want to fully consider. What would Delilah do with me after that? And no matter how things turned out, as long as Hilger was out there, I'd be not just a burden to Delilah, but a danger, too. It wasn't fair to her.

Not two days earlier, I'd decided I should just break things off with her, I'd accepted that it had to be done. Then, stupidly, I'd let her come see me, and it had been so good that I'd temporarily forgotten my resolve. But already, as I drove east into West Hollywood on Sunset Boulevard, the sun flaring behind me as it sank in the sky, my evening with Delilah was beginning to feel meaningless, even foolish. She was an attractive woman, yes, more attractive than any I'd ever known. And she had a lot of good qualities, along with a few maddening ones. But what did any of that have to do with me, really, and the life I had to lead? Drunk on liquor at the time, and intoxicated by her nearness, I'd nearly been beguiled by her talk of choices. But I saw clearly now all that was foolish. Some things go beyond choice. Some deeds have such power and resonance that they become your own nature, and eclipse everything else you do. Delilah didn't understand that. Because part of me cared about her, and always would, I was glad she could indulge such illusions, and took some quiet pride in maintaining them for her. What I couldn't and wouldn't do was share them.

I stopped at an Internet café with no great hope and checked the Kanezaki bulletin board. Still nothing. I stared at the empty text box for a few moments, unsurprised. I would just have to go on to the next target. It felt natural. It felt like fate.

At another café, I checked on Hilger. There was a message waiting, as I had expected. I smiled to myself, ruefully. *You see?* I thought, as though I was talking to Delilah. *You see?*

A name, Michael Accinelli. A timetable: five days
again. *Shit.* I wondered what the short fuses meant. For
now, no way to know. I supposed I should count myself
lucky that Hilger hadn't made the deadline even
sooner, after learning how quickly I'd managed to
do Jannick.

There was a business address in Mineola, New York;
a home address in Sands Point, New York. I didn't recognize the name of either town. Phone numbers. The
make and model of the cars he drove—a 2007 Mercedes
S600 and a 2007 Range Rover HSE—along with license
plate numbers. Several photos of a fit-looking guy in his
late fifties, with a full head of steel-gray hair and dark,
piercing eyes. In one of the shots, Accinelli was wearing
an expensive-looking charcoal chalk-striped suit; a
white, spread-collared shirt; a navy tie; and a white linen
handkerchief. He was sitting, both hands folded on a
knee, leaning forward slightly, smiling confidently. Very
chairman of the board, and in fact the photo looked like
something lifted from a corporate brochure or website.
In the other photos, he was behind a lectern in similar
business attire, probably at an investors' conference or
some industry event.

I Googled him. The first hit was for a company called
Global Pyrochemical Industries, and sure enough, there
was the shot of Accinelli in the charcoal suit, right on
the home page. He was indeed the chairman of the
board, and the CEO, too. I clicked on his bio: born and
raised in Oyster Bay, Long Island, 1950; graduated with
honors from West Point, 1972; served in Grenada,
Panama, and the first Gulf War, winning a Silver Star in
the second of the three conflicts; retired from the Army
a bird colonel after twenty years of service. Founded
GPI in 1993, took it public in 2001.

I wondered about Iraq. That was Hilger's war, too. Could be a coincidence; could be a connection. A long shot, but I tried searching for Hilger/Accinelli. Nothing. Likewise Jannick/Accinelli and Jannick/Hilger. Well, maybe Kanezaki could do better.

GPI described itself as a specialty chemical supplier to companies all over the world. They had four product lines: intermediates for pharmaceuticals; automotive airbags; industrial cellulosic polymers; and pyrotechnic and military. I didn't know much about any of it. The only applications I recognized were car airbags, and the various military uses: rocket propellant, explosives, white phosphorus grenades.

I checked on the business and home addresses. Mineola was on Long Island, about twenty-five miles east of Manhattan. Sands Point was ten miles north of Mineola, on the north shore of Long Island at the tip of the Port Washington peninsula. Mineola sounded solidly middle class; Sands Point, on the other hand, apparently was the model for the town of East Egg in *The Great Gatsby*. Fitzgerald's mansion was still there, I discovered, on Hoffstots Lane, and was currently for sale for $28 million. It seemed Accinelli had done well with GPI. He certainly wasn't living in Sands Point on his military pension.

Manhattan made me think of Midori, living in Greenwich Village with our son, Koichiro. He would be . . . about two and a half now. I'd seen him only once, a year earlier, and after Midori's betrayal I knew there was no way I could have either of them in my life. A permanent gulf was best for all of us, even, much as it saddened me to admit it, for Koichiro. I thought of him, of course, late at night, when sleep wouldn't come, and the way he looked and felt the one time I had held him in my arms.

Sometimes I would open up a small vein of hope about the far-off future, and imagine going to him, explaining who I was, building a relationship, however uncertain, being part of his life. Those tenuous hopes and fragile aspirations seemed ridiculous now, weak and naive in equal measure, and I could have laughed at myself for ever having indulged them.

Sands Point had its own website, which boasted that the community was entirely residential: just eight hundred fifty families; a few houses of worship; a primary and a secondary school; and unsurprisingly, a country club with an eighteen-hole golf course. The country club was called the Village Club, and I had a strong suspicion that Accinelli, an ethnic kid who had grown up on the other side of the tracks in nearby Oyster Bay and then gone on to make something of himself, would be a member. I checked the club's website. There was no directory of members, but there was a collection of photos from a recent New Year's Eve party, Accinelli prominent in several of them. An attractive woman of about his age, whom I assumed was his wife, was on his arm in all the photos. The people around them were well dressed, looked well fed, and must certainly have been blessed by fortune. I made them as low-tax Republicans and limousine liberals. Probably there was more to them than that, but the shorthand would get me started as I determined how to invisibly infiltrate their society.

I thought about posting the information to Kanezaki. The sooner he had the name of the second target, the sooner he could apply the new data to the nexus we were trying to build with Hilger, and, by extension, Dox. There wasn't an obvious connection to the CIA, as there had been with Jannick, but . . . I hated the thought of tipping off a government agency to an impending hit, even if the tip-off was to someone with a good track record, like Kanezaki. It was just too dangerous. I decided to play it by ear again. Worst case, I'd tell him immediately afterward, and find a way to placate him, as I had before.

Because I had accessed the bulletin board and then researched Accinelli from computers in L.A., I had to assume Hilger might now be able to place me here. I imagined how he would try to anticipate me, if that's what he wanted to do: *He's coming from L.A. The most obvious airport would be LAX, but of course there's Orange County, too, and Burbank. On the other end, JFK, La Guardia, and Newark are all pretty much equally possible. I haven't given him much time, so assume he goes straight to the airport after accessing the bulletin board . . .*

No. With a minimum of three airports on either side, the whole thing was too unpredictable. He couldn't narrow it down enough to make it operational, not unless he had a small army of people to rotate through all three possible destination airports for surveillance of multiple incoming arrivals. Even so, as always, I would assume the presence of a welcoming party, and use extra caution leaving whatever airport I flew into.

I purged the nav system for a last time, input LAX as my next destination, and returned the car at the airport. I caught a bus to the terminal, where I discovered that United offered three red-eyes: two to JFK and another to Newark. First class was sold out on the JFK-bound flights, but there was one first-class seat left on the 10:30 to Newark. I bought a ticket, spent two hours reading the latest *Economist* in the departure lounge, and slept for a few hours before arriving in Newark at six-thirty the following morning.

I waited in the arrivals area with my carry-on after getting off the plane, until the passengers from my flight had cleared out. Among the people who remained, all presumably waiting for other flights, no one set off my radar, but there was no way yet to be sure. I started walking toward the baggage area, and no one followed me out. So far, so good.

I took the tram to another terminal and noted again I wasn't followed. If someone was waiting for me, he was outside the terminal, not inside. That, or they had enough manpower for a static approach. Regardless, there were a few more things I could do to make sure.

I went to a pay phone and used the Yellow Pages to find a place called Image Rent-A-Car that specialized in exotics. I was looking to rent a Mercedes for a few days, I told them, the S Class. Did they have one I could pick up today? Unfortunately, the Mercedes rentals were all out, the helpful gentleman on the other end informed me. But they could have a navy 2006 BMW 750Li delivered to me in most places in the tristate area in less than an hour—four days, four hundred free miles, seventeen hundred fifty dollars. I told him the BMW would do, and that I'd be happy to come to him, if he could give me an address.

I went outside, and the East Coast winter cold hit me immediately. I felt my nostrils prickle, and a sudden wind cut right through the cashmere blazer I was wearing. I wanted to hunch my shoulders and jam my hands in my pockets, but didn't, in case I'd missed something and needed to react quickly. I scanned the area as I moved. There were people around, getting in and out of cars, fumbling with luggage, but no danger signals. Damn, it was cold. The airport workers were all in gloves and hats and bulky parkas, and the exhaust coming from cars and taxis was billowing out as white steam. I'd have to pick up some warmer clothing as soon as I could.

I got in a cab and, in a thick Japanese accent, told the driver I was concerned my suspicious wife was following me. Could he take a strange route so I could make sure she wasn't?

"Anything you want, buddy," he said. "I'll just put it on the meter."

I smiled, slipping on the leather gloves I had bought in Mountain View, and thought, *I love New York.*

ONE HOUR, TWO CABS, and a foot route later, confident I was clean, I picked up the BMW. Among the mansions of Sands Point, it would be familiar, comforting, and invisible. I threw my bag in the trunk, turned the seat warmer on high, plugged Accinelli's work coordinates into the nav system, and followed the directions out to Long Island.

It was Sunday morning, so traffic was light, and the trip took about an hour. Global Pyrochemical Industries was on a four-lane road called the East Jericho Turnpike, which sliced east to west through a mixed residential neighborhood about a mile south of the Long Island Expressway. The immediate area consisted of modest single-family houses, compressed into regular clusters alongside one another, set slightly back from their streets on small, rectangular patches of lawn. There were a few apartment buildings; a school and a baseball field; train tracks and a lumberyard. East Jericho itself was zoned for businesses: real estate and other professional buildings; an office-supply store; restaurants; a bowling alley. And, at the east end of it, six H-shaped buildings, arranged in two rows of three, surrounded by a chain-link fence topped with razor wire. Global Pyrochemical Industries.

I drove past, looking for anything that smelled of a setup. With Accinelli as the target, it wouldn't be difficult for Hilger to predict my fundamental moves, such as initial surveillance of the target's workplace and residence. There could be a team here, waiting for me. But for now, nothing set off my radar.

Operationally, I wasn't wild about what I saw. First, the parking lot was accessible only through a gated station, currently manned by a guard. Probably a rent-a-cop, possibly half asleep, true, but it complicated things. And the presence of all that razor wire, and the fence, and the access control, and of course the guard, all hinted at other measures I would prefer not to encounter.

I drove through the area, getting a feel for it. I noted some possibilities, all involving setting up in a nearby parking lot and waiting to tail Accinelli's Mercedes when I saw it leave the premises. The one advantage of the controlled access meant there was only one place I had to key on to know when he was coming and going. Well, it was a start. I decided to take a look at his home.

Sands Point turned out to be possibly the most moneyed town I'd ever seen. Mansion after mansion on plots the size of small countries, some of them set so far back from the road they were nearly invisible through the bare branches of all the winter trees. Because the town was set on the Port Washington peninsula, many of the homes fronted Long Island Sound and had their own marinas, the better to dock, of course, private sailboats and yachts. The cars I saw were all Mercedes, BMWs, and Lexuses, along with one antique Bentley, and I was glad to have a ride that felt at home among them.

I was on high alert as I approached Accinelli's house, on a quiet, tree-lined road called Hilldale Lane. If Hilger had decided to set up a welcoming reception, the area around the residence would be a key choke point. But the street was entirely quiet. I rolled up just past the driveway and took a peek.

Accinelli's was one of the town's more modest dwellings, but his home was still a mansion by any definition: a massive, Romanesque-style building of gray stone set a hundred yards back from the road; a rolling, manicured lawn, frosted over now, with a circular driveway cutting through it; old-growth trees and plots of flower gardens, empty now but for a few hardy perennials hanging grimly on in the frozen dirt. The air of the place was ease, a relaxed confidence in the rightness of the natural order, money and status untouchable by the vicissitudes of the outside world.

Next to the house was a detached two-car garage of the same stone as the main structure. At the driveway's center, at the front of the house, there was a stone portico, and under it, a black Mercedes S Class, the 2007. The way it was parked, I couldn't see the license plate, but most likely it was his. Was someone coming, going, or did they typically just park the car there? No, there was no frost on the windows, so it hadn't been there all night. Someone had just come from somewhere, some errand, maybe, maybe grocery shopping, and they had parked the car in front of the house to carry something inside.

Just then, the front door opened and I saw Accinelli. *Son of a bitch.* I eased off the brake and let the BMW roll forward. But not before I saw what he was carrying: golf clubs.

He hadn't looked out toward the street, and I didn't think he'd noticed me. Even if he had, I doubted he would have made anything of a fancy BMW driving past. I kept driving, thinking, weighing the possibilities. I hadn't expected anything actionable to happen so fast—I had planned only on a drive-by, a get-acquainted-with-the-neighborhood visit—but this looked like too good an opportunity to pass up.

Golf clubs suggested an outing, and the clothes he'd been wearing . . . it hadn't fully registered at first, but he was in black-and-gray polypropylene or something similar, zipped to the neck. "Technical gear," some of the sporting-goods outfitters like to call it, a fancy way of saying cold-weather sporting clothes. Yeah. He was on his way to the links.

Shit, I didn't remember the address of his club. If I did, I could have gotten ahead of him, which is almost always preferable to tracking from behind. The Village Club, it was called, but where was it? As I drove back down Hilldale, then right on Middle Neck, the same way I had come in, I looked for local points of interest on the nav system. *Country clubs, country clubs, come on . . .* I couldn't find it. Okay, the hell with it, plan B.

I pulled over onto the shoulder and stopped. If Accinelli came this way, I'd let him go right past me, then fall in behind. A few minutes of a big BMW behind him, especially if he were heading to Sands Point's golf club, as I expected, wouldn't alarm him. And if he went the other way on Middle Neck, I would just swing around and follow him in the other direction.

Sudden paranoia jolted me: what if the Hilger team I'd been so watchful for turned out to be Accinelli?

Maybe they know each other from the war. Maybe Accinelli owes a favor. Hilger tells him roughly when to expect me; Accinelli watches the road from the house, with the car warmed up; he sees me, then walks out pretending not to, with a golf club bag that's actually holding a 12-gauge shotgun loaded with sabot slugs.

I scanned the area. A black SUV was coming toward me down Middle Neck, and I started to get that deep-down *Oh, fuck* feeling. I held down the brake with my left foot and put my right over the gas, ready to floor it if the SUV slowed, or sped up, or swerved. But it didn't, and as it came closer I could see the occupants were just an elderly couple. Shit, they were probably on their way to church.

I let the SUV pass and checked the rearview. There was the Mercedes, pulling out of Hilldale and making a left on Middle Neck, away from me. For a moment, I'd been so keyed up that I was surprised he wasn't coming at me. Then I realized I was being ridiculous. What was Accinelli going to do, blow someone away from his own car a hundred yards out from his $10 million home, right in front of the horrified neighbors? No. Hilger might have been trying to set me up, but it wouldn't be that way.

I did a U-turn on Middle Neck and followed from about a hundred fifty yards back. It was a long, straight road that gradually curved from east to south, and tailing him from far back was easy. I continued to scan for surprises as I drove.

After about two miles, Accinelli made a left onto Thayer Lane. Thayer, right, now I remembered, that was the address of the club. I followed along behind him. About eight hundred yards up, Thayer curved around to the right and I lost sight of him for a moment. Then I came around the curve, too, and saw Accinelli's car again, stopped next to an island with a guard post at the center of it. Beyond the post was a parking lot; beyond the parking lot, a compound of enormous tile-roofed brick buildings that I remembered from the website comprised the former estate of Isaac Guggenheim. This was it, then, the entrance to the club. Accinelli moved forward past the post. I swung around on Thayer and headed back out.

I recognized there was an opening here, if I could move fast enough to exploit it. I input the coordinates for Midtown Manhattan into the nav system. Twenty-five miles. Allowing time for parking and the purchase I planned to make, with just a little luck and light traffic I could be back here in not much more than an hour and a half.

I took the Long Island Expressway west as fast as I could without risking a ticket. What was Accinelli planning today—nine holes, or eighteen? And how long would he be playing regardless? Surely no less than two hours, even for a shorter game. And it would be lunchtime after that. Maybe he'd grab a bite at the club. Maybe this was a Sunday ritual for him, leaving his wife a golf widow, spending two, three, maybe four hours on the links, and with his cronies thereafter. It made sense. Anyone who played in these temperatures had to be a fanatic.

Maybe. But of course I couldn't really know. There was no time to hone in on his patterns, and all my suppositions were just that. But with only five days to work with, I had to exploit whatever openings presented themselves, no matter how narrow.

It took me less than forty minutes to reach the Spy Shop on 34th between Third and Lexington. I remembered it, along with a few other handy places, from the

last time I'd reconnoitered New York. Predictably, there
were no parking spaces anywhere nearby. I considered
parking illegally—I was going to be in the store for only
a few minutes—but decided it wasn't worth the admit-
tedly small risk of having the BMW's presence here
logged in a New York City law enforcement database. I
found a garage around the corner, gave the attendant a
twenty to keep the car on the main floor for fifteen minutes, and jogged over to the Spy Shop. It was a bit
warmer now than when I'd arrived that morning, but I
was still going to have to make time to buy some proper
clothes when I had a chance.

The store was well outfitted with various options for
vehicle tracking, overt and surreptitious. I chose a top-
of-the-line model I was familiar with, the Pro Trak Digital, a magnetically emplaceable real-time GPS system,
and was suddenly down another twenty-six hundred
dollars. Along with warm clothes, I was going to have to
find a bank.

I picked up the car and headed back to the Village
Club. Traffic was manageable again and I made good
time. While I drove, I unpacked the unit, placed the
eight D cells I had also bought into the battery pack, assembled everything, and tested it for power. It all
seemed to be working. I put the unit in the glove box
and stuffed the empty packaging under the passenger
seat. I was wearing the gloves, not just because of the
weather, but to keep my prints off the device, too.

As I turned onto Thayer Lane again, exactly ninety-
seven minutes after I'd left it, I started thinking in
Japanese, like my good friend Yamada, who this time
was being transferred to New York and would live on
Long Island. Like many Japanese, I was an ardent
golfer, and relished the chance to become a member of

a top club for less than the million dollars entry cost in Japan. I was hoping to take a look at the Village Club because it sounded so good on the Internet. . . . Would that be all right?

I pulled up to the guard post and rolled down the window. The guy inside, about seventy with ruddy cheeks and fading blue eyes, leaned toward me, away from a portable space heater. Something about him felt like retired law enforcement, but I took in the impression only in the most fleeting mental shorthand. I was too deeply in character to consciously consider anything operational, although of course I was still aware of and responsive to it.

He looked me over, and again in some compartmented part of my consciousness I realized he wasn't used to seeing Asians pull in here. "May I help you, sir?" he asked.

"Yes, please," I said, in the thickest Japanese accent I could muster, with an accompanying helpless, timid expression. "I move soon Long Island. Want club member become. Can pick up . . . brochure here?"

The guard smiled. Amazing the generosity of spirit a little helplessness can bring out in some people. "Certainly, sir," he said. "The main facility is directly in front of you. Just park anywhere you can find a spot and they'll help you inside."

"Thank you very much," I said, nodding. The gate went up and I drove forward, my heart starting to beat hard.

The parking lot was on my right. I pulled in, driving slowly through. Damn, it was full. The place was popular.

Black Mercedeses weren't exactly in short supply in the parking lot, and I had a couple of false starts before seeing each time that the license plate of the car I was looking at was wrong. But the third time proved to be the charm. There was Accinelli's car, in one of the lot's center spaces, next to a deep green Aston Martin Vanquish S. Perfect.

I kept going until I found an open spot, at the farthest edge of the lot. I parked and took the unit out of the glove box. The battery pack and accessories went into my front pockets. The GPS and cellular modem housing I tucked into the back of my pants, under the jacket. I took two quick breaths and got out of the car.

I walked slowly, my breath fogging in the cold, swiveling my head as though taking in the view of the lovely golf course and grounds surrounding the lot. In fact, I was checking for people. The cold was on my side at the moment—it wasn't the sort of day anyone sane would linger in a parking lot. And if there were people waiting in one of the cars for some reason, they'd certainly have the engine running, with a billow of exhaust rising up from the tailpipe.

No, the lot was empty. It was lunchtime; that was also on my side. I reached Accinelli's car, scanned it and the surrounding vehicles to ensure I hadn't missed anyone, then took a step in next to the Vanquish, easing the GPS unit from my waistband as I moved. I doubted I was the first person to pause for a closer look at that gorgeous emerald of a race car. It was built to be ogled as much as to be driven.

I leaned closer, my hands on my thighs, then dropped into a squat. I pivoted, and in less than fifteen seconds, had emplaced the main unit and battery pack on the Mercedes' undercarriage, the GPS antenna to the underside of the rear bumper, and the miniature cellular antenna underneath the side skirting. I glanced around from the squat and saw no one, then stood and, for the benefit of anyone who might just possibly have seen me disappear for a moment, shook my head at the Vanquish one last time in envious admiration.

For form's sake, I continued on toward the main building. Continue all the way through with the charade, or pull out now? There were risks and benefits both ways. The more time I spent here and the more people I engaged, the greater the chance I would be remembered. On the other hand, if that former cop of a guard asked anyone inside about a Japanese visitor looking for a brochure, it would look odd if no one remembered me.

I decided there was less risk in just killing five minutes walking along the golf course, then waving my thanks to the guard as I left. I had parked so far down that I was out of his view in any event.

I strolled along the access road, my hands in my pockets, shoes crunching the frozen gravel, breath fogging, ears numb. A group of four well-insulated diehards was leaving the course in my direction, golf bags slung over their backs. I kept my head down, and from the cadences of their conversation as they passed I sensed they had paid me no mind.

I stopped at the edge of the access road and admired the green for three minutes, freezing my ass off. Then I turned around and headed back to the BMW. I waved to the guard as I drove past, but he seemed not even to notice. His attention was directed at cars coming in, not ones that were leaving.

There were a few things I still needed, things I could probably find in the suburbs, but I wanted to do the bulk of my shopping in the more anonymous city. So I drove back, stopping first at a military-surplus store I knew—Galaxy, on Sixth Avenue between 30th and 31st.

I went inside, and emerged fifteen minutes later wearing polypropylene long underwear under a new pair of jeans and a wool turtleneck sweater; wool socks and work boots; a black wool watch cap and a navy peacoat; and a pair of ski gloves. Thank God. I also had on a pair of sports shades, the swept-back style bikers and marathoners use, which would cut the winter glare and, not coincidentally, obscure my appearance. In my pocket was a Victorinox Swiss Army knife with a four-inch blade. Not exactly a fighting knife, but the kind of tool I preferred was hard to find in New York and this was better than nothing. The clothes I'd been wearing I carried in a store bag, along with a few extra pairs of socks and underwear.

Next, I stopped at a Citibank ATM for a cash infusion. Then a low-end men's clothing store for a shirt, jacket, and tie, and another pair of sunglasses, this time with large, round lenses that would hide my eyes and change the contours of my face. Finally, the Apple store on Fifth Avenue, where I used one of the store's computers to check the Kanezaki bulletin board. Nothing. I wondered whether he really was coming up empty, or whether he was holding back from me, the way I was from him. No way to know. And nothing to do about it. But it was still irritating as hell.

Now that I was properly outfitted and had a little time, I realized how hungry I was. I hadn't eaten since the plane. I walked two blocks west to the Carnegie Deli and, over a tureen of chicken soup and a roast beef sandwich that could have faced down Godzilla, I configured the iPhone to work with the GPS transmitter. By the time I was washing down a gigantic slice of apple pie with a second cup of coffee, I had everything up and running, and checked Accinelli's position. I had ex-

pected to find him still at the club, or perhaps back
home. Instead, I was surprised to see that he, or his car,
anyway, was right here in Manhattan. I zoomed in on
the location—downtown, corner of Bowery and Prince. I
watched for three minutes, but the car didn't move.
Okay, a fair bet he wasn't at a light or stuck in traffic.
The car was parked.

I paid the check and went back to the garage where
I'd left the BMW. I headed down Broadway, the iPhone
plugged into the cigarette lighter, faceup on the passenger seat en route. The Mercedes didn't move.

I made a left on Spring, then another left on Bowery.
I drifted north a block, and there, on the east side of
Bowery just north of Prince, a parking lot. I didn't see
Accinelli's car as I drove past, but according to the
transmitter it was there.

I parked in another lot three blocks north of Houston
and walked south back down Bowery, the watch cap
pulled low, the shades in place. Thick traffic rolled by in
both directions, and I heard engines and tires on pavement, the sounds somehow amplified, compressed by
the dull background roar of the wider city. Down the
street, someone laid on a horn, and three horns answered, like some bizarre mating call. A truck was backing up to a loading bay on 1st Street, beeping loudly and
incessantly enough to warn all Manhattan. Two men
stood behind it, gesturing to guide it in.

I slowed when I reached the lot. An attendant
manned a booth at the front. Behind him were eight
rows of cars, parked grill to tail, each about five deep.
And there was Accinelli's Mercedes, second from the
front of one of the rows.

The cars were clustered tightly to use as much of the
small lot as possible. When you came for your vehicle,

they'd have to move others to access it. Meaning they would ask when you were returning, so they could put short-timers up front and latecomers farther back, and thereby minimize the need to shift vehicles every time a customer arrived for his car. Wherever Accinelli was, he wasn't planning on staying long.

I circled the block on foot, considering. There was no way I could act here. Too many people, too much light, too little control over the environment. I supposed it would have been too much to ask for Accinelli to be parked in some deserted spot in the Meadowlands.

Still, it might be useful to see which direction he came from when he returned to his car. I would have a good view of the parking lot from up to a block north on Bowery and from up to a block south, and from as far away as a block west on Prince. I checked my watch and began slowly walking a T pattern along the two streets. I figured I could keep it up for an hour before someone might find the behavior suspicious. This was New York, after all. If I'd been near a high-value terror target, the Time Warner building at Columbus Circle or the New York Stock Exchange, for example, I wouldn't have risked loitering. But on a cold Sunday afternoon just north of Little Italy, I didn't expect any problems.

As it happened, I didn't have to wait long. Twenty minutes after I'd started the T pattern, as I was heading west on Prince, Accinelli made a left from Mott, just a block away and walking briskly toward me on the other side of the street. He was still in the black-and-gray polypropylene golf attire. I kept my face away from him and turned left onto Elizabeth before we reached each other. Then, when he'd passed my position, I turned around and headed north on Elizabeth, back to the

BMW. There was no particular hurry now; I could track him remotely from the iPhone.

I did. I stayed behind him, hoping for a crazy, random opportunity, a toilet break at a highway rest stop, something like that, but he didn't stop or turn off, he just headed straight home. As we proceeded, I fell farther and farther behind, and I realized he was speeding. I didn't want to risk going more than nine miles an hour over the limit, and I estimated Accinelli was doing something like eighty-five, maybe better. Either the speeding was habitual for him, or he was in a hurry.

I tracked him to Sands Point, but didn't follow him all the way to his house. There was no benefit to doing so. I already knew it wasn't a good place to get to him, although if I had to choose between his office and his home, I marginally preferred the latter. With the GPS tracker in place, though, I had a feeling I'd find an opening somewhere else. It was just a question of when.

21

I HEADED BACK toward New York, thinking. The sun was beginning to get low in the sky. Stay in the city? I knew it better than Long Island, but I wanted to be close to Accinelli so I could react quickly if an opportunity presented itself.

I stopped at a gas station and found a hotel called the Andrew in the phone booth Yellow Pages. It was in Great Neck—about five miles equidistant from Accinelli's home and office. That would work. I called the hotel and confirmed they had a room, but didn't make a reservation. The room would probably still be available later, and I'm always more comfortable denying a potential datapoint to the opposition.

I decided to drive back into New York. I could check the bulletin boards anonymously there, and I doubted Accinelli would be going out again today. I monitored the transmitter just in case, but his car stayed put on Hilldale Lane.

Part of my mind wanted to go to Dox, but I wouldn't let it. There was nothing I could do for him that I wasn't doing already, and imagining his circumstances was just going to wear me down. I needed to stay sharp, keep doing what I was doing, and get the job done.

Delilah. My thoughts wanted to drift to her, too. I found myself remembering the Bel-Air, remembering it with regret, and with longing. I shook my head, irritated at my weakness. *Let it go,* I said to myself. *Forget her. Focus.*

I rubbed my eyes. I was just tired, that was all. A good night's sleep and I'd be okay again. First the bulletin boards and then fuck it, I was done for the day.

I entered the city through the Queens Midtown Tunnel. I didn't have any particular destination; pretty much any couple of Internet cafés would do. I went south on Park Avenue, then drifted down Broadway. It was only when I was heading west on Ninth, toward Greenwich Village, that I realized where I was going. To Midori, and Koichiro.

Oh come on, I thought. *What are you doing? Don't you have enough to deal with right now?*

Yeah, but I was so close. I'd been aware of it the moment I stepped into the frigid New Jersey air outside Newark airport. And it wasn't like I was going to ring her bell or anything. I would just . . . park, for a few minutes. Near her apartment on Christopher Street. I wouldn't even get out of the car. I would just sit, and think, and feel what it felt like to be near my son. That wasn't so much, was it? People did stranger things. They went to grave sites, and knelt in front of tombstones, and ornamented the earth above the bones with flowers, and why, if not to establish some frail communion with the shifting shadows of memory? This would be like that. Just a little while. To feel him nearby. To decant and briefly savor the vanished moment when I held that small child in my arms.

I saw an open space just east of Waverly and decided it was an omen. I parked the car and angled the side mirror so I had a view of her apartment, a seventeen-story prewar building a block away. It was cold the last time I had been here, the way it was now. I remembered everything from that last time. I remembered every word.

When he's old enough, I'll tell him you're dead. That's what I was planning to do anyway, after tonight. And you are. You really are.

And was he old enough, now? Had she already told him the father who now sat not a hundred yards away died before he was born, and so for the son had never even existed?

I sighed. It was Koichiro I wanted to think of, not Midori. I thought of a line I'd once read somewhere: *You forget the things you want to remember and remember the things you want to forget.*

What the hell was I doing, anyway. It was going to be dark soon. I was tired, and I wanted to be up at dawn in case Accinelli was an early riser. I should go.

But I lingered a few minutes more, watching the building, watching the windows I knew were hers, wishing I could undo the past and make a different present. Just a few tweaks, a few different decisions, and maybe I would be walking up to the doorman now, announcing myself, a present under my arm, knowing my son and his mother were expecting me and eager for my arrival.

I glanced at the iPhone screen. Accinelli's car hadn't moved. All right, it was time for me to go. Check the bulletin boards, a quick bite, then sleep.

I looked up and saw a couple walking down Christopher toward me on the other side of the street, a small child between them. They were all wearing hats and gloves in the cold, an Asian woman and a Caucasian man, and the child was laughing, swinging by their arms. I blinked and looked harder, then, instinct kicking in, slumped lower in my seat. It was Midori. And the child was Koichiro.

My heart started hammering. I glanced out again, conflicted, wanting to watch, wanting to hide, wanting to get out of the car, afraid to, resentful that I couldn't, ashamed of my hesitation. And who was the white guy, walking with Midori, holding my son's hand?

I sat there, slumped and cowering and impotent, and watched as they passed me on the other side of the street, then as they stood talking in front of Midori's apartment. After a minute, the man leaned in and kissed her. It wasn't a long kiss, but there was an intimacy to it, a familiarity, that enraged me. The man leaned over and said something to Koichiro, smiling. Koichiro laughed, and the man turned and walked away. Midori and Koichiro watched him for a moment, then went into the building.

The rage drained suddenly out of me, replaced by a hard, cold clarity. The man was on foot. I could leave the car here, get out right now and follow him. I was already wearing a hat and sunglasses, so no one would remember my face. And gloves, so there wouldn't be prints. I didn't need any time, or any special control over the environment because nothing had to look natural. I didn't want it to look natural, I wanted it to look like what it would be, like some faceless anonymous someone came up behind him and broke his neck and was walking away unnoticed before the body even hit the pavement.

Midori would know, of course. But what could she do? She had no way of finding me. How could she punish me? Keep me from Koichiro, maybe? Tell him I was dead? Go ahead, tell him that, if you haven't already. I'll show you what dead really is.

I watched him in the side-view, walking down Christopher. Maybe he was taking the subway. Follow him down the stairs, then close around the corner, no one in front of us, *bam,* drop him and keep moving, up another set of stairs to the street again. Back to the car and gone like a ghost five minutes after.

Okay. I got out, locked the door, put the iPhone and keys in my pocket, and headed smoothly after him. I wasn't angry now. It didn't feel personal. It was just a job, like always. And I knew how to do it.

He was fifty yards up the street, moving quickly in the cold. He crossed to the other side of Christopher at Seventh Avenue, heading south. My gut told me he was going to the Sheridan Square subway station. Walking more quickly, I cut over onto Grove to intercept him.

He passed right in front of me when I was ten yards from West 4th Street. I fell in behind him, closing the distance. I logged my surroundings: moderate traffic on Seventh Avenue, none at all on West 4th. A handful of pedestrians going both ways on West 4th, talking, laughing, the usual New York polyglot. Storefronts, empty. Nothing out of place. It was near twilight now, and cold. People had their heads down, they were hurrying home to dinner, or even just to get inside. Nobody was going to notice, much less remember, one man in a watch cap and shades in the midst of the vast metropolis.

Sure enough, he took the stairs at the Sheridan Square subway entrance. I rotated my neck, cracking the joints, taking a last look behind me as I hit the stairs. All clear.

I followed him down, taking the ground noiselessly along the outer edges of my boot soles, my heart pounding now. Five steps behind. Four. Three.

He turned the corner. I glanced behind. Empty. I followed him around. Empty. I took a step closer. The range was perfect. Reach for his face with one hand, the other in his lower back. Pull him onto his heels, circle the neck, arch, crack, drop, done.

I was an eye blink away, a routine electrical command, a single fired synapse. In a thousand parallel universes, I did it and it was already done.

But here, in this life, I hesitated. In my eyes, I saw an empty subway station corridor and a perfect moment to act; in my mind, I saw Koichiro, laughing at whatever the man had said to him. My breath caught in my throat and my hands froze half outstretched in front of me. I stopped, my stomach clenching, my shoulders rolling forward as though at war with my rooted feet.

I watched him move down the corridor and turn another corner. Then he was gone.

I walked back to the car on unsteady legs. I got inside, slumped in the seat, put my face in my hands, and was suddenly convulsed in tears.

Maybe the man was like a father to Koichiro, or would be. Maybe he was as close to a father as my son would ever know. And I was about to take that away. Because I could? Because it would numb some hurt part of me?

I stayed there for a long time, feeling confused and helpless and miserable. Finally I got it under control. I fired up the car and drove away and I didn't look back.

22

I FOUND A COUPLE Internet cafés and checked the bulletin boards. Nothing on either. Then, on foolish impulse, I Googled: "Jan Jannick bicycle Palo Alto." The first hit was a front-page article in the *Palo Alto Daily News*. A bizarre accident, the article reported. Bicycle. Night. Rain. A tragedy. Jannick was survived by a wife and two small children, a boy and girl, all of whom were being cared for by relatives during this difficult time.

I purged the browser and rubbed my eyes. *No choice,* I reminded myself. *It was Jannick or Dox. Jannick or Dox.*

I stopped at a place called Katz's Delicatessen at Houston and Ludlow. The food was good, but I ate with neither hunger nor relish, only to keep my body going. Finally, I drove out to Great Neck and checked in at the Andrew, where I took the hottest bath I could stand, trying to boil the tension out of myself.

I lay in bed afterward, exhausted but unable to sleep. A thousand fragmented images and voices pressed close inside my head, each a hungry demon, gnawing at my mind. Then, in the midst of that mental cacophony, I heard a single voice, Delilah's, telling me about choice, how it was within me to make the right one, that it was my choices that would make me who and what I am. I seized on her voice, followed it, and it began to drown out the others.

And then, for the second time that evening, my eyes filled with tears, this time at the tenuous, terrifying hope that maybe Delilah had been right. That, improbably, even accidentally, I had proved her right. And that, if I could do it once, I could do it another time. And another after that.

You can, I told myself, again and again, my lips forming the words like a prayer, an incantation. *You can. You can.* And, breathing that silent mantra, clutching it as though it was my last and only hope, finally, fitfully, I slept.

23

I GOT UP AT five the next morning. The first thing I did was check the transmitter. Accinelli's car hadn't moved—it was still at his house in Sands Point. I showered, shaved, and got dressed, then went down to the restaurant for breakfast. I kept the iPhone open in front of me while I ate, in case Accinelli moved earlier than I thought likely.

At six o'clock, I started driving circuits on 25A and the Long Island Expressway between Mineola and Sands Point. At six-thirty, the transmitter started moving. I wasn't surprised. Accinelli was a self-made man, with all the ambition self-made success implied. I hadn't expected him to show up and punch a time clock at nine.

I watched on the iPhone as he came down Searingtown Road, then fell in behind him on the LIE. Traffic was already thick in the other direction, toward New York, and I supposed one of the benefits of living in Sands Point and working in Mineola was that doing so offered him a reverse commute.

As I followed him I hoped, but didn't really expect, that he might pull over at a rest stop, or a favorite diner, or some other place where I might find an opportunistic few minutes alone with him. But he didn't. From the LIE, he went south on the Northern State Parkway, then onto East Jericho. By the numbers, from home to the office. I went past as he waved to the guard in front of the parking lot, then watched him drive inside.

I picked up some sandwiches and fruit at a supermarket and went back to the hotel room. If Accinelli didn't go anywhere until he was done at work, it was apt to be a long day of watching and waiting.

But at just before eleven o'clock, he moved. I went to the car, watching on the iPhone as he headed west on the LIE, toward New York. On the Brooklyn-Queens Expressway, I came close enough to spot his car, and stayed behind him across the Williamsburg Bridge. Downtown again. Interesting.

I followed him onto Delancey, keeping several cars between us. *Where are you going?* I wondered. *Same place as yesterday?*

I expected him to go right on Bowery and park at the lot I'd seen him use the day before. Instead, he continued onto Kenmare, then made a left on Mott, going the opposite direction from where I'd spotted him yesterday. Then right on Broome, right on Crosby, and into a parking lot between Spring and Prince. And all at once it came together for me. I knew why he was here.

I drove past the lot, made a right onto Houston, then another right onto Mott, the same block I'd seen him turn off yesterday. I paused at the corner of Mott and Prince, but didn't see him coming. If I was wrong, I had already lost him, and wouldn't be able to reacquire him until he was moving in the car again. But I knew I wasn't wrong. The signs had all been there; I was just too distracted by thoughts of Midori and Koichiro to put them together.

Accinelli had a mistress.

Why had he still been in his golf clothes when I saw him yesterday? Why was he hurrying, first on foot, then on the highway? And he hadn't been shopping here—he was carrying no packages.

I pictured it: he tells his wife he'll be golfing at the club, and he will be, too, because it's important that he's seen there, that his buddies will unintentionally vouch for him, unwittingly provide an alibi. But he's only staying for nine holes, not eighteen. The difference creates a two-hour window for him. He wants to make the most of it, so he doesn't even change his clothes. In fact, he wants to stay in the clothes, wants to be wearing them when he gets home later. And then he stays too long, and hurries to return before his wife gets suspicious.

And why the different parking lot today? Everything else I'd seen about Accinelli indicated he was comfortable with patterns—foolishly comfortable, in my opinion, because even aside from the fact that Hilger wanted him dead, his wealth and stature made him an inviting target for kidnapping. But today, he'd practically driven right past the lot on Bowery, in favor of another that wasn't a half-mile away. Why the change, and why only now? Could it be because he didn't want to be seen by the same attendant every time he came here?

I'd come across this kind of thing before. When a large part of your job involves following people surreptitiously, discovering patterns you can exploit, you see a lot of behavior that goes unnoticed by the outside world. Drugs. Prostitution. Gambling. Affairs. Closet homosexuality. Addictions and compulsions, cravings and lust. The real world, the id, the dark constants of our nature.

Maybe it wasn't a mistress. Maybe it was a gay lover, or a catamite, or some such thing. My gut told me a mistress, but it didn't really matter. What mattered was that I had a new focal point, one potentially more accessible than his home or his office.

I crossed Prince and parked in front of a hydrant on the other side of Mott. I didn't expect to be more than five minutes, and confirming my suspicions would be worth the small chance of a ticket, and the even smaller chance that the BMW's presence here today would ever be discovered as meaningful.

I got out, the hat and shades already on, and headed north on Mott, my breath fogging in the cold. Cars and trucks lurched along on Prince in front of me, gears grinding, the occasional horn honking. I heard children yelling and laughing somewhere, probably at a nearby school. A construction team was tearing up a sewer line, and for a moment the explosive pounding of a jackhammer drowned out everything else. I glanced left at the corner of Prince and bingo, there he was, wearing a navy suit, coming toward me. The light across Prince was red, and I was happy to be a good, law-abiding citizen and wait for it. It gave Accinelli time to make a left on Mott and get ahead of me.

The light changed. I crossed Prince with a dozen other people and stayed on the west side of Mott, the opposite side from Accinelli, and therefore the more likely to escape his notice if he were to glance behind. To my left was a church, the grounds around it enclosed by an old brick wall. On the right side of the street, various awnings and signs for ground-level stores and cafés; above them, fashionable, red brick apartment

buildings that had once been tenements and ware-
houses, dark fire escapes zigzagging down their façades.
I counted four floors of living space on some of the
buildings; others had five. My eyes tracked everywhere
as I walked. Two men and a woman stood smoking and
shivering in front of a place called Café Gitane, but they
were too young, too hipster-looking, and I didn't make
them as a problem. An attractive brunette in a long
leather coat was rolling up the metal gate in front of a
store, opening for the day's business. She displayed no
awareness of anything around her and again I detected
no problems. A bike messenger in dreadlocks and
shades was taking a package from a woman in an apron
in the doorway of a florist called Polux. Like everyone
else I'd seen so far, they paid no attention to the street
scene around them. They felt like civilians, and nothing more.

As he walked, Accinelli reached into his pocket and
took out a set of keys. Right, keys out now for faster
entry, don't want to linger on the street where you might
be seen. About halfway down the street, he turned and
went up a flight of four granite stairs to an apartment
building entranceway. He unlocked the metal-framed
glass door and went in.

I continued on Mott to Houston, then crossed the
street and came back, checking hot spots. Everything
still seemed fine. No good hides for a sniper, I was glad
to see: this stretch of Mott offered no parking; the
crosstown traffic on Houston and Prince rendered un-
tenable a shot from a vehicle farther away; and with the
church grounds across the street from the apartment,
the only accessible windows and rooftops were directly
overhead, too sharp an angle to be useful.

I stopped in front of the building Accinelli had entered. It was sandwiched between two stores: a high-fashion men's clothing consignment shop called INA Men, and a tiny place called A Détacher that looked equal parts fashion gallery and couture boutique. If I were Accinelli, paying my mistress's rent, I would have selected a spot very much like this, with the church across the street, so no apartment windows from which someone might look down and see me, and the easy access to the Williamsburg Bridge and the LIE beyond it. Also, the nearby boutiques that would provide cover for action if I were seen: "Yeah, what a surprise running into you here, Bob; right, I'm just buying a present for the wife at A Détacher. And you?"

I walked up the steps and looked through the door, putting my hands up and my face close because the light from outside was mirroring the glass. The first thing I noted was the absence of a doorman. Good for Accinelli—he wouldn't want to have to announce or explain himself, or to be noticed or remembered. And maybe good for me, too.

There was a narrow corridor stretching for about twenty-five feet past a group of metal mailboxes and back to an elevator. Fluorescent lighting. No cameras I could see—another plus, from Accinelli's standpoint.

I stepped back. There were no hinges visible, and there was a push handle on the left. The door would open inward from that side. To the door's left was a metal call box. A few FedEx and postal service signs were taped to it. So package and mail delivery occurred before—I glanced at my watch—eleven-thirty, at least today. I counted thirty buttons from among which a visitor would select to call his host and be buzzed in. Each had a last name next to it. I read through the list quickly. None of the names meant anything to me, and I doubted any of them would prove relevant for what came next regardless.

I walked up and down the street twice more, taking in the details: where I—or someone else—might set up to wait and observe; which stores and cafés would offer a view of the street; how people were dressed and what they were doing. The vibe wasn't quiet, exactly, but it wasn't bustling, either. It was still a little early for lunch, and even some of the shops hadn't yet opened. Accinelli probably favored visits at this hour as much for the relative lack of crowds as for the built-in "going out for a business lunch" excuse the time afforded him.

I went back to the car and was relieved to find that no passing law enforcement official had noticed my parking peccadillo. I drove around the block several times, cementing details in my mind, then widened my perambulations to include more of the neighborhood. Then I found a parking space on Bleecker Street, where I waited and monitored the transmitter. At twelve thirty-five, the Mercedes pulled out. I followed from a distance just in case he stopped somewhere and an opportunity presented itself. But I doubted he would. As it was, the whole thing could have been a two-hour "lunch." I doubted he wanted to be away longer than that.

I was right. He went straight back, pulling past the guard post at one o'clock sharp.

I drove around for a while, going nowhere in particular, letting all the details of what I'd just seen—the layout, the openings, the flow, the risks—run through my mind. Accinelli would be back to his secret spot on Mott Street, of that I had no doubt. Probably his schedule, and his ability to fabricate plausible reasons for two-hour absences, would be the only limiting factors. Lunchtime would typically be convenient. And if a secretary harbored suspicions about why certain appointments were always made directly, rather than through her, so what? Did she really want to risk her job through an indiscreet comment that got back to a powerful man like her boss?

I thought of the bike messenger I'd seen, and felt a plan beginning to cohere. I started with the general parameters, then built in details. I asked what-if questions, and played when/then games. I liked what I was coming up with. It wasn't perfect, and there were risks. But there always are. I doubted I was going to have a better opportunity than Mott Street.

I found a bike shop in Great Neck, where I bought the cheapest twelve-speed they sold, along with a pair of long neoprene biking gloves; a fleece balaclava and a helmet to go over it; a nifty side-view mirror called Third Eye that attached to the earpiece of a pair of sunglasses; and a three-foot, case-hardened, steel bike chain called the Kryptonite Fahgettaboudit. Next, an Office Depot, where I bought a large box of styrofoam peanuts. Finally, a hardware store, where I picked up a file, a paintbrush, and two cans of paint—black, and mud brown. I wiped down everything and didn't handle any of it afterward except with the gloves.

At a nearby park, not far from young mothers pushing their toddlers in strollers and on swings, I slathered paint all over the bike frame. I started with the can of black, using little care in my application. I just wanted the bike to look old, or as though someone had tried to make it a less enticing target for theft. Later, in a more private setting, I would file down the serial number until there was a hole in the metal beneath.

I ran the brush back and forth, back and forth, letting

my mind drift. Of course it was impossible not to think of Koichiro. To have just seen him, to know that he was so near. To be within earshot now of all these young mothers with their children, hearing them laugh and chat and gossip about goings-on in the neighborhood. To have read of the fallout, the consequences, of what I'd done to Jannick.

I opened the can of brown and kept at it, the sun providing a hint of warmth to the otherwise chill air. Midori's parents were dead, and she had no brothers or sisters. If something happened to her, who would take care of Koichiro? No one but Midori knew I was his father. Even if someone did, there was no way to find me. What would happen to my son? Who would step forward?

My hand stopped in midstroke and I stood completely still for a moment, frozen by sudden insight. It had been right in front of me, and I'd missed it. I'd been too focused on the CIA funding of Jannick's company, that was the problem. It seemed like a connection. But it wasn't impossible that it was nothing but a distracting coincidence.

Who would step forward? The article said Jannick's wife and children were being cared for by relatives. Who, though? Grandparents? Brothers? Sisters? Uncles? Aunts? Whoever they were, they were like pieces on a chessboard, and Jannick's death had rearranged their positions. Maybe that new positioning was what Hilger was really after.

I finished the bike. As soon as it was dry, I threw it in the trunk and drove to the Great Neck Public Library, where I posted a message to Kanezaki: *What relatives are staying with Jannick's family now? Parents, siblings, whoever. Names, addresses, most of all, their jobs. Cross-*

reference with everything else we have. Hilger might have been after a secondary effect.

THE NEXT FORTY-EIGHT HOURS were uneventful. I continued to tail Accinelli, but he never left the office during the day and always went straight home at night. I figured he was too busy for an assignation, or couldn't come up with a believable excuse. I heard from Kanezaki. He told me he was running down the leads I had sent him, but that was all.

I started to get concerned. Hilger had given me five days, and I had only one left. I thought about contacting him, insisting on talking to Dox again. But I decided not to. Hilger wouldn't have done anything yet: he needed Dox, at least until I was finished with Accinelli. Besides, right now, it would be too easy for him to say no. I wasn't devoid of leverage, but what I had, I needed to use sparingly.

ON THE MORNING of the deadline, I was waiting in the BMW near Sara D. Roosevelt Park, about ten blocks from the Mott Street apartment, watching the readout on the iPhone. I'd been there since following Accinelli to his office as always, and so far he hadn't moved. It was past eleven now, and I was beginning to think I might have to contact Hilger and tell him I needed more time. And then, just like that, the little light that represented Accinelli's car on the phone started moving. *Come on*, I thought. *Come this way. A little afternoon delight.*

I watched as he headed west on the LIE, then the Brooklyn-Queens Expressway. When I saw him approaching the Williamsburg Bridge, I was sure.

I affixed the little side-view mirror to the shades I had

on and stepped out of the car. Almost every inch of me was covered in something: thermal underwear, work boots, the wool turtleneck sweater, the peacoat, the balaclava, the neoprene gloves. I put the chain over my neck, secured the bike helmet over the balaclava, and set the box of styrofoam peanuts on the ground. I took the bike out of the trunk, propped it against the car, and looked around. There were a couple of pickup basketball games going on at the park. Construction on a nearby street. No one was paying me any attention. I waited for a break in the traffic, for the intermittent clusters of passing pedestrians to thin, and then picked up the box by a plastic strap across its top and walked the bike away from the car. The box was large and awkward, but with only styrofoam peanuts inside, it weighed almost nothing. I had stripped off all the labeling; the box was now bare, and there was no way to tell what was inside it.

Two blocks from the car, I got on the bike and rode it one-handed to Mott, just another bike messenger in eclectic cold-weather gear, a heavy chain across my chest, pedaling an old bicycle I'd painted ugly like all the messengers do so no one would want to steal it. I rolled slowly down the street, checking the hot spots, finding nothing out of place. Like the last time I was here, daylight mirrored the exterior of the glass door, making the apartment corridor invisible from the sidewalk. The call box in front of the apartment was once again festooned with notices from deliverymen, and I nodded, satisfied to have one less thing to worry about.

I leaned the bike against the wall of the apartment building, to the left of the door, the side that would open when Accinelli unlocked it. I set the box down and arranged the chain around the bicycle frame but didn't actually lock it. I wouldn't have cared if someone stole the bike right then, and I certainly didn't want to have to waste time unlocking it when this was done. I just needed something to look busy with for the few minutes I waited for Accinelli.

I faced north on Mott, expecting him to arrive from the south side as he had before. The little side-view mirror gave me an excellent view of the street to my rear. From Accinelli's standpoint, it would seem that my back was to him, that I was paying him no attention at all.

A minute later, I saw him turn the corner from Prince, heading toward me on my side of the street, gradually growing larger in the side view. A hot rush of adrenaline spread out from my gut and my heart started kicking. I glanced ahead and saw no problems.

I watched him come closer in the mirror. A charcoal suit today, and a yellow tie. His keys came out, like last time. Ten yards. Five. Three.

Just as he hit the bottom of the stairs, I straightened and picked up the box, struggling with it, exaggerating its heft and awkwardness. I turned toward him. He was at the top of the stairs now. I started up behind him. He put the key in the door and turned it. I was one step below him now. He pushed the door open.

"Can you hold that for me for a sec?" I asked, stepping across the threshold and thereby not giving him much of a choice.

I saw a second's uncertainty ripple across his expression. Letting a stranger into a New York apartment building is a no-no. But with the outfit, the helmet, the box, I looked legit. And it would have been impolite to not even hold the door, to leave me standing outside in the cold with that heavy, awkward parcel. I knew that somewhere, deep in his instincts, he was wondering why the bike messenger didn't just buzz the apartment of whoever the big box was for. But because more than anything else he wanted to end this transaction quickly, to get inside and be on his way with the least fuss possible, he would tell himself that surely I would have, could have, buzzed the apartment, but just happened to see him there, opening the door, and hoped he would be kind enough to help me. . . .

"Sure," he said, stepping to the right and holding the door as I passed him.

"Appreciate it," I said, looking ahead over the box. A straight, plaster-walled corridor, empty. The only danger of interruption, someone coming down the elevator or in from the street. But at a little before noon, the middle of the workday, and with only thirty units in the building, the risk was small, and in any event unavoidable.

I set the box down next to the wall on my left with a grunt, leaving only a narrow space for Accinelli to get by me on the other side. I stood there as though catching my breath, ready for him to squeeze past.

Sudden, sickening doubt hammered me in the gut. A series of thoughts shot through my mind in preconscious shorthand, laser sharp and klaxon loud, the entire message delivered and received in a millisecond:

The whole thing's a setup. There's no mistress. Accinelli's on the payroll. They staged it so you would follow him here, where he could take you out.

I spun counterclockwise to face him, my hands up, so sure I would be facing a gun or knife that as I came about and saw something in his fist, I didn't stop, I just slapped it aside with my left hand. At the instant I made contact and the object broke loose to my left, I saw what it had been: his keys, and no more than that. *Oh, shit.*

The keys flew through the air. Accinelli's head tracked them as they bounced off the corridor wall and hit the floor, his mouth wide open in surprise.

Oh, shit, I thought again. My paranoia had finally taken me over the edge. The setup had been so perfect— he'd been a half-second away from stepping past me, unconcernedly giving me his back. Now his expression was hardening, his arms coming up, his body blading to the left, the old soldier's instincts kicking in, readying him to fight.

I wasn't worried about whether I could handle him; I knew I could. But if I'd lost the element of surprise, if he fought me, there was no way it was going to look natural.

Decades of experience and underlying instinct took over. I stepped back and in a high voice said, "Oh my God, I'm so sorry! I thought . . . I thought you had a knife. Oh, my God, another flashback, I can't believe this. I was mugged once, and . . . I'm so sorry."

He looked at me, confused and incredulous. No doubt part of his mind was still screaming that I was a threat, but if I were, why had I stepped back instead of pressing the attack? And my manner now was passive, even submissive in the abjectness of my tone and my apologies. Before he had a chance to put it all together, I said, "Here, let me just pick those up for you. I'm so sorry."

"No!" he said, his hands still up, palms forward. "No, it's fine. I'll get them myself." He turned and took a step toward where the keys had landed.

"No, really," I said, moving with him, the words tumbling out in urgent cadences. "I feel so bad. I can't believe this happened to me again. It's so embarrassing. The hospital told me with the medications it wouldn't, and it's been three months since the last one so why would I expect a problem? But I guess I should have . . ."

"It's fine, it's fine," he said, now thoroughly convinced I was insane, and no doubt wanting more than ever just to be away from me.

I didn't stop my agitated rant for a second. It's difficult to talk and attack at the same time. The average person needs to get his mind right, focus, concentrate first, even if only for a moment. Accinelli would recognize this, on some level, and would therefore find my mad logorrhea comforting by comparison with what he'd feared a moment before.

He picked up his keys and shouldered past me. He kept his head turned toward me for an extra-long beat as he moved by, but I showed him my hands, palms forward, my arms held back, to demonstrate my harmlessness, and kept up my blathering.

Finally, his head turned. At the instant I was in his blind side, I shot in and looped my right arm around his neck, yanking him toward me, getting him back on his heels, off his base. The inside of my elbow centered on his windpipe, just hard enough for positioning, not hard enough to crush anything. I caught my left biceps in my right palm, brought my left hand around to the back of his head, and squeezed. I had learned the technique at the Kodokan as *hadaka jime,* naked choke, better known in the West as a sleeper hold.

Accinelli grunted and backed into me, trying to get his weight under him, to find his balance. His left hand scratched at my right forearm but found only the slippery neoprene gauntlet of the bicycle glove. He dropped his keys and reached back with his right, by instinct or long-ago training going for my eyes, but I buried my face in his shoulder and his scrabbling fingers were stymied by the bicycle helmet.

It was over in less than five seconds. Some people last a bit longer, some a bit shorter, but no one can go very long once the carotids have been closed off and oxygen is no longer reaching the brain. His groping hands abruptly fell away and he slumped in my arms. I leaned back against the wall, supporting some of his weight with my body, and held him there.

I was very conscious of how much pressure I was using. In the heat of the moment, it would be easy to apply too much, which at a minimum would cause bruises. The purpose of the choke was just to deny his brain oxygen. Anything more than that was unnecessary and would leave signs. I had a lot of experience with *hadaka jime* from my judo days, and always had a knack for it. I could feel just how firmly to squeeze.

I remained like that, controlling my breathing, counting off the seconds. Someone might have come down the elevator or in through the door, but the possibility didn't trouble me. If it happened, I would just drop Accinelli, walk away, and deal with Hilger and everything else afterward. In any event, there was nothing I could do to influence, let alone control, the eventuality. I knew how I would react if it happened and that was enough.

I imagined what would come next: his mistress tries him on his cell phone, then checks downstairs when there's no answer. Or some other resident finds him here. No sign of foul play—no gunshot, stab wounds, or blunt trauma—and therefore no justification to expend resources on an autopsy. There would be questions, of course, but he was a prominent man, and his family would be only too eager to close the matter quickly and obscure the details of where he died and what he might

have been doing there. The cause would remain unknown, and would probably be treated as an embolism
or some other such story that doctors proffer to families
to help them find closure when death can't otherwise
be explained.

After four minutes, I knew he was past any attempt
at resuscitation. I eased him down on the floor and
looked outside. Two women in wool coats and fur ear-
muffs walked by, laughing about something, maybe on
their way to an early lunch. I watched them pass. No
one else was coming. Okay.

I picked up the box and stepped outside. I left the
keys where they had fallen. Logical enough that Accinelli had been holding them when he was struck down
by his mysterious embolic event, and that they would
wind up on the floor beside him.

I headed down the stairs, glancing south on Mott as I
moved. All clear. I glanced north. Then, only by virtue of
years of experience, I turned my head away and continued down the stairs as though I had noticed nothing of
any relevance.

What I had noticed, in fact, was the blond guy from
Saigon. Hilger's backup. And he was walking straight
toward me.

24

DOX WAS STANDING next to his cot, doing isometric exercises against his chains. He knew from the sounds on the boat that they were in a port somewhere; that, unusually, three of them were off the boat; that the one who'd stayed behind was Uncle Fester. Despite knowing it was a victory for the psycho, he couldn't help feeling dread. Fester was going to give him the "surprise" now, he could feel it. That, or something worse.

Things were quiet for a while, and then he heard Fester's footsteps, coming down the stairs, heading his way. He sat up on the cot and pulled futilely against the chains, not for the first time. Goddamnit, if there had been just a little more slack. He'd thought a hundred times about improvising a weapon, something sharp, but there wasn't a single thing in the cabin, not a doorstop or a window crank, the workings in the toilet tank, nothing. With a weapon, he might, just might, have had a chance. But as it was, he couldn't stand straight, he could barely fucking move, he couldn't even defend himself against Fester's knees and elbows when the psycho paid him a visit, how the hell was he going to take the man out like he needed to?

Fester looked in through the window, then opened the door. He was carrying a large canvas bag and smiling, and Dox thought, *Nothing good can come of this.*

"I was just thinking about you, Uncle Fester," Dox said.

Fester smiled. "Yeah? I'm glad I didn't find you touching yourself, then. It would have been embarrassing."

"Well, funny you should say that, 'cause that's exactly the thing I was thinking about. I was wondering if you'd ever had any kind of psychosexual workup. I think you might be intrigued by the insights. Did you know that eighty-five percent of people with an inclination to torture were bed wetters and fire setters?"

Fester's eyes narrowed and his ears flattened against his scalp, and Dox was pleasantly surprised. He was making this shit up as he went along, but who could say what kind of fucked-up childhood might produce an adult specimen like Uncle Fester? Anyway, it seemed like he'd just hit a nerve.

"No," Fester said. "I didn't know that."

"Oh, yeah. It's all in the *New England Journal of Medicine* and the *Harvard Psychiatric Review.* You ought to read the articles, you could learn something about your nature."

"Yeah, *cabrón*? I wonder why you enjoy reading those articles."

"Oh, psychos like you are a hobby of mine. For example, did you know that almost eighty percent of soldiers who volunteered for work as interrogators in World War Two were denied the necessary security clearances because the tests proved they were latent homosexuals?

Not that there's anything wrong with that, of course. Gay será, será."

Fester smiled and one of his eyes twitched. "Remember how we talked about these?" he said, reaching into the bag and taking out a car battery and alligator clips. "When we waterboarded you and you screamed like a girl. It made me think . . . why not?"

"Oh, Fester, you shouldn't have. Sharing your toys with me like this, it's touching."

"Keep talking, motherfucker. It's a nice warm-up for screaming."

Dox smiled, continuing to play the game, but inside he felt a rush of adrenaline at the possibility that had just suggested itself. So this was the "surprise." Fester wasn't going to settle for a few well-balanced pops today. He wanted to use electricity, instead, which would involve getting close and staying close while he fucked around with a bunch of wires.

No one else was on the boat. There was never going to be a better chance.

"See, that's what I'm talking about," Dox said. "Don't you ever wonder why you enjoy this shit so much? Or were you afraid if people found out about it back in old Mexico they'd have turned you out good and made you somebody's bitch? And the worst part is—admit now, it's just the two of us—you secretly wish somebody would."

Fester smiled his psychopath smile again. "Turn around, *cabrón*."

"Sorry, amigo, but giving my back to someone with your documented proclivities would likely spoil my whole weekend."

"Turn around, *cabrón*. Or I'll turn you around."

Dox felt a dip in the boat that told him someone had

just stepped onto it. Then footsteps on the stairs. *Shit.* He'd been so close to provoking Fester into a heedless charge. Well, maybe he could cause a little more animosity, enough to guarantee another encounter like this one.

"Come on, Fester, tell me the truth. You like those photos, don't you? Where the men are wearing black leather masks and holding cat-o'-nine-tails? Maybe some Nazi SS uniforms, you know what I'm talking about, the good stuff. I'll bet you've got yourself a collection, I'll bet you know all the best Internet sites."

Fester's face went white and Dox thought, *Damn, I've nailed you dead to rights, you damn pervert.*

The door opened and the young-looking guy walked in. He looked at Fester, then at the battery he was holding. "What are you doing?" he asked.

"Nothing," Fester said. "Why are you back so soon?"

"What's with the battery?" the young guy asked, his expression indicating he had a good idea of the answer and didn't like it at all.

"Uncle Fester finds gratification in getting in some extra licks when he thinks no one's looking," Dox said. "This is just the first time he's been caught in the act. You are all aware he's homosexual, right? Ask him about his photo collection."

"Shut the fuck up," Fester snarled, and took a step toward Dox.

The young guy had a gun in his hands, and was pointing it at Fester, so fast it seemed like a magic trick. Dox blinked, wondering for a second whether he was seeing this right.

"I can't allow that," the young guy said, his voice perfectly calm.

"Mind your own fucking business," Fester said, and

the look in his eyes was so hate-filled and dangerous that Dox decided the young guy had shown first-rate judgment in not waiting to draw his weapon.

"I am," the young guy said, still in the same no-nonsense tone. "And you'll thank me for it later, when you've had a chance to cool off. For now, I want you to back up and go through that door. If you do anything other than comply with my clear instructions, I will shoot you dead."

For one second, the room was perfectly silent. Then Dox said, "This is a difficult way to come out of the closet, Fester, but there are organizations that can help you with the transition. Hotlines, things like that. You just have to . . ."

The young guy took a step back. Keeping the gun on Fester, he turned his head to Dox. "You, shut the fuck up," he said, and something in his tone made Dox decide he ought to comply.

Fester backed out as directed, and the young guy followed a moment later. Dox heard the door lock, then their footsteps going up the stairs.

He sat there for a long time after, thinking. He wasn't sure whether he'd just created an opportunity for himself, or a death sentence. The one thing he did know was the next time Fester managed to be alone on the boat with him, he was going to find out.

25

A BEGINNER WOULD HAVE looked more closely, checking his perceptions, telling himself until it was too late it couldn't be so. Someone with a bit more seasoning would have glanced away, but only after a startled reaction, and some visible effort, which would have warned the enemy he'd been spotted. A real survivor understands the essentials instantly. And what couldn't be understood now, I would consider later.

I took the steps to the sidewalk and set down the box so I was standing between it and the bike. I put my back to Mr. Blond and started "unlocking" the bike chain, watching him in the side-view mirror attached to my shades. He was twenty yards away, not hurrying, but not taking his time, either. He was wearing a black wool hat, not so much against the cold, I was sure, as to make him harder to describe if there were witnesses. It might have been enough to throw me off, too, but his gait had that same liquid ease I remembered from Saigon, and that was all I'd needed to make him here.

How he'd found me didn't matter for the moment. What he was here for, I could assume. My main advantage was clear: not only had I given no sign I spotted him, he didn't even realize I knew who he was.

Now that my back was to him and he didn't know I was watching, I looked more closely in the side-view mirror attached to the helmet. He had on a black, waist-length leather coat and, I now noted, gloves. It was how I would have done it. The hat to obscure features; the gloves to prevent prints; the coat as light armor in case something goes awry and the target rallies with a weapon. He was wearing shoes with thick soles, almost certainly rubber, and his footfalls were noiseless.

However he planned to do it, it would be close. If it were a gun, it would be small caliber for reduced noise profile, and he'd want the muzzle right against my head. Even if it were a suppressed larger caliber, he'd want to be as close as possible to be sure of the shot. A knife, of course, would be quietest of all. Regardless, by giving him my back, I would increase his confidence, change the implicit risk/reward calculus I knew was running through his mind, reduce the apparent dangers of proximity and thereby encourage him to enter the range I wanted.

I watched in the side-view. Ten yards now. A fresh dump of adrenaline surged through my gut and my limbs.

Eight yards. I unwound the bike chain from the frame. It was over three feet long and close to ten pounds, and attached at both ends by a heavy steel lock. I took hold of the end opposite the lock, pretending to wrap the chain around the stalk under the seat, letting him see my hands at work, keeping his confidence high.

Five yards. His right hand dipped into his coat pocket and eased out, his arm staying close to his body, his hand just in front of his thigh. His thumb flicked a lever and a blade appeared. A decent bet, I thought, that he'd decided to exploit the apparent opportunity to take me from behind by cutting my throat. The advantages would be certainty of lethality, and blood spurting away from him rather than onto his clothes.

Three yards. My heart was thudding like a war drum in my chest. I fought the screaming urge to turn and face him before he got any closer.

Two yards. He started to ease to the right to get around the box I'd set down. *Now.*

I spun clockwise, the chain in my right hand, the lock on the end of it coming around like the racket on the world's nastiest tennis backhand. Mr. Blond's reaction was instantaneous and showed a lot of training: he brought his left hand up to the right side of his face, turtled his shoulders, dropped through his hips, and, most important, stepped forward, inside the arc of the chain, where a blow would deliver less force. But I'd anticipated all of it, and action beats reaction every time. Between the length of my arm, the length of the chain, and the flex of my hips and legs, I had a lot of room to adjust. I drew in by an equivalent distance, and the lock snaked around and blasted into his upraised left hand and right temple like the end of a medieval flail.

His head snapped to the left and he staggered in the same direction. The chain came about, and as it passed my centerline, I swiveled my hips and swung it in again, forehand this time, coming in from my right. Mr. Blond's weight was on his left foot and he couldn't move out of the way. But somehow, even with his circuits scrambled as they must have been, he managed to drop his weight and get his left hand up again, high this time, palm out, his forearm protecting his face. The lock blasted his arm back into his head and rocked him to the right. But with a wounded quickness that amazed me, he managed to snake his arm around the chain and get a hold of it before it bounced past him.

I tried to yank the chain away. Mistake: he pulled in the other direction and used the counterforce to find his balance. His left foot was forward now, a few inches from my right, our bodies mirror images attached by the short length of chain. He took a half-step in with his right foot, and a left sidekick blurred into my ribs. The impact knocked the wind out of me and plowed me backward into the bike. Only my grip on the chain kept me from going over.

He still had the knife in his right hand, close to his body. I felt what he was about to do: shuffle step in, engage me with his left hand, stab with his right. And my side was wide open.

I reached back with my left hand. He shot forward off his left leg, the right foot trailing, closing the distance, the knife coming into range. My groping fingers closed around the bike frame. His weight was carrying him forward now, the momentum channeled through his legs and into his knife hand. Supercharged with fear and adrenaline, I swung the bike around like a discus thrower, getting it between us just as he closed and went for my guts with the knife. His hand punched through the wheel spokes and I twisted away a half-inch from the blade.

He froze there for a split second, his left hand still gripping the chain, his right caught in the bike wheel, trying to process these novel circumstances. I didn't know what kind of training he had, but it was a safe bet getting a bicycle wrapped around you wasn't part of the curriculum. Plunge forward? Jerk back? Let go of the chain? So many options, so few neurons . . .

I didn't give him time to come up with something effective. I sacrificed my hold on the chain and grabbed the bike wheel with both hands, twisting and rotating it to my left. His elbow was pushed into his body, and his hand cranked past his shoulder. He howled in pain, his fingers came open, and he lost the knife. I twisted harder, and he bent sideways at the waist to keep his elbow from being broken. His right knee was torqued at almost ninety and twisted in, and he had too much weight on it to get it out of the way. I rotated counterclockwise, raised my right foot, and stomped down through the back of his knee, breaking it. He howled again and as he collapsed over his ruined leg, I twisted the wheel harder, and his elbow snapped, too.

I let go of the wheel and he went down on his back, the bike on top of him. He made a hell of an effort to scramble out from under it, but he was short two functioning limbs and his progress was minimal. I stepped wide of him, my eyes scanning the ground. There, the knife. I scooped it up, a distant part of my brain registering from the distinctive logo on the blade that it was an Emerson, the recurve edge making it the Commander model, one of Dox's favorites.

Mr. Blond managed to sit up. He took hold of the bike frame with his left hand and jerked his ruined arm out of the spokes, screaming with the effort. He stared at me, panting, his nostrils flaring with exertion, his face glistening with sweat. He pushed the bike forward as though to shield himself, but he had only one good arm and his mobility was destroyed.

"One chance," I said. "Tell me where Dox is and I'll let you live."

"Jakarta," he said, through clenched teeth.

No. They wouldn't keep the boat in the same place after a call. He was lying.

Then again, so was I.

I feinted left and he overreacted, and I stepped easily behind him. He dropped the bike and tried to spin, but I stepped in close and shoved a knee in his back, rotating with him as he frantically continued to try to turn and face me. I covered his eyes with my left hand and cut his throat with my right.

The cut was deep but fast, and I had my hand out of the way just ahead of the geyser that followed. A horrible gurgling sound poured forth, an interrupted, bubbling scream. He fell to his side and turtled his chin in and clasped his neck with his good hand, blood pouring through his fingers. I stepped back, but that hot, acrid smell filled the air and invaded my senses, enrapturing me for an instant in the insane killing joy I had first felt in Vietnam, that almost orgasmic rush that only comes from killing a man who has just been trying his hardest to do the same to you.

I stood there for a moment, the iceman propitiated, exulting, watching as Mr. Blond struggled to get up, his legs kicking, a pool of blood spreading on the sidewalk all around him. Then the kicking slowed and his hands fell away. A long, burbling sigh issued forth, his head dropped to the pavement, and the tension drained out of his limbs. One foot continued to scrape slowly back and forth, back and forth, whether reflex or the body's last, futile efforts to fight I couldn't say and didn't care.

I glanced around. A dozen bystanders stood rooted, mouths agape, shocked, not comprehending, struggling to come to grips with the evidence of their own senses. They were all twenty- and thirtysomethings with fashionable bags and trimmed goatees who'd come here for an upscale lunch of Moroccan couscous or to acquire a fabulous pair of Italian platform shoes. A safe bet none of them had ever even witnessed a dead body, let alone one newly created with a knife before their very eyes. I saw no immediate problems, neither accomplices nor anyone who looked the least bit likely to try to intervene. I would have expected more than one, but ... Dox had said four people on the boat. Maybe Hilger couldn't spare more than Mr. Blond.

I badly wanted to check for ID, but there were too many people, and not enough time. Besides, it was almost certain he was traveling sterile. I closed the knife and pocketed it, threw the chain over my head, and picked up the box. I righted the bike and almost got on, but looked down at the front wheel in time. It was too badly bent to rotate cleanly through the metal struts on either side of it. *Shit.*

I laid the bike down flat and stomped on the wheel, truing it sufficiently to turn. I could have just jettisoned it, and the box, too, but I preferred to leave nothing behind. And besides, I could create more distance faster on the bike.

In my peripheral vision, I saw people taking out cell phones now, snapping pictures, shooting video, and I was glad for the balaclava, helmet, and sunglasses. Keeping my head down, I got on the bike and pedaled away north on Mott, against traffic so no one in a car could try to follow me. The front wheel wobbled but it held.

I made a right on Houston, rode as fast as I could four blocks to Forsyth, then made another right, again against traffic. There was a dumpster at the northeast end of Sara D. Roosevelt Park and I stopped next to it. I used Mr. Blond's knife to open the box and upended it into the dumpster, spilling out the styrofoam peanuts. Then I sliced open the box's other end, folded it flat, and threw it into the dumpster, too. Witnesses would describe the box the bike messenger had been carrying, and doubtless it had been captured on some cell phone cameras, too. It couldn't be traced back to me, but there was no advantage to making it easy to find, either. Layers of defense. Always layers.

I cut east on Stanton. Two blocks further on, I paused just long enough to dump the knife and the bike chain in a sewer. I pedaled south on Allen until I found another dumpster, this one for the bike helmet and sideview mirror. When I reached Canal, I got off the bike and leaned it against a building, confident someone would appropriate it inside fifteen minutes. Even if no one did, and the police picked it up, it was sterile. The serial number was gone, I'd paid cash when I bought it, and I'd wiped it down completely for prints before setting off that morning. More layers.

On foot now, I headed west on Canal, then north on Eldridge, then west again on Hester and into the park. As I walked, I pulled off the balaclava and the shades and stripped off the peacoat. Underneath, I was wearing my new shirt, sport jacket, and tie. Shorn of the bulky coat, my build now appeared considerably slimmer. I carried myself differently, too, imagining myself as a professional, a man who wore a tie and jacket every day and worked in an office. Anyone looking for a bike messenger now would go right by me. I took the gloves off last, and left everything on the ground near a trash can. There were homeless men in the park, and I expected the remnants of my bike messenger persona would disappear no less quickly than the bike itself.

I pulled out the second pair of sunglasses, the round

ones, from inside the jacket and slipped them on, then checked the iPhone to see where Accinelli had parked. The Bowery lot, the same place I'd seen him the first time. A little closer to Mott Street than I would have liked, but no one was going to make me now. Regardless, I couldn't leave the transmitter under his car. Probably no one would find it, and even if someone did, no one could trace it back to me, but . . . the way I saw it, there was still a slim chance Accinelli's death could be ruled accidental. Maybe a heart attack from the fright of witnessing a bloody murder not ten steps from where he stood, something like that. Not likely, but . . . things were happening too fast for me to consider it all right now. I didn't want to leave behind evidence suggesting Accinelli had been targeted. I'd stick with the original plan and figure out the rest later.

I heard sirens from west on Prince Street, and glanced over as I came to the Bowery lot. There was a police barricade in place, a uniformed cop directing traffic from in front of it. The lot attendant was standing outside his booth, watching.

"Excuse me," I said, walking over. "I think I dropped my MP3 player the last time I parked here. Can I take a quick look?"

"Sure, man," he said, barely glancing away from the spectacle west on Prince. I thanked him and went to Accinelli's car. I squatted down, quickly retrieved and pocketed the equipment, and slipped away without another word.

I drove back to Great Neck. Once I was out of the city and the immediate exigency had passed, I got the shakes—the usual aftereffect of an overdose of adrenaline, this time compounded by my awareness of how close I had just come to dying. I pulled over at a rest stop to wait for it to pass.

I sat in the car for almost an hour. When the shaking was no more than a slight vibration in my fingertips, I started thinking. I needed to consider three things: How Hilger had gotten to me. Why. And what it meant for Dox.

How was the easiest. He must have known about Accinelli's mistress. If he knew about her, he would be aware of the unfavorable home and work terrain, as well. Not so difficult to anticipate that I'd learn of the mistress, too, and that I'd make my move at her apartment. Mr. Blond had probably been setting up there for days, maybe in a van a block or two north, watching the area in front of her apartment through binoculars. When he saw me go in after Accinelli, he knew what I was there for. At which point, he gets out of the van to intercept me and take me out. It was a good plan. If I hadn't seen him in Saigon, and remembered that smooth gait, it might have been me right now, lying on the cold sidewalk in a pool of my own blood.

Why was harder. By killing me in the immediate vicinity of Accinelli's cooling body, Hilger would have significantly reduced the chances that Accinelli's death would be viewed as natural causes. Two deaths so close together is a hell of a coincidence. That meant that the naturalness of Accinelli's demise wasn't a priority for Hilger. Which raised the question of why he wanted me for the job in the first place.

There was another thing. The third job was bullshit. There was no third job: it was just an illusion, a way to get me to drop my guard.

Finally, Dox. I wanted to worry, knowing Hilger might already have killed him, but the iceman wouldn't permit it. *Just work the problem,* a voice in my mind said. *Be cool. Be analytical. The rest won't help you, or Dox, either.*

I put myself in Hilger's shoes. He was smart. How would he plot this out?

There are only two targets. As soon as the second one is done, Mr. Blond takes out Rain. Kill Dox first? Risky. What if Rain demands to talk to him again before the Accinelli hit? And what if something goes wrong with the hit on Rain? Without Dox, I'll have lost all my leverage. Better to wait. When Mr. Blond confirms Rain is done, I put Dox to sleep right after.

That felt right. It's how I would have done it. Which meant Dox was still okay.

Probably.

I rubbed my eyes. Now that the adrenaline surge was depleted, the inevitable parasympathetic backlash was kicking in. My mind felt dull, and I badly wanted to sleep.

How to handle this. That was the only other thing I needed to figure out now. If I did things right, Dox still had a chance. If I fucked it up, he was done.

One way or the other, I needed to contact Hilger. I had to keep him moving, keep trying to generate new datapoints until there were enough for a breakthrough.

How. How.

I could pretend everything went fine. Accinelli is dead, apparently of an embolism. Let me talk to Dox. Give me the particulars on the third target.

But no, that would unsettle him. He'd learn soon enough about Mr. Blond. He might already suspect the worst, because his man sure as hell hadn't reported in since I'd last seen him. He'd know I was gaming him somehow if I didn't acknowledge what had happened.

Play it straight, then. Accuse him, threaten him, fly off the handle. That's what he'd be expecting, what he'd be ready for. If I gave him the predictable stimulus, he'd give me the predictable response.

Which would be . . . what? I wasn't sure. Some form of denying everything, stalling for time, finding a way to get at me again. He didn't know I'd seen Mr. Blond in Saigon—if he did, he would have sent someone else to ambush me in New York—so he would probably believe he could bluff his way through.

I'd insist on talking to Dox again, of course. And if Hilger wouldn't let me? Well, that would mean only one thing. And I would spend the rest of my life finding a way to make him pay for it.

I drove to the Great Neck Public Library and posted an update to Kanezaki. Then I called him from a pay phone. It wasn't yet five in the morning there. Well, he was going to start his day early.

The phone rang only once, then I heard his voice: "Yeah."

"What, do you sleep with that thing on your pillow?"

"Sometimes."

"You need to check the bulletin board right away. All the particulars for the second person on the list are there now. But he's already been taken care of. Things are moving fast."

"Already been . . . you did it again. You waited to tell me."

"I don't have time to argue with you now. Remember the blond guy in the photos I sent you?"

"Of course. I haven't been able to find out anything."

"You'll be able to now. He had a bad accident in New York City not two hours ago."

"Oh, God."

"Yeah, our friend sent him to anticipate me. I got lucky."

"Our friend . . . that means . . ."

"Right. There's no number three on the list. Or rather, I was number three."

"What about . . ."

"I don't know yet. But I'm hoping he's still okay. He's our friend's leverage, remember? I'm going to set up another call to find out. But we'll get to that in a minute. Are you up now? Are you listening?"

"Of course," he said, sounding as though my question might have offended his dignity.

"Good. The blond guy was probably traveling sterile. But I have a strong feeling he was driving something, probably a van, that's still parked on the street. If the cops were to find it, they might be able to associate it with a name. If we get a name, we can find out who applied for that visa to a certain Asian country recently. You following me?"

"Of course," he said again.

I realized I was being too didactic. He wasn't green anymore, and he'd never been stupid.

"You haven't had time to think about this yet," I said. "I have. That's the only reason I'm asking."

"Don't worry about it," he said, and I imagined a reluctant smile on the other end of the phone.

"Anyway. If we have a name and visa application for Mr. Blond, we'll be awfully close to our friend."

"Understood."

I paused, thinking there were other things. Christ, I needed to sleep.

"What about those secondary effects we talked about?" I asked. "You know, the family."

"Almost done. I should have something later this morning."

"All right, great. One other thing that occurs to me. I have a feeling our friend knew the second guy on the list. They served in the same theater of operations, you'll see that. I don't know what it means, exactly, but . . . my gut tells me it's significant. Part of the nexus we're trying to establish."

"All right, good. I'll follow up on that. What's next?"

"I'm going to send a message to our friend to set up another call. I'll slow things down as best as I can, but if I don't push to do the call quickly, he'll smell a setup. So my guess is, if you can come up with a breakthrough about his location, we need it within forty-eight hours. No, less than that. Because I'm going to have to travel to wherever he is."

"Why don't you leave now?"

"I don't know where . . ."

"You don't need to know, at least not exactly. We know he's on a boat, still probably within reasonable proximity to the last place he called from. Get going now, you'll be that much closer when we have his position. Wait in a hub city, a place nearby with a lot of flight connections. It'll save time."

"You're right," I said. "I'm tired, I should have seen that."

"Yeah, well, apparently nobody's perfect."

I laughed, glad to see he was counterpunching. "All right, I'll set up that call and then catch a plane. I'm going to need a few items from you, though."

"Let me guess. Something from Santa."

"Right. Same kind of toys he brought down the chimney last year, minus the tranq gun. You remember, or do you want me to post it?"

The "toys" I was talking about included a suppressed pistol with infrared laser and night sights, spare magazine, a hundred rounds of hollow point, a tactical thigh rig for carry, and night-vision goggles. I might have some refinements once I knew the terrain—assuming we learned the terrain in advance—but it paid to get him moving on the fundamentals now.

"I remember," he said.

"Smaller this time, too, more concealable. I'm probably going to be operating in an urban environment. Body armor, too. And a medical kit. I don't know what kind of shape my buddy's going to be in."

"Got it."

I thought for another moment, feeling I was missing something. Then I realized.

"Papers," I said. "I doubt my buddy's been traveling with a passport, and wherever he is, most likely he's going to have to clear customs in a country he hasn't officially entered."

"I can take care of that."

"Good, good. All right, as soon as you have anything on those family members or anything else, post it. And I'll be in touch as soon as I hear from our friend."

"Okay. Good luck."

I checked online. The only nonstop flight I could find from the East Coast to Southeast Asia was on Singapore Air, Newark to Singapore Changi, leaving at eleven o'clock that night, arriving in Singapore eighteen hours, forty minutes later, at 6:40 A.M. local time. Long flight, but it would save time compared to changing planes on the West Coast or in Tokyo or Hong Kong. Besides, the way I felt just then, if I could snag a first-class seat, I could probably sleep the entire way. And Singapore would put me within an hour flight, two at most, of the likely radius of Hilger's boat.

I called the airline on the way back to the hotel. I was

in luck—first class was available that evening. At over twelve grand for a round-trip ticket, I was surprised they sold any at all. I didn't know about their other customers, but for me the extra comfort would be worth the expense. In my line of work, the difference between arriving exhausted from a nineteen-hour flight and arriving well rested could easily turn out to be a life-or-death thing.

I checked out of the hotel and found another Internet café, where I left Hilger a message:

If you were hoping to hear from Mr. Blond, you might have to wait for a while. He wasn't doing well last time I saw him.

You have one chance to live through this. Let Dox go. Now.

I hoped it was the right message. I thought it would engage him the way I wanted, but I couldn't be sure. It was possible he'd double down: kill Dox, come at me with everything he had, try to finish the game that way.

But I didn't worry about it. Not really. I was too tired, for one thing. For another, I wasn't in charge. The iceman was running this show now, and the word worry had never been part of his lexicon. After all, to worry, at a minimum you have to care.

26

HILGER SAT ON THE FLYBRIDGE, flanked by Pancho and Guthrie. They'd made port in Singapore the day before and were docked now in a berth at the Republic of Singapore Yacht Club. It was past one in the morning, though still hot and humid, and the other seventy boats berthed around them were all silent, rising and falling on the harbor swells as though breathing in their sleep.

Demeere had called fifteen minutes earlier, just before noon New York time. He'd spotted Rain at the Mott Street apartment. No surprise there; they'd known Rain was in New York from the bulletin board access, just as they'd known he was in California before that and Paris originally. So far, so good.

Accinelli had shown up five minutes later. Demeere told them Rain had followed Accinelli in, and they all knew that meant the man was as good as dead. Demeere was setting out to intercept Rain, and would take him when he left the apartment. He told them he would check in again right after, and then he clicked off.

That had been fifteen minutes ago, a very long fifteen minutes. Hilger imagined the sequence: Demeere had called just as Rain went in. Rain would be inside for, at most, five minutes. Demeere wouldn't fuck around when he came out, he'd engage him immediately and be done with it. A one-minute walk back to the van, drive off, call from a few blocks away. It was hard to imagine a way for the whole thing to take more than ten minutes.

Another fifteen minutes went by. No one said a word. Hilger thought about calling Demeere, but didn't want to risk it. Demeere would have purged his mobile phone before going out. If something had happened to him and Hilger called him now, the call would remain in the log. Not likely anyone could do anything with the number, but Hilger wasn't going to take the risk. Besides, if Demeere were able to call, he would have already.

Hilger turned to Pancho. "Can you access New York City police band through the satellite?"

Pancho nodded. "It'll take a little doing, but yeah."

"All right. Let's see if we can learn anything that way."

Pancho disappeared. Guthrie and Hilger remained silent.

Ten minutes later, Pancho returned. From the set of his jaw, Hilger knew even before he spoke.

"They've got a killing on Mott Street," Pancho said. "No ID on the body, they're calling it a John Doe. But the victim is a Caucasian male. Blond Caucasian, about thirty-five."

Hilger nodded, betraying no emotion. "How?" he asked, and that would be his only concession to a concern for something nonoperational.

"Throat cut," Pancho said.

Guthrie shook his head. "Goddamn," he said. "Goddamn."

Hilger sighed. He never got upset in these situations, never. He'd lost men before, and knew by instinct and training not to indulge his grief until later, when the immediate situation had been dealt with and new plans set in motion. His men had always looked to him for leadership, and leadership meant focusing on the problem, not on your own feelings.

"What do you think Rain's going to do?" Pancho asked.

"Hard to say," Hilger said. "But he'll check in. We've still got his friend."

"You think he did Accinelli before he got to Demeere?"

Hilger nodded. "I'd say so. Monitor the police band, and we'll know soon enough."

"What kind of vulnerabilities does this create?" Guthrie asked. "I mean, Demeere was operating sterile, right?"

"No doubt about that," Hilger said. "And even if someone could attach a name to him, it wouldn't be a real one. And even if the false name could lead to anything . . . Rain doesn't have the kind of resources to do anything with it. And even if he did, we're moving around too much for him to pinpoint us. We'll only be in Singapore for another day, and then we'll move on. Operationally, we're okay."

"If Accinelli's done," Pancho said, "we don't need Rain. If we don't need Rain, we don't need Dox. Say the word, and I'll take us out toward the Riau Islands, weight him, and throw him over the side."

Guthrie shot Pancho a look that Pancho ignored.

Hilger had a reasonably good idea of what the exchange meant.

"No," he said. "Not yet. I want to hear what Rain has to say first."

"Are you . . . are you going to call Demeere's wife?" Guthrie asked.

Among the four of them, Demeere had been the only one who was married. An American woman, JoAnne Kartchner, who lived with Demeere in Brussels. Hilger had met her once. She had lively eyes and he could see the attraction between her and her husband. Demeere's work kept him away from home a lot, but Hilger had never known him to be unfaithful.

He wouldn't say anything now, but before Demeere left for New York, he had given Hilger the number where he could reach JoAnne. "I'm not planning on going anywhere," he had said, with a small smile. "This is just in case." Now Hilger wondered whether the man had sensed something, some premonition.

He wondered for a moment whom he would want called on his own behalf, if the worst should happen. Or whom he would want to call himself, if he knew his own end was imminent. No doubt his sister, Susan. She was married and living in New York, a third kid on the way. He visited her and her family every time he was on the East Coast. After all, with their parents gone and no other siblings, there wasn't much other family to stay in touch with, and her two sons, Hilger's wonderful nephews, were the whole future of the clan. Yeah. If he knew it was all over, if he had time, it would be a comfort if Susan's was the last voice he heard.

He nodded. "Yeah. I'll call his wife."

Nobody moved. The night's humidity had grown

heavier, a pall of wet heat that pressed down on them from above and all sides.

"Demeere was a good man," Hilger said. "As good and reliable as any I've had the privilege to work with. We're going to miss him. And we're going to honor his memory by finishing what we started, and what he cared about enough to be part of."

Pancho and Guthrie nodded. Hilger looked at them, satisfied they were going to be all right.

My God, but Rain was going to pay. And that fucking Dox, too. Between the two of them, they'd cost Hilger dearly. He was so angry just now that he was tempted to let Pancho do as he'd asked, take the boat out to deeper water and dump Dox over to the sharks. He was angry enough to leave the two of them alone for a while first, knowing how Pancho was likely to use the time.

But the operation had to come first, as always. Demeere had been the point man in Amsterdam, and with him gone, someone else would have to go there for the final steps. He didn't like the idea of sending Pancho; the man was capable, but his forte was muscle, and he lacked Demeere's finesse. For one second, Hilger wished he had sent Pancho to New York instead of Demeere. It was Pancho's aura of dangerousness that had persuaded him not to—Rain would have made him too easily. Demeere, he had thought, would have a better chance at surprise. Well, that hadn't worked out, but there was nothing to be gained from agonizing over it now.

And Guthrie . . . he was definitely good, definitely reliable. But Hilger hadn't known him as long as the others, and wasn't sure he trusted him for something as critical as Amsterdam.

In the end, he might have to go himself. Yeah, that

would probably be the best way. Despite everything, the operation was still on track. Best to see it through personally.

For the moment, that meant holding on to Dox for a little while longer.

But only a little.

27

THE LONG FLIGHT TURNED out to be exactly what I needed. There was nothing I could do about anything until I was on the ground again, and knowing that, and accepting it, enabled me to unwind for the first time since receiving Hilger's message in Paris. I fueled up on the first-class dinner, then slept like a dead man for nearly twelve hours after. I woke up feeling reasonably fresh, with less than five hours remaining to Singapore.

I thought about what I would do after landing. I'd stay in the terminal, at least to begin with. If Kanezaki had gotten a fix on Hilger's position, and depending on when Hilger wanted to do the call, I might have to fly immediately to Jakarta, or Kuala Lumpur, or wherever. I didn't want to waste time clearing customs twice, or be forced to explain such a rapid back-and-forth to an immigration official, either.

Okay, find an Internet connection in the terminal after we land, access the bulletin boards, see what Hilger . . .

My thoughts stopped there, snagged on a problem I hadn't anticipated. If Hilger had a way of knowing where I was accessing the board, and he saw the access in Singapore, or anywhere else in Southeast Asia, he'd know I was coming for him.

Shit. Stupid to have missed something so obvious. There had been a lot going on, and I was tired, but still . . .

Delilah. I didn't see an alternative. I could give her the URL, and she could cut and paste Hilger's message onto the bulletin board she used with me. Or read it over the phone, either way. And then I could dictate the response to her, and she could type it in. Hilger would think I'd gone back to Paris after New York. There were actually some advantages this way. If he thought I was in Paris, it would lull him, get him to lower his guard.

But what if she told her organization? Maybe she wouldn't, but I couldn't count on her not to. On the other hand, if they wanted Hilger dead, as she had told me, I supposed there was at least a decent chance they'd stay out of my way. And if they interfered . . . well, I'd just have to take the risk. I might have turned to Kanezaki, but I didn't trust him enough to have him filtering my messages from Hilger, not on this. He had an agenda, and saving Dox was only tangentially a part of it. For a dozen reasons, personal as well as professional, I didn't want to go to her. But there was no one else but Delilah.

As soon as we landed and I was off the plane, I headed to a pay phone in the terminal to call her. It was midnight in Paris, but she was a night owl, and I knew she'd be awake. The only question was whether she was alone. If she was operational, she wasn't going to answer the phone.

But luck was with me. She picked up right away with a throaty *"Allo."*

"Allo," I said. *"C'est moi."*

There was a pause. She said, "Is everything okay?"

"No breakthroughs, but some movement. I . . . need your help with something. Is that okay?"

"You know it is."

"All right. Our friend uses a bulletin board to contact me. But he may have a way to check the location from which I'm accessing it. I don't want him to know where I am now. So I need you to access it for me."

"That's nothing. I thought you were going to ask for more."

"I might. But this is all I need for now. Just for you to access it, cut and paste the message into the bulletin board you and I use, and then cut and paste my response back into the bulletin board I use with him. If we do it this way and he checks as I expect, he'll think I'm in Paris. That'll give me an advantage."

"I understand."

"You have to go someplace sterile. You don't want him to be able to trace . . ."

"Yes, I know that."

I thought of Kanezaki's peeved "of course" responses for a second, and some of the comments I'd received from Dox over the years, too.

"Do I . . . micromanage?" I asked.

"Yes."

I cleared my throat. "Listen, don't sugarcoat it. I can handle it straight."

She laughed. "I'll leave right now. Give me a half-hour."

I went to an Internet terminal. After the usual check for spyware, I uploaded the Hilger URL to Delilah. Then I checked the Kanezaki bulletin board. I'd found nothing on it so many times in the last week that I was expecting nothing now.

I was wrong. Kanezaki had hit the jackpot.

The dead man in NYC was named Wim Demeere. He applied for a Vietnamese visa under the name William Detts and traveled to Saigon at the same time as you. Here's the photo from the visa application.

There was a postage stamp–size photo attached. It was him: the blond man I'd seen in Saigon, then killed in New York.

A James Hillman applied and traveled at the same time. Here's his photo. Look familiar?

There was a second photo. I recognized it instantly. Hilger.

Here's the best part. You were right, Dox was trying to tell you about a Marine. The guy's name is Frank "Pancho" Garza, and Hilger knows him from Iraq. There's a thirty-foot fishing boat, Ocean Emerald, *registered to Garza in Shanghai, berthing privileges at the Shanghai Boat and Yacht Club.* Ocean Emerald *docked in Jakarta last week, and two days ago made a port call at the Republic of Singapore Yacht Club. As far as I know, it hasn't left Singapore.*

I realized I was gripping the mouse hard and made myself stop. Singapore . . . damn, they were right here. I didn't even have to make the short hop to Jakarta, Kuala Lumpur, wherever. It was the best omen I'd felt since this whole thing started.

Now, secondary effects: Jannick had a brother, Henk Jannick, who cleared customs in San Francisco last week, apparently to take care of his brother's family and help with burial and estate matters. Henk is the head of security at the port at Rotterdam. Henk's number two is another Dutch national, Joop Boezeman.

Two things about Boezeman. First, presumably he's in charge of security while Henk Jannick is away. Second,

*he attended a conference in New York City in Sep-
tember last year: the U.S. Maritime Security Expo. Accinelli was one of the speakers. Demeere was another
attendee.*

*Here's my take: Boezeman works for Hilger. What-
ever Hilger is up to, it involves something in Rotterdam,
something that the head of port security there could prevent. But a hit on the security head himself is too difficult, or too high profile, or both. So Hilger kills Henk's
brother in California, forcing Henk to take leave, and in
Henk's absence, the #2 guy, Boezeman, is in charge.
Boezeman in charge creates an opening for Hilger to do
something. The question is what.*

*Other questions: Why did Hilger have Accinelli killed?
Why were Demeere, Accinelli, and Boezeman at the Maritime Security Expo in New York at the same time?*

*I know you're in the air. Call me as soon as you get
this. This thing is bigger than just Hilger, I can feel it.*

It was what I'd been hoping for. A bunch of disconnected pieces that, with just one additional datapoint, or
one fresh perspective, suddenly cohere into meaningful
intelligence. But Accinelli, and now Boezeman and the
rest . . . I didn't care about any of it. Hilger had Dox
right here in Singapore. That was all that mattered.

I gave Delilah the half-hour she'd asked for, then accessed our bulletin board. She had pasted in Hilger's
message:

*I don't know what you're talking about. Good work
on Accinelli, but you still have one more to do before
Dox walks. I know you'll want to talk to him. Call me
like last time at 08:00 GMT. That's 24 hours from the time
I'm leaving this message.*

I smiled. Stimulus, response. By leading with threats
and accusations, I'd created an opening for him to deny

everything and try to dissuade me. And maybe I'd bought Dox a little time in the process.

I checked the time/date stamp. He'd left the message at 08:00 GMT the previous day. That was four in the afternoon in Singapore, while I'd been in the air. So I had—I looked at my watch—a little over eight hours before the call.

I purged the browser, went to another pay phone, and called Kanezaki.

He picked up right away. "Where are you?"

"Not over the . . ."

"I'm using a scrambler, it's okay. Where are you?"

"Singapore."

"Perfect, perfect. I was hoping you'd catch the non-stop from Newark. I'm here, too."

"What are you . . ."

"You saw the bulletin board, right?"

"Yeah."

"You were already in the air when I got the information. I had to leave right away—assemble the gear you need, charter a plane . . . there wasn't much time."

"Where are you?"

"Grand Hyatt, Scotts Road and Orchard. Can you meet me here?"

Ordinarily, I would have declined. It's inherently uncomfortable for me to allow someone else to choose a meeting place. But it made no sense for Kanezaki to try to set me up now. Maybe another time, but not now. I suppressed my paranoia and said, "Yeah. Give me two hours."

"Room seven-oh-four. I'll be here."

I hung up and called Delilah from another phone.

"You get it?" she asked.

"I got it. Thank you."

"Let me give you another number, a sterile line, scrambled. I need to talk to you, it's important."

"You can just put it on the . . ."

"I'll put the number on the bulletin board. But I need to talk to you."

I hung up, checked the bulletin board, and called her back on the sterile line.

"What is it?" I said.

"Do you know where Dox is?"

"I . . . have a good idea."

"You said he's on a boat. How are you going to get him off?"

Why was she asking me this? "How do you think?" I said.

"I think you're so angry and afraid that you're planning on going in with both guns blazing."

I frowned. "That's not exactly the way I'd put it."

"Without solid intelligence about the layout, and the numbers and placement of opposition on the boat, you might as well be wearing a blindfold. It's suicide, for you and Dox. You can't do this alone."

"Look, I appreciate the offer, but this is going down today. You're too far away."

"I'm not talking about me. I'm talking about Boaz."

"What?"

"He's in Jakarta now. And he has something you need."

"What the hell is he doing in Jakarta?"

"You know what he's doing there. Waiting for your call."

I felt something go cold inside me. "You told him," I said quietly. "About Dox. About Hilger."

"Yes, I told him. My people want Hilger dead. They'll help you."

"Hilger dead is secondary. All I'm trying to do for now is save Dox."

"It amounts to the same thing. And if you get killed storming that boat, you won't save anyone."

I didn't respond. *First Midori,* I was thinking. *Now you. I drop my guard a little, and look what happens. Every damn time.*

"Do you understand?" she said.

"I don't need your help," I said, barely managing to modulate my voice. "I don't need you second-guessing me and deciding what's best behind my back. I've lived a long time, through shit you wouldn't believe if I tried to tell you, and I've managed it with my own instincts and my own judgment."

"Good. Keep living that way. Don't ever change your tactics. It'll all work just fine for you, right up until the day you die from it."

Maybe it's for the best, I thought. *This is your way out, your reason. You always knew you couldn't trust her. Now she's given you the proof. Just say goodbye and you're done.*

"You had no right," I said, getting ready.

"No, John, I do have the right. You see, I'm in love with you. And that means I have the right, and the obligation, and yes, the fucking self-interest not to let you do something stupid that gets you killed!"

"You ... you're ..." I said, stupidly, my game plan suddenly shredded.

"I love you," she said again.

There was a long pause.

"I don't know what to say," I managed to mumble.

"The traditional response is, 'I love you, too.' You can try that, if you want."

I swallowed. "Tell me about Boaz," I said, hoping she would accept it as a kind of answer.

"He has something that can get you onto the boat safely. And Dox off it. He's on a private plane. It's fueled and ready to go, and he can meet you anywhere. You just have to call him and tell him where."

There was another long pause. I said, "Give me the number."

She did. I jotted it down.

"I, uh, I'll . . ." I said.

"Just help Dox. And protect yourself. We can talk about the rest later."

"Wait," I said. "I . . ."

But she had already clicked off.

I called the number. A voice I recognized said in gruffly accented English, "Boaz here."

"Hello, Boaz," I said.

"Shalom, Rain-san," he said, and I imagined his irrepressible smile. "I was hoping you would call."

"This line is secure?" I asked, hoping the answer was yes now that he had used my name.

"Of course. Where are you?"

"That depends. What do you have for me?"

"Delilah didn't tell you?"

"Not specifically."

"Then I'll just say this. It's a hostage rescue technology developed by our Sayeret Matkal commandos. Top secret. And just what you need."

"What's it going to cost me?"

"We want Hilger dead. He killed Gil in Hong Kong, as you know, and we've been looking for him ever since. Delilah says you have actionable intelligence pinpointing his location. If that's true, the Sayeret technology is yours to use. I can bring it to you."

Actionable intelligence? I thought. Maybe now, but not when Delilah had contacted Boaz. Well, she'd told him what she thought was necessary to get him involved.

"You're not worried about CIA retaliation?" I said, stalling for time so I could think about whether to tell him where to find me.

"Hilger's not CIA anymore, as you know. He's a freelancer now. That makes him vulnerable."

Not exactly a comforting statement, from my perspective. Goddamnit, how was I going to handle this....

"I'm in Singapore," I said, feeling I was losing control of the situation. First Kanezaki, then Delilah, now Boaz ... Christ, why not just throw a party?

"I'll be there in three hours. Tell me where."

"Can I reach you on this number?" I asked.

"Of course, it's a mobile, GSM."

"I'll call you. Be somewhere in the Orchard Road shopping center."

After the usual assuming-the-worst precautions at and en route from the airport, adjusted to account for the extensive public camera coverage courtesy of the Singapore government, I made my way to the Grand Hyatt near Orchard Road, Singapore's upscale shopping district. It was about eighty degrees and humid, and I relished the tropical heat after the arctic conditions in New York. The area in front of the Towers was bustling with well-dressed Chinese, Malays, Indians, and foreigners, and I caught snatches of conversation in a half-dozen tongues. Cars and taxis were lined up patiently at traffic lights in the rush-hour congestion, and I almost smiled at the distinct absence of honking horns. It seemed these people had found a way to get along.

I took the elevator to the tenth floor, then the stairs down to seven. I moved along the empty hallway watchfully until I came to Kanezaki's door. I knocked, then took several steps back. Despite what my rational mind was telling me, I hated showing up where I was expected. Especially after what had happened outside Accinelli's apartment.

Kanezaki opened the door and looked out at me, a slightly quizzical expression on his face. "You going to come in?" he said.

I nodded and made my way into the room. The shades were down, and I noticed immediately the sliding doors to the bathroom were open. Likewise the closet. He was being courteous, as well as sensible. When you're dealing with someone looking for a threat, you're asking for trouble if you don't let him see your hands.

Kanezaki locked the door and turned on the DO NOT DISTURB sign. Then he put a nylon duffel bag on one of the twin beds and gestured for me to help myself. Inviting me to reach into the bag, instead of doing it himself, again showed experience and good sense.

I dropped my carry-on and took a look. Inside was a 45 SOCOM HK Mark 23 with Trijicon night sights, a laser aiming module, Knight's Armament suppressor, two spare mags, one hundred rounds of Federal Hydra-Shok, and a Wilcox tactical thigh holster. Also night-vision equipment. Same gear he'd gotten Dox and me for our raid at Wajima a year earlier.

"I told you, something concealable," I said, hefting the HK, racking the slide to check that the chamber was empty. With the attached suppressor, the damned thing would be a foot and a half long.

"I do the best I can," he said. "I thought you liked the SOCOM."

"I like it fine. I just don't want to walk down the street with it in broad daylight."

"This is going to go down during the day? We don't need the night-vision equipment, then."

"No. Although better to have it and not need it."

"Well, the SOCOM is what I can borrow from the armory without anyone asking questions. Look, there's a pair of fishing coveralls, too. The thigh rig will fit inside with room to spare. Slice a hole at the hip and you'll have easy access."

I pulled out the coveralls he was talking about and draped them open. Yeah, I supposed they would serve. He even had disassembled rods and a tackle box inside, obviously for cover at the yacht club. I saw a baseball cap and shades, too, along with gloves, binoculars, and the requested medical kit.

"You've thought of everything," I said, not displeased.

He shrugged. "Two heads are better than one. Look in the tackle box."

I did. In addition to a full complement of fishing gear, there was a Benchmade Mini-Reflex with a three-inch blade. I pressed the catch and the blade sprung into place.

"Nice," I said.

"Don't get caught with it. It's illegal except for active duty military and law enforcement. You could get in trouble."

I laughed and pocketed the knife. "What about the body armor?"

"In the closet."

I glanced over. Two blue vests hung from a pair of hangers. I walked over and hefted one. "Christ, it's light," I said. "You sure this is any good?"

"Dragon Skin. It'll stop a 7.62 round at twenty-four hundred feet per second."

I nodded, liking the sound of that. "You've got two in here," I said.

"I'm going with you."

I looked at him, and saw he was serious.

"No," I said. "It's not necessary. It's not even a good idea."

"I've thought it through. I don't see how you can do it alone. Figure at least two fixed defenders, maybe more, and . . ."

"Do I seem to be getting old?" I asked.

"What? No. I mean, the same as usual."

"At the rate I'm going, I half expect someone to try to take my arm when I go to cross the street."

"Why, who else is trying to help you?"

"Never mind."

"Anyway, it wouldn't matter if you were twenty. That's not the point."

I thought of Boaz. "I've got something that'll change the odds."

"What?"

"Let's just say you're not my only low friend in high places."

He didn't say anything.

"Look," I said, "it's not that I'm not grateful. But you and I have never operated together before, not when it comes to kicking down doors, anyway. We're as likely to get in each other's way as we are to do each other any good. Trust me on this, okay?"

He didn't answer.

"You're an ops guy, Tom, and you've turned into a damned good one. But you're not a shooter. Play to your strengths. You'll live longer."

We were quiet for a moment. He said, "You're still going to need someone to drive. I've got a van."

I thought for a minute. I had been planning to rent a car myself. If I managed to drop everyone cleanly inside the boat and Dox was in good shape, we could walk leisurely out to the parking lot when it was done. If he wasn't in good shape, or if there was pursuit, having a car waiting with the engine running could make all the difference.

"All right," I said. "You drive, and I go in."

"Deal. How about the rest?"

"Hilger wants to do the call at sixteen hundred local time. That gives me the rest of the morning and early afternoon to pick up the other equipment I need, get a feel for the layout of the yacht club with Google Earth, reconnoiter the perimeter, and go in."

"You sure he'll make the call from the boat?"

I paused, seeing a disconnect between us that I'd missed until just now. "Yeah, I'm sure. The purpose of the call is proof of life. He's got to be able to put Dox on, assuming Dox is even still alive, and there's no way they're going to move Dox off the boat. So the boat is where the call happens. But the call isn't when I want to go in. I want Hilger off the boat, not on it."

"I don't get it. How . . ."

"Hilger is secondary. If I hit the boat early, maybe he won't be there. It's one less person shooting back at me, and Hilger is a damn good shot. If I wait until the call, their numbers likely go up, and my odds of getting Dox out go down."

Not that I hadn't been tempted to go for the "two birds with one stone" scenario. Certainly, the iceman wanted to do Hilger badly enough to wait until he was sure to be on the boat. But if Dox got killed because of my lust to kill Hilger, I wouldn't be able to live with it. We could always pick him up later. One thing at a time.

Kanezaki almost said something, didn't, then almost said it again.

"What?" I said.

"If you're not going to do Hilger, help me with something else."

"What are you talking about?"

"I told you in the bulletin board message, this is bigger than just Hilger. The kind of thing I was hoping to prevent by taking him out, I think it's already under way."

I said nothing, and he went on. "Hilger used to be military, and after that, the Agency. You know what the difference is now?"

I shook my head.

"There's no oversight now, and he's running a for-profit outfit. Translation: He can do anything, for anybody. Look what he was mixed up with in Macau—radiological-tipped missiles with that arms merchant, Belghazi. Then in Hong Kong, nuclear matériel to the terrorist, Al-Jib. Do you see a pattern here?"

"I suppose so, but . . ."

"So what do you think it means that he's found a way to put his own agent temporarily in charge of Rotterdam port security?"

"I don't know." I might have added that I didn't care, but there was no advantage in provoking him.

"It means he can bring anything he wants into the port."

"So . . ."

"Rotterdam is the largest container port in Europe, and every one of the world's leading oil and chemical companies is active there. You've got four world-class oil refineries and more than forty chemical and petrochemical companies. We're talking jet fuel, gasoline, everything. It's a major terrorist target."

"Because . . ."

"Because if something shuts down the refineries, the price of refined petrochemical products skyrockets. Driving, flying, heating oil, you name it. Shortages of everything, and the world economy drops to its knees."

"You think that's what Hilger's up to?"

"I think that's what he's being paid to do, although I don't know by whom. But here's the way I see it. Accinelli's company sells chemicals, right?"

"I know."

"Including radioactive materials like cesium 137, which is used in oil drilling, atomic clocks, certain medical applications . . . and dirty bombs."

I was quiet, waiting for him to go on.

"Hilger and Accinelli went way back, all the way to the first Gulf War. I think they were friends, as you suggested. I think Accinelli introduced Demeere and Boezeman at that security conference in New York, and I think Accinelli procured cesium, or something like it, for Hilger, maybe under false pretenses. I think the reason Hilger had Accinelli killed was because he knew too much, he'd be able to connect Rotterdam to Hilger if something happened there."

"That's a lot of speculation."

"There's more. Remember the British Petroleum Prudhoe Bay shutdown? Because the pipes were rusty? That was Hilger."

"Hilger put rust in the pipes?"

"There was no rust. Hilger has information on everyone, he blackmailed the people who make those decisions at BP. All pipes have some rust, just not enough to matter. But who could contradict the company? It was the perfect excuse. I think Hilger wanted to see the global impact of an interruption. And I think he found it unsatisfactory. He wants something bigger—not just a pipeline, a whole refinery complex. Like the one at Rotterdam."

I sighed. "Why can't you deal with him through channels?"

He laughed. "I've got a friend in the Inspector General's Office. I talked to him about Hilger once. He told me the man is untouchable. No one even wants to mention his name. The word is, he's got leverage on a lot of people, and powerful friends, too. No one's willing to go after him at the top, and if you try from down below you'll run into obstructions, or worse. Do you get it now? The system's broken."

We were quiet for a moment. I said, "What are you asking me?"

"Boezeman lives in Amsterdam. Go there. Brace him. Find out what Hilger's been up to and help me stop it."

"Don't you have real secret agents who are paid to do this kind of thing?"

"Yeah, we have lots of them. All I have to do is fill out the necessary paperwork explaining where my intel comes from—that means you, by the way. Except . . . oh, shit . . . no one knows about you. Since the first time you helped me with my treasonous boss in Tokyo, I haven't reported our contacts, which is a felony, by the way. I've shredded files on you—oops, another felony. But I'm sure the bureaucrats who run the CIA and are beholden to Hilger will be happy to overlook all that and do whatever I ask of them in Amsterdam or anywhere else as long as I say please."

He was quiet for a moment, breathing hard.

"Look," I said. "It's not that I don't want to help. But we had a deal. You help me with Dox, I take out Hilger."

"You're breaking the deal. You're letting Hilger walk away. I'm saying okay, just help me in Amsterdam, instead."

I shook my head. "No."

"You killed two people. Both with families. Don't you even want to try to prevent whatever all that was intended to foster?"

I wasn't even aware of crossing the room. It was like I was gone for a second, and when I came back, I had him against the wall, my hand gripping his shirt, my forearm jammed against his throat.

"I did that for my friend," I snarled. "Not to help Hilger, or anyone else. For my friend. Because I didn't have a choice."

"Does that mean you don't care?" he rasped, his mouth a grimace.

I held him there a second longer, then let him go. He coughed and massaged his throat, but he didn't take his accusing eyes off me.

"Tell me something," I said. "The difference between you and Hilger."

He cleared his throat and swallowed. "The ends, Rain. It's all about the ends."

I looked at him. "I bet he'd say the same thing."

"He'd be right."

We stood there for a moment in silence. Finally, I said, "I'll think about it."

"That's all I'm asking."

"You sound like Tatsu. And you're manipulating me the way he did, too, you bastard."

He smiled. "Thank you."

"Yeah, he would have said that, too."

I borrowed his shower, changed into fresh clothes, and got ready to head out. "I've got some things to do," I said. "I'll leave my bag here, if that's okay. Why don't you load the gear into your van and reconnoiter the yacht club. Don't get too close. You don't need to know the interior layout. That's my job. You do need to know the streets, ingress, egress, everything."

He started to say something, but I cut him off. "Sorry," I said. "I know you know that. I'll meet you back here in two hours."

He smiled and held out his hand. I shook it. He started to say something again, and again I cut him off.

"Don't tell me to do the right thing," I said. "I already told you I'd think about it. Don't sell past the close."

He looked at me. "What, are you psychic now?"

I frowned. "What, then?"

"I was just going to say good luck. Is that okay?"

I told him it was. We were going to need it. And so was Dox.

28

I DID A ROUTE from the hotel to make sure I was still clean. Then I stopped at Orchard Towers, a nondescript office complex in the city's shopping district. No one would know from the utter diurnal blandness of the place that every night it was overrun by a raucous throng of calculating prostitutes and eager johns. For now, the wall-to-wall bars in the basement and on the first two floors were shuttered, and the atrium was quiet enough to be in a coma. I took the escalator to an Internet shop I knew on the second floor.

I used one of the terminals to check out the Republic of Singapore Yacht Club, first through the club's own website, then from the air with Google Earth. Amazing, the information that's publicly available these days. Not long ago, you needed a top secret clearance to access Keyhole satellite photographs. Not anymore.

The club had berths for about seventy boats of varying sizes. A long pier extended out from the marina facilities, with five perpendicular quays leading off it. Kanezaki had said *Ocean Emerald* was a thirty-footer. That meant the boat could have been in any of the perpendicular berths. I would try to find a way to narrow it down. Even if I couldn't, five general possibilities wasn't insurmountable.

The club also had three restaurants and a bar; twenty-eight guestrooms; and boat rentals. All of which meant that, however exclusive the place might otherwise be, they welcomed, and were used to, visitors on the premises.

So far, so good. I called Boaz from a pay phone.

"Where are you?" I asked.

"A food court, in a shopping center at the corner of Orchard and Scotts."

"You know where Orchard Towers is?"

"Orchard Road?"

"Yeah, a half-mile west of you, across the street from the Hilton. Meet me out front in five minutes. You in a car or on foot?"

"On foot."

"All right. See you in five."

Five minutes didn't give him a lot of time to scramble an ambush team, if that's what this was about. But I still wasn't going to wait exactly where I'd told him.

I headed out and walked a hundred yards east, then ducked into an alley. I put my back to the east side of a loading dock, where anyone moving west would have to look backward to see me. Four minutes later, I watched Boaz go past. He was wearing shorts, a loud Hawaiian shirt, and sandals, and a large backpack was slung over both shoulders. He might have been a European tourist on his way to a hostel somewhere.

I eased out, checking behind and across the street. I didn't see any problems.

"Boaz," I called out.

He turned, keeping his hands at his sides.

"Ah, I didn't think you'd be where you told me," he said.

"Just come this way. And keep your hands where I can see them."

He complied. We cut down Claymore Road. I glanced behind as we moved. No one was following.

Harry's bug detector was buzzing in my pocket. "You have a mobile phone?" I asked him.

"Of course."

"Reach for it slowly and turn it off."

He shrugged and slipped his hand into one of the front pockets of his shorts. Harry's detector fell silent.

"Are you armed?" I asked.

"Only with something sharp. Nothing that goes bang."

I steered us into another alley. "Face the wall," I said. "I'm going to pat you down."

"I don't see how we can accomplish our objectives with this level of mistrust," he said, his expression grave.

"Boaz, a year ago, your organization was trying to kill me. Turn around."

He shrugged. While I patted him down, he said, "That was situational, you know, and personally I regretted it."

He was wearing an FS HideAway knife in a sheath around his neck, the same kind Delilah had introduced Dox to a year earlier. For the moment, I didn't bother with the backpack. He couldn't access it quickly enough for anything in it to present a threat.

"I'll let you keep the knife," I said, straightening. "Just don't reach for your neck suddenly. What's in the backpack?"

He smiled. "Camera gear. Take a look."

"I will as soon as we're settled. Come on, let's keep moving."

"You're wasting time," he said, shaking his head. "I'm alone. And if I weren't, I wouldn't have a team follow me now. I'd have them waiting wherever Hilger is, as soon as you told me. They would know to expect you there eventually."

I looked at him, disturbed by the truth of his words. Goddamnit, I was in a box. And Delilah had caused it.

"We want Hilger," he said. "Why would we want you? That situation is over. Our interests are aligned now."

All right, the hell with it. I didn't have a choice.

"What do you have for me?" I asked.

He broke out in a big, boyish grin. "Wait'll you see it."

We took a cab to a hawker's market, one of the outdoor food courts that dot the city and serve cheap, delicious Singaporean food. The centers are popular and can be crowded and noisy well past midnight, but we were ahead of the lunchtime crowd and had no trouble getting a table. We sat on plastic chairs under the shade of a big beach umbrella and enjoyed skewers of chicken and beef satay washed down with mango juice. While we ate, Boaz invited me to take a look in the backpack, which he had placed on the concrete floor between us.

I did. As he'd mentioned, the pack seemed to be full of camera equipment: a Nikon camera body, a variety of lenses, portable lighting equipment, a tripod, and battery packs.

"I don't get it," I said. "What am I supposed to be looking at?"

He gave me the boyish grin again. "Have you heard of an 'active denial system'?"

"No. Should I have?"

"ADS is the Pentagon's name for a nonlethal millimeter wave energy weapon. America's troops have used it in Iraq."

"Okay . . ." I said, getting interested.

"It shoots electromagnetic radiation at ninety-five gigahertz. Boils moisture in the skin, but only to a depth of one sixty-fourth of an inch. So it hurts like hell, but doesn't cause damage."

I glanced down at the backpack. "Your guys have developed a portable version."

"Correct. The Pentagon's unit, which they had developed by Raytheon, is truck-mounted. Very powerful—the range is over a kilometer—but big. What I've got here has to be employed close up, but you can carry it on your back."

"It goes through walls?" I asked, doubtful.

"That's . . . the tricky part. You can adjust the frequency. Shorter-range frequencies go through walls, yes. But they also cause more damage."

"So if you don't calibrate it right . . ."

"Right, you can cook the hostages along with the terrorists. It looks bad on TV after. Do it right, though, and no one gets worse than a sunburn."

I nodded. "What does it feel like?"

He smiled. "You want to try?"

"Just tell me."

He laughed. "A wise decision. I had it done to me—once. It feels like your skin is on fire, simple as that. The Sayeret Matkal had a little competition. Five thousand shekels to anyone who could group three rounds in a five-inch cluster from ten yards away while being hit with the beam. This is a joke for these men, they're expert shooters. Ordinarily they group in one inch from much farther."

"What happened?"

He laughed again. "They couldn't shoot at all. They were too busy writhing and running away. No one asked to try twice. When word got around about what it felt like, people stopped volunteering."

"I like it," I said.

He nodded. "You should. Without intelligence . . ."

"Yes, I know. Delilah's already been persuasive on that point."

He looked at me. "You're treating her right?"

I returned the look. "That's really none of your business, is it?"

He shrugged. "She's my colleague, and as close as a sister. We watch each other's backs."

I nodded. "It's good of you to ask, then."

"So? You're treating her right?"

I couldn't help laughing. He laughed, too. "I know, I know," he said. "We Israelis are pushy. You know, there's no word for 'Excuse me' in Hebrew?"

"What?"

He shrugged. "An old joke. But with some truth. If I put my nose where it doesn't belong, forgive me."

"We're . . . managing," I told him, thinking of what she had said to me on the phone just a few hours earlier. "It's not easy, though."

He laughed again. "It never is, my friend. It never is."

We were quiet for a moment. I said, "You . . . have a family?"

He nodded. "Three sons and a baby daughter. Thank God we finally had a girl. My wife was ready to give up. And you?"

"It's a long story," I said, after a moment.

We were quiet again, and this time he didn't push.

"Why did Hilger take your friend?" he asked.

"Does it matter?"

He shrugged. "It won't affect what happens to Hilger."

"It did affect it. It guaranteed it."

"Good."

We finished the food. He said, "So? How do you want to do it?"

I shrugged. "Show me how to use the device. I'll take care of the rest."

He nodded. "I owe Delilah a hundred shekels."

"What?"

"She told me you would say that."

I looked at him, nonplussed.

"I can't show you. It takes training and experience. I have to see the terrain. Set the controls wrong one way, and it has no effect. Wrong the other way, and you boil your friend's internal organs. And while you're trying to get it right, probably people on the boat will be shooting at you. Don't be stupid."

I didn't answer.

"Besides," he went on, "I've already got a van, a driver . . ."

"Jesus, you're not alone?"

"No one works alone anymore, Rain. You're the only one I know."

Again I didn't answer. I was trying to account for how quickly and thoroughly I'd lost control of this op. And at the same time thinking, admitting, really, that my odds of success were better because of it.

"You'll like Naftali," he said. "He's, what do you call it, a wheelman?"

"You could call it that, I guess, yeah," I said.

"Very serious. I don't think he knows how to talk."

"That'll be refreshing."

He laughed. "Here's what I propose. Naftali drives. I operate the device. You do the shooting. I assume you're equipped?"

"With a cannon."

"I'm sorry?"

"Nothing. I'm equipped. And I already have a driver."

"You're bullshitting me."

"I'm not. I think we're all going to have to sit down together. If we don't coordinate . . ."

"You're right, it will be a cluster fuck."

He raised his eyebrows and looked at me, and I nodded to show that I appreciated his use of the idiom. "Yes," I said. "A cluster fuck."

He smiled. "And you're sure Hilger will be on the boat, as Delilah says?"

I didn't hesitate, or give any other indication that I was lying. "Yeah," I said. "I'm sure."

"Good. Then let's sit down with our two drivers. We don't have much time."

29

HILGER STEPPED OFF THE BOAT, leaving Guthrie and Pancho with Dox. He needed to check the bulletin board, and preferred to do so from anonymous points like Internet cafés. He was able to tell where Rain was accessing it, and although he had taken steps to ensure that Rain couldn't do the same thing on the other end, a little extra caution never hurt.

He did a surveillance detection route, then caught a cab to the Ritz-Carlton, where he logged in at their business center. No response from Rain, but . . .

He checked, and sure enough, Rain had accessed the board a few hours earlier, from Paris. He must have gone back there after New York. That's where he'd been when they first grabbed Dox. Maybe he was living there these days. Something to consider, if they didn't wrap him up soon somewhere else.

He wondered why Rain hadn't responded. Maybe he hadn't felt the need to. Hilger had told him to call at 08:00 GMT; maybe Rain simply planned to comply.

Or maybe Rain had found unpersuasive Hilger's protestations of innocence about what had happened outside Accinelli's apartment. So what, though? They still had Dox, meaning Rain had no choice but to play along. Playing along meant, at a minimum, calling in to make sure Dox was still okay. At which point, Hilger would deny everything again, assure Rain there was a third target, and just keep stringing the man along for another couple of days. Once Rotterdam was done, he'd give Rain a fictitious target and finish him off when he showed up for the job. But for now, Rotterdam was the main thing. He needed to focus on that.

He went to a pay phone and called Boezeman. They had never met—Demeere had recruited and run Boezeman precisely to keep his knowledge of Hilger's operation as limited as possible—but they also had a backup plan, just in case. Agency SOP, and Hilger still followed it. Because if something happens to the primary case officer, how do you make contact with his assets? And how do you establish your bona fides when you do?

Demeere had implied to Boezeman that he was fronting a heroin operation. Demeere had never said so in so many words, of course; just a wink here and a nudge there, and Boezeman had filled in the details he was most comfortable with. Why else would the blond Belgian want a Rotterdam port security official to escort him onto the facilities, look the other way while he removed something from a shipping container, and escort him out? For a million dollars U.S., it had to be drugs, and a big shipment at that. And it wasn't as though anyone was going to be hurt by it. Holland's drug laws were the most liberal in the world, but they were still fundamentally silly, distinguishing between "soft" drugs, like cannabis and magic mushrooms, on the one hand, and heroin and cocaine, on the other. But people wanted them all, and what right did the government have to interfere with that? Or with a man's right to profit so handsomely from the government's hypocrisy?

The problem, Boezeman had explained to Demeere, was access. Only the head of security had the authority, official and perceived, to move an unauthorized person around the way the Belgian wanted. Didn't the head of security take vacation? Demeere had asked. Boezeman had laughed at that, pointing out that Henk Jannick hadn't taken a vacation in more than two years. Well, we can wait, Demeere had assured him. Maybe something will come up, and you'll find yourself in a position where you can help me.

The phone rang twice on the other end, then three times. It was six in the morning in Amsterdam. Maybe Boezeman turned his mobile off at night, although most Europeans Hilger knew never did.

Then a voice cut in: *"Hoi."*

"Hello, Mister Boezeman?" Hilger said.

"Yes, speaking," the man said, switching to English.

"My name is James Hillman, and I'm a friend of William Detts. He told you I might be calling, right?"

"Uh, yes, he did."

"Well, unfortunately, William can't make it to Amsterdam as he was hoping. But perhaps you could hold open that rental property he discussed for me? The one with the western view and the sunsets?"

The reference to rental property and the rest was a prearranged signal that would establish Hilger's bona fides. He waited for the prearranged response.

"Yes," Boezeman said. "It's a good property, and the sunrises are even better than the sunsets. I can hold it for you."

"Wonderful. I expect to travel to Amsterdam in the

next two days. Perhaps you could show me the property then?"

"I'd be happy to. Just let me know your itinerary."

"I'll call again as soon as I have the details. I assume you take cash?"

"Yes, of course."

"Perfect. I'll make the arrangements, and call you again shortly."

He hung up, relieved that it had gone smoothly. It wouldn't have been the first time an asset forgot his fallback instructions, but Demeere had clearly drilled the man well. Damn, he would be hard to replace. He'd reeled in Boezeman so efficiently after Accinelli had introduced them at that conference in New York, and then managed him perfectly afterward.

It had taken a while to get everything else in place. First, they'd needed the material. Accinelli had come through there. Cesium 137 was a radioactive element and therefore highly regulated, but Accinelli was willing to fudge the paperwork at Global Pyrochemical Industries and provide it to a fellow Gulf War veteran he trusted, who he believed was still with the Agency. Hilger had hinted that the cesium was being used to develop a new kind of ion propulsion engine for the military, a black program, totally off the books, everything acquired from private sources without any official government funding. Accinelli was a patriot, and was pleased to be able to leverage his success in the private sector in the interests of national security.

The only problem was that Accinelli knew of the Hilger–Demeere–Boezeman link. When the operation was completed at Rotterdam, it would be worldwide news. The initial explosion would be trivial—only a hundred pounds of TNT—and, with a little luck, wouldn't even produce casualties. It was the fallout, literal and figurative, that would get all the attention.

Cesium 137 emitted gamma rays. Less toxic than the alpha rays emitted by, say, uranium, but prone to travel farther. Even better, cesium was hugely reactive, and combined eagerly with other elements. Roofing materials, concrete, soil . . . none of it could be cleaned afterward.

Thankfully, the people exposed to the radiation would be at minimal risk. The body could process half a cesium exposure in less than a hundred days. Strontium 90, another ingredient they had considered, would have been absorbed by bone, and the body would need thirty years to excrete half a dose of that. Overall, a one-mile swath—not coincidentally, the heart of Rotterdam's refinery facilities—would see an increase of cancer rates to one in ten thousand. Only a .05 percent jump, and that would only be for anyone stupid enough to stick around afterward, but it would be enough to turn the area into a no-go zone for decades. Very low casualties, but a very high fear factor. No wonder people called radiological bombs "weapons of mass disruption."

The key was to detonate the device at the very center of the refinery facilities. To do that, someone needed to access it on the premises, ensure that it was properly placed, arm it, and leave before it exploded. That meant cooperation from an inside man. It meant Boezeman.

But knowing the connection to Boezeman, Accinelli would have suspected his cesium had been involved. With Accinelli gone, that link was severed. He had been a good man, and was now another unfortunate casualty, another Hilger would have to live with. But the alternatives—the costs of inaction—were infinitely worse. And he wasn't asking anyone to make a sacrifice he wasn't willing to make himself.

It had gone so smoothly at first. They'd taken possession of the cesium, assembled the device, and sealed it in a lead-and-concrete container to prevent detection by the port radiation scanners that were coming into vogue since 9/11. As soon as Dox was taken and they'd made contact with Rain, they sent the device to an accommodation address in Rotterdam by commercial sea shipping, knowing it would have to go through the port. While it was on its voyage, Rain had killed Jannick. The man was so damn efficient that he'd actually gotten ahead of schedule, and they had to make him wait so Demeere could set up in New York to ambush him when he came for Accinelli.

Hilger knew Accinelli well, well enough to know his friend always kept some pretty young thing, usually a struggling artist or aspiring actress, in an apartment or loft. Demeere had traveled to New York a few weeks earlier, tailed Accinelli, and discovered the whereabouts of Accinelli's latest. They had discussed it, and decided that, capable as he was, Rain would discover her existence, too, and that because the woman's apartment represented more favorable terrain than either Accinelli's home or office, Rain would likely hit Accinelli when he went to visit the woman. That's where Demeere had decided to lay the ambush. But something had gone wrong. Somehow, Rain had seen it coming.

Hilger realized now he'd been too ambitious. Demeere could have silenced Accinelli, and they could have taken Rain out another time, another place. But the opportunity to have Accinelli dispatched naturally, like Jannick, raising no questions, and to set Rain up simultaneously, had been so perfect . . . too perfect, he understood in retrospect. After all, the perfect is always the enemy of the good.

So, yes, there had been losses, but there always are in war. And on balance, things could be worse. Boezeman was still game. They still had Dox. And Rain . . . the man was resilient, no doubt. But no one was bullet-proof. He was going down. And Hilger would relish it when it happened.

30

THIS TIME, when Kanezaki opened his door in response to my knock, he didn't have any smart comments about whether I was coming in. He just stood there, looking at Boaz, Naftali, and me. He didn't say a word, but I didn't need to be psychic to know what he was thinking: some variation on the time-honored What the fuck?

I smiled. "May we come in?"

"I guess so," he said, moving aside so we could all file past him.

We all sat across from each other along the edges of the beds. "Tom, Boaz, Naftali," I said, gesturing as appropriate. Boaz had been right about Naftali. The man hadn't said a word since I'd met him. There was something familiar about him, but I couldn't place what.

There was a round of uneasy handshakes, and I went on. "I'm sure we can imagine our various affiliations, and they don't really matter anyway. What matters is, we all showed up here for the same thing and we don't want to trip over each other's dicks trying to get it. With me so far?"

Everyone nodded. Boaz smiled and said, "Trip over our dicks?"

"Yeah," I said. "It means ..."

"No, no, I get it. I like it. It's better than 'cluster fuck.'"

"They're a little different," Kanezaki said, and Boaz nodded to show he was eager to hear more. "A cluster fuck is ..."

"Not that it's not important, but why don't we do the language lesson later?" I said.

No one responded, and I went on. "I want my friend safely off that boat. You all want Hilger dead." I paused again, locking eyes just for an instant with Kanezaki. "We know Hilger's on the boat now, but don't know for how much longer. So we need to move fast."

Kanezaki's face betrayed nothing, and I went on. "We know the general layout of the yacht club. What we don't know is the precise location of Hilger's boat, the nature of the opposition on board, whether any sentries are posted off the boat, and where Dox is being held on the boat. What I propose is this. We've got two vans. We use both, arriving separately. Naftali and Tom, you wait in the vans, engines running. Hilger knows my face, and probably Tom's, too, so we're the wrong guys for recon-naissance. That's Boaz's job. So far, so good?"

Everyone nodded. Kanezaki said, "What do we know about club security? Can Boaz just walk in?"

"Let's find out," Boaz said. He nodded to Naftali, who tossed him a mobile phone. "Sterile unit," Boaz said. He dialed a number from memory.

"Hello," he said, "I'm interested in chartering a fishing boat. Is that possible? No, not for today. You do, good. Two boats? Oh, the twenty-two-footer should be fine. Look, this is for an important client and I'd like to see the facilities. Can I do that? Yes? Right, Chan, I'll ask for you, thank you. I'll be by tomorrow or the next day. Yes, of course, my name is Vanya. If you're not there, though, can I just . . . stroll around by myself, take a look at the boats? Of course, of course, I would never board a boat without the captain's permission. Yes, thank you."

He clicked off and looked at us. "The operation is off. Chan says we can't board a boat without the captain's permission."

No one said anything, and he shrugged. "Just a joke. Security's not an obstacle, at least not initially. But this raises a question. If we have to . . . disable security, how far do we go?"

The answer was so obvious to me that for a second, I didn't follow him. "You mean . . ."

"At all costs, we want to avoid the loss of innocent life. It's our most important rule of engagement."

"Sorry, can you define that phrase, 'all costs'?" I said. "And what do you mean, 'rule'?"

He sighed. "Well, sometimes it's more of a guideline than a rule. The real world can be messy. But we try very hard."

"All right, I agree to try hard," I said. "Fair enough?" He nodded, and I went on. "Tom's got some fishing equipment. You carry it with you and scope the area, checking all the spots where you would place a sentry if you were Hilger. Have you got a wireless earpiece to use with one of those phones?"

He nodded. "Of course."

"Good, so do I, and that's how we'll stay in touch as you stroll around. No telling what you'll find, so you'll just have to inform me and we'll improvise."

He nodded again.

"You keep wandering around, looking the part of afternoon-fishing hobbyist, until you spot *Ocean Emerald*. When you find her, you get your equipment ready. While you're doing that, I move in."

"What equipment?" Kanezaki asked.

"What's your security clearance?" Boaz asked.

Kanezaki scowled at him, and Boaz sighed. "Am I the only one here with a sense of humor?" he said. He turned to Naftali. "Naftali, was that not funny?"

Naftali might have been made of stone.

Boaz sighed again and turned to Kanezaki. "Well, what can you do . . . these secrets always get out sooner or later anyway. Have you heard of an 'active denial system'?"

"Of course. The Raytheon technology. Nonlethal millimeter wave energy weapon."

Boaz laughed and looked at me. "Smart guy." He gave a quick rundown on the particulars of his device.

"Okay," I said when he was done. "When I'm in position, you zap the boat. Either it'll fuck up the people on board, increasing my chances of surprising them, or they'll haul ass off the boat like their hair's on fire. Either way, I drop whoever I encounter and extract Dox."

"Dox will be locked inside while I'm zapping," Boaz said.

I nodded. "I'll apologize to him later."

"Have you considered how they might have secured him?" Kanezaki asked.

I nodded. "If it's just a locked door, I'll shoot the lock out. If it's ropes, I've got a knife. But you're right, if he's in manacles . . ."

Kanezaki smiled. "I've got a pair of four-foot bolt cutters in a nylon case in the van. Boaz can carry it. We need you mobile, and shooting straight."

I nodded and gave him a slight smile. "Two heads really are better than one."

I imagined the terrain for a moment. We were working on the fly. It would be so easy to miss something.

"I come off the boat with Dox," I said. "He's a big guy, and if he needs assistance my hands are going to be full. Boaz, you'll be armed?"

"How do you say it? 'Fuckin' A,' I think?"

"That's how it's said. You cover the retreat to the vans. Tom, we ride with you. Naftali, if anyone tries to follow, you ram. Clear?"

Everyone nodded.

"Whatever you need to bug out, have it with you. Bags, papers, everything. Assume we can't come back to our hotels. Now, what are we missing?"

"Probably a dozen things," Boaz said.

"I know. But there's no time. We're not going to get a better chance than this. Let's go through it one more time, and then we roll."

31

DOX SAT ON HIS COT, his eyes closed, his head cocked. He'd felt someone step off the boat a half-hour earlier. The remaining footsteps told him the one who'd gotten off had been Hilger. The blond dude had been gone for days now. If the young guy left, too, that would leave just Uncle Fester. Dox had no doubt the sick bastard would come calling shortly after that—the taunts had worked the man to nearly foaming at the mouth before. Well, this time he had a plan. It wasn't much, and it was likely to fail, but it was better than nothing.

He'd wondered many times in his life whether, if the worst happened, he'd fall apart, or if he'd have the courage to go out swinging. He'd heard stories of brave men who'd lost it, their nerve, their backbone, whatever, at the moment of truth. He hoped he wouldn't be one of them, but he supposed you could never really know until that moment came.

He listened, grimacing slightly with the effort of straining for even the tiniest sounds. Footsteps, a door opening ... then a heavy thud, like something big falling

to the deck. A body, maybe. Then a door again, this time
closing, followed by the click of a lock.

Son of a bitch. It sounded like Fester had dropped the
young guy and locked him in a room somewhere. That
could mean only one thing.

He felt a hot rush of adrenaline surge through his
torso. This was it. His moment of truth was on its way
right now.

He took two deep breaths and strained against the
chains, first left, then right. He'd been doing what iso-
metrics he could every day since they'd grabbed him,
hoping there would actually be some use to keeping his
body from tightening up. Well, it looked like the effort
had been worth it, and he wanted to be warmed up now.
If this had even a prayer of working, he was going to
have to go from zero to a hundred with nothing in between.

Half a minute went by. He heard Fester's footsteps
coming along the corridor. Then there he was, smiling
his psycho smile through the door window while he
turned a key in the lock.

"Hola, maricón," he said, coming in, holding the battery and wires again. "We didn't get to finish our conversation." He turned and used the key to lock the door
from the inside. "And now no one can interrupt us like
last time." He slipped the key into his pocket.

"Wait a minute," Dox said, controlling his voice to
keep his pounding heart from creeping into it. "You
mean you've had a whole day to stew, a hundred options
to consider, and the best line you could come up with to
get some of your mojo back is"—he switched to an er-
satz Mexican accent—" 'We didn't get to finish our conversation'?"

Uncle Fester looked at him, nonplussed.

"I mean, you might have said, 'I like the way you talk, now let's hear you scream,' or, 'You're right, I do like to torture people, but I've never tortured anyone like I'm going to torture you.' What do you think of those? You can try one, if you like. I won't tell anyone you got it from me. Go on back out, we can start over."

Fester stood there, his eyes burning with hate.

"Well, shit. If you're going to get your rocks off with me, at least sing to me. I'm partial to that Lou Rawls number. You know the one . . ." He paused, then broke into song: "You'll never find, dah dah, dah dah dah . . . as long as you live . . . someone who loves you, tender like I dooooo . . ."

Fester didn't move. Whatever script he had in mind, Dox was so far off it the man couldn't figure out what he was supposed to do next. Which was exactly the idea. Now the trick was to flummox him even worse.

"You're crazy," Fester managed to spit out.

"Come on, man, admit what you're here for. You want my dick, don't you? It's all right. You can have it. Here."

His heart was pounding so hard now he could feel it in his neck. He stood up and pulled down the front of the track pants.

"What the fuck?" Fester said.

"It's all right, man," Dox said, shuffling toward him. "I'm attracted to you, too."

"You're fucking sick!" Fester hissed, rooted to the spot.

Dox kept moving forward. Eight feet, six . . .

"Here," he said, reaching inside with a manacled hand and freeing what a long-ago girlfriend had christened Nessie, the Loch Ness Monster. "There you go, it's okay."

Five feet. Fester's face was contorted in horror and confusion.

Three feet. Dox let the track pants snap back in position. He bent at the waist, aimed with his shoulder—

Fester's paralysis broke. He turned to the door as though to escape.

With a wild yell, Dox hit him in the back with his full two twenty-five. Fester slammed face forward into the door and the battery and wires hit the deck. Dox shuffled back, ready to launch himself again, but the chains slowed him. Fester turned. Dox shot up from underneath, and the top of his head nailed Fester in the face with a satisfying crunch. The impact rocked Fester back into the door. He grabbed Dox's shoulders on the rebound to try to shove him away, but Dox surged up against him, his palms forward, the chains cutting into his wrists. His straining hands found Fester's package, and he latched on and squeezed for all he was worth. Fester screamed and tried to jerk away, but he was up against the door now, Dox's weight pressed against him. He managed to shove Dox's shoulders back but couldn't break the death grip on his balls. Dox twisted inside Fester's hands and slammed up against him again, then shifted his grip and squeezed harder, yelling now with the effort.

Fester braced his temple against the side of Dox's head and tried to lever him away. Dox retracted a fraction and as Fester's face slipped past him he lunged forward like an adder and bit down on Fester's nose. Blood spurted into his mouth and Fester, shrieking now, managed to jerk to the side and create space. Dox tried to adjust but again the chains slowed him. An elbow connected with his cheek but he hung on. He could barely hear Fester screaming now, the whole of his being was focused on squeezing, squeezing . . . it was all he had and if he lost it, if this didn't put Fester down, where he could bronco stomp him or knee drop him, he was done.

Fester hit him with another elbow, then a third time, and suddenly Dox was falling. He couldn't break the drop with his manacled hands and took the impact on his shoulder. He brought his legs in, trying to roll away and get to his feet, but Fester stayed with him, kicking him now, wildly, out of control.

Dox kept rolling, but Fester, screaming, didn't let up for a second. One of the kicks connected with the back of his head and he saw an explosion of white. When the flash faded, Fester had stepped in front of him, and the next kick caught him squarely in the face. His head rocked back but he couldn't do anything to cover up. He tried rolling away again, dazed, but Fester easily stepped around him and just kept kicking.

Dox managed to roll to one of the walls and fetal up with his face to it, and for the next minute Fester vented his rage at Dox's back and legs. The blows didn't really hurt, exactly; he was too jacked on adrenaline and fear to feel much, and anyway there were too many impacts to distinguish. Mostly what he felt was a series of cascading thuds that reverberated through his body, like he'd fallen down under a rock slide.

Finally it stopped. Dox blinked and spat out a mouthful of blood, his or Fester's or both, he didn't know. He tried to get his feet under him, but he couldn't move. He wondered distantly whether Fester had cracked his spine. Well, it didn't really matter now.

He felt the heel of Fester's boot in his shoulder, easily turning him onto his back. He lay there, numb and exhausted and helpless. Fester squatted next to him, his breath heaving, his nose mangled and his face a bloody mask, and presto—a blade appeared in his hand. He took Dox by the hair and brought his face close.

"You like showing your dick, motherfucker?" he hissed, his teeth strangely white through all the blood. "You know what I'm going to do now? Cut it off for you and stuff it in your mouth. And your balls with it."

Dox spat a huge wad of blood and phlegm into Fester's face. He did it without thinking, but he was immediately glad. Without exactly meaning to, he'd answered the question of how he would leave this world, and he'd answered it well. Maybe it wasn't much, but it was all he had now, and he held on to it tight, hoping it would carry him through the rest.

Fester wiped the glob from his face and flung it away. He kneeled on Dox's chest, driving the breath out of him. Dox tried to twist away, but he might as well have been nailed to the deck.

"Here it comes, motherfucker," Fester said. "I hope you like the taste."

32

"HOW'S IT COMING?" I said, into the wireless earpiece I was wearing.

"Good," Boaz answered. His words were slightly slurred, and I understood it was because he was talking without moving his lips. "A lovely afternoon. So far no one who looks like a sentry."

"I can see you now," I said, and it was true, his Hawaiian shirt was impossible to miss, even without the binoculars. That was part of the point—he looked like the antithesis of someone trying not to be spotted. If you're going to be noticed anyway, you're better off hiding in plain sight.

I was kneeling in the back of Kanezaki's van. The van was configured for cargo, not passengers, and had no seats beyond the two in front. We were parked nose out in the yacht club parking lot. Naftali was diagonal to us, facing us from twenty feet away. Both vans had a pair of fake plates magnetically attached over the real ones. Layers again.

"Good, good, everything is good," Boaz said, taking his time, a fishing pole slung over his shoulder, the camera pack and the bolt cutter case hanging off his back, the Nikon dangling from his neck. He was wearing a baseball cap and shades, a sensible enough precaution against the strong tropical sun. The blond wig protruding from the back and sides of the cap would be a little more difficult to explain on practical grounds alone, but it would certainly throw off witnesses. The rest of us were similarly attired.

I watched him go down the first perpendicular pier. With the binoculars, I could make out the names of a few of the boats, but not many. I didn't see *Ocean Emerald*.

"Don't see it yet," I heard him say, and watched him turn around. He walked back to the main pier, then repeated the operation on the second perpendicular. I scanned the area, looking for anyone reacting to him. Everything seemed okay.

I watched him walk down the third perpendicular, then the fourth. I started to get nervous. What if they'd put to sea? Maybe Hilger got spooked, decided they'd been in Singapore too long, put the boat in north to Malaysia, south to Indonesia. Or he'd changed the boat's name somehow. Or Kanezaki's intel was off . . .

Boaz walked to the very end of the pier and made a right on the last perpendicular. He strolled slowly along. The bows of the boats were facing toward me, and so was Boaz, as he examined their sterns.

"It's here," he said, continuing to walk to the end of the perpendicular as though appreciating all the lovely yachts. "Halfway. I just went to the other side of it."

"I'm on my way," I said. I stepped out of the van, a fishing rod in my hand, the coveralls concealing the HK on my thigh, my heart starting to kick with adrenaline.

I crossed the parking lot, my pores immediately

yawning open in the sticky heat. Ahead of me was a red brick building; behind it, I knew from the satellite photos, a swimming pool, from which the sounds of children's laughter carried over to me now. Two Chinese men in golf clothes came through the doors to the club, presumably heading to a nearby course. They ignored me as they passed.

I walked straight down the access road to the pier, my head swiveling as I moved, searching for danger, so far spotting none.

"No sentries I can see on the craft," Boaz said, avoiding the *b*'s and *p*'s and *m*'s that would force him to purse his lips.

"Roger that," I said. "Near the second line now."

"I think this is a good location to take a few photos."

I kept moving, looking for problems. Several of the boats had little parties in progress on their decks, prosperous middle-aged Chinese and foreign men in white captain's hats, women in shorts and bathing-suit tops, the smell of beer and barbecue, the sounds of carefree laughter. I passed several people moving to and from the main clubhouse, everyone in shorts and boating shoes, suntans and white smiles. Life was good for these people. Not one of them gave me even a second glance.

I passed the fourth perpendicular. I could see Boaz now, halfway down the fifth. He had erected a tripod with what looked like a professional photographer's auxiliary light set atop it, the light set in the center of a large metallic umbrella, the whole thing connected to an exceptionally large rectangular battery pack. He was working the controls of a device the average person would assume was a light meter.

"You ready?" I said.

"Ready."

I turned onto the fifth perpendicular and began heading toward Boaz. The gloves Kanezaki had thoughtfully provided were in my pocket, and I pulled them on as I walked. I set down the fishing pole, then reached inside the coveralls and came out with the HK. I held it along my leg, the muzzle of the suppressor past my knee, and kept moving in. I wished there were some cover or concealment, but the terrain was what it was. I hoped Boaz's ray gun was as good as he claimed.

"Five, four, three, two, one," I said, still walking casually toward him. "Go."

33

A T FIRST, Dox thought the hot flush was a fear reaction. After all, a sadistic sociopath he'd provoked to murderous rage was athwart his chest, a second away from gelding him. The only thing that could have surprised him at that point was the wonder that he'd managed not to piss himself.

But within a half-second, he understood it wasn't a hot flush, although he had no better explanation. It felt like he'd touched a burning lightbulb, except not just with his fingertips, but with his whole body. Then, before he could even complete the *What the fuck?* thought he was forming, his entire body was on fire, like someone had doused him head-to-toe in kerosene and set him alight. He howled in agony and writhed under Fester's knee. Then Fester was off him, shrieking, rolling on the deck as though his clothes were ablaze and he was trying to put himself out.

Dox strained against the chains, sure he was on fire and utterly confused about where it had come from and why he couldn't see the flames. He managed one coherent thought—*Out of the frying pan, into the fire*—and then all he could do was howl and hope it would be over soon.

34

A SECOND AFTER Boaz engaged the device, a cacophony of shrieks emanated from belowdecks on the boat. Among them, I recognized Dox's baritone roar, and was seized with conflicting emotions: relief that he was alive, horror at the level of pain that could have produced that agonized wail.

I stood there, helpless, the HK in front of me now in a two-handed grip, waiting for someone to stumble off the boat so I could shoot. Nothing happened. If anything, the screaming got worse.

In my peripheral vision, I saw movement on the adjacent craft. I glanced left and right to confirm there was no danger. Civilians, looking out from their boats now to see what was causing the ruckus.

"What's happening over there?" a Caucasian man yelled in English from the boat to my left.

"Police matter, sir," I called back in my best command voice. "Please just stay on your craft and keep your head down. There could be shooting and I wouldn't want you or your family injured."

The man disappeared without another word.

The screaming went on. *Goddamnit, why aren't they trying to get off the boat?*

"Turn it off!" I said. "They must be stuck belowdecks. I'm going in."

"It's off," I heard him say. In my peripheral vision, I saw him pull a pistol from a bellyband. I half turned to him, but he was pointing the gun at the boat, not at me.

"Stay there," I said. "We might need heat again." I jumped onto the deck and moved to the stairs.

The screaming had stopped. I paused at the edge of the entrance, glanced down, and pulled my head back. With my eyes adjusted to the glare outside, I couldn't see what was below. I pulled off the shades and jammed them in a pocket.

Another quick peek. Nothing. Still no screaming.

There were only six stairs. I leaped over all of them and landed in a squat on the deck below. I pivoted, the gun out, tracking for danger. Still nothing. I was in a narrow corridor. There were three doors, all closed, all on my right, all with small windows.

I moved up next to the first of them and snuck a quick peek through the window, then away. Nothing.

I checked the second one the same way. Again, nothing.

I checked the third. Dox, lying on his back, in shackles. A bald guy, his face covered in blood, holding a knife, staggering toward him.

I grabbed the knob. It was locked. *Fuck.*

I stepped to the side, closed one eye to ensure that if I got hit with debris I'd only be half-blinded, brought up the HK, and fired three rapid shots into the door jamb inside the knob. The HK whispered and kicked in my hands. Wood splinters exploded past me.

I stepped back and launched a front kick just to the

side of the knob. The door blasted inward. The bald guy spun to face me. I put two rounds in his chest. He staggered back to the wall and crumbled to the deck.

There was no one else in the room but Dox. I knelt beside him, the gun up, facing the door. "How many others on the boat?" I said. "Do you know?"

"One other," he grunted. "One other."

"Hilger?"

"No. Someone else. I think he's locked in one of the ..."

From two doors down came the staccato crack of a half-dozen rapid pistol shots. The guy Dox was talking about, in one of the rooms I'd passed. The windows were small, and I'd been moving quickly. I must have missed him.

There was no cover in the room. I moved up stealthily along the wall, keeping the HK aimed at the door, waiting.

Nothing happened. Whoever he was, he was smart. The defender in a fixed position has a significant advantage over the aggressor who comes looking for him. He knew it, and he was waiting for me to pass him on the way out.

Fuck, I didn't have time to play it this way. Club security, cops ... we had to get out of here.

"Give me five seconds of heat," I whispered into the earpiece. "Exactly five seconds."

"Jesus Christ, not again," Dox mumbled from behind me.

"Three, two, one," I heard Boaz say, and then my skin was on fire.

An involuntary scream tore loose from my throat, with Dox offering a chorus from the deck behind me. I fought the illusion that the gun was red-hot and battled the overwhelming urge to drop it. It was all I could do to stay on my feet. Whoever was down the hall, the only advantage I had was that I knew what this was, and that it would last only five seconds.

It seemed like a lot longer. But then it was gone, as suddenly as it had started. I gritted my teeth and charged into the hallway.

There—the first door I had passed. It was open, the wood around the jamb torn up by pistol shots. I sprinted down to the edge of the frame and stopped.

"Again—three seconds," I whispered.

"Three, two, one," I heard again, and again my nerve endings exploded in fire. I shook with pain, with the effort of not screaming. From inside the room, I heard a long wail. Then, so suddenly it seemed a miracle, the pain was gone. I took a deep breath and spun into the room.

There he was, on the right, splayed on the floor. I brought the HK around.

Whoever he was, he was as quick as I've ever seen. He snapped the gun forward and simultaneously rolled to his left. I felt something slam into my chest and heard the double crack of successive pistol shots. I staggered back into the wall and returned fire. My first two shots landed short, but they made him flinch. I walked the muzzle up an inch and kept firing. Again, I was short, but the second two rounds ricocheted along the deck and into his body. He curled up and I kept firing, three times more, two to his torso, the last in his head. He dropped his gun and lay still.

I could barely breathe. Gritting my teeth, I dropped the empty magazine, slammed in a spare, and released the slide. I pressed my left palm to my chest, then brought it to my eyes, fully expecting it to be covered with blood. But it wasn't. The Dragon Skin. I'd gotten the wind knocked out of me, but it seemed that was all.

I picked up and pocketed the empty mag and staggered back down the hallway. Dox had gotten to his knees, but hadn't managed any further than that. Amazingly, the bald guy was holding onto the cot, halfway to standing. I brought up the HK.

"Don't," Dox said. "Don't, don't, don't do that."

I turned my head, but kept the muzzle of the gun on the bald guy. "What?" I said.

"Don't you kill him," Dox said, coming shakily to his feet. "Give me the gun."

"There's no time . . ."

"Give me the fucking gun!" he screamed.

You have to know when to argue with people, and when not to. This was clearly a "not to" situation.

Dox staggered toward me, and I leaped forward and grabbed his arm before he could fall. I placed the gun in his manacled hands and walked him over to the bald guy. The bald guy watched us coming. His arms shook, and he lost his hold on the cot. He sank to his knees, then slumped to his side, panting and trembling.

Dox stood directly over him. He aimed the gun.

"Just so you know," he said, "even if I had time, I wouldn't do to you what you were going to do to me."

The bald guy started to say something. Dox didn't wait to hear what. Without another word, he emptied the full magazine into the bald guy's face. Twelve muffled shots, each fading into the next. Bone and brain matter flew.

He stood for a second, swaying slightly, looking down at what he had done. Then he handed me the smoking pistol. He buckled, and I grabbed his arm to support him.

"Good," he said. "That was worth ten thousand dollars in therapy right there."

"Don't worry, I've got a spare mag."

He nodded. "I figured you did."

I swapped in a fresh magazine, then pulled out an extra baseball hat and jammed it on his head. I eased a pair of shades over his eyes. "You look good," I said.

"Just get me out of here, man."

I squeezed his shoulder. "That's what I'm here for."

I put on my own shades, took his arm, and helped him down the corridor. "We're on our way," I said, into the earpiece. "Just the two of us. Get out the bolt cutters, be ready."

"Hurry," Boaz said. "We have a lot of attention."

I holstered the HK and kept us going. I didn't know the nature of Dox's injuries, but he was having a hard time moving, even beyond the limits of the shackles. It took a full minute to get him up the stairs.

Crossing the deck, I saw Boaz was right. There were people staring at us from half a dozen boats. Several groups on foot had stopped and were watching to see what the commotion was. *Come on,* I thought. *Come on, come on. . . .*

Boaz reached out and helped Dox hop onto the pier. The chains were heavy, but there's not much that will stand up to four feet of bolt cutters. Boaz moved in and, three well-placed snaps later, Dox had the use of his hands and feet again. The manacles themselves we could worry about later.

Boaz had already packed up the heater. He shouldered the gear while I scanned the crowd for danger, so far seeing nothing worse than gawkers. Then we set off toward the main pier, hurrying now, Dox's giant arms around our shoulders, his chains clanking as we moved.

"This man's hurt!" I called out to the people who were staring at us. "Somebody call a doctor!" There, that ought to make us look more like the good guys and lower the chances of someone disputing our passage. Theoretically.

We made a left onto the main pier and kept moving. I saw that Kanezaki had backed all the way to the edge of the pier. Boaz must have called him. But Christ, it was taking us forever. *Why the fuck did the boat have to be on the farthest perpendicular?* I thought. *Murphy's Law. Unbelievable.*

People stared at us as we walked by. No one said anything, or tried to interfere.

Fifty feet out from the access road, I started to think we were going to make it. I could see the exhaust drifting from Kanezaki's idling engine.

Two uniformed security guys burst through the main clubhouse doors and onto the pier. They sprinted straight at us. Each was wearing a sidearm, still holstered.

"They're shooting back there!" I cried out in a high voice. "Hurry!"

For one second, I thought they were going to buy it. They looked down the pier and I could feel their attention shifting. Then their eyes came back to us, their expressions hardening.

For all his concern about rules of engagement, Boaz had his pistol out as fast as I did. "Do not reach for your weapons," I said, loudly and evenly, pointing the HK at the guy in front of me, while Boaz covered the other man.

Neither said a word. Their mouths dropped open and their hands crept north. Whatever they were paid to provide "security" at the yacht club, this wasn't part of the job description.

"Over the side," I said. "Into the water." Neither moved. I pointed the gigantic suppressed muzzle of the HK directly at the guy's face, suddenly pleased at the intimidating size of the thing, and shouted, "Now!"

He jumped in without another word. The other guy followed him an instant later.

"Very humane of you," Boaz said, and we kept hustling forward down the pier. The automatic side door of Kanezaki's van slid open. We helped Dox in, then followed inside. Kanezaki pulled smoothly away.

"You got him?" Boaz said to me.

For an instant, I didn't even know what he was talking about. "Who?"

"Hilger."

I shook my head. "He wasn't on the boat."

"Damn it," he said. "Delilah told me . . ." He stopped and smiled. "Well, I guess she was wrong."

"Intel," I said. "What can you do."

He laughed. "I think maybe things between you two are better than you let on."

Dox was lying on his back on the floor. I used the bolt cutters to get the manacles off him. While I cut, Boaz called Naftali. He was a half-mile behind us, and there was no pursuit.

Kanezaki pulled over. I removed the fake plates and we set out again.

We kept driving. Naftali called again. Still all clear.

It looked like we were going to make it. I pulled off the hat and shades and patted Dox's shoulder. "How are you doing?"

"I feel like shit."

He looked it, too. He was pale and he was having trouble breathing. Adrenaline was probably masking a lot of his pain, but that wasn't going to last much longer.

I knew Kanezaki had morphine in the medical kit. I go
out a syringe and gave Dox a hit.

"How's that?" I asked.

"Oo-rah," he said. "John Rain, my angel of mercy."

I laughed.

"Who's driving this thing, anyway?" he said.

"It's me, Dox," Kanezaki called from up front. "Tom."

"Good to have you here, man," Dox said, his voice a
little stronger now, rallying from the morphine. "I'd
shake your hand and thank you properly, but I'm a lit
tle laid up at the moment. And who's this?"

Boaz pulled off the hat, wig, and shades. "Boaz,"
he said.

Dox held up his hand and Boaz shook it.

"I didn't know John had other friends," Dox said, the
words slurring slightly. "I thought I was his only one."

Boaz smiled. "I guess that's why he wanted to get you
off that boat so much."

"My skin's starting to hurt," Dox said. "What did you
guys use, some kind of millimeter wave device?"

"Am I the only one who's never heard of these
things?" I said, and heard Kanezaki laugh.

"Sorry," Boaz said. "Calibrating the waves isn't an
exact science. You probably have first-degree burns,
maybe second."

Dox laughed, grimacing as he did so. "Jesus Christ,
you think I give a rat's ass about a sunburn? Uncle Fes
ter back there was fixing to decapitate Nessie."

Kanezaki glanced back. "Nessie?"

"Please don't ask him," I said.

"If you'd shown up ten seconds later, I'd be singing in
a girl's choir somewhere, I'll tell you that," he said,
laughing and grimacing harder. "Goddamn, I'm telling
you, that was a near, near thing."

Then his voice cracked. "I . . . ah, fuck, this is embarrassing," he said. "I really thought I was dead, though, I . . . ah, fuck."

He lay there, gritting his teeth and shaking, and the tears rolled silently down his face. I put a hand on his shoulder. "Go ahead," I said. "Get it out."

"Why did it have to be in front of you?" he said, half laughing, half crying. "You never puke, you never cry, and you're going to make fun of me for this for the rest of my life."

"I'm going to tell all your lady friends, too," I said, and he laughed again through the tears.

It lasted another minute, then played itself out. "Thanks for bailing me out," he said, looking around. "All of you. You too, Boaz, whoever you are. I will not, ever, forget it."

"I'm glad we could help," Boaz said. "And I'm sorry about the sunburn."

Dox tilted his head back toward Kanezaki. "Where are we, anyway?"

"Singapore," Kanezaki said. "On the way to a private jet at Changi. We'll be there in five minutes."

"Five minutes," Dox said. "Good. 'Cause I've got a joke to tell."

"You don't really have to," I said, familiar with Dox's notions of comedy.

"Tell me," Boaz said, with the boyish grin.

"I swore I'd tell John the *kabunga* joke if I came out of this alive, and I mean to keep my word, even high on morphine."

"You really don't have to . . ." I tried again, but he was already rolling.

"There are these three missionaries," he said, "and they get captured by a nasty tribe of aborigines deep in the jungle." He looked at Boaz. "You don't know this one, do you?"

Boaz shook his head. "Keep going."

"Well, the aborigines tie them up and set them down before the chief, who as it happens speaks a little English. The chief says to them, 'We are a hostile tribe, and we despise you and your missionary ways. So you have only two choices. Death or . . . *kabunga.*' Then he gestures to the first missionary and says, 'Choose!'

"Well, the man doesn't know what this *kabunga* business is, but he knows what death is, all right, and he knows he doesn't want that. So he looks at the chief and says, 'I choose . . . *kabunga.*'

"The chief raises his arms and cries out, '*Kabunga!*' And a dozen warriors rush out. They throw this boy down, pull off his clothes, and sodomize him but good."

"There's a theme in your jokes, are you aware of that?" I said.

Boaz said, "Shhh. I like it. Keep going."

"So now the chief looks at the second missionary, and he says, 'My friend, what do you choose? Will it be death, or . . . *kabunga*?'

"Well, this boy knows what *kabunga* is now, and he doesn't want any of it. But choosing death, well, that'd be suicide, and suicide is against his religious principles. So he swallows hard and says to the chief, 'I . . . I choose . . . *kabunga.*'

"The chief raises his arms and cries out, '*Kabunga!*' And once again, a dozen warriors rush out, and they have their way with this boy, and it goes on for an awful hour. Finally, it's over. The chief looks at the third missionary and says, 'What will it be, my friend? Death, or . . . *kabunga*?'

"Now this boy's seen just about all the *kabunga* he

can stand. And even though it's against his religious principles, and even though he knows death is the end, he just can't face *kabunga*. So he screws up all his courage, sticks out his chin, looks the chief straight in the eye, and says, 'I choose death!'

"The chief raises his arms and cries out, 'Death! But first, *kabunga!*' "

Boaz threw back his head and roared, and his hilarity was infectious. Within seconds, the inside of the van reverberated with laughter. As Dox had said, it had been a near, near thing. Laughter was one of the reactions. There would be others.

"Wait, wait," Boaz said, wiping his eyes. "I've got one, too. These three missionaries . . ."

And it went on from there. I had a feeling we would be seeing Boaz again when all of this was done.

I didn't mind the thought at all.

35

At Changi, Kanezaki showed his credentials to a uniformed guard. The man spoke into a radio and waved us through the gate.

"That worked well," I said.

Kanezaki called someone from his mobile. "We're on our way," he said. "Two minutes." Then he glanced back at me and smiled. "Low friends in high places."

We drove through another gate to the part of the airport I assumed was reserved for private planes. There were two dozen small jets parked on the tarmac. Kanezaki drove up to one of them. The hatch opened, and a young, crew-cut man came down the stairs. His back was ramrod straight, his civilian trousers were creased, and if he wasn't a Marine, the Marines didn't exist.

Kanezaki pressed a button and the van's side door slid open. He got out and met the Marine around the side.

"Two to transport," Kanezaki said. "Plus me."

"Sir," the Marine said, "I'm not authorized for other passengers."

"Come over here," Kanezaki said, and walked the

man out of earshot. I watched them talking. Kanezaki gestured and spoke; the Marine nodded and listened.

After a minute, they came back. The Marine extended a hand to Dox. "Sir, can I help you aboard?"

"Yes you can, son, and I'm glad to see they sent the Marines. Just give me five minutes with these reprobates first, all right?"

"Yes, sir," the man said, and stood off a respectful distance.

"Well, this is the VIP treatment," Dox said. "What did I do to qualify?"

"The jet is part of a small CIA fleet," Kanezaki said, "used to render very bad people to very secret places. You might have read a bit about it in the newspapers. And that's all I'm going to say."

"We know about the program," Boaz said.

Kanezaki smiled. "I know you do. You're part of it."

"What did you tell the pilot?" I asked.

He shrugged. "Mostly I reminded him of the shame he would bear for the rest of his life if he flew off leaving a wounded Marine behind."

"That would be me," Dox said. "Hope you didn't mention John here was Army."

Kanezaki laughed. "I didn't. It must have slipped my mind."

I watched Kanezaki, strangely moved. He reminded me so much of Tatsu. The way he was willing to work outside the system to fix the system. The way he connived to make other people complicit in his nefarious means and noble ends.

"Am I right in assuming," Boaz said, "that despite Jim Hilger's surprising failure to be on the boat as we all expected, we all still want him to take . . . early retirement?"

"Hell, yes, you can assume that," Dox said. He turned to me. "Do you know where to find him?"

"Feel free to ask me after we're on the plane," I said. "You know, when we're not right in front of a foreign intelligence operative." I looked at Boaz. "No offense."

Boaz smiled. "None taken."

"I don't care if Boaz is from Mars," Dox said. "I'd trust him to watch my back anytime. And I hope he'd trust me to watch his." He looked at Boaz, who nodded back. "Plus the man appreciates a good joke. Unlike some people I could mention, despite their possession of other positive attributes. So tell me: where do we find this miserable, trouser-shitting little dick-puller of a whining, chickenshit, yellow-bellied, squealing, pissing, piglet motherfucker and put him down like the rabid dog he is?"

Boaz looked awed. Before he could ask Dox to repeat it all with annotations, I said, "'We' don't find anyone. You can barely walk. From the way you're breathing, your ribs are probably broken and morphine is masking the worst of it."

"It's just a flesh wound," Dox said with a grimace. "I've had worse."

"You lie," Boaz said, in a weird British accent. The two of them broke up, Dox half laughing, half groaning. I didn't get it.

When they stopped, Boaz said, "It's true I'm a foreign intelligence operative. But that's my, what do you call it, a day job. This operation . . . let's just say, it wasn't sanctioned by my organization."

"What do you mean?" I said.

"Naftali. He's Gil's brother."

"I'll be damned," I said. "I thought he looked familiar."

"Yes, he looks a bit like Gil. And he's dangerous like Gil. He doesn't think our management has been sufficiently motivated about avenging his brother's death."

"That's management for you," Dox said. "If they're not doing nothing, they're overreacting. Never anything in between."

"You're on your own on this?" I asked Boaz.

He shrugged. "Certain people . . . are happy to look the other way while Naftali and I are on vacation. You know how it works. Sometimes people want something done, but don't want to know about it. They don't want their fingerprints on it. I believe America's former defense secretary Rumsfeld was known for this. The 'rubber glove syndrome.' No fingerprints, no attribution."

"Christ," I said, "doesn't anyone just work for the government anymore?"

Dox groaned. "I told you once, man. Privatization is the wave of the future. Hey, you don't think we still have a shot at Hilger here in Singapore, do you?"

I shook my head. "I doubt Hilger goes to the grocery store for a quart of milk without five different currencies and three different passports. He'll come back to the yacht club, hear the sirens, and just melt away."

Kanezaki said, "And we can't wait for him at the club. It's too hot right now. We can't go back."

"All right, forget Singapore," Boaz said. "But if you have information about where we can find Hilger after this, Naftali and I will act on it. Privately, discreetly, and immediately. You can count on that."

Kanezaki shrugged. "These secrets always get out sooner or later anyway," he said, and Boaz grinned.

I wasn't surprised. Kanezaki wanted Hilger dead enough to bring me in for it. Why not the Israelis, too? And it wasn't as though he would be sharing classified intel. Everything he knew on this op, he had generated with me.

Kanezaki briefed Boaz on what we knew. When he was done, Boaz said, "So this port security guy in Amsterdam, Boezeman, you think he's integral to whatever Hilger is planning."

"That's right," Kanezaki said.

"And you have his particulars? Work and home addresses, telephone numbers, photographs?"

"Of course."

"Who is Hilger working for?"

"I don't know. There are a lot of groups that would love to take down the refineries at Rotterdam. AQ, Hamas, Hezbollah . . . and Hilger is mixed up with all of them."

Boaz pursed his lips and blew out. "If you're right about what Hilger's been doing, how long do you think we've got before this whole thing goes down?"

Kanezaki nodded as though this was exactly what he'd been considering. "It's hard to say. We know he's been planning Rotterdam for a while, that it's important to him. With the losses he's taken, my guess is, he'll get to the Netherlands as soon as he can to see it through."

Dox said, "If he shipped a device, why not just use a timer? Or a detonator rigged to a mobile phone? Call the number from wherever and whenever, and boom."

Boaz shook his head. "Too many potential problems. The timer isn't good because he wouldn't know precisely when the package arrived. The mobile phone isn't good because there might be no reception inside the container. And either way, he'd be taking a chance that the device might have been damaged or otherwise rendered inoperable if the container were dropped or mishandled at sea."

"Boaz's specialty is bombs," I said.

Boaz smiled. "These days, people call them Improvised Explosive Devices. It sounds more impressive. But nobody gave me a raise for it."

"Besides," Kanezaki said, "if he could have done the whole thing remotely, he wouldn't have needed Boezeman or any other inside man in the first place."

Dox nodded. "Right, right. And even if Hilger's not in town, I'll bet Boezeman will have plenty of information that could lead us to him. If he's asked nicely, that is."

"What about your organization?" I said to Boaz. "Feed this to them, they'll feed it to . . ."

"To the Agency," Boaz said. "Our counterpart relations with the Dutch are . . . not strong."

I shrugged. "Then the Agency will feed it to the Dutch."

"You can't be serious," Kanezaki said. "The Agency's not going to pass along anything without studying it first. Most of what we're going on comes from unvetted sources and the rest is speculation. They'll probably never pass it along at all. Even if they did, I'd say the time frame is a month, minimum. No one wants to send a warning like this and have it turn out to be false. Believe me, in a bureaucracy, the fear of looking stupid is stronger than the fear of losing Rotterdam. Official channels are a waste of time on this."

We were all quiet for a moment. Boaz said, "This whole thing may be . . . a wild-goose chase, true. But my gut tells me it's worth looking into. Besides, I've been thinking about visiting Amsterdam. Rain, what about you?"

I looked at Dox. He said, "If you're not going, I am, I don't care if I have to crawl. It's not just because of whatever nefarious shit Hilger's up to there. And it's not just because I want revenge, either, although hell yes I do. It's because Hilger knows we're going to come after him. First chance he gets, he'll be looking to preempt us to improve his own longevity. I refuse to live my life wondering whether that bastard's managed to acquire me again. I'll take him out first, thank you, and I'll sleep better because of it."

We were all quiet again. Dox said, "Besides, if Tom is right, Hilger's fixing to do something nasty in Rotterdam, and we're the only ones in a position to stop it."

I thought for a moment. What Dox had said was right, I knew. I didn't want Hilger to live any more than he did.

But I was keenly aware also of Kanezaki's point about doing something to thwart what Jannick's and Accinelli's deaths were intended to foster. I hated that he'd hit a nerve with that shit. I knew he was manipulating me. But I also wanted to believe there was some way to undo what I'd done.

I sighed and tilted my head toward Dox. "Let's get him on the plane."

Dox shook his head. "I ain't going anywhere unless you're going to Amsterdam."

"I'm going," I said.

Dox smiled. "All right, good, 'cause I could use a good nurse about now. Boaz, watch out that he doesn't sneak off to the red-light district."

Boaz grinned. "I'll be careful."

Dox shook his head. "Goddamn, I wish I could join you boys. The thought of looking at that little spot between Hilger's eyes through a Leupold scope . . . man, it's giving me wood right now."

"All right, time to go," I said.

Kanezaki called out, "Marine!" The crew-cut guy appeared a second later. He reached into the van and helped Dox to his feet. Despite his bravado, the big sniper looked awful. His face was red and blistering and he could barely support his own weight. But he was alive, and that in itself was a wonderful thing.

"Good hunting, amigo," Dox said to Boaz. "When you're done, I'm going to owe you a few beers, and then some. We'll get together and tell each other a few more jokes."

Boaz smiled. "I'll look forward to it."

We all got out of the van. The Marine helped Dox onto the plane.

"What about Naftali?" I asked Boaz.

"He's returning the other van," Boaz said. "Better not to leave loose ends." He looked at Kanezaki. "What about yours?"

"I've got someone to take care of it," Kanezaki said.

Boaz laughed. "It must be nice to work for a big organization."

On cue, another young guy came off the plane, a civilian this time, from his appearance. Probably low-level CIA. Kanezaki tossed him the van keys. "You know what to do," he said. The young guy nodded, closed the doors, got in the van, and drove off.

"I'll meet you in Amsterdam," I said to Boaz. "I'll get the first flight I can."

He nodded. "Likewise. I'd offer you a ride, but if I don't return the plane I borrowed soon, someone will step on my dick."

Kanezaki said, "That's not quite how it's ..."

"All right, let's get out of here," I said. "Boaz, I'll call you on your mobile. If for some reason I can't reach you, the backup will be the lobby of the Grand Hotel Krasnapolsky, seven in the morning, then seven at night until we find each other."

"You know Amsterdam," Boaz said.

"I've been there," I said, deliberately noncommittal. I was beginning to trust Boaz, at least "situationally," as he might put it, but I still wanted a backup location with plenty of exits, entrances, and security. In other words, a difficult place for a hit.

He shook my hand, then Kanezaki's, and then walked off, presumably to whichever of the private jets was his. Kanezaki and I got on the plane. The Marine went to the cockpit, and five minutes later, Singapore was a thousand feet below us, and getting farther away by the second.

36

A S THE TAXI PULLED into the parking lot of the Republic of Singapore Yacht Club, Hilger saw the flashing police lights and the gawkers lined up in front of the club entrance. He instantly understood and accepted what it all meant. His heartbeat kicked up a notch, but he didn't show anything.

"Oh my God, I can't believe this," he said to the driver. "I left my laptop at the hotel. Can you take me back right away?"

The driver swung around. Hilger punched some digits into his mobile phone but never pressed the "Call" button. He waited a moment, and then, for the driver's benefit, said, "Hi, I was just using the computer center and I think I left my . . . oh, you found it? Oh, thank God. Yes, I'll be there in five minutes to pick it up."

Next, he called Guthrie's mobile. No response. That was bad; Guthrie was always reachable. He tried Pancho next. Again, no answer.

He clicked off. The first thing he thought was that he'd have to ditch the phone right away. The number would show up in the call logs of Pancho's and Guthrie's units.

He knew they were dead. He didn't know how Rain found the boat, but somehow he had. It was the same as in Hong Kong. He'd known Rain would be looking for a way to counterattack, of course, but he thought with the boat as a shell game, and with Dox as a hostage, Rain would be neutralized. Everything he knew about Rain indicated that Dox was his only partner. But Rain couldn't have tracked him like this without help, and Hilger wondered for a moment where it might have come from.

Fuck. Fuck. Fuck.

He breathed in and out, slowly and deeply, calming himself, focusing. If Rain had learned about the boat, could he have learned about the Rotterdam op? Not that Rain would care about the op itself; the man was a mercenary and nothing more. But he might use its existence as a way to track Hilger again. Or he might share his knowledge with someone else who might be inclined to interfere. It didn't seem likely, but neither had the calamity that had just occurred here on Singapore.

For one bad second, he was gripped with self-doubt. Maybe he'd made a mistake in treating Rain like an enemy. Maybe he should have just tried to recruit the man, and Dox, too, even after what had happened in Hong Kong. He wondered if he'd let his anger about that blown op color his judgment, the personal interfere with the professional. After all, it wasn't as though Rain had affiliations, or stupid loyalties, or anything else that would have inhibited him from working with Hilger. Maybe if he understood the importance of Hilger's work, he could have taken it up for himself. Nihilism was unnatural. Maybe the right cause could have brought Rain around.

He squeezed his eyes shut and pinched the bridge of his nose. Or maybe not. Because almost nobody else really got it. Where were the realists in the government, the men who would do what was necessary? Instead, we had a bunch of chicken hawks peddling fantasy solutions to imaginary problems, who called their solution the "Patriot Act" and sold it to an ignorant public eager to believe the tough talkers were actually protecting them. It made Hilger want to puke.

Well, he would take care of it, take care of all of it. He was so close now.

He closed his eyes and focused on his breathing again. Slowly, in and out.

All right. Assume the op is blown. Assume Rain knows about Boezeman. Hard to imagine how, but still . . . what does Rain do with the information?

Hilger smiled. He knew Rain now. It had taken him a while and cost him a lot, but now he knew his enemy. Rain would use the information to track Hilger. It was the predator in him, the relentlessness he'd seen in Rain's eyes in Saigon and in his actions everywhere else. Lots of other things were uncertain, but this one Hilger knew he could take to the bank.

Two courses of action immediately presented themselves. One was an imperative; the other, an opportunity.

The imperative: get to Amsterdam immediately. On a chartered jet if there was nothing immediately available commercially. Meet Boezeman, access the device, ensure proper placement, arm the detonator.

The opportunity: stay in Amsterdam for just a short while after, to double back on the man, or men, who he was certain would be tracking him there.

Maybe he was miscalculating again. Maybe Rain, and

Dox, too, if they were together, would get the better of him. Certainly not impossible to imagine; they were skilled, they were ruthless, and they were pissed.

But he would take that chance. As soon as he finished his business with Boezeman, nothing would be able to stop the operation, and the operation was always what mattered. More than the lives of any of his men. More, of course, even than his own.

If it came to that.

As the taxi pulled into the hotel parking lot, Hilger's mind felt as cool and clear as a pristine mountain stream. He knew exactly what he needed to do, and he knew exactly how to do it.

37

KANEZAKI HAD the Marine pilot take us to Hong Kong. Along the way, he used a satellite phone to make various arrangements: a doctor for Dox, a 12:25 A.M. first-class Cathay Pacific flight to Amsterdam for me.

"I can't get you the kind of hardware you like in Amsterdam," Kanezaki told me, just after we'd landed. "My reach outside Asia isn't great."

I thought of the way he'd handled his pilot, the way he reminded me of Tatsu. "It will be," I said.

"Why do you say that?" he asked.

I smiled. "Just a feeling. Anyway, I expect Boaz and Naftali will be carrying enough hardware to make them clank when they walk."

"Sounds like you've been to Amsterdam, am I right?"

"I know the general layout. But I haven't been to Rotterdam at all."

"Well, our man lives near Vondelpark in Amsterdam, if you know where that is. A duplex at 15 Vossiusstraat. Commutes to work in Rotterdam."

"I know Vondelpark."

"I'll upload the dossier to the bulletin board. It'll be waiting for you when you arrive."

"Good."

He hesitated, then said, "Tatsu would be proud of you."

I nodded. Maybe it was manipulation; maybe it was heartfelt. Either way, I suspected it was true. "He was a good influence," I said. "On both of us."

I shook his hand, then turned to Dox. The big sniper was lying on his back on some folded blankets on the cabin floor, zonked from the morphine we'd been administering. I squatted down and took his hand. "Enjoy your vacation, you malingerer."

He groaned. "You know there's nowhere I'd rather be going right now than to Amsterdam. You put him down good, all right?"

I squeezed his hand. "I will. I'll see you soon."

An ambulance was pulling up even as I got off the plane. I walked across the tarmac and then through the airport, and by the time I reached the Cathay Pacific counter, I was Taro Yamada again, and checked in for my flight without a hitch.

I thought about calling Delilah. I was still unsettled by what she had said to me. I didn't know how I felt, or even how to respond, and felt stupid for it. Just a few days earlier, I had decided the whole thing was ridiculous, unsustainable. And then there was that night at the Bel-Air, and . . . shit, I just didn't know.

But in the end, the thought of Delilah getting a report from Boaz and radio silence from me was just too uncomfortable. I didn't want to seem to disrespect her. Because I did respect her, I was grateful to her, I . . . ah, Jesus Christ. I found a pay phone and called her.

She picked up immediately. *"Allo?"*

"It's me. We got him. He's safe."

"Oh, John."

"Yeah, it's all right. He's going to be okay."

"When are you coming back here?"

"Soon. There's just one thing I have to finish first."
Under the circumstances, she would know what that
thing was.

There was a pause. "Are you sure it's . . . necessary?"

"I have no choice. He'll come after us if I don't."

"Let me help you, then."

"No, it's not a good idea."

"I'm afraid."

That threw me.

"What are you afraid of? You're never afraid."

"I'm afraid you've been pushing your luck. I want to
be with you on this."

I paused, trying to think of what to say, of a way to explain.

"I don't want you involved," I said. "I don't want you
to come into the place I'm in, the place where I have to
be. I think . . . you're the only thing that can pull me
out."

"John . . ."

"Okay? I have help. Talk to your people, you'll see.
Don't come. I need you after."

I hung up then, afraid of what I might say next. I
stood there for a long time, my eyes closed, wondering
about what I had just said to her and where the words
had come from. So much was happening, I couldn't stay
on top of it. I wanted to find some dark, safe place
where I could hide from everything and try to figure it
all out.

But I had to stay focused. I had to finish this. I had
no choice.

I was practically comatose on the thirteen-hour flight to Amsterdam, arriving at six-thirty in the morning local time. I doubted Boaz and Naftali could have made it as fast, but I bought a prepaid card and tried Boaz from a pay phone anyway. No answer. Yeah, they were probably in the air.

I used the Cathay Pacific arrivals lounge to shower and change. Kanezaki had given me the second Dragon Skin vest, and I put it on now, half for protection, half against the likely cold outside. I took the usual precautions leaving the airport, then caught the train to Amsterdam's Centraal Station.

I arrived to find a rainy, chilly, gloomy morning. Commuters shuffled past me on the slick pavement, umbrellas dripping, chins tucked into scarves. I was struck by the relative absence of conversation. Maybe it was the hour, maybe the chill, but the mood of the area was quiet, even dour.

I bought a hat, scarf, gloves, an umbrella, and a map at a station shop. None of the shops that were open sold jackets—or knives, which I wanted almost as much. I'd have to wait until something opened later, when I could outfit myself properly. In the meantime, I was going to be cold again.

I took the GVB tram to Leidseplein, near Vondelpark, where Boezeman lived. I knew the square was a lively spot at night, but it wasn't quite nine in the morning now, and the dozens of bars and restaurants and coffee shops were shuttered. I paused on a bridge over one of the antique canals that circled back from the harbor like concentric strands on a spider's web, looking down briefly at the wet leaves floating on the murky water, a pair of geese gliding by, improbably white and pure in contrast to the Stygian waters around them. Cars passed me, their headlights weak against the wet winter morning gloom, their tires spraying water from giant puddles onto the sidewalks. Bicyclists pedaled stoically through the chill rain.

Vossiusstraat was only a five-minute walk from the tram stop. I found the street, a narrow, one-way, cobblestoned thoroughfare, and walked down it. I was entering an area where Hilger might anticipate me, and my alertness sharpened.

On the left side of the street was a long row of centuries-old, four- and five-story brick-and-stone buildings, one joined to the next. None of the doorways was set in deeply enough to offer someone a place to hide and wait. On the right side was the mile-long green strip of Vondelpark, separated from Vossiusstraat by a spiked, wrought-iron fence. I checked the park through the bars of the fence, pausing in front of parked cars for cover as I moved, and saw nothing out of place. A few people passed me, but their hands were visible and their vibe not dangerous. In the rain, shrouded by umbrellas, they gave me not even a glance.

I slowed and squatted with a parked car to my back as I passed number fifteen—an old, heavy wooden door with decorative carvings and a stained-glass window at its center. I looked at the exterior wall around the doorjamb, then inside the stained glass at the vestibule within. No buzzers, mailboxes, or other signs of individual units. Apparently Boezeman, or more probably the Boezeman family, owned the building, and the entranceway was theirs alone. Good to know.

The lock was new, and might have presented an impediment. But from my initial assessment of the terrain, I thought I'd prefer to force him into the vestibule when he arrived at or left the apartment, rather than try to gain entry in advance and wait for him inside. Without more intelligence on his circumstances and habits, waiting inside would have involved too many uncertainties, primary among them the potential comings and goings of family members. By contrast, the long, narrow street, with the park on one side, created various solid opportunities for watching and waiting, and surprising him at the entrance. It was too bad, really. If I could have been here two hours earlier, maybe even only one, I might have had a chance to greet Boezeman as he left his apartment on his way to work. I didn't know what he looked like, but how many people would be coming and going from this one apartment? It would have been improvised, ad hoc, and involved some risk, but it could have been done.

I walked the streets for two hours more, absorbing the vibe of the area, focusing on Vossiusstraat. From Vondelpark I had a clear view of Boezeman's apartment. That was useful, but only up to a point. I'd be able to see him coming and going, but wouldn't be able to get to him in time to force him back into the entranceway, where I could talk to him privately. Waiting on the street itself, close to his building, was possible, but would look suspicious if I had to stay for very long.

I wondered how security conscious he might be. Responsibility for facilities security didn't often translate into the kind of personal awareness that might have protected him from someone like me. On the job, he would think one way; off the job, thinking himself free of enemies, his habits might be lax. With Boaz and Naftali to help, we might be able to set up a watcher at each end of the narrow street. The third person would walk up and down the street, and we would trade positions periodically to avoid being too conspicuous. If Boezeman commuted by train, he would leave the street in the morning and arrive in the evening on foot or on a bicycle. If he drove, it would be the same thing in a car: Either way, with someone posted at each end of the street, we'd be able to see him coming and get the third person in position near his apartment before he arrived.

Assuming he didn't carpool. Assuming he wasn't married and didn't leave with his wife or arrive in the evening after picking up the kids from day care. Assuming a thousand things, none of which we had time to properly screen for.

I bought a heavy wool jacket in a Leidseplein shop, then called Boaz from a pay phone. This time he picked up.

"Are you here?" I asked.

"We just landed."

"Good. Your phone is scrambled?"

"Yes, but I still want to be careful not to disturb the other passengers."

"I understand, there are people around you. All right, I've been having a look around. I see some possibilities. When can you meet?"

"How about tonight, the hotel we talked about before, and, say, two hours earlier?"

"Even earlier would be better. It would give us a window to meet Boezeman when he comes home from work."

"Maybe. I have a local friend who's going to give us presents. I don't think we'll want to show up empty-handed."

He had a point. There were already so many unknowns. With guns, we'd at least improve our chances of quietly getting Boezeman into his apartment, of controlling him and anyone else we found there, and of establishing the necessary fear that might induce the proper talkativeness. And there were other tools we would probably need to track Hilger, if in fact he were in town.

"I'll call you again at fifteen hundred," I said. "We'll see how far along you are then."

I found an Internet coffee shop, or *koffieshop,* as the locals knew them, a place called Get Down To It, on a side street off Leidseplein, and descended the stairs to find a terminal and see what Kanezaki had for me. Halfway down, the rich, heady smell of cannabis enveloped me, and for the second time in not much more than a week I was back in Saigon, a young man this time, a boy, really, on leave and smoking the Thai Stick an enterprising rear-echelon type had smuggled in on a military flight from Bangkok. The iceman breathed it in, exulting in an almost physical sense of recall, the memory of what it was to be a teenager with skills and a license to use them, ten thousand miles from home and making it up as we went along, knowing no one had ever been here before us, like Neil Armstrong on the moon but better, juiced with hormones and adrenaline, excitement and fear, an adolescent's curious mind and a predator's deadly instincts. We knew we were special, anointed for our role, baptized by our experience, our childhoods shed, as lost and useless to us now as empty snakeskins. Everything else would come later—the horror, the cost of it, the regret. But on leave in Saigon, in the back of a dark Dong Khoi bar, high on Thai Stick and our status as gods, we had no idea what was being mortgaged, or what we would have to pay for it.

The *koffieshop* was a quietly lit space with a low beamed ceiling and a red-tiled floor, the walls darkened by years of accumulated smoke. There was a pinball ma-

chine, pool tables, a dark wood bar and a handful of
black stools in front of it. In one corner were cushioned
seats, a half-dozen young people sitting on them, absorbed in their smoking and conversation; in the other,
three Internet terminals, all empty. Soft house music
played in the background. I used one of the terminals to
access the Kanezaki bulletin board. As promised, he
had left me a full dossier on Boezeman, including photographs. I wrote down what I needed to and memo-
rized the rest. Then I purged the browser and, without
really thinking, took a seat at the bar. A sign was taped
to the counter:

SPECIAL OFFER: WHITE WIDOW AND SUPER PALM POWER
HASH, 24 EUROS. DUTCH, 12 EUROS. THAI, 3 GRAMS,
12 EUROS.

Thai, huh. That shit was still around.

I looked at my watch. Close to five hours until I
needed to call Boaz.

The bartender came over, a tall guy with thinning
brown hair. "What can I get you?"

Fuck it. "Thai," I said. "And some papers."

I rolled a single joint. *Just a little,* I thought. *Just to see
what it feels like after so long away.*

I took a very small hit and coughed anyway, and the
bartender smiled. Not the first time he'd seen a coughing patron, no doubt. He brought over a glass of water
and moved off again.

The iceman liked it, I could tell. I gave him another
small one, which went down easier, and then a third.

What the fuck are you doing? I thought. I looked at
the joint with horror and stubbed it out. I was exhausted, I'd let my guard down, but shit, I was in the
middle of an op. Was I trying to get myself killed?

Amazing, though, the association of the smell, and

now the taste, with Saigon. I'd never smoked dope before or after. It was purely a Vietnam thing for me.

You'll be okay, I told myself. *It was only a little. What the hell . . .*

I felt the outer edges of my perception beginning to fuzz over. It was nice, actually. It reminded me of a time I hadn't realized I'd missed. And it made me aware of how strung out I'd been since receiving Hilger's message in Paris. Sex with Delilah, and all the booze that night . . . it was like I had been trying to get outside myself, or anesthetize something within.

Sometimes you need the anesthesia. Because what you learn about yourself when fear finally overtakes you isn't pretty. You understand that the person you thought of as yourself, your immutable, indivisible self, is just an overlay, fragile and frail. Fear strips away the façade. And having to see what lies beneath, and accept it, makes you different from everyone who hasn't been similarly forged. You've been aged; they remain neophytes. You have brutal clarity; they, comforting illusions. You've looked into the abyss, and can still feel it looking back; they don't even know such a place exists. And for all of it, you hate them.

Why had I insisted on Saigon with Hilger? There were other places we could have gone, places that offered the same operational advantages. But the iceman wanted Vietnam. He wanted to take me back, back to the place he was born, where he thrived, the place that was purely him. Why?

Because you need me.

I started. The voice was whispered, intense, familiar.

I looked around. No one had spoken. The bartender was at the other end of the bar, talking to one of the girls at the corner tables. The house music seemed far away.

What are you talking about? I thought. *I know I need you.*

No. You've been trying to kill me.

I've been trying to accommodate you.

Bullshit. You're ignoring me. Smothering me. Letting me run loose at night in Paris like I'm a fucking dog that needs to be walked so it won't crap the house. And then when you need me for Dox, you second-guess me, fight me, tolerate me like I'm the hired help and you can't wait until I'm finished with the chores so you can send me off again. That shit is over. Get the fuck out of my way.

No. You don't own me.

The hell I don't. You'd be dead now if it weren't for me. You would have died the first night you pissed your pants in a firefight. Your life is mine. I don't own you? I fucking am you.

"You okay?"

I jumped to the side and my right hand went to clear a blade clipped to my pocket, a blade that wasn't there. Before I knew it, I had the stool in my hands, cocked back like a baseball bat.

It had been the bartender talking to me. He took a step back and raised his hands, his eyes wide.

"Hey, man," he said. "It's cool. It's cool."

Fear had blown away the marijuana trance like an arctic wind. I looked around and realized where I was. And what I was doing.

I put the stool down. Everyone was looking at me.

The bartender slowly lowered his hands. "You were pretty zoned out there, man. That Thai weed can be strong."

"Yeah, it can be," I said, nodding. "I don't think I'll be having any more of it."

I walked in the wet, cold air until I found a cheap

hotel, where I slept for several hours. When I woke, I
still felt exhausted, the way you do from a post-combat
parasympathetic backlash, but at least my head was
clear again. All the flying, the stalking, the near catastro-
phes. Then getting Dox out, knowing he was all right.
And now that thing in the coffeehouse . . . it was like facing off with your worst enemy, then getting pulled apart
with everybody still armed, nothing really resolved.

I stopped for some food and coffee at a place called
Café Bouwman, on Utrechtsestraat along the Prinsen-
gracht canal. It was good—a neighborhood kind of
place, low-key, unpretentious, with old wooden tables
and leather seats, and a bartender who knew her customers. When I was done, I called Boaz from a pay
phone.

"How are we doing?" I said.

"We finished up ahead of schedule. We were waiting
for your call."

"Good. How soon can you be in the place we
talked about?"

"We're here now. But we have a car, we can meet
you anywhere."

Ordinarily, I wouldn't have accepted the proposal.
But I wasn't worried about Boaz right now. And the
Krasnapolsky was less than a fifteen-minute walk from
where I was. It would save time to go straight there.

"I'll meet you in front in fifteen minutes," I said.

BOAZ AND NAFTALI were waiting out front as promised.
Boaz had lost the Hawaiian shirt and was wearing a
bulky down jacket and jeans. He looked thoroughly unremarkable, nondescript, unmemorable. Naftali had on
a nylon windbreaker and a backpack. But for a certain
hard look in his eyes that not everyone would know

what to make of, Gil's brother looked like a young European tourist on a budget. We walked down the street to a pizza place. Boaz and Naftali ordered a few slices, and we sat in back to talk.

"Do you celebrate Christmas or Hanukkah?" Boaz asked.

"Neither."

"Well, you'll like our presents regardless. USP tacticals and suppressors, and some sharp pointy things, too. I love the holidays."

I briefed them on the layout around Boezeman's building, then we discussed how to proceed. Boaz agreed that intercepting Boezeman as he came home tonight, or failing that as he left in the morning, was our best bet. But as we started talking about Hilger, I began to feel uneasy. We weren't taking his possible presence adequately into account.

"If this whole thing is real," I said, "and he really does have a radiological device that he needs to arm, he could be here already. He might already have contacted Boezeman. Hell, he might already have armed the bomb for all we know."

"All right," Boaz said. "Let's assume he did. What does he do next?"

"He gets the hell out of Dodge. The op is done. Maybe the device is on a timer; maybe it's mobile-phone-activated. Either way, he'd want to leave town before detonation, otherwise there's too much chance of getting caught up in a security sweep. So he catches the train to Brussels, straight from Rotterdam."

"No," Naftali said.

Boaz and I both looked at him. Boaz said, "I knew you could talk."

"He doesn't leave right away," Naftali said, ignoring

the commentary. "He's lost all his cutouts and he's dealing with Boezeman directly now. Boezeman can connect the operation to him. First, he kills Boezeman. *Then* he gets the hell out of Dodge."

We were all quiet for a moment. Naftali had just made a damn good point.

"All right," I said. "Where does he get to Boezeman?"

Naftali shrugged. "Where are we talking about getting to him?"

Boaz nodded. "You're right. And I don't like the idea of waiting for Boezeman in the same place and at the same time as Hilger. A lot of things could go wrong."

"Why don't we call him?" I said. "Boezeman. Flush him out. If he knows anything, we'll be able to tell."

"It's risky," Boaz said. "It would be warning him."

I shrugged. "He's still got to come home tonight. If the call doesn't get the results we want, we can always use the apartment as plan B."

I took out the notes I had made from the information on the Kanezaki bulletin board. "Here's his mobile," I said. "Let's see what happens if our friend Boezeman gets an unexpected phone call."

Boaz handed me a mobile. "Sterile," he said.

I input the number. Two rings, then a deep voice: *"Hoi."*

"Hello, Mister Boezeman?"

"Yes, speaking."

I thought of the names Kanezaki had mentioned on the bulletin board. "I'm a friend of our mutual acquaintances, James Hillman and William Detts."

I paused. Boezeman said, "Yes?"

Not an "I'm sorry?" or a "Who?" Something about the word choice, and his tone, told me I'd hit pay dirt.

I waited longer, seeing what the pressure of silence might produce.

"Uh, is this about the rental property?" he said.

Goddamn, it was working. That was a bona fide if ever I'd heard one.

"I'm supposed to give you a signal in return, right?" I said.

"Who . . . who is this?"

"I'll explain who I am, Mister Boezeman. Right now, I'm either your best friend or your worst enemy. I've been investigating James Hillman for more than two years. I know what he's doing in Rotterdam. I know how he's using you to do it. Cooperate with me, right now, or the next call you get will be from the national police and security services."

There was a long pause. I could hear his breathing. It was fast.

"I . . . what do you want?" he said.

"To meet you. Right now. To tell you what Hillman has really been up to and for you to brief me. In return for that, I won't make that phone call to the police. But one thing first. It's very important. It's for your safety. Did you meet with Hillman earlier today?"

"I . . . I . . . why?"

He met him. It was all right there in his voice.

"You're not safe," I said. "You can't go home tonight. Not until we've taken care of this."

"How . . . I don't even know who you are."

"Are you at work now?"

"Yes."

"Good. You'll have an hour to think about all this, and you'll see that trusting me is your only option. I'm on my way to Rotterdam now. I'll call when I arrive. We can meet anywhere you like. You'll want to choose somewhere public." I clicked off.

Boaz frowned. "You're going to let him choose the place?"

"Of course not. I just want to get him moving. Once he takes some action, he'll take more. Now let's go. I'll brief you on the way."

Their car was parked near the hotel, a Mercedes C Class with a navigation system. Naftali drove. Boaz input Boezeman's work address. We were there in less than an hour—not the city of Rotterdam, which I'd heard was pretty, nor even the port itself, but instead the refinery complex, a sprawling network of waterways plied by freighters and garbage scows; thousands of miles of pipes twisting in all directions, carrying who knows what to God knows where; squat oil tanks and rotating power turbines and towers belching smoke into a sky the color of lead.

I called Boezeman again. He answered immediately.

"I'm here," I said. "Near your office at the refinery." I gave him the address of a gas station we had just passed, and he said he was coming.

"Told you," I said to Boaz, and he smiled.

We drove a little ways off and parked on a rise with a view of the gas station parking lot. Like his apartment, Boezeman himself was a Hilger nexus, and we had to be careful.

Five minutes later, a blue Fiat pulled into the corner of the gas station lot, eschewing the pumps. We waited a minute, watching through the binoculars, and saw no cars following.

Naftali drove us in. Boaz and I had the USPs out and ready. As we pulled into the gas station, we saw Boezeman, sitting alone in the car.

I rolled down my window. "Let me see your hands, Mister Boezeman," I said. He complied, and we crept closer. I could see the backseat now. It was empty. Okay.

"Watch my back," I said to Boaz. Never a phrase that made me particularly comfortable. But if it was good enough for Dox with Boaz, it would have to be good enough for me.

"We've got you," Boaz said, and I stepped out of the car. Boezeman got out, too.

We stood there in the rain, looking at each other, Boezeman's expression plainly afraid. "What kind of trouble am I in?" he said to me, and I thought, *Thank God this guy's just a civilian and not a hard case.*

"I'm going to give you some information," I said, "and then you're going to give me information in return. Fair enough?"

Boezeman nodded, looking nervously at Boaz and Naftali.

"The man you know as James Hillman also goes by Jim Hilger. He's working for radical Islamic interests. He's smuggled a radiological device into Rotterdam. A dirty bomb."

The color fled Boezeman's face. "Oh, my God."

"I can tell by your reaction that you didn't know what you were mixed up in," I said. I expected that in his distressed state, he would pick up the possibility of exculpation and run with it.

He did. "I never knew. Never. They never told me, but I thought . . ."

"Drugs?" I offered.

"Yes, only drugs. Oh, my God." His face had gone from white to green. It looked like he might puke.

"Mister Boezeman. This is important. You met with Hilger today, didn't you?"

He nodded. I waved to Boaz and he got out of the car.

"Did you give him access to the refinery facilities?" I said.

"He . . . had to retrieve something from a container. I had the container brought from the port and stored on the refinery grounds."

"Why?"

"I have more access at the refinery. And Hillman— Hilger—he told me to do it that way."

"Did you ever take a look at what's inside the container?"

"I tried once. There were cases, but both were locked."

"All right. Did you let Hilger into the container?"

His frozen expression was all the answer we needed.

Boaz said, "The bomb is armed."

Boezeman turned away, doubled over, and vomited.

I looked at Boaz. "Can you disarm it?"

He shrugged. "I can disarm anything. With proper tools. And enough time. And with access, of course."

"Well, you're only going to get one out of three," I said. "If we're lucky." I turned to Boezeman. "Listen," I said. "You have to pull yourself together. We can still rectify this if we hurry. But we need more information. Where is Hilger now?"

"I . . . I don't know."

I wasn't asking the questions right. Boezeman was so agitated, he was getting the mental equivalent of tunnel vision. He was responding too narrowly, I could feel it.

"But did he give you any indication?" I said. "Did he say he was leaving town, or that he would meet you later, anything like that?"

"He has to come back tomorrow," Boezeman said.

"He told me . . . he couldn't move everything all at once. He had a big duffel bag, and it was full when he left."

"Probably with newspaper," I said. "They shipped it over with the bomb so you would think he was carrying something important out of the container. But he told you he had to come back?"

"Yes, to pick up the rest."

"There is no rest. The only reason he hasn't detonated the bomb yet is because he needs to kill you first. Where did you last see him? Someplace public?"

"Yes, it was . . . outside the gate. There were guards near. And he tried to . . . he wanted . . ."

"What?"

"He wanted me to come to the station with him. But I couldn't."

"He was looking for someplace private enough to kill you. That's all."

"But if he wants to kill me, and he knows I'm here, why doesn't he just . . ."

"It's not that kind of bomb," Boaz said. "The conventional explosion is small. It might not kill anybody. It's the radiation that does all the damage, mostly by causing panic."

Boezeman moaned softly, but said nothing.

I put myself in Hilger's shoes for a moment. *The bomb is armed; all that's left is to silence Boezeman. How do I get to him? Time and place . . .*

"Mister Boezeman. Did Hilger ask you any questions about what time you leave work, what time you get home, how you commute, that sort of thing?"

For a moment, he didn't answer. Then he said, "Yes. All those things. I thought . . ."

"That he was just making conversation, learning

about life in the Netherlands, yes. Tell me exactly what you told him. Be specific."

"I told him . . . I'm usually home by six o'clock. That I commute by car."

That was all I needed. With a nod of my head toward Boaz, I said, "Can you get this man into the container?"

"Not again, I don't . . ."

"This man is a bomb-disposal expert. If he can disarm the bomb, you walk away from this without anyone ever even knowing. You can even keep whatever Hilger paid you. If the bomb goes off, you burn in hell."

Boezeman stood there, struggling not to hyperventilate. "I . . . all right, I can take him."

Boaz looked at me. "Go. Take the car."

"You . . ."

"You take care of Hilger. I'll take care of the bomb."

Naftali got out of the Mercedes. The keys were in and the engine was still running. I looked at my watch. It was five o'clock. With luck, I could intercept Hilger. With luck, Boaz wasn't about to die in a radiological explosion.

With luck.

38

RUSH-HOUR TRAFFIC wasn't kind to me, and I didn't make it back to Leidseplein until six-thirty. I hoped Hilger, who knew he would get another try tomorrow, hadn't given up for the night. But I had a feeling he'd stick it out for a while longer. Silencing Boezeman was important, and he'd want to do it as soon as possible so he could complete the op.

The real question wasn't whether, but where. I put myself in his shoes again.

No need for anything to look natural. Just a bullet in the back of the head, or a knife in the liver, ideally while he's going in his own front door.

But you couldn't wait right by his front door. There were too many apartments, too many passersby. It would be too suspicious. The end of the street? Similar problem. You might miss the target entirely.

Vondelpark would be ideal. It was big, dark, and had lots of bushes and trees for concealment. You could lurk there for hours, with a view of Boezeman's apartment. If you had a sniper rifle, all you'd need would be line of sight. With a pistol, maybe you could drop the target

from just on the other side of the Vondelpark fence.
With a knife, the trick would be getting from the park to
Boezeman's door before he got inside. At a run, it
would take ninety seconds, considerably longer than it
takes a man to let himself in with a key.

Unless, of course, someone's broken off something inside the lock.

That was it. That's how I would do it. Even with a
rifle, you'd want to slow the target down, give yourself
extra time for the shot.

I parked the car and set off, pulling my wool hat down
low over my ears and turning up the coat collar as
I walked.

I started walking down Overtoom street, thinking I
would enter the park from Van Baerlestraat, the north-
west side of the eastern quadrant of the park, and a
good distance from Boezeman's apartment. That would
maximize my chances of seeing Hilger while he was focused on spotting Boezeman, before he had a chance to
see me.

It made sense, but suddenly it felt wrong. The iceman
didn't like it, and he was trying to tell me why.

And then I knew. I'd considered the possibility that
Hilger would be here. Why couldn't he, with all his experience, have come to similar, mirror-image conclusions?
Sure, by all means, jam Boezeman's lock. But then monitor the door some other way, from somewhere else in
the park—from where he could ambush me.

I thought for a moment. What about another man? I
doubted he had any left. Dox had said four on that first
phone call. After New York and Singapore, that left
Hilger.

A camera, then? A magnetic mount, or even duct
tape, on the iron fence would work. And then he could

wait anywhere. He could set up at Van Baerlestraat, the
direction from which he knew I would hunt him. Lie flat
on the ground, the muzzle of the gun up, waiting
and watching.

I changed direction and entered the park from
Stadhouderskade, the eastern end. As soon as I was inside the gate, I moved off the path and into a line of
trees. I dropped into a squat, waiting for my eyes to adjust to the dark. There were a few people about, all with
umbrellas, all hurrying through the rain, doubtless on
their way home from work. I saw no one loitering anywhere.

I moved slowly along the trees at the northeastern
edge of the park, knees and elbows the whole way, my
face an inch from the sodden ground. It felt like coming
home. I paused frequently to check my surroundings. A
few bicyclists went by on the path to my left, but that
was all.

A hundred yards in, I stopped. Straight ahead of me
was a thick cluster of trees. It was where I would have
waited for me. I crept closer. There, at the base of the
thickest of them. Prone on the ground. Hilger.

I waited and watched him. He was on the eastern side
of the tree, taking cover and concealment from anyone
approaching from the west. It was as I'd thought: he'd
anticipated me. Only I, and the iceman, had played one
step further ahead.

It was hard to tell in the dim light, but it looked like
he was holding a pistol in his right hand. Something
glowed periodically on his left. A small monitor, maybe
a mobile phone. I'd been right about the camera setup,
too, which meant he had no one with him.

Slowly, painstakingly, I circled behind him, and then
gradually moved in. The rain muffled sound, but I didn't

need it. If there was one thing my body had learned and would never forget, it was how to move silently through the mud. Hilger had said his conflict had been in the desert. Too bad for him.

Twelve yards. Ten. It was easy to get overeager at the moment of the kill, and I forced myself to stay slow and steady.

"Don't move," I heard from behind me, in a commanding tone.

It was Hilger's voice. I froze and didn't try to turn. The person on the ground in front of me remained still.

"Very slowly, place the gun on the ground, far from your body. Then get your hands up high, fingers spread."

I did as he had asked, then snuck a glance back. I couldn't see much more than a silhouette holding a pistol, ten feet away. The muzzle was abnormally long, and I realized it was a suppressor. With the gun on me, it was too far to rush him. If he shot center mass, the Dragon Skin might carry the day. But if he aimed low or high, I'd be done.

"Who's the guy on the ground?" I asked, wanting to engage him, see if I could create an opening.

"I have no idea."

"You just shot someone to use as a decoy?"

I heard him laugh. "It worked, didn't it?"

I couldn't deny it.

"Are you going to give me a hard time about it?" I heard him say. "How many people did you kill this week?"

"I didn't have a choice."

He laughed again, and I felt a slow-burning rage ignite deep within me. He hadn't moved to pat me down, probably because he was wary of getting too close after our run-in in Saigon. I had the knife Boaz gave me clipped to my front pocket. If I rushed him, I could probably open him up even as he was shooting me. I might die, but I'd take him with me to hell.

Do it. Do it now.

It was the iceman talking.

No. There's a better way.

A distraction. That's what I needed. Something to buy myself the extra second.

"Tell me where Dox is," I heard him say, and I realized that was my opening. He didn't know how messed up the big sniper was. He thought he was here.

"He's with Boezeman," I said. "Boezeman let him into the container. He disarmed the bomb."

There was a second of silence while his mind grappled with his new understanding of just how much I knew. Boezeman, container, bomb, disarmed . . . it was a lot to process. It required thought, and made it hard to focus.

"You're lying," he said.

This time I was the one to laugh. "You're right. You want to know where he is? Dox. Take him out."

Hilger had spent enough time in the military, and was sufficiently acquainted with Dox's deadly skills, for the words *take him out* to have an almost Pavlovian effect. Klaxons were going off in his mind now: *Rain must be wearing commo gear, Dox is close by with a scoped rifle, where's the line of sight, get off the X—*

I spun and rushed him. I was five feet away when the first slug hit my chest. I felt like I'd run into a tree, and the air was driven out of my lungs. He got off two more, both to my torso, and then I had both hands wrapped around the gun. I twisted hard to the left, forcing the muzzle out to his right. He rotated his body to keep his

wrist from breaking, and two more shots went off to the
side. We struggled with the gun.

I couldn't draw breath. It felt like I'd been kicked by
a horse, by three horses. Hilger snapped a knee into my
groin and pain rocketed through my abdomen. I got a
hand around the long suppressor and shoved back and
over, toward Hilger's right shoulder. He couldn't get out
of the way, and he couldn't let go. His wrist snapped. He
howled and I tore the gun away from him.

I took a step back, and with my last strength blasted
a desperate side kick into his knee. He yelled again and
collapsed. I fell to my knees a few feet away, fumbling
with the pistol, trying to breathe, breathe . . .

I bobbled the gun and dropped it in the mud. Hilger,
his face a rictus of pain, was struggling with his belt
buckle with his left hand. I remembered Saigon, and
thought, *belt knife.*

Of course, no backup pistol. That's what I'd seen in
the dead guy's hand.

Breathe, breathe . . .

I groped for the gun. I couldn't find it. The outer
edges of my vision were going dark.

Hilger twisted the buckle, and suddenly there was a
blade in his hand.

I gritted my teeth, and with all my strength tried to
suck air into my lungs. No go. Tiny red dots danced before my eyes. My phony command to Dox had unbal-
anced Hilger enough to deny him the time and the focus
to shoot for my head or pelvic girdle, but the rounds had
reverberated through the Dragon Skin to hammer my
diaphragm into spasm. The knee to my groin had made
it worse. My brain wasn't getting oxygen, and it was beginning to shut down.

Hilger slid toward me, the knife in his left hand, his

left forearm digging into the mud, pulling himself forward like an injured reptile.

I rubbed frantically at my diaphragm. A tiny whistle of air made its way into my lungs.

Hilger slashed with the knife. I fell away from him to my back, getting my feet between us, still rubbing, trying to coax my diaphragm out of spasm. Another snatch of air stole down my throat, like a prisoner dashing across a mine field.

Another slash. The blade hit my boot. I drew a tiny, hitching breath. Hilger screamed and slashed again. Again he hit a boot.

I put my hands down to shove away from him, and my right fingers touched cold metal. The gun. I grabbed it and kicked away to create a precious extra two feet, then got it out in front of me with my right hand, my left still massaging my abdomen. I drew an inch of breath. Then another. The red dots disappeared, and the darkness retreated.

Hilger saw the gun, saw that he couldn't reach me. His body sagged and he dropped the knife in the mud.

We sat there like that, neither of us able to move. After a few moments, Hilger laughed and said, "I guess you are bulletproof, after all. Body armor, right?"

I didn't answer. I was still working on getting my breath back.

We sat there like that for almost a minute, neither of us able to move. When I could finally speak, I sighted down the muzzle and said, "Tell me how to disarm it."

He smiled. "Then you haven't yet. You were lying."

"I don't know. Somebody's been working on it. Tell me, and I'll let you live."

He laughed.

I thought about calling Boaz. But without Hilger's co-

operation, there was nothing I could do to help him
And a phone call could distract him at a delicate mo
ment. I would have to wait.

"Who are you working for?" I asked. "AQ? Hamas
Hezbollah?"

He laughed again.

"What?" I said.

"I work for my country."

"I don't get it."

He sighed. "Someone has to deny America's enemie
their funding, Rain. How can the country prevail agains
radical Islam while simultaneously underwriting it?"

"What does this have to do with Rotterdam?"

"It has everything to do with Rotterdam. America'
oil addiction is a sickness that's killing the patien
Christ, Americans would rather send soldiers to wa
than carpool to work. And Congress is worse. The idiot
actually proposed to offer taxpayers a hundred-dolla
rebate to buy more gasoline—they want to give the ad
dicts more money for a fix, more money to send to th
mullahs and the al Saud, our enemies."

"So Rotterdam is an inoculation."

"Yes. That's well put. You increase the price of o
enough to lower demand and create market incentive
for alternatives, but not so much that the patient goe
into the shock of economic depression. It's a shame th
patient doesn't have the sense or the will to inoculat
himself through a carbon tax, but denial is the nature c
addiction, and doesn't change the fact that the patien
badly needs help."

"What about British Petroleum, then? Prudho
Bay?"

He looked at me. "How do you know about that?"

"What difference does it make?"

There was a pause, and I thought he would refuse. But I'd told him I might let him live. No matter how tough you are, in extremis, it doesn't take much for a drop of hope to blossom into a full-blown mirage of salvation.

"Prudhoe Bay was a test of the new treatment," he said. "On the one hand, it was a failure because it didn't have the desired effect. But it was successful, too, because it demonstrated that for the patient to get well a higher dose was needed. There were other possibilities, including Ras Tanura in Saudi Arabia. But . . ."

"You had an unwitting access agent in Rotterdam. Boezeman."

"That's right. And I wanted to keep casualties to a minimum. The layout at Rotterdam is good for that."

"So with Rotterdam inoperable . . ."

"Right. The price of oil would spike, demand would slacken, and I would single-handedly have hastened the advent of a post-oil, post-OPEC world economy. You get it now? Do you understand what's at stake? We live in perilous times. We're battling a new kind of enemy. An enemy that can't be deterred. What do we do to fight him? Become like him?"

"Haven't you?"

"I didn't say 'me.' I said 'we.' Someone has to do what needs to be done, Rain. Someone has to live in the shadows so others can enjoy the light. Someone has to sin so others can enjoy innocence. Now, if you don't understand my reasons, go ahead. Do the only thing you're good for. You beat me. You won. Again."

I didn't say anything. *The only thing you're good for.* It was stupid, but the words cut into me.

"But grant me a last request," he said. "Let me call my sister. She's the only one I have to say goodbye to. Or is a small mercy against your code of killing?"

I watched him, the front sight of the pistol even with his forehead. I thought about how easy it is to retract a fingertip, how easy to take a life.

It had always been easy for me. What others could accomplish only with the greatest encouragement, with fear and regret and swallowed revulsion, I could just . . . do. And I'd kept on doing it. There would always be a reason, it seemed. And if there weren't, maybe I would invent one.

"My mobile phone is over there," he said, inclining his head toward the dead guy by the tree. "My knee is broken, I can't get to it. Would you lend me yours? Please?"

What difference did it make? A small mercy, like he said. I pulled my mobile out and tossed it to him.

"Thank you," he said. He grimaced and flipped it open with his good hand.

If I was going to stop, I had to find a way to stop, a time and place to stop. I would have to make a decision to stop. The decision would carry risks, it was true. But so, always, would the alternative.

Maybe this was what Delilah had been talking about, when she told me about choices, and how I would make the right one.

Hilger was supporting himself on his left elbow, inputting his sister's number with his left thumb. It embarrassed me to have to hear whatever he might say to her.

Yes, that was it. I'd been telling myself for so long I had no choice, that maybe my choice reflex had atrophied. But I could reawaken it. I could let him live. By walking away, I would prove that Dox and I were no threat to him. He'd have no incentive to come after us after that.

It made sense. I could do this. It was up to me. My choice. Everything would be possible. A thousand new directions. I thought about how I would tell Delilah, how she had been right, and how much her confidence had meant to me, how much it had helped me. I would tell her . . .

The phone! Not his sister, he's detonating the bomb!

Without any other thought, I brought the gun up and shot him in the face. Again. Three times. He jerked and twitched and dropped the phone.

I sat there dumbly for a long moment in the sudden silence, the rain beating a steady drumbeat on my arms and shoulders. A tendril of smoke curled coyly from the muzzle of the gun.

I stood and picked up the mobile. I checked the screen. An access code, then 1, for America, 212, for New York . . . and six more digits. Christ, he'd been one digit away.

But was it the bomb? Or did he really have . . .

It didn't matter. For all I knew, Boaz was elbow deep in the device right now. If Hilger had detonated it, Boaz would have died. Even if I was wrong, I had no choice.

The rain beat harder. And through the echo of that sodden drumbeat, I thought I heard a whispered voice, at once familiar and distant.

No choice.

I stood there in the cold and dark and rain. I'd known, at some level, of the possible danger if he made a call. But I'd let him make it anyway. Because once he had the phone in his hands, I had . . .

No choice.

My mobile buzzed. I looked and saw that it was Boaz.
I picked up. "You okay?" I asked.

"Did you hear a boom?"

"No, I didn't. But I wasn't listening closely."

He laughed. "I have a simple rule. If there's no boom,
it's good news."

"You disarmed it."

"Disarmed and disabled. We'll need experts to handle
the radioactive material and make sure it's disposed of
properly, but that's someone else's concern."

I started walking toward the car. Jesus, I didn't know
I had so many places that could hurt. "Whose?" I asked.

"Let's just say Mister Boezeman is very eager for no
one ever to learn of this incident. And my organization
is very eager to own a Rotterdam port official. It's going
to be a beautiful friendship."

"You're going to bring the organization in on
this?"

"Of course. With results like these, a little—what do
you call it, moonlighting?—is easily forgiven. But
enough about me. I'm so relieved not to be blown into
a million pieces that I'm forgetting to ask you
about Hilger."

"He's dead."

"How?"

"How do you think? Bullets."

"And you're okay? You're not hurt, you're out
of danger?"

"I'm okay."

"Fantastic! Naftali will be so pleased he might talk
again. He was hoping to do it himself, but he's a big boy,
he understands that what matters is, it's done."

"Where are you?"

"On the train, on the way back to Amsterdam. Let's ave a beer. Debrief, decompress."

"I've . . . got a lot to think about."

"Bullshit. No one should be alone after something ke this. Besides, you have our car and all our shiny oys. You have to give them back or we'll get in trouble."

I tried to smile, but I felt sick. "I'll meet you at the sta- on and give you the keys. But I can't stay long."

PARKED NEAR Centraal Station, took my bag from ne trunk, and locked the car. As I walked along one f the canals, I dropped Hilger's gun over the side. I ad left the USP in Vondelpark. I didn't have time to earch for it in the mud, but it was okay. I hadn't even red it, and if Boaz was using it, it must have been terile.

I met them inside the station, as they came down the airs from the Rotterdam train. Naftali shook my hand. I owe you, Mister Rain," he said.

"No, you don't. You had my back. That's good nough."

He shook his head. "I know my brother was sent to ill you. I'm glad now he didn't succeed."

"Yeah, me too," I said, and Naftali actually smiled.

"I told you he would be excited," Boaz said.

I laughed weakly, then grimaced. My chest felt like I'd opped a truck with it.

"Where will you go now?" Boaz asked. "To Delilah?"

I couldn't have fooled him even if I'd been in- lined. "Yeah."

"I didn't call her, you know. After Singapore. It was p to you."

"Well, do you want me to go see her?" I said, handing

him the car keys. "Or do you want to stand here ta▌
ing?"

He laughed. I explained about the USP and told the▌
where they could find the car, then went to the tick▌
booth to see about a train to Paris.

There was a nine o'clock that arrived at Paris Nord▌
one in the morning. I bought a ticket and headed to t▌
platform. I called Kanezaki just before boardi▌
the train.

"How is he?" I asked.

"He's going to be okay. A lot of bruises, some fra▌
tured ribs, and a hell of a sunburn."

Yeah, my skin was itching, too. I'd been so busy▌
hadn't noticed until now.

"Good."

"How about you?" he asked. "Did . . ."

"You were right about everything. And everything v▌
came here to do, we did, including rendering our frie▌
defunct. I'll post the details. But you can probably rea▌
the Israelis on their mobiles right now."

"I may do that."

"You did well, Tom."

"And you did good."

"Well, no good deed goes unpunished. I'll be▌
touch, okay?"

"I hope so."

I took my seat on the train and five minutes later, v▌
pulled out of the station. I was wet and shivering fro▌
crawling through Vondelpark, and my chest ached. I ju▌
wanted to get somewhere warm and dry, somewhere▌
could close my eyes.

I leaned my head against the window. As we left t▌
lights of the city behind and the world outside gre▌
darker, my reflection appeared in the glass.

For so long, I'd been asking myself whether I had a
choice, and always answering no. But maybe the real
question was why I never had a choice. Why I always
put myself in a position where I had no alternative
but killing.

What was that saying of Henry Ford's? "You can
have any color you like, as long as it's black."

I thought I heard the iceman: *You can have any choice
you want, as long as it's mine.*

Maybe. But I'd made at least one right choice, in New
York when I'd walked away from Midori's boyfriend.
And maybe I was making another right now, in going
to Delilah.

I thought about those three small words she had ut-
tered, the ones I didn't know how to respond to. I'd
think of something, maybe even what she had called
"the traditional response," although the thought of it
scared me. I had told her I needed her to guide me back,
and staring at that ghostly image in the glass, I knew I
did need her, that without her I would just give up and
surrender to the iceman. It would be so easy. I was used
to it. A part of me even wanted it.

But there was something I wanted more. And with
Delilah . . .

That was it. *With Delilah.*

The iceman was a loner. Why was I fighting him
alone? That was what he wanted, the nature of the fight
was itself his victory. But I had allies, Delilah foremost
among them. Maybe if I could just be a little less stupid
about accepting what they wanted to give me, I could
stack the odds in my favor.

I didn't need to kill the iceman. I didn't even need to
fight him. I just needed to make more of myself, so that
he would be less of me.

I didn't know how, exactly, and I was too tired to fig
ure it out now. But I wouldn't have to figure it out o
my own. That was the point.

I closed my eyes. The reflection was still there,
course. I just couldn't see it. And for the moment, th
was enough.

AUTHOR'S NOTE

The Bali, Paris, Saigon, Tokyo, Los Angeles, Bay Area, New York, Singapore, Rotterdam, and Amsterdam locales that appear in this book are described, as always, as I have found them. The nonlethal millimeter wave "area denial system" technology Rain and Boaz use in Singapore is real, but I don't know if there are yet versions as portable, or as able to penetrate walls, as the one in this book.

ACKNOWLEDGMENTS

Once again, I've written a book that has been made much better through the generous contributions of many friends. My thanks to:

My agents, Nat Sobel and Judith Weber of Sobel Weber Associates, and my editor, Dan Conaway of Putnam, for helping me keep the stories fresh and the prose sharp.

Michael Barson (master of Yubiwaza), Carroll Beaurais, Katie Grinch, Summer Smith, Caroline Sun, and Matthew Venzon of Putnam, for doing such an amazing job of getting out the word on the books. Go, Barsonians!

Massad Ayoob of the Lethal Force Institute, for sharing his awe-inspiring knowledge of and experience with firearms tools and tactics, for the great instruction at the LFI I and II (see you at III, Mas), and for helpful comments on the manuscript.

Tony Blauer, for teaching Rain and Dox some of the pattern interrupt / verbal distraction techniques they use several times in this book to gain a tactical advantage.

Matt Furey, for again providing some of the Combat

Conditioning bodyweight exercises Rain uses to stay i
top shape (and that his author uses, too).

Peyton Quinn of Rocky Mountain Combat Applica
tions Training and author of *A Bouncer's Guide to Bar
room Brawling* and *Real Fighting,* for his concept of th
previolence "interview," in this case the fast intervie
Rain receives in chapter 3.

Ernie Tibaldi, a thirty-one-year veteran agent of th
FBI and now a top security consultant, for continuing t
generously share his encyclopedic knowledge of law en
forcement and personal safety issues, for turning Rai
on to Katz's Deli in New York, and for helpful com
ments on the manuscript.

Jonathan Shay, for *Achilles in Vietnam: Comb*
Trauma and the Undoing of Character, from which I de
rived a greater understanding of Rain's own Vietnar
experiences, related in chapter 8, and their long-term et
fects.

When I visited Saigon to research this book, it wa
my first time. Rain, of course, had been there lon
before, and I needed to see the city through his eye
The website When from Our Exile: Ivan in Việt Nar
(www.pauahtun.org/Exile/Default.htm) was an enormou
help.

Sensei Koichiro Fukasawa of Wasabi Communica
tions, for continuing to guide Rain in Japan, for lifelon
friendship, and for helpful comments on the manu
script.

Laurent Boudin, Marie Jeanne Denis, François Lau
rent, and Françoise Triffaux of my French publisher
Belfond and Univers Poche, for introducing Rain to L
Petit Célestin on the quai des Célestins and La Closeri
des Lilas in Montparnasse.

Naomi Andrews, for guiding me on all things Frenc

and Parisian, and for helpful comments on the manuscript.

Lori (aka Laure) Kupfer, for continued insights into what sophisticated, sexy women like Delilah wear and how they think, and for helpful comments on the manuscript.

Paul Guyot, for inspiring Rain horologically.

Roberta Parks, M.D., Owen Rennert, M.D., Evan Rosen, M.D., Ph.D., and Peter Zimetbaum, M.D., for continuing to answer my strange questions about the medical implications of unarmed killing techniques, and for helpful comments on the manuscript.

The extraordinarily eclectic group of "foodies with a violence problem" who hang out at Marc "Animal" MacYoung's and Dianna Gordon's www.nononsense selfdefense.com. A special thanks to Marc himself, for sharing his thoughts on leaving the life and coming to grips with the "dragon" within and the "gray man"—thoughts that inspired and helped shape my notion of the iceman, with whom Rain struggles in this book—and for helpful comments on the manuscript.

Dox's stunning stream of invective in chapter 35 is courtesy of a rant by one David Jefferson Bean, philosopher, iconoclast, owner and operator of the Bean Machine, and brilliant blogger (mygreenhell.typepad.com). When Dave gets up a head of steam, you'll want to set down your coffee, lest you spew it on your keyboard laughing—and nodding your head in stunned agreement.

Terry Trahan, who no longer clanks when he walks (but then again, he doesn't need to), for his insights on getting out of the life and on the fine art of Weaselcraft.

Three men I count myself privileged to know have characters named after them in this book: Wim Deneere, Frank "Pancho" Garza, and Montie Guthrie. In

addition to their names, the characters share some pos
itive characteristics with their real-world namesakes
But the characters also have certain . . . negative charac
teristics, which are entirely fictional and have nothing to
do with these gentlemen as I know them. I say this be
cause I wouldn't want anyone to mistakenly conclude
that I hold Wim, Pancho, or Montie—friends and teach
ers all—in anything other than the highest regard. Plus
they might beat me up or shoot me if I didn't provide a
disclaimer. Special thanks to Montie, for always taking
my calls about firearms tools and tactics, and for helpfu
comments on the manuscript. I hope it goes withou
saying that any firearms mistakes in the manuscript are
entirely Montie's fault.

The line Rain recollects in Chapter 6, "Hell, I'll kill a
man in a fair fight . . . or if I think he's gonna start a fai
fight," is from Joss Whedon's terrific movie *Serenity*.

Eve Bridberg, Vivian Brown, Alan Eisler, Judith
Eisler, Jack "Spook" Finch (no pregnant yak he), Ton
Hayes, Rachel Holtzman, Mike Killman, Yukie Kito
novelist J. A. Konrath, Dan Levin, Doug Patteson, Mat
Powers, Sandy Rennert, Ted Schlein, Hank Shiffman
The Man Called Slugg, Pete Wenzel, and Caryn Wise
man, for helpful comments on the manuscript and man
valuable suggestions and insights along the way.

I feel like I'm forgetting to mention someone . . .

Kidding. My wife, Laura, helps with, suffers through
and then enjoys these books like no one else. Thanks fo
everything, babe.

BARRY EISLER

RAIN FALL

Born of an American mother and a Japanese father, John Rain is a businessman based in Tokyo, living a life of meticulously planned anonymity. There are few who know who he is or what he does. Trained by the U.S. Special Forces and a veteran of Vietnam, he is a cool, self-contained loner—and he has built a steady business over the past twenty-five years specializing in death by "natural causes." After the assassination of a government official in a crowded subway car, Rain's carefully ordered world comes under siege. Agents within and without the international intelligence communities have been circling him for some time and, having connected him to the subway incident, may now have the scent they have been seeking. At the same time, Rain is drawn outside his private world by an alluring jazz pianist, the dead man's daughter, who is the key to the very secrets her father was trying to reveal when he died.

Also Available:

Hard Rain

Rain Storm

Killing Rain

The Last Assassin

Available wherever books are sold or at
penguin.com